Nine Planets

Greg Byrne

Dragonwell Publishing

This is a work of fiction. All of the characters, organizations, and events portrayed in this novel are either products of the author's imagination or are used fictitiously.

Cover art by Dragonwell Publishing

Published by Dragonwell Publishing
(www.dragonwellpublishing.com)

ISBN 978-1-940076-17-1

Contents

PGFWABF
PHACHB
PHAYHH
PFSAHG
A.

Before

Curse

Father Nick's Day minus seventeen hundred years
The harbour town of Patara
Province of Lycia
late evening

The thought comes upon Nikolas so abruptly and with such potency that he halts, astonished, panting with fright.

Take his own life? Drive steel into his own belly?

He almost laughs to drive out such mischievous wickedness, but it persists.

Kill yourself, Nikolas. There is no hope.

Chills crevice into the parts of his body where until now were only the delights of wine and the many pleasures of food, for the party he has just farewelled was lavish and he spent much. So was his wine cup poisoned with some venom of despair? Were thieves and slavemasters even now following him? For certainly the riches of his parents, dead only this month gone, are substantial and tempting, and now they are his.

It is then that he notices the sudden silence of the streets of Patara—so strange! If pursuers are abroad, they are making no noise of it. Only Nikolas and the wind are out this night, and it troubles him.

Still, there is only a mile to his house, and certainly the morning sun after sleep will settle such afflictions of the soul. But perhaps, he ponders as he strides, it is the same bleak despair that killed Umit his friend barely two weeks ago. For even Umit's youth and great cheer and strength were not guard enough against hopelessness.

Nikolas is fighting the mad lust for steel and blood—his own—when he catches wind of something so wickedly foul it almost makes him retch.

He turns, curious.

Fish left to rot in a fisherman's net?

He knows immediately it is not. Not even the most odorous catch could threaten to overpower him so violently.

He stops for a moment, covering his mouth, distracted from knives. This is no quirk of the wind, not the product of natural decay or ferment. Nor the acrid stink of a forge. But nothing obvious presents itself. The moon, a rich coin of promise and plenty, stands a handspan or so over the Acropolis up on the hill. The town breathes. A dog barks once, as though watchful.

Curious, Nikolas thinks, but as he turns to go, a dark figure emerges from the alley he has just passed, out past the house of Besim the leather worker.

Nikolas stares, thinking for a moment it must be an unwashed fisherman returning home. Yet the figure casts no shadow, seems instead to suck in light. And the stink surges at him in a putrid tide.

This is no fisherman. Thoughts of knives vanish. He should be away from this place with all speed.

The figure sees him and stops.

Nikolas draws shocked breath and his muscles lock. Neither is it human, he is sure, nor even the tormented spirit of Umit. No living thing could cast out so much smoke, a vile cloud that shudders the night and stops Nikolas' breath.

Nikolas turns for home and hastens, very afraid.

But when he glances back at the next corner, in a blurred pounding of disbelief and panic and still half a mile from his house, the thing is following, and now it is gaining.

Nikolas rises to a sprint, though it is not much faster than he is already running. This is no common thief, that much is certain. And unless Nikolas can outrun it or hide, then he is sure his life will be forfeit as well, and he would rather take his own. He thinks of shouting, but the town seems bewitched, all too silent, dangerously so, and he doubts anyone will hear.

A hundred paces from his house, Nikolas turns the last corner, sees his house.

He is thinking how he will barricade his door and kindle fire to fight the thing off when, without any warning, his heart rises to a wild sprint, gallops at a rate he thinks must surely kill him, then slows. He stumbles, shocked, his chest swelling with space that it cannot possibly hold. His vision blurs.

The bark of a dog is cut off cleanly. Knife-clean. Without echo.

The wind drops.

Nikolas sucks air, stares frantically around and sees something he just doesn't believe.

Only about thirty paces behind him, the figure has paused midway through a stride. Amid the smoke and fume, now strangely still, a single leg extends in a peculiar and quite impossible jut. It cannot balance there, surely. But it is, as though the world has halted for a moment.

Nikolas listens, more than a little afraid. Why can he move when his pursuer cannot?

And there, deep below hearing, in resonant strata he cannot even guess at, the world adjusts its stride, reconsiders its rhythm, pauses.

The world has turned aside for a moment, Nikolas thinks.

And he has turned with it.

His vision cleared.

And there, motionless, the shadowed figure remained. Nikolas stared. It could not be possible! The gods must prevent such a twisting of the laws that governed nature and movement and time! He was in another world, surely.

Or a mad dream. He blinked, trying to orient himself but realized he could hear nothing. Not old Deniz coughing. Nor dogs barking, arguing their territories. All the houses of his neighbors stood dark and silent, as if abandoned.

Even the wind was still, gone whispering and wandering through other towns perhaps. As though Patara were midway between breaths. He listened, imagining that all her neighborhoods had sunk deep, drowned under sleep.

A dream? No—the bits of crust between his teeth tasted more of olive than sleep. No dream this, not unless dreams offered him the barnacled smells of fish and harbor or the gritty skid of sand under his feet.

He spat on the ground and rolled a glob of mud around his fingers. *That* was no other world. Nor the moonlight on the hilltop Acropolis overlooking Patara, although the moon seemed very reluctant to rise. Nikolas rubbed his eyes and stared at it. An anchored moon, he thought. Surely it had been higher than a handspan above the hills earlier.

None of it made any sense! He glanced back once to the shadowed figure—he dared not approach it—shook his head in disbelief and took himself inside and barred every door and window. He knew he would not sleep—his heart was pounding too hard for that—though he might still find a knife to stop it.

Then he checked that his inherited treasure was still locked away in the place where his father had kept it. The time was once when Nikolas had wanted to use it in acts of charity. He was not one to luxuriate when so much need and poverty surrounded him. But now he was not so sure. What was the point in generosity when he was going to die anyway?

Having kindled fire in his hearth and found a stout stick, he placed a chair before the door and sat down, the stick across his knees.

A knock startled him. He jerked, his arms flailing, though he kept hold of the stick, and realized instantly that no bandit would be so polite as to knock.

Yet whoever stood outside had approached with remarkable stealth and silence. Nikolas thought quickly and looked through a crack in a shuttered window. The shadowed figure still remained where Nikolas had last seen him, though the person at the door could still have been a different thief. The world was full of them.

A second knock sounded, and then a voice. "Nikolas of Patara."

Nikolas went to the door, the stick ready for blows.

"Who might you be?" he asked, one hand on the barred door.

"A poor man."

Though his voice didn't *sound* poor; it was calm and steady, not stricken with the croaks of age or the mumblings of wine. And neither was his accent local, though Nikolas had difficulty placing it. No sailor, certainly, not even in those three words. Nor one of the nomadic merchants who filled the markets with exotic smells and sounds. *This* voice seemed oddly clean of any accent at all, and it troubled Nikolas.

"What would you ask of me, poor man?"

Nikolas worried at the stranger's pause. "Much and nothing, *kyrie*."

Much and nothing? Nikolas mouthed the words, debating with himself. He had not spoken of his inheritance to anyone since his parents' untimely deaths, so he doubted the stranger would be wanting to rob him. The man, strange though his accent was, might simply want a meal and a place out of the night.

Then why hide a simple request in riddles? The door-bar creaked under the pressure of his hand. "It is late, poor man."

"And all the lamps of your neighbors are dark, and their doors bolted. All are sleeping but you, Nikolas of Patara. Will you unbolt your door?"

"There are strangers abroad tonight, poor man. You can see the one that followed me home if you turn to your right a little."

And, to Nikolas' surprise, a gentle chuckle sounded on the far side of the door. "Yet it was not you he was pursuing, but me. His lion and my lamb, a comparison he did not care for when I told him of it. And if you look out, you will see he will be no further threat this night. And all I am asking is a favor, *kyrie,* not your life. Much if you agree, nothing if you don't."

Nikolas's breath caught. "And you will not speak of this favor with the door closed?"

"I might, but we cannot achieve anything with it so. And I have often been told of your kindness, Nikolas. Many speak well of your hospitality towards strangers."

Nikolas slipped over to the cracked shutter. The shadowed figure remained.

Well, he thought. *A night for marvels and terrors both. If I am to die, then may it be quick.* Then he eased up the bar and opened the door.

Before him stood a small man with an enormous smile. Perhaps the man's yellowed shards of teeth disarmed him, or his bare scrap of a body. There was certainly nowhere he could have hidden a knife or cudgel. The stench of the man made him cough, though. He was glad for the dark to hide the holes in the man's rags that the moon wasn't shining through. More hole than cloth, more dirt than stitching. Old, barefoot and scabrous, wizened and grinning, the poor man stood there on tiptoe as though he was peering through crowds at parading kings. He did not seem to mind that his unbound hair got into his eyes; his smile took up all the space on his face. He barely reached Nikolas's chest.

"I can boil water for washing," offered Nikolas and immediately regretted it, but the man was waving a pair of enormous leathery hands and grinning.

"No water for me, *kyrie,* or I will wash away. Nay nay, there is indeed little time." He glanced up at the moon with his face bright. "Will you aid me, Nikolas of Patara, or will you go in to your bed and your dreams?"

"You say there is little time?"

"The person of smoke and evil will not remain forever as he is now." The man peered at Nikolas with a curious gleam in his eye and Nikolas realized.

"You stopped him!"

The man smiled. "Indeed I did. And the moon too, though it will not wait all night for us as I have told it to wait now."

Nikolas gaped. Bizarre upon bizarre. "He...he was going...going to kill me! And you...stopped him!"

"No, he has not the power of death, though he desires it. He will always be the second, though he aches to be the first. No, he has already done something far worse than murder. He has made *you* want to kill yourself. Hopelessness is far worse than violence. For have you not seen how bleak things have become in recent days? Why is it that the world has lost its sweetness and has become foul, a place without hope?" He reached up and held Nikolas' arm with a surprisingly strong grip. "Why is it that you are thinking even now of taking a knife to your heart? You are too young for such despair."

"You know?"

The old man squeezed Nikolas' forearm. "Why?"

Nikolas had to confess he did not know, though he was not surprised by the question. Not only in Patara had folk begun to speak with resignation of the futility of existence that had taken root in their hearts and minds. Hundreds had wasted their coin on wine and dance, or chariots and fine horses, or fine silks and costly jewels, or unspeakable debauchery, then slipped knives into their own hearts. Or refused to eat, the methods were many. Some had even gone to the mountains and climbed above the snowline to remain there until they perished. Or walked off piers, such as Umit had done.

Men and women of note or of unimportance—it mattered little. And it was true of other towns, other cities, indeed other countries.

But no-one knew why. Patara and Anatolia were not ravaged by plague or war, certainly not enough to cause a widespread hopelessness.

He looked at the poor man, deeply troubled. It was unlikely that the man had come to his house simply to discuss the heart of man and its failings. "Do *you* know, then?"

The old man's voice was soft, though Nikolas remembered every word. "The person of smoke who pursues us has placed a curse of hopelessness on mankind, and most lately on *you*."

Nikolas could hardly speak.

"He hopes that you will kill yourself." He reached into some hidden place in his garment and withdrew a long knife, beautiful, glimmering and deliciously curved.

Part of Nikolas longed for it.

"And here is the weapon with which you will do it." He stared at Nikolas for a moment. "If you choose to."

Nikolas sputtered, confused and angry, and pushed the knife away. "No! How did you—? What is—?"

The poor man seemed ridiculously calm. "For have you not already wasted your coin tonight in the fruitless pursuit of things that do not last, and found no lasting truth in them?"

Nikolas nodded, bewildered.

"Now, having found no purpose, you will take your own life." He held out the knife again, his eyes level and steady.

"No! This is foolishness!"

"It is not, *kyrie*. Our pursuer controls some of the powerful merchant houses in Turkey and Arabia, and even countries further again. From many things you paid for this night, he will derive a small part. One copper coin out of a hundred—it seems insignificant, but many copper coins from many bazaars and markets and lavish feasts are sufficient to make him rich. So his curse will rob you first of your wealth and then of your life. And his power is spreading."

"Then what can be done?" demanded Nikolas. "You speak with knowledge of this person, you know his evils, so can you stop this curse?"

The old man grinned. "Nothing of this earth can stop the curse, *kyrie*."

"Are there others then? Who else knows of this?" Though he knew the answer as soon as he spoke the question.

"Only you and I, *kyrie*. Only Nikolas of Patara and a poor man who has nothing. In time, there will be others, but that time is not now."

Nikolas frowned. "I don't understand. Surely the Lycene Council will—"

"There is a man of your town who has three daughters but no cattle or coin to offer for their dowries. His name is Fahrettin, a dear friend of your father and mother."

"Fahrettin? Yes, I know him and his daughters." The youngest, Tezer who was born early, and her sisters Verda and Tülay.

"In the last weeks, his fortunes have turned poorly. Without dowries, his daughters cannot marry, and he must sell them into slavery come morning." The man paused and looked up appraisingly at Nikolas and he held out the knife again. "A third time, Nikolas of Patara."

But Nikolas was angry now, at knives and injustice and this bizarre little man. "What…what can be done? Appeal to the governor? The magistrates?" Even as he spoke, he thought of his parents' wealth. He had coin with which to bless, just as he had been blessed.

The man shook his head. "They could—would do nothing."

Nikolas took the man's hand and pulled him inside. "Then *we* must! He was a friend of my parents! Wait here a moment."

His gold was well hidden, but he had placed three or four bags close at hand if he ever needed to flee fire or thieves. "And your name, friend?" he called.

"'Friend' will be quite sufficient, *kyrie*."

The bags were heavy, but Nikolas carried them to the door and gave one to the man. "Is this enough, do you think? We can go back later with more."

The man hefted the bag and his eyes widened. "Your heart is full of gifts, *kyrie*."

"As I have been blessed, friend. Now let us go. The thought of those maidens losing their freedom galls me more than I can say."

"Before we go, giver of gifts, lay your hand upon this door and speak the words I speak." He took Nikolas' hand and laid it on the door, and Nikolas, at the touch of the poor man's hand, felt a strong and marvelous wind clear out the hopeless sludge in his heart. Amazed, he realized he would not kill himself now. The thought just disgusted him.

And then he repeated the five strange words after the man, still giddy with lightness, his heart swelling with more than blood.

Avein en deisum senkudis neim.

He understood none of them, but remembered them all.

He peered at the man, amazed he was not deeply suspicious. "You ask a lot of a stranger, friend. What was it I just did?"

The man's smile occupied most of his face, a wide dawn of happiness. "You learned the words to stop the moon yourself. 'Tis a simple deed when you know it, and yon moon is an obedient creature when you speak her tongue. So when you give again, you may do so in secret. For giving is best done without trumpets and acclamation. And for your safety also. The person of smoke will certainly oppose you, as he has long opposed me."

The old man chuckled as he pulled Nikolas out into the street and kicked the door closed. "Now come, giver!"

Nikolas followed the man at a run through the town. Even with a bag of gold in one hand, the man ran without panting, with speed strangely disconnected from his appearance. Once Nikolas glanced up at the moon to see it resting, as though waiting, a handspan above the hills. Not a dog barked in the night, nor a lamp flickered. Not even the moored boats in the harbor murmured against the water. Eventually the poor man stopped in front of a house with windows above his head. He grinned. "We are here," he said.

"Come, then," puffed Nikolas. "I shall lift you and you can throw the bags in. We cannot leave them at the door for thieves."

"You will throw the bags in, not I. This is your gift, *kyrie,* not mine. Reach up; you are tall, and a gentle swing should do it. The master will find the bags in the morning and bless the stranger who put them there."

"I want no thanks!" whispered Nikolas.

"Of course not. But men will hear of the deed nevertheless, those good of heart whom you will teach the words you learned from me."

"And this single gift will stop the curse?"

"For this man and for this moment, yes."

"For this moment only? But we cannot give gifts forever."

"There is a way."

"Tell me!"

The old man was silent for a moment. "Why does our adversary pursue us with such fury? Because he rightly believes that I know how to break the curse and, no matter how much I deny or protest, he believes that I have slipped outside of time to pass this secret to you."

Nikolas realized. "But you have not! So when you are gone and he still pursues me, what protection will I have then? Or must I remain in this half-world forever?"

"Nikolas of Patara, I must ask of you a sacrifice." He lifted his eyes to meet Nikolas', and small though he was, he held Nikolas' gaze with power and certainty. "This is the very night on which the world balances. Into this night, we might place a lantern of hope into the stories of men, a lantern whose light will inspire hope and draw many. Or we might not, and permit the curse of your adversary to have its way, and kill countless. So if you could, by your own actions, give hope to many, would you?"

"Of course!" Nikolas said. "I will not be responsible for so much death!" And when he realized, he added, "Neither will I permit my parents' death to go unremembered, for certainly they died of this curse also."

"A sacrifice then, Nikolas of Patara," The old man's sad face glimmered in the moonlight, "and three shields."

"It is no sacrifice if I can restore hope." Nikolas gripped the bag with fierce courage. "Just the shields, friend."

The old man grinned. "It is good, then. These are for you and those you will call as your allies and brothers, a brotherhood of poor men you must gather about you to continue the task. Give again and again on this one day of the year, sacrificing time and coin and comfort at need, being always constant and courageous, all the while speaking the five words I taught you so that you might slip outside time and avoid your adversary. The first shield is your house, for now it stands under a different time to the rest of humanity. Within it, you will be protected from your adversary. Even a mere splinter of your door will suffice to protect the houses of your allies and those who make the gifts you give. The second is the five words which I taught you earlier. When you deliver gifts or you have need of protection, speak them. The third is this. The curse cannot touch you now."

"But those are only for now! What of the secret, the way to break the curse forever?"

"You already have it, deeply locked within the secret chambers of your soul, in a place your adversary will never find. For it is not *where* it is hidden, but *when*. Now I must command you twice, Nikolas of Patara. Do not speak of this secret to anyone. And do not die childless, for there will come a morning when you will wake to find that the door of the secret has opened within you and you know how to break the curse. If it is not you, it will be your son, or perhaps the son of your son of your son."

Nikolas could only stare. A man who stopped the moon, who had powers too strange to speak, who fought curses outside of sight. "Who are you?"

"I know who I am." He gestured to the window. "Now come. There is giving to be done."

Surprised at how suddenly calm he felt, Nikolas stood on tiptoe and swung a bag over the lintel, knocking his elbow. The bag swung and landed softly inside.

The old man whispered, "I heard nothing, *kyrie*."

Nikolas hesitated, then pulled himself up to the window ledge and peered in. The moon illuminated the room enough for him to see the bag resting on something near a fireplace. Boots? Sandals? Stockings? He could not tell, but he aimed the next bag at the same place, and the third, then slid down next to the man.

"It's done," he whispered triumphantly, feeling light-headed with generosity.

"So it is," said an oddly distant voice.

Nikolas looked around in amazement, but the old man was gone.

His heart skipped again to a far-off music.

A dog barked.

And over the rooftops, the moon cast off its anchors and went rising up into heaven.

One

Remember

Father Nick's Day minus twenty-eight days
North American Space and Air Defence Central HQ
Walton, USA

The man woke to the panic of blindness and the coolness on his skin as someone unwrapped bandages from his head and eyes. Spaces inside his head echoed. His vision blurred, then cleared, and he saw a man in a white coat next to his bed, and a second man in a blue jacket on the other side. Two men in suits stood further away. The room was white and sterile. Air-conditioning hummed. His palm itched. The taste of blue felt soft on his tongue.

"Where?" he croaked, wondering, *Blue?* "Where is this?" Had he been sick? Injured? *Taste?*

Blue Jacket did something with his Scout, a dark unit about the size of his hand, with several recessed ports and access tools along its sides that marked it as government issue. He was surprised he knew that. The suits looked impassive. One was taller than the other. One wore glasses. Both wore grey ties.

"You're in the medical facility in NASAD," said the white-coated man. "You work here. Perhaps you can tell us your name?"

Name. His name. That should have been a necessary part of him, identity infused through every cell, yet in the space where he expected to find it was only a dark shape, without form or color and submerged under grey mists and shadows.

He knew instinctively the shape represented his identity, though he could not taste it, access it. It puzzled him. "I don't know."

"Corporal Peter Blackwell," said White Coat.

Blackwell, he thought, mouthing the word, tasting its sounds, trying to make it fit into the echoing spaces of his mind. *Corporal Peter Blackwell.* It felt awkward, clumsy, though he knew what a corporal was.

"I'm a soldier?"

"You're a Dungeon watcher, Scandinavia Desk, Watch Four at the North American Space and Air Defence Central HQ. NASAD. You're twenty-nine years old, single."

NASAD? He remembered no such place. He worked at...His boss was... He was a...

White Coat glanced around at the suits, and one of them nodded slightly.

Blackwell realized that they were communicating with glances and facial expressions, but he couldn't understand them. *A watcher?*

"How did I get here? Was I injured?"

"You had an accident."

Blue Jacket put away his Scout but said nothing. The two suits looked still enough to be furniture.

He concentrated. He remembered nothing about an accident. When he scanned back, searching for memories—*What did I do yesterday?*—every verb was null, every place void, everything...blank. Instead, brown shapes formed in his mind. Formed, moved, transfigured, faded, re-formed, as though they were trying to signify something, as though he should be able to recognize them. Shapes that were blurred and intergrown in strange ways in his head. Different to what he imagined them to be. Senses re-skinned. He tasted brown, he heard sweetness.

He tried to sit up, confused. "An accident? Where?"

White Coat put pillows behind his back, and said, "We don't know. One of your friends brought you here after you were injured."

"Who? Where is he now?"

"He didn't leave any details, but you've been comatose for about two weeks. Your scans show that you won't remember much of your past...as well as something, well, a little unusual. The reports are inconclusive, and we are still waiting on some neural analyses, but..."

He shrugged. "To be honest, we don't quite understand what's happened to you."

Shapes with *taste*. "I don't remember."

"Your brain has been…reconfigured. We don't know the cause, or the full extent."

"Reconfigured? What does that mean? I've lost *all* my memory?" He reached up and felt his head, though it felt normal.

"And what else do you rememb—?" White Coat asked.

Blue Jacket said quickly, "He remembers nothing. You heard what he said."

Blackwell didn't understand why Blue Jacket had not allowed White Coat to finish, but he remembered nothing anyway. Words drained out of his head, and nothing filled it. "I don't know. Nothing."

"Don't worry," White Coat said, and Blackwell wasn't sure why the sides of his mouth moved upwards. "You'll remember *everything*. We're hoping it will be sooner rather than later, obviously."

The way the lines and shapes on his face changed fascinated Blackwell. There were thoughts and emotions governing them, he knew, though he had no idea which ones. Just lines and shapes. White Coat talked a lot, and Blue Jacket's face rarely varied from its still calm. Their faces moved but he didn't understand what their expressions meant. Sound and movement without meaning. A world full of it.

Blue Jacket laid a hand on Blackwell's shoulder. "Remember in your own time, Corporal. No need to be rushed by Doctor Sullivan there. I'm Cox, by the way. Gary Cox, Senior Training Advisor with NASAD."

Sullivan stared at Cox, but his eyes narrowed this time. Blackwell wished he understood what it meant. He thought perhaps the two men were opposed, though did not understand why.

"Robert Sullivan, Doctor," said Sullivan. "It's my job to help you regain your memory. If you feel up to it, perhaps you wouldn't mind a brief visit to your workstation. No objections, Mister Cox?"

Cox's eyes narrowed again. "We all know the answer to that."

"Well, then," said Sullivan slowly. "Let's go. Perhaps something there might prompt a memory."

Blackwell hoped so, though an appearance from his mysterious friend would serve better. He put on the boots given him, then one of the suits helped him stand, though he felt fine.

"And when you've looked around there, we'll take you…home."

Home. Another memory he should have. But nothing attached itself to the word, no lover or children. No house or car, lawnmower, cracked bathroom tiles in need of repair, renovation plans, dog. He felt incomplete.

They led him out like a tame beast. He was dressed in a workblue coverall that held no memories. A patch of skin on his right palm seemed distinctly darker than the rest. He had burned himself? It looked cleanly and expertly healed, but unlocked no memories. His boots looked new, though he had no recollection of purchasing them. Cox followed Blackwell closely, never more than a foot from his shoulder. Blackwell could hear him breathing.

As they passed an internal window, Blackwell saw a brief reflection of the body he occupied. Moderately tall, dark messy hair, bearded face, powerful physique. It raised no memories.

Who am I?

As they passed through corridors and down through many humming levels, he said, "I don't remember NASAD."

"It's a Government monitoring station," said Sullivan, "an early warning post. The nerves of the President, if you like. We—you monitor real-time satellite feeds for unexplained military movements, weapons testing or launches. Most of the analysis is done in the Mission Room four levels up, but all the feeds are monitored on separate Desks below the MR and the most critical data channeled into the Pulpit. You're a hundred meters underground, Corporal."

"And my job is to watch the satellite images?"

"Do you remember the Dungeon, the monitors, anything…else?"

Cox spoke quickly. "You don't have to answer, Corporal."

Blackwell didn't understand why he shouldn't, though looking at Cox's still face made him feel calm. "I'm sorry. No."

They halted at a steel grey sliding door in a small lobby opposite two elevators. One of the suits opened the door by keying a code on an access panel - *7 - 5 - 5 - 1 - 6 - 4 - 0 - 2 - 3 - 1 - 1 - 0 - 2 - 6 - 0* - 2. Blackwell watched him key in the access code, and felt it on his tongue as it played itself out in his head without any conscious thought, flowing through the circuitry of his brain according to its own laws, more like a landscape of color and texture and taste than a series of digits.

"You'll get your own access code on your replacement watchcard tomorrow," said Sullivan. "The manual keypad is a failsafe if you misplace your card. It will take a while to remember the sequence."

But Blackwell could not forget if he tried. The sequence began with the cool sharpness of orange rain, then accelerated into a sweet humming that tasted of guava, and concluded with rich and deep singing. Mountain singing, he thought. A choir of operatic baritones standing on a summit.

"Your card will only get you into certain areas—the Dungeon, elevators, MR, access and service areas, lower admin zones," said Sullivan. "The HR people are still working on replacing your other cards."

"I lost them?"

The way Sullivan hesitated made Blackwell realize he had other words beneath those he was speaking. Other words which perhaps meant something different.

"Not lost them, no. Not as far as we know. You were brought in without so much as a wallet. There was some talk that the police would be called in to interview you about your assailants, but I don't think—"

"That's not essential information!" said Cox loudly. "You're overstepping, Doctor."

Essential or not, Blackwell wondered if the attack had injured his brain, deleted his memory. "Someone attacked me, then." Though the idea triggered no memories. "I was in a fight? How? What happened?"

Sullivan's voice was noticeably louder. "Part of your recovery is to discover these things on your own—the neural connections become stronger when they form that way."

They ushered Blackwell into a small room. Three workstations circled a central concrete pillar painted blue, but it was devoid of anything else. No graffiti, management memos, Post-It notes. No charts, data panels, warning signs.

"This is the Dungeon, home of the Scandinavia Desk," Sullivan said. "You work as a Watch Four specialist, monitoring satcams. You're very good at it, though you might find it unfamiliar for a week or two. I will mentor you through your first shift when you start in a few days, monitor you closely and re-integrate you back into normal life."

"Doctor Sullivan neglected to mention that I will be here as well," said Cox.

It occurred to Blackwell then that something deeper was passing between the two men, a dispute out of his sight. The suit guided him to a chair in front of a bank of screens. A chronometer above them read 0147.

Blackwell sat. Nothing was familiar. "I don't remember any of this."

"You are our first warning of trouble in Scandinavia," said a suit as if Blackwell had not spoken.

"What's important in Scandinavia?"

"Nothing you see is unimportant, not even the smallest incident," said the suit. He wore black unframed glasses. A mole near his left ear looked like a grenade. "Monitor and report to the Pulpit. National security. You'll start when you feel better."

"No," said Blackwell, troubled by something he could not yet identify. "I want to remember. I feel fine. I want to start now."

"I think you should rest first," said Cox. "You've just woken from a coma. Too many new experiences and…memories would be harmful right now. Best to start tomorrow."

The silence that followed puzzled Blackwell. Sullivan and Cox stared at each other for eighteen seconds—Blackwell smelled the time calibrating neatly in his mind—and then Sullivan called the two suits to the door, where they conferred.

But Cox looked over Blackwell's shoulder to where Sullivan stood in the doorway. His eyes narrowed. He leaned forward and whispered quickly, "I only have a few seconds, so listen and don't speak. Do you remember who you are, Tower?"

Blackwell felt disturbed by the closeness of his face, the staleness of his breath. "What? Tower? Who are you?"

"Tower is your real name, and I am one of the few allies you have remaining." His face and voice were both as steady as lines of latitude. "Hear me. You must *not* try to remember who you are. If you—"

"Why not?"

Cox looked around hurriedly. "Bound up with your identity is a vital secret that must remain concealed. For the lives of millions across the world, you must not remember it. And if you *do*," Cox twitched his head towards Sullivan, "cut out your tongue before you tell *him* anything. If he and his masters learn your secret, then all is lost. Say nothing to anyone until we talk further. Things are not as they seem."

Tower? His mind was a tractionless surface where no information gripped. "I don't remember anything."

"Good. Keep it that way. As much as possible, avoid going out—"

"Why?"

"Because what you may see will stir memories, and those memories will kill millions. It's only for a day or so until we have stabilised your situation. Tell him *nothing*."

At the thought of killing, though, a dark deathly yellow throbbed in Blackwell's throat like toxic mushrooms. He almost choked, but Sullivan and one of the suits appeared at the door where the suit stood, one hand inside his jacket. Blackwell instinctively dropped to a crouch, amazed to find himself calculating attack angles and distances. In less than a second, should he need to escape, he knew he could fight off one suit and use Sullivan as a shield to get to the second. Three seconds to disable three and be clear.

One of the suits stepped between Cox and Blackwell. "Excuse me, Corporal," he said. "Mister Cox is needed elsewhere." He reached an arm behind Cox's back. "You'll come with me, Senior Training Advisor."

Cox turned to Blackwell. "Do not *remember,*" he hissed, but if there was any message in his face, Blackwell could not decipher it.

Even so, Cox's warning aligned strongly with his lack of identity. Though his brain was no more than a hollow echoing cavern, it was possible that something was hidden deep down. Not only twenty-nine years of his own memories, but if he was responsible for warning the President of threats against the US, then possibly something worse.

He paused. Something did not add up.

If the secret could kill millions—and NASAD was there to ensure national security—why had Cox told him not to remember it?

And why had Sullivan removed the one man who knew of it?

"Ready to start?" Sullivan asked when they were alone in the room. "Are you sure you're OK?"

"Yes."

The first blurred hour seemed to consume a week. With Cox's warning pulsing endlessly in his brain—he found he could segment his brain to consider it separately—he listened to Sullivan describe seismic registers and zoom factors, temperature gradients and satellite orbit nodes. Sullivan was thorough, methodical, calm.

"Did I really know all this?" Blackwell asked him. None of it felt right, though he had no idea what constituted *right*. "I don't remember any of it."

Sullivan's smile was full of teeth. "All of it," he said. "It will come back."

So how could I be good at this? Blackwell wondered. *How can there be degrees of skill in looking at a screen for six hours?*

But something massive was building under his skin, and it caught him off guard. When he identified it, it sat him back in his chair.

Almost all of his past was gone, but something new was forming up in its place.

He remembered *everything since he had woken.*

No millions-killing secret, but every single moment of the last two hours instead, preserved without corruption or flaw in his head in a moving landscape, in graduations of *color* and *taste,* dancing data-banners in the chambers behind his eyes. A beautiful thing it was, more beautiful than any music. And instantly accessible, he realized, with no need for backups, no system validation tests, no maintenance.

Startled, he checked as Sullivan was telling him about something else, surprised how easy it was. Not only could he smell and taste every word spoken, but also everything he had been taught and shown. The start time of the practice sim they had done in the first two hours? *0116.* The data crossover period between the MAYFLOWER and COLUMBUS satellites? *0145—0151.* The incident duration of the troop movements: *0149—0234.* The incident itself: two units of the Finnish Ranger regiment, border patrol, with light mortars and rocket launchers identified by their heat sigs and curious *tastes.* Temp ranges: minus 14—minus 7 Celsius, cloud cover: two eighths, wind speed: 14km/h nor-north easterly. And the data were just *there* in his mind.

The next practice sim, though considerably more complex, was just as easy to remember. And the next. And the one after that. Even when he went back to the first, the data were still there. Undegraded.

No recall necessary. No effort. He just went to the place where the data were and accessed it.

He sat back. Was that who he had been before his accident? A human database, a freak? Did the bosses know about his prodigious memory? Was that why he was so good?

He had already realized that his mental chronometer continued to keep time behind his other thoughts. *Six fifty three.* Counting even when he wasn't conscious of it. *Six fifty three and thirty eight seconds. Thirty nine. Forty.*

"Who sits in the other two seats?" he asked Sullivan.

"Your watch-partner in one, and the other workstation is for backup."

"Who is my partner?"

"The position has become recently vacant. We will commence interviewing shortly, and your partner will start when you've regained full proficiency." Sullivan smiled. "For the moment, we've shifted the Scandinavian Desk to another location with temporary staff. We thought we should start your rehabilitation here in the hope it might spark a memory. All the monitors and functions are live, but we've cut the link to the Pulpit for the time being. How do you feel?"

"Fine. Why did my partner leave?"

Sullivan looked at his Scout, then at Blackwell. "That's not important. Any triggers yet? Any...resurfacing memories?"

"No memories. Just tastes and smells."

Sullivan scribbled something on his Scout, erased it, and wrote something else. "Well, that's a start, I suppose." He pocketed his Scout and smiled. "Enough for now. You need a good night's sleep, I think. Normally at this time, you'd hand over to Watch One," said Sullivan, "but we'll train you in that later."

In the elevator, as a woman's voice declared their ascent, he realized that he was different. Different in ways he could not measure.

Reconfigured.

"We've assigned you a new home and prepared new...ah, security measures for the foreseeable future."

"Security?" echoed Blackwell as a sharp memory stirred deep within him. "Why?"

"Just a precaution," said Sullivan.

The woman's voice announced *Mission Room,* and Sullivan escorted him from the elevator into a glassed gallery overlooking a vast chamber of screens arrayed around a raised platform. Dozens of uniformed staffers sat at terminals, strode purposefully between stations, clustered in small groups. "Now, this is the MR, the Pulpit in the middle, and the Nest is up on the far side, where the generals meet."

Blackwell stopped, fascinated, forgetting security for a moment.

Seven levels above the Mission Room, Sullivan led him out of the second-last elevator and down the long access tunnel, carding through the five steel doors that protected NASAD from public access.

"These doors and the dome shield are build to withstand fire, flood, direct rocket attack, low yield blast," said Sullivan. "Almost everything short of a nuclear detonation."

Back in the elevator, Sullivan keyed the ground floor. "There are several access points from the outside into NASAD, all disguised.

You'll learn all of them in time. Tonight, we'll use the alley. When we get out, walk casually. We are two workers returning home after a late shift."

They exited the elevator into a bare and dimly-lit room with a single door and a monitor showing the alley outside.

Sullivan checked the monitor, then keyed a sequence of digits into the keypad on the door, and pushed open the door. The room went dark.

"Quick," he said, followed Blackwell out into the cool darkness, puddles and smells of rubbish, then pulled the door closed. There was no handle on the outside. "The bus stop is this way," he said.

"I don't have a car?"

"Your bus is the 33," said Sullivan. "There's a timetable at your apartment. I'll drive you there tonight, though."

As they started down the alley, Blackwell saw a figure slouched against a wall, a bottle in one hand, and streetlight glinting on something long and metal in his other hand. Blackwell stared, but as they passed the slumped figure and came to the alley entrance, a gurgled cry and heavy thud made Blackwell turn. The figure was crumpled in a heap on the ground, the bottle rolling away with a hollow tinkling. The heavy slump of the figure disgusted him with an angry pity. Orange anger flared in his head as he swung around to cradle the man in his arms, comfort him, though it was too late to tell him that nothing was so bad that suicide was the only answer, but Sullivan held him back. "It's just an Early," he said. "He's gone. There's nothing you can do. The cops will pick him up, issue a 104, clean up."

"A what? He...he just killed himself! You're not shocked by this?"

"We get a couple every now and then, especially at night for those who don't want an audience."

"People killing themselves is *normal* in this world?"

Sullivan peered at Blackwell for a long moment before he spoke. "You don't remember this?"

This was a vile world, and his anger tasted of bitter coffee. "No! I...but...I was *part* of this? I *knew* about this?"

"*Everyone* knows. He got the Black Despair, woke up one morning and didn't have any reason to keep going. No *hope*. Nothing anyone can do. Best just let them go."

Blackwell was deeply shaken as he followed Sullivan out of the alley and onto the main street. If this was his world, he would rather be comatose. "But what causes it?"

"Come on," said Sullivan, opening car doors. "No-one knows. There's no medical explanation. Just wake up one morning and life seems pointless. No cure, although most go out on mad shopping sprees, hoping to find some meaning in possessions. Worst single cause of death on the planet—kills millions every year. Governments let it go so long as you don't kill anyone else when you go, and if you want to go out in style, just call Cable Co and they'll send out your own personal assassin. This guy must have been a loner, so he found a dark spot and killed himself."

Sullivan got in.

Blackwell barely had the strength to get into the car. "No cure at all? That's *it*? How can that be the end of everything?"

"Come on," said Cox. "No-one knows why. It's been around for almost two thousand years, and no-one can cure it. It just is." He paused. "Is this important to you?"

Blackwell inhaled twice. "Yes," he said, realizing that somehow, vile and horrifying as it was now, suicide had been a part of his life *then*.

Walton, USA

Home was a two-bedroom NASAD apartment on the ground floor of an apartment building a few minutes from the town center. Home was neat, comfortable, furnished, equipped with everything he would need. Home had cream colored walls, except the bathroom, whose walls were white. Home had a TV with a selection of current movies, books, music, news tiles. Home had a small empty garage. Home's fridge and pantry were both neatly stacked with a variety of food items and utensils. Home had a wardrobe of clean and neat shirts, shoes, ties, work clothing, athletics, casuals, none of them worn.

Hoping for jolts, resonances, stirrings, Blackwell went flicking slowly through the apartment, touching objects, sniffing the bindings of books, hoping to see his name written on the flyleaf of a book. A photo of him with a lover, a friend, parents. A shirt he would remember wearing, stained with pasta sauce or red wine from an Italian restaurant somewhere. *Anything.*

But nothing in Home resonated with him. The apartment was full of the new smells of fabric and electric appliances instead.

"For security reasons," said Sullivan, flicking on the TV, "external and internal threat detectors have been installed. You don't need to call or trigger an alarm—everything that passes into and out of this apartment is monitored, and armed guards will be on site within minutes. We can't protect you when you venture out, but when you're here or on shift, you'll be safe. I'll have the threat detectors activated now." He took a Scout from his pocket, tapped at it for a few moments, then said, "OK, safeties are on."

Blackwell shook his head. *Safeties? Armed guards?* "I don't remember this place."

Sullivan's face was unreadable. He gestured to the TV, where a panel of suited people were discussing something. "Maybe something will spark a memory."

Something on TV caught Blackwell's ear. The suits were discussing impact zones, climatic upheaval and underground bunkers. "What is this?"

Sullivan hesitated. "You don't remember?"

"Nothing."

"I'm sorry no-one told you, although it's rather shocking news for someone who's just woken from a coma. It's the Melcassar Comet. Torino Level 7. Some lost comet that appeared out of nowhere. Catastrophic end of all life on Earth if it hits. We've known about it for a year or so, although scientists weren't sure if it would hit Earth or just skim past. A group of governments combined to build and send up a nuclear device to shatter it, but it only destroyed a small part. It knocked it off course, though, so we should be safe."

"Should?"

"Governments are saying there's no problem, that it should slide past on its way to the sun, but people still talk."

"Comet or Black Despair, then?"

"I'm sorry. It's an ugly world. Listen, relax, get some dinner and maybe watch a movie. I'll come past in the morning at about ten and take you into town for a look around. Help you remember things."

Blackwell clenched his mouth closed. *Bound up with your identity is a vital secret that must remain concealed. For the lives of millions, you must not remember it.*

This was the vital secret? The possible impact point of the comet? Blackwell almost immediately dismissed it. No secret that could save millions should remain concealed. And Cox had given clear commands.

Cut out your tongue before you tell him anything. If he and his masters learn your secret, then all is lost. Say nothing to anyone until we talk further.

Sullivan turned to leave. "See you at ten," he said.

Blackwell said goodbye at the door. To clear his head, he looked up into the cool black night sky, hoping to see the comet.

Instead, the wide blaze of stars triggered something else. His heart leaped to a mad race, and deep, pure resonances thrummed within him. His cheeks warmed, even in the cool evening air. The world was foreign and vile, but the vast swathe of stars was *so* beautiful, so wonderfully *real*.

Shocked, he looked down. *Stars?* Stars had meaning? No. Perhaps the coma had unbalanced his body chemistry. Perhaps he was just tired. He risked another look upwards, and color returned to his brain with such fabulous force and significance he could barely keep his eyes open.

Stars.

And then he realized. Everything else in the world was ugly, but something about stars was tantalisingly important, dangling just out of reach. It was a pointer to his *memory*, he realized. Stars were relevant in his life in some way, but how? He had been a student... studying astronomy? Astrophysics? He had studied the comet? Although how would that—or suicide—be relevant to a secret that would kill millions and had to be concealed?

He stood there until 11.32, pondering without resolution, then went inside, dressed for bed in pyjamas that smelled like the NASAD medical room, and got between sheets that smelled newly washed. But as he lay there in the dark, something like continental plates shifted inside the echoing cavern of his memory. At first, he only saw, behind grey mists and shadows in the center of everything, the dark mass of his identity, but now, a single shape that tasted of stars was orbiting like a tiny hopeful planet, ablaze with significance.

Alone in his apartment, in a thrill of excitement and sick disgust, Sullivan made coffee, sat on his sofa and waited. His pulse raced. The coffee tasted of rank bilious wickedness. No matter how much The Third had promised him for this mission, some small remnant of his humanity rebelled against murder, and Blackwell was dead for sure.

Tortured first, almost certainly with The Third's new machinery, and then executed. All because of what he knew. That small secret that would only take a day or so to extract. This combat would be without honor or mercy, and Blackwell the innocent to the slaughter.

Sullivan pushed the coffee away. A car braked sharply down the street. A neighbor laughed at something.

The phone rang once, then fell silent.

Fear roared in Sullivan's ears as he picked up the handset, sure that the act would pollute him.

The Third's voice came on without delay. Simultaneously, on the handset panel, chronometer digits began counting. Sullivan hated it fiercely, that methodical, relentless, entropic march. Although it was only a connection counter, he regarded it as the decay of his own life measured there in silicon black against the pale cream display. Second by second, down into death or failure.

"We have begun his training," Sullivan said, his eyes closed tightly shut to keep his vision from being sucked down the secure line as well. Even with a phone line between them—no-one knew where The Third could be found—the voice seemed to emerge from a cloud of malice so poisonous as to nearly choke him. "Yes, the Brotherhood have made contact with him as well. They sent a protector, as you expected. He spoke to the target, but we removed him quickly." He remembered Cox's manner and winced. "Yes, he knew who I was. It should only take a day or so to extract the information you need from the target."

He listened, with his gut warping and twisting like a speared fish in a steel bucket. "I understand. Extract the secret, then kill him."

Extract the secret.

Plain as the words were, they sounded as unlovely as a dog coughing up its last blood and breath. Sullivan gagged, and when the voice closed the link and the handset pulsed hot against his ear, he could not move for an hour.

Blackwell went back inside. Alone in the enormous cavity of his brain, Cox's warning continued.

Bound up with your identity is a vital secret that must remain concealed. For the lives of millions, you must not remember it.

He was so focused on it that he did not at first notice the tall lean man standing in his living room. Two straps over the man's chest indicated a pack of some kind on his back.

"Hello, Peter," he said. "I'm the friend who brought you to NASAD."

Blackwell swallowed. "My friend?" He knew he mustn't ask, but…his friend would know these things! His words tumbled out in a guilty rush of relief. "I don't—How did you get in here? What's your name?"

"Ed." He stood there, leaning slightly backward, his brown eyes steady. What little hair remained on his head drifted and floated in a way that reassured Blackwell, though he did not know why.

"How did you get in?"

Ed smiled faintly. "Stay still." He reached out to Blackwell's head with both hands—"This won't hurt"—and probed with his fingers at points around Blackwell's head, looking intently at a point somewhere beyond Blackwell.

"Any headaches?" he asked. "The NASAD people told me you might have suffered cerebral damage. Dizziness, blackouts, nausea?"

"No. Are you a doctor?"

"More a plumber," said Ed, and dropped his hands. Blackwell's temples and head tingled.

Ed narrowed his eyes as he considered Blackwell. Blackwell watched his every movement.

"Who was I before my accident?"

Ed didn't move. His voice was even and quiet. "The same man you are now."

Blackwell frowned at that, unable to extract any meaning from it. "Did I work at NASAD?"

"No."

The suits and white coats lied, he realized. *And that's why nothing in this apartment is familiar.* "Where did I work, then?"

Ed slipped off the straps. "Work is hardly the word for what you used to do. You were a student."

"What was I studying? What subjects? At university?"

"No."

"Was I like this before the accident? What is the secret in my head? Why will it kill millions? *Who am I?*"

Ed swung a faded green rucksack around and held it out to Blackwell. "Do you recognize this?"

Blackwell realized that Ed expected a positive answer, but with great effort, he resisted answering. "Who am I? Tell me about my accident, about my life before the accident. What is the secret!"

Ed held the rucksack closer. Black straps dangled.

Blackwell's focus was on Ed's face, though it presented as much information as a black hole. "Tell me. *Please*."

Ed nodded. "It's yours. You used to keep your things in it. Open it."

Blackwell took it, as much annoyed as troubled. It was heavier than he expected. He hefted it, expecting Ed to explain, though the taller man simply stood and watched. Blackwell unzipped the top compartment and looked inside.

"I have to *know*."

"Take them out," said Ed.

Blackwell stared, but Ed's face was blank.

He reached into the rucksack. The first item was a Scout, similar to those used by NASAD staffers, though larger, formed from a darker casing, and with extra touch panels on one side. The second was a simple data tile, though slightly thicker than those commercially available, and with a small screen.

Blackwell put the rucksack down, and noticed that it remained rigid as he leaned it against the wall. The Scout fitted neatly into his palm, its screen blank until his body warmth activated it.

"Don't put it down," said Ed. "It will key to your *theta* waves shortly—just keep physical contact until it does."

Blackwell watched the screen illuminate in fascination. "Why are you giving them to me? What are they for?"

The technical and practical details of the Scout and tile took about an hour. Blackwell listened in silence, remembering everything Ed told him.

Ed looked to the door. "We put you at NASAD to watch for trouble."

"I was a *spy*?"

Ed laughed, and Blackwell chose to interpret it as positive. "It sounds exciting, but no. You just have an extraordinary memory and an eye for detail, and we need you to keep a watch on our interests in Scandinavia. We're the good guys in this game—the bad guys you don't want to cross. Both of us are worldwide and very secret, though, and both have infiltrated NASAD as well as governments, armies, international organisations. We're both fairly evenly balanced, but things are changing, Peter. After centuries of war, things are going to get very ugly very soon."

"Why?" He felt as though he was on a ten second delay from reality. "Where was I before this? Who else is like me?"

Ed considered him. "You weren't here in Walton. And you're one of a kind. Now, don't worry too much about your NASAD…ah, *colleagues,* but be careful nevertheless. You won't have much to do with the generals, and most of your workmates are neutral, but be very careful of anyone in the Pulpit. Don't speak of me to anyone. Keep to yourself."

"Who is 'us'? Your—our—?"

Ed smiled. "Do you mean, 'Can I trust you?'"

Blackwell nodded. "Yes."

"Your real name is Tower."

Tower is your real name, and I am one of the few allies you have remaining.

"But it's best that you don't know any more than that. Now, getting back to the equipment. You must remember all data from your Watch, and tile everything from the other Watches. You must *not* lose a single moment of data. And there are two situations in which you must use the tile and Scout as I instructed you. Firstly, when you see anything unusual in Scandinavia, any military escalation, any unexplained combat activity not covered by the Diplomatic Lists, anything unusual at all. And secondly, and most importantly, when you remember who you are."

"I was told not to remember."

"Of course, but the time will come when you must."

"Soon?"

Ed smiled and grasped his shoulder. "Whoever is in the Pulpit will try to prevent you. You must not permit yourself to be diverted. If the situation becomes…ah, untenable, the Scout and rucksack will keep you alive until we get you out."

"Untenable? What does that mean?"

"Dangerous."

With a thrill that surprised him, Blackwell tasted yellow and the muzzles of war. "How will I know?"

"I'm not permitted to tell you, I'm sorry. Nor anything about your past."

"Because millions will die? Is that true?"

Ed only smiled. "You'll learn everything you want to know after your extraction." He shook Blackwell's hand. "In the meantime, good luck, and don't forget what I told you to do."

Remembering every word Ed had said, Blackwell watched him walk down the street. None of it made sense! It was all just a blast of noise, and he did not know how to turn it off.

Father Nick's Day minus twenty-seven days
Walton, USA

At 9.15 exactly, his internal alarm woke him. Sullivan was coming to take him into town to help him regain his memory, though Cox's warning still pulsed behind his eyes.

Bound up with your identity is a vital secret that must remain concealed. For the lives of millions, you must not remember it.

If Cox and Ed were both correct, he was a trainee agent with an unknown organisation, friendly with NASAD. He had an amazing ability to remember, and he had been placed in a monitoring installation to watch for something in Scandinavia. And though his long-term memory had been erased, a deeply-buried secret would cause enormous casualties if Sullivan got hold of it, though it was unclear who Sullivan was working for. Perhaps, as Cox had warned him, his placement at NASAD was part of a witness protection program and Sullivan had followed him.

But if he hadn't been in Walton before his coma, anything he saw today with Sullivan wouldn't matter. That gave him a quiet relief. If colors flared matchbright behind his eyes at some random sight or smell, he would school himself not to react and not to speak. Then Cox would return and explain what on earth was going on. He was sure the world had not been so obscene before his coma. Suicide as normal? It was not only disgusting, but deeply wrong. Even more so that he seemed to be the only one who saw it.

After eating food he didn't taste, he sat down on the bed they said was his, and looked for his shoes.

It was then that he saw on his right ankle, faded and blue and quite simple, a tattoo. It looked like a Japanese *kanji*. He couldn't read it, and it didn't raise the excitement of stars, so maybe it was just a youthful dare from his hidden past. But it was too small for that.

He considered. Perhaps an identifying clan or family mark?

A visual database would surely have it listed, and the local library would have one. Perhaps Sullivan would give him a moment to check.

At 9.52, he opened the front door, and stood on his front step, taking his bearings. A short old man, dressed in a shabby coat, passed with a beagle. The sun moved behind clouds.

Sullivan arrived on foot at 9.59, wearing an blue open neck shirt and business trousers. He looked down the street both ways before looking at Blackwell. "Did you sleep well?"

"Yes, thank you."

"I thought we would walk into town. It's not far, and perhaps you'll see something you recognize."

Blackwell nodded. He might, but he would not speak of it.

The neighborhood seemed new, modern apartment buildings interspersed with older houses, along roads lined with spreading trees. Uniformed supermarket workers made him stare, their noses and ears and lips pierced with metalware that looked like explorers' tools. Until they reached the post office, though, everything was just flat skin over void. If he turned them side-on, the wind would blow them away. Nothing had substance.

But then, at the Walton Post Office, three gold letters changed everything.

FND.

Emblazoned on the side of a green mailbox, they sent his heart racing. Colors flared like stars, gorgeous, significant and so *real*. Reality disengaged a little. Silence hazed his hearing. He stumbled, frightened at his response, but dimly aware that he must not tell Sullivan anything.

A hand gripping his arm. Sullivan helping him stand. The world resuming. "Everything OK? You look faint."

Blackwell stood, forced his attention away from the mailbox.

Say nothing.

"Peter, you OK? Here, sit down, take it easy for a minute."

Unspeaking, Blackwell allowed himself to be guided to a row of green plastic chairs near a bus stop. Sullivan sat next to him, faced him. His voice was soft, his face close. "So what happened?"

Say nothing. He prepared his words, *Nothing. Just a turn. Maybe just a little weak.* But the words that came off his tongue, tasting of limes and sounding like gentle rain, were not those. "The letters FND on the mailbox sparked a memory." Shocked, he bit his tongue, but the words were out, right in Sullivan's face. It was his tongue, but not his will. "I remember Father Nick's Day."

Sullivan leaned forward. "Really?" he said quietly. "What do you remember?"

Blackwell's mind was already racing with Cox's warning and deeper still, plans of escape. "I need to go," he said, but even as he stood, Sullivan took his arm and guided him back down again.

"You're still a little faint," said Sullivan. "Stay for a while."

Say nothing.

"Tell me about Father Nick's Day. It will help you regain your memory."

"But Cox told me not to say anything!"

Sullivan's laugh was soft, and his hand on Blackwell's shoulder gentle. "I'm sorry you were subjected to his conspiracy theories. You won't have to put up with him again. He's quite harmless, but to someone just woken from a coma, his crazy ideas must have been disturbing, to say the least." He removed his hand. "Come on, tell me. Talking is good therapy for someone in your position."

Blackwell tasted limes and heard gentle rain a second time and this time knew what they meant. Somewhere in his reconfigured brain, the synapses that permitted him to lie had been disabled. He *had* to tell the truth. Falsehood would taste sour, purple and spiky.

All his plans not to speak were now hopeless.

Cut out your tongue before you tell him anything. If he and his masters learn your secret, then all is lost.

"I can't." For a brief moment, an alarming desire to disable Sullivan beckoned—a quick jab to the neck would do it—but a stronger instinct shoved that idea down, the faint noises of a deeper battle echoing up from the shadowed gorge of his memory.

"*Can't* and *won't* are very different words, Peter. Speaking is good for you. Whatever Cox told you is complete nonsense."

Blackwell thought fast. He still believed Cox, but the minefield ahead of him was dark and pathless, and although any step he took could bring the disaster Cox feared, the alternatives seemed no better. Ed was not going to tell him anything, so perhaps he could tread carefully through the minefield and learn something as he went.

"Alright," he said, tasting limes in every word.

Sullivan folded his hands in his lap. "Let's hear it."

But then a young girl approached with her parents. She had a yellow envelope in her hand, and she slipped away from her father's hand and dropped it into the FND mailbox slot. Then she splashed in puddles until her parents called her back into the hurry of people. It disturbed him that he didn't understand these people. His world was diagonal to theirs. He spoke a different language to them—theirs was commerce and cars and money and purchases, and his was a private grammar of sounds and smells and a single negative verb: *I don't remember.*

But he *did* remember Father Nick's Day. Memories unribboned in brightening color. "The man in the alley killed himself because of the Black Despair. He had no hope. But parents...parents register their children at birth for Father Nick's Day!" The cascade strengthened. "And if they do, they...you can beat the Black Despair until the next Father Nick's Day! Without it, you'll kill yourself. The man in the alley probably didn't register."

Sullivan smiled. "That's great, Peter. Really good, although everyone knows that stuff. But you had a very strong reaction to that mailbox, so can you go a bit deeper? There might be something in the Father Nick's Day concept that links with your past life." He paused. "Anything?"

Blackwell thought, genuinely curious. "Nothing, I'm sorry."

A businessman arrived, dropped in his envelope and stood there for a few moments afterwards, his eyes closed and hands clasped. Blackwell wondered what he was doing.

"But something in your memory links with the idea, yes?"

Even now, the three gold letters still made Blackwell's pulse race. "Yes."

Sullivan was silent for a moment. "Any other memories?

Blackwell could not hold it back. Even with Cox's warning like screaming jets on all horizons, he said it anyway. "Stars. I had the same reaction when I looked up last night and saw stars."

Sullivan's eyes narrowed. "All stars? Or one in particular?"

"I don't know."

"Anything else?"

Blackwell could not stop himself. "I have a tattoo. On my ankle."

"Show me."

Blackwell did. He wondered what passers by would think of a man showing such interest in another man's ankle. "I thought I could look for it on a visual database in the local library."

Sullivan only looked for a moment. "You won't find it there."

"Do you know what it means?"

"Yes, but I can't tell you, I'm sorry. Your memory will return stronger if you discover things without being told. But you can look if you like. The library is a few blocks along this road."

On the way to the library, though, between a grocer and a sports store, a poster of a frozen lake in a suicide agent's window stopped him. He cried out and stepped back, the powerful yellow of finishing surging up within him, twisting his gut, and knocked over someone carrying groceries. Fleeing breaking glass and yells, he hurried away, panting. The world dimmed slightly. Noises and sight blurred.

"Peter?" Sullivan hurried after him. "A memory?"

"Ice," muttered Blackwell, and Sullivan took his arm and guided him to a park bench in Walton's Memorial Park. Blackwell sat, his hands on his knees, his back rigid.

Sullivan sat next to him. "Tell me when you're ready."

Blackwell barely heard him, staring at a tree he was not the slightest bit interested in, the world a hazy afterthought on the outskirts of his vision. It was not until Sullivan laid a hand on his shoulder, and the side of his hand made contact with Blackwell's skin that the world resumed. Black clouds appeared on the horizon.

"Peter?" said Sullivan softly. "Ice is a memory?"

"There's darkness in it," gritted Blackwell, still remembering the overwhelming despair, the powerful yellow of death, and the appearance of a second planet around his darkened identity-sun. Two planets, stars and ice, though he hated the second with a wild passionate fear.

"That's all?"

"No." The thought was like rape across the clean flesh of his memory, but he had to speak it. "The poster was in a suicide agents' window," he breathed. "So there…there are people who *help* people kill themselves?"

"Just like wedding planners, financial consultants, mortgage brokers. It's a service."

Blackwell processed the idea with reluctance. "I don't want to think about it any more."

Sullivan was silent for a few seconds. "Are you OK? Do you want to stay here while I get us something to eat?"

Blackwell nodded, his voice an unreliable instrument.

"What would you like?"

Although people were walking past him, or sitting on the grass with lunches in paper bags and boxes, wafting Thai and Chinese and several different dialects of curry past him, Blackwell realized he had no preferences. Everything was nutrition, nothing was taste. "Anything."

"OK. I'll be back soon."

Both his body and mind taut and stiff, Blackwell heard a rustle of fabric, the squeak of Sullivan's boot soles and footsteps. He remained motionless, though, watching dog walkers, mothers and complaining children, suited men and women, trying to think of nothing.

Until he saw the man and woman, he was successful. But there, among officeworkers and friends sitting on the grass eating lunch, a man and a woman were standing near a wall, talking to each other with their faces only a handspan apart. The sun was in her eyes—she was holding up one hand against it—but her whole focus was on the man. He moved forward, kissed her, then reached into his pocket, drew out a small box and gave it to her.

At that instant, as the woman received the gift and smiled, Blackwell's heart shifted orbits with a great planetary movement. He jumped up, so excited he almost danced in place.

Under the thin paper of his world, in the place where things were real, the idea of gifts formed and swung into orbit as his third planet, a real memory, with substance and depth so wonderful it forced him to sit and think.

And with one new breathless planet came another…something about words.

Secret words.

Five secret words.

And then another—a door, a…*strange* door.

Gloriously relieved that Sullivan was not there to rape these memories, he hid them deep down in a place he hoped he could defend. And there, as his five planets began their tiny hopeful orbits, their assembled mass generated something new.

He breathed out a great whoosh of excitement as some mad, dizzy recognition sprang up inside him: he had been with a woman! He couldn't remember her name. They were standing watch behind his strange door! When she moved, when the air around her shifted, he smelled her jasmine perfume. And the gifts and the five words were somehow connected.

Millions will die.

And the last thought was just *there* as he stood, stronger and more present than breath.

The jasmine woman *loved* him. His internal reality outshone the sunlight. He closed his eyes to harbor the memory, but there was no losing this, no unanchoring. This had its own sweet heavenlies, swelling out in a secret place in his mind, fixing its own constellations in his heart.

He must have been laughing. He opened his eyes into sunlight and a staring crowd, but it didn't matter. People nudged each other into polite dispersings.

Glad to be free of Sullivan's constant presence, he went striding, with all his sails galleoned, and excitement swelling under his skin.

There was *substance* in him. Real memory. He was as much a man as those he saw, a deserving member of the Walton citizenry. Not only were there memories now in the hollow cavern of his heart, but a woman as well.

He was so excited that he broke into a run, liberty a breathy gold fruit in his mouth.

But on the way, he stopped on the sidewalk, curious about a group gathered around TVs in a shop window. He paused and eased his way forward until he could see the screen, ignoring muttered complaints. Amid graphics of trajectories, the screen showed a faint fuzzy white patch amid blackness.

"Ugly thing," someone said.

But inside Blackwell's head, the planet named stars flared matchbright, glowing with significance. It wasn't a star that was significant, but the *comet*.

Clouds burst over him midway to the library. He loved the place from the moment he stepped inside the doors. Like a warm mother, he thought wryly. The automatic doors opened and closed on him several times—cold, warm, rain, warm—as he stood in the entrance, wondering what he had thought of his own mother. A librarian came and asked him if he would mind stepping forward and keeping the rain outside.

Blackwell did. The woman's name badge read 'Kay.' Her smile lit him up. She had short brown hair with blonde flecks. His pulse could have powered a city. He wondered if the woman of his memory were similar.

She asked him what he was looking for. He tried a serene smile, but it probably appeared as a grimace. The signboard rescued him.

"The Searchbase?" She followed his pointing finger. "Yes, down on the left. Have you used it before?"

Blackwell shook his head. *Maybe, but I don't remember.* He could not interpret the shapes her eyes and mouth made. Completely beautiful, but without any meaning at all.

She looked back at the main desk, and the women behind it, their fingers moving across keyboards as they chattered and laughed. "Come on, then. I've got a moment."

She settled him into a booth, explained how it worked and left, decorating the air with sweet fragrances, though not jasmine.

Blackwell liked the feel of the library. Quiet. The tactile hum of dataflow—a different hum to the cautious secretive silences of NASAD.

He sketched the shape of his tattoo on the touchpad with a stylus, and set the search to include the major visual databases, but he found nothing even remotely similar.

Well, he thought. *Let's change things,* although Cox's warning clamored in his skull.

You must not try to remember who you are. Millions will die.

But the momentum was strong. If he was not the NASAD worker, then who was he?

'Peter Blackwell', he keyed in, and set the parameters to *worldwide*. The screen filled with census returns, suicide listings, BMD registrations, Father Nick's Day listings, political officeholders and, if he had the correct passwords, credit checks, criminal records, police records. Too many. He typed *Corporal* Peter Blackwell.

Ah. Seventy-nine records: several American Blackwells, amongst them a Senator Blackwell from Iowa who once served with the US army. An Australian Corporal Blackwell, mentioned in despatches in the junglerot defense of the Kokoda Trail. And a British Blackwell, once of the Coldstream Guard, who had served as a diplomat in Moscow before he walked in front of a freight train twenty years ago.

Blackwell sat up, unaccountably frightened. He read back, uncertain.

Moscow. The word shook him, not the noxious taste of yellow, or the almost-demonic thought of ice, but another terror.

Something about...the...smell of...the smell of planes.

He blinked. Smell? Why not the sound, the terminal screaming of jets captured by gravity? A plane crash would explain his coma and head injuries. Or the particular whine of a troop carrier reactor under load? *Troop carrier? Where did that come from?* The memory evaporated before he could examine it.

The smell of planes. While not as awful as ice, another tiny planet swung into orbit.

He wiped his mouth, turned away. What was it about Moscow that had such powerful tones of ending? Perhaps the letters of the name that were so similar to the infinity symbol. Either that or the muzzles of a firing squad.

He sat back. No. Perhaps he had been to Moscow in his hidden life. The idea tasted brown to him, the root word for mystery in his private mental etymology of images and textures.

When he left hours later, Kay was not at the front desk. He had no idea what to say to her if she had been there.

But Sullivan and the rain were, both waiting at the front door. Blackwell knew the angles on his face did not represent pleasure, though they quickly changed to a smile. A librarian locked the sliding glass doors behind him, and Sullivan blocked the way forward.

"Did you find anything?"

Beyond him, cars splashed through evening-shiny puddles. Black umbrellas mourned and bobbed. Blackwell realized he was hungry, and that reduced the distress at telling Sullivan his secrets. "No, but I have new memories now."

"Tell me."

Blackwell could have hacked at his tongue with an axe, but the words came out independent of his horrified will. "Ice. The smell of planes. Stars."

"Stars is the comet, right?"

Blackwell was shocked. "Yes, but how did you know?"

Sullivan waved a hand. "Doesn't matter. Let's continue."

"Something about gifts is important. Five—"

"Gifts? That's interesting. How are they important?"

Was this the information that would kill millions? Blackwell didn't think so. Sullivan had said everyone knew that, although Blackwell thought it bizarre and pathetic, yet another face of the bleak and ugly world he inhabited. Magical gifts that appeared out of thin air on living room tables one morning every year. Gifts of encouragement, of wonder. Gifts that kept hope alive, that barricaded life against the Black Despair. He told Sullivan. "December sixth. Father Nick's Day. But no-one knows how the gifts get there, or who puts them there."

"Good, although that's common knowledge."

"Common?" It was disturbing how alien this world was. "How can gifts be the only way you people keep hope alive?"

"Maybe you can tell us that. Do you remember getting a Father Nick's Day gift?"

"No."

"So why do gifts excite you so?" He paused. His voice lowered. "Maybe you know how they get there?"

"No! How could I? No-one knows that. I only know that they are very important."

"OK. What else?"

Blackwell's tongue was already speaking the words. "Five secret words. A—"

"What words?" Sullivan's voice was a little louder, his face slightly closer. He smelled of stale curry. "Do you remember the words themselves?"

"No, I'm—"

"Not even the rhythm? Nothing at all?"

Blackwell hesitated. "Is it important?"

Sullivan leaned back, gave a short barking laugh. "No," he said. "No, I just thought…well, words are rather more concrete than vague images, so they could trigger more memories." He smiled. "Anything else?"

"A secret door. The jasmine woman who loved me. And Moscow."

Sullivan moved his head sharply to one side. "Detail please."

"I've told you everything I know, I'm sorry. But if I think of anything else, I'll tell you." The promise came off his tongue completely without his permission.

Sullivan held up hands and counted memories off fingers. "Eight memories. You sure that's all? It's not a lot to build a life on."

Ice. The smell of planes. Stars. A jasmine woman. Five secret words. A strange door. Moscow. Gifts. Eight planets. The only residues of memory from his hidden life. An unwalked geography.

But as he turned his attention inwards and watched their slow revolutions around the grey mass of his darkened identity-sun, he realized there was a ninth planet, one he had not seen before, one without taste or smell, but hiding itself with armored shadows. He approached it cautiously. The world and Sullivan dimmed. His inner solar system moved according to its own geometries and laws. He thought it immensely beautiful.

Who are you? He prodded the new planet gently, but it rotated away, locked down tight. From a hazed distance, he heard Sullivan's voice.

"Peter? You OK?"

For once, with reality so distant, he was able to keep silent. The shape intrigued him with its impenetrable defences. How could it have formed without being born of a memory? What did it represent?

Bound up with your identity is a vital secret that must remain concealed. For the lives of millions, you must not remember it.

With all his strength, he resisted surfacing, certain above all things he should speak no more. Talking to Sullivan was a minefield, dark and trackless, and should he return, he would be striding naked and unshielded into it.

If he and his masters learn your secret, then all is lost.

He would have rather stayed inside himself forever. It was safe and well-ordered in there. As the rain sucked him back out, everything was wet noise, grey shadows and dizzy splinters of shine. Sullivan's hand was on Blackwell's shoulder, shaking. "Peter!"

Blackwell blinked, unfocused.

"Are you OK? What happened?"

"There's another memory." The words gritted out through every barrier Blackwell could raise. *Cut out your tongue.*

Sullivan slipped his hand inside his coat. Perhaps he was cold. His eyes widened a little, then narrowed. "What is it?"

"I don't know, I'm so—"

"Try! This is important!"

"I can't taste it."

"Taste? OK, what does it look like?"

"Black. Armored. It won't let me in."

Sullivan breathed out, then took his hand out of his coat.

"OK." The wind ruffled his hair. "It's late. We'd better get you home. We'll do some more tomorrow."

But Blackwell knew better, and though he tried to armor himself like his planet had, the words came blithe and light off his tongue. "That's all there is. I've only got those nine planets. There won't be any more. But..." He tried desperately to suck it in—*Cut out your tongue*—but couldn't. "The ninth planet is hiding something."

The voice answered even before Sullivan had keyed the number.

Sullivan *hated* calling The Third. He collected himself with an effort. "He's begun to remember," he said, and the handset sucked his words in. "He has nine memories, eight of which we already know. It's the ninth that's interesting. He can't access it—he says it won't let him in, but it's almost certainly the information you want."

Sullivan could barely keep the handset near his ear. Assassin that he was, he realized he had warmed to Blackwell, and just could not bring himself to send him to his death. "I can't press him for memories much further. He will almost certainly close up when he realizes what we are doing. With your permission, when I finish his training, I will assign a Watch-partner to monitor him and extract the information. Yes, one of us, of course, but someone who appears trustworthy and friendly."

A pause. Sullivan listened, certain that the memory of the voice would keep him off food for days. "So soon? Begging your pardon, but may I ask for two weeks? Yes, I should be able to extract the information by then." *But you will have to send in the assassins to do the killing, for I will refuse you, Third.*

Sullivan listened, sweating with violent cold, certain not only that this conversation would be reported to The Second, who controlled everything, but that Blackwell would not get his two weeks. For the price of the single piece of information somewhere in Blackwell's head, Sullivan would receive wealth beyond counting and measureless accolades from his Cabal peers. And half the world would die.

And then the handset held only a deathly silence. Sullivan could not control his shuddering.

Walton, USA

When Blackwell entered his street, the night had lost its bearings behind clouds dense enough to sway planets. Wind tracked along streets with a cargo of darkness and wet treesmell. Though Blackwell loved it, he wanted only a hot shower and bed, and time to go back inside himself and prod once again at the armored planet. Perhaps it would explain this mad, pointless, hopeless world.

A police car was parked further along the street from Blackwell's apartment. Streetlight huddled in wet pools. Neighbors clustered at doors with yellow light behind them, watching two rainjacketed officers speaking with an old man in striped pyjamas. A woman in a grey tracksuit held an umbrella over them both. Blackwell wondered if it had been a suicide who had taken someone unwillingly with him.

The officers retreated towards the car. The umbrella popped open in a gust. The woman struggled with the umbrella. The man in the dressing gown began hobbling towards his door, his combover hair flicking in the wind.

Blackwell's mental chronometer registered 1956. Wet and cold as he walked up the path to his apartment, he was thinking about a hot shower and bed when his heart accelerated without warning.

The rain and wind halted, along with the officers, the old man and the tracksuited woman midstep. The umbrella froze in a snarl of rainflicking fabric and bent spars. Neighbors were caught halfway through turns to go inside, hands pushing on doors. Halted. Photo-frozen even as Blackwell moved freely in his own private movie, shocked. His heart settled.

And in the utter silence, a dog yelped.

The old man with the beagle was waiting at Blackwell's door when he reached it. The beagle sniffed at Blackwell's trouser leg and wagged its tail. The old man was wearing a threadbare coat, no more than a brown stitchery of holes. His smile was wider than most of them. He barely reached Blackwell's shoulder.

"You!" breathed Blackwell. Drips from his clothing fell on the doorstep into puddles glistening with streetlight, until the old man laid his hand flat on Blackwell's forehead with leathery and surprisingly strong fingers. Blackwell resisted for a moment, but the man's smile was so vivid and real and *genuine,* so vastly different to Sullivan's.

Then heat from the man's hand sparked in Blackwell's skin and spread through fibre and muscle, bone and organ, and he realized he was completely dry, even his shoes. Something else triggered inside him in a place he didn't recognize, but bewildered didn't even start to explain it.

"You are so different to the man you once were."

Blackwell's heart skidded in a mad race. "Who are you?"

"I know who I am." For someone with such a cargo of wrinkles, his voice was surprisingly young and, though soft, it had remarkable carry. "But it is you upon whom the light rests. Do you know who you are?"

Blackwell shook his head, hoping to make things line up. "Tower?" he offered weakly. "Is that who you mean? What Doctor Cox called me?"

"Some call you that. The good Doctor was one." He paused a moment. "The good Doctor that others have ridiculed and mocked, whose warnings you have been unable to ignore. Did you not believe him?"

Blackwell's mind skidded. "Who are you?"

The old man cocked his head. "The one who sent Doctor Cox to warn you not to speak of your nine memories."

The skid avalanched. "You know?"

"Listen closely. For seventeen hundred years, unknown to humanity, two powerful adversaries have been warring over a single secret. The Cabal wants that secret, and with it, they will unleash a supernatural darkness upon the world from which it will never again emerge."

Blackwell stared. "This makes no sense! Why would anyone want to destroy the world?"

The old man smiled. "Oh, the world will remain. Your planet is sturdy enough for that. But this is not a natural disaster the Cabal desires, or even one started with any form of visible weaponry. The Second—the Cabal master—seeks something far darker. He wants a disease of the *spirit*. Why fight your enemies when you can rob them of hope? Why permit people, in the face of terrible adversity, to build up resolve and determination and patriotic hope when you can simply kill such feelings at their source? Why not just destroy hope with a curse of hopelessness? Without hope, there is only death."

Blackwell was aghast. "Wait wait wait! There's a curse on us all?" Despite the information transforming into colors and tastes in his mind, he wanted desperately for it not to be true. Data were good, but these data were nothing but threat.

"It's been there since the original Father Nikolas gave the first gifts in Patara seventeen hundred years ago. The curse is a vile and vicious thing. It sucks the joy from everything that gives meaning to human existence, such as relationships and purpose, and when that joy is gone, people seek vainly instead to find happiness in objects, even though nothing ever eases the despair, and the only certainty is suicide. And people think it's a normal part of life! That's the sad and terrible thing. But what they don't know is that, for seventeen hundred years, unseen, unknown, unthanked, the Brotherhood of Poor Men is all that has shielded them from disaster." He held out his arms. "Until now."

Blackwell stared. "Now?"

"Now you have woken and everything has changed. Your mind is a beautiful and orderly place, yet hidden there is the secret the Cabal seek. Your ninth planet."

"But how? How did it get there?"

"It was there before your coma. I cannot tell you more except this. Your ninth planet is both weapon and shield, both despair and hope. As a shield, it is all that is protecting you and uncountable millions from the chaotic and terminal suicidal darkness that Sullivan and his master wants. You cannot lie, my friend. You cannot refuse a question. The Tower for which you are named is defenseless. So ignorance must be your shield. Make every effort not to unlock your ninth planet. If you *do*, by chance or will, given your inability to lie, cut out your tongue before you speak a *word*." His face and voice were both as steady as lines of latitude. "If they learn your secret before the right time, then all is lost." His smile then was faint but glimmering. "But if they do not, then we can break the curse and restore hope to humanity. This is our weapon against the curse."

Blackwell did not even want to know how the old man knew such things. "The right time," he whispered. "There's going to be a right time?"

The old man looked up to the heavens. "And it will be soon, within fourteen days. In that time, you *must* keep your silence. Now I must go. Trust no-one and be cautious who you befriend, for there are more than two players in this game, Tower."

"What if I tell them about you? Are you a secret too?"

The old man chuckled. "I am an old man with a beagle, so ordinary that no-one knows or remembers me. You may speak about me to whomever you please."

The beagle licked Blackwell's ankle. "Then what do you want me to do?"

The old man's smile could have ignited furnaces. "Refuse to remember. Do your job. Watch and wait. You will know when the time comes. I will see you again."

"Who *are* you?"

The old man smiled. At his feet, the beagle got up. "I know who I am." He reached out, laid a hand on Blackwell's forehead and spoke something in another language perhaps. Blackwell's heart skidded strangely. Blood ignited in his arteries like a city grid firing up. Then the old man was gone, slipped into the crevices between blinking. Blackwell turned, checked on the porch, on the steps. Nothing. How could he have disappeared so quickly?

As the rain started again, brooming down the street, Blackwell ran down to the sidewalk and stared hard along it, both ways. Apart from the police and neighbors, the sidewalk was empty. Impossibly empty. The old man hadn't looked like a sprinter.

The wreckage of the umbrella launched into the night. The pyjama man stumbled and fell, then got up and staggered off, his shirt soaked and torn, his tracksuit confederate glancing around for her umbrella. Neighbor noises disappeared behind rain and closing doors. The police car pulled away from the kerb. A chill wet wind raced across Blackwell's back.

And his mental chrono, when he realized, still registered the same time as when time had stopped.

1956.

Time outside of time.

Uncountable millions will die the most horrible death possible.

Cold penetrated his heart.

Cut out your tongue before you speak a word.

Later, lying in bed, watching shadows track across his ceiling like spies, certain that at any moment, they would coalesce, enlarge and become a darkness that would engulf homes, towns, countries and then the world.

But the something that had triggered inside him was stirring. In his private solar system, as he turned his gaze inwards, the armored planet was brightening. Only slightly, but it was enough for Blackwell to taste the overwhelming flavour of a cobbled courtyard, the smell of a muddy river, the far-off noise of a freeway and city, and closer at hand the sounds of engines firing up, taking off and landing.

Father Nick's Day minus twenty-six days
Walton, USA

On the fourth day of his training, after Blackwell had got unprecedented perfect scores on every single sim, Sullivan announced the Scandinavia Desk would resume normal operations, with Blackwell and a new Watch-partner. He spoke into the earpiece. "Send him in." He laid his Scout on the workbench. "I'll get the techs to reroute the signals. Your partner is Corporal Carl Randall. He should be here soon."

Corporal Carl Randall looked as though two flights of stairs would kill him. Tall, round-faced, ample-bellied, he came in grinning and humming something operatic. He had brown eyes. He hastily straightened his blue tie.

"You're in safe hands, Corporal," Sullivan declared. "Your new Watch-partner scored one hundred percent. Even in advanced mode."

"Pleased ta meet ya," said Corporal Carl Randall. His hand, as soft and cool as a thawed steak, enclosed Blackwell's entirely. He had far more hair than he needed, all of it messy, although his chin was clean. "I got ninety-five."

"Corporal Peter Blackwell," said Blackwell. *Or Tower. Or my real name that I don't remember.* He kept his face steady.

A tech called Sullivan to the door, where they conferred. Carl's chair whoofed as he sat in it. "Sullivan told me all about you."

Careful.

"Heard you lost your memory."

"Yes."

Carl leaned forward with a grumble of chairframe. "Could he handy in the right circumstances," he whispered, winking.

Blackwell studied his face for signs of treachery without knowing what he was looking for. A curl of the lip? Redness in the cheeks? Sweat on the forehead? Carl had all those, yet his words seemed friendly.

"You OK, buddy?"

"I'm fine, thanks."

"Just you looked like...well, you were staring. Thought maybe I had ketchup on my face or something."

Unable to lie, Blackwell told the truth. "I can't read faces." He turned away.

"Read? You mean you...what? Like smiles mean you're happy, that kind of thing?"

"I was in a coma. My brain is different. Sorry."

Carl raised a hand. Sure he was Sullivan's agent, Blackwell expected weaponry.

"No need to be sorry," said Carl. "Coma, eh? Happens to the best of us. Married?"

"No."

"Girlfriend?"

The thought of Kay and the jasmine woman were both sweet and incisive. "No."

"OK. But if you can't read my open and honest face, you've got no chance with women, so Uncle Carl is going to help. We'll start with Female Facial Expressions 101. It ain't easy, but there's benefits to be had. Exams are pretty tough, though."

Blackwell stared, forgetting secrets for the moment. For an agent, Carl was rather *unusual*. Even unable as he was to read faces, Blackwell was sure Carl was softening him up with friendship first. "You can teach this?"

"Well, maybe. But ya gotta start somewhere, and I sorta got a knack for it. Marriage will do that. It's a big project, this language that no-one speaks with their mouths. Not only are there the angles and sizes of the eyes and mouth, but also head angles and—"

"Head angles?"

"You ain't seen the half of it! Then there's the meanings behind cosmetics, posture and clothing… the combinations are pretty well endless."

Blackwell stared. It was amazing how people learned all this without being taught. Data were so much simpler. They were reliable, infinite, never suicided and lacked facial expressions.

"I'll bring in some movies for when it gets quiet. Got a small player. Just don't tell the boss, eh?"

At the door, the tech left. "Signals have been re-routed," Sullivan said. "Gentlemen, we're live."

The next day, after coaching from Carl, Blackwell made courage out of scraps, went into a department store and bought two jars of Marietta's jasmine oil. He kept one. The sales assistant wrapped the other and asked if it was a gift. He nodded, too overwhelmed by its fragrance to speak.

The jasmine woman.

And thus armed, he slipped into the library, uncaring if anyone was following. The Searchbase section was there to his left, but he avoided its lure. *Must not,* he told himself, pulling away with immense reluctance.

Instead, he put the cream-colored box on the counter in front of Kay.

"For me?" she said, with an expression that he might have interpreted as favorable. "I remember…you're the…the Searchbase man!"

The smell of jasmine as she opened the jar almost unligamented his bones. He nodded. "It's jasmine."

"You're very kind. It smells beautiful. Did you find what you were looking for?"

"Not yet." *Not for another twelve days.* The words Carl had taught him came out easily. "Would you like to get some coffee?"

She laughed. "Now? I'd love to but I can't, sorry, and I don't get off work until late. I have a training conference tomorrow and Wednesday, so how about Thursday?"

"I'd like that. How does ten o'clock sound?"

"I have a break at ten thirty."

"Ten thirty it is. See you then."

The sun was too dim for the joy he felt. Surely it was another universe he was in. Carl was delighted when Blackwell told him, and launched into *Wie will ich triumphiren* as sweetly as a bird caught in joyous uplift. Blackwell spent the next two days resisting Carl's invitations to dinner, fishing and drinking, certain friendship would be the first step before disaster, though he had to admit at times that Carl seemed more like a giant panda than a predator. No predator would talk so much.

On Thursday, another woman was at the front desk. The chatter Blackwell remembered from the work area behind was absent, although the staffers were still there, staring at monitors. The woman's name badge read *Tracy.*

"I'm looking for Kay."

"She's gone." Tracy looked away quickly.

"She said she would meet me here."

"No, sorry. Not that. *Gone.*"

"Oh." Even Blackwell understood the glimmer of tears in her eyes. Carl's coaching hadn't prepared him for this, although a voice hardened inside him, the darker voice of troop carriers and Moscow.

"Gone," he repeated, both understanding and hating the word. "The Black Despair."

Tracy looked away. Her mouth quivered, distorting the words. "Last night. Sorry."

Perhaps he stood there for one minute or ten. For once, his internal chronometer did not register. When at last he walked out and the airhushing doors cut off the memory of her voice—forever, he thought, for he vowed never to go back—soft things separated away from the hard core inside him. *I am not allowed to remember things. But I will never forget you.* Words intended, but never spoken. They spooled in his head like loose film.

A different Blackwell emerged onto the footpath, the troop carrier Blackwell, the harder man.

Hidden in your mind is the secret the Cabal seek. Your ninth planet.

He knew, though, that he would not seek out anything from his past. Curious as he was to the location of the muddy river, freeway and airstrip, a stronger desire had replaced it. He found the place he was looking for and walked there. It was a run-down apartment building with ground floor offices; the nameplate read 'Walton Counseling.'

"I'd like to register as a counselor," he told the old man behind the desk and was glad he couldn't tell whether the expression on the man's face was pleasure or amazement.

The old man reached out a hand. "Bill Smythe."

"Peter Blackwell."

"What's your training, Peter?"

"I have no training."

The old man's eyebrows went up. "Sorry, to work here, you will need a degree in social work, although we will take undergraduates as volunteers to do minor tasks or non-participant observation." He picked up a pen. "Have you done any certificates or non-degree courses?"

"No."

"Nothing? Could I ask your interest in counseling, then?"

"Life is far too precious to slash away with a knife. I want to stop the Black Despair."

"Stop?" The pen fell from his hands. His eyes widened. "Sorry? The Black Despair can't be stopped. No-one ever recovers. Our counseling is in marriage, family, relationships. We do what we can in those areas, remembering that the Black Despair stops everything."

"Nevertheless."

Bill leaned back. "Nevertheless? You seem very determined. Well, alright. You seem genuine, if a little ambitious. OK. I'll start you next week with some filing, if you'd like. Monday OK?"

Each day of the old man's fourteen breathed in and out. Life incremented by seconds, all of which registered. His planets orbited in an orderly fashion, the ninth armored but still pulsing with faint, steady promise. He learned how to close off the vacuum of his mind from Watch Four data. He remembered everything, spoke to almost no-one.

With all the world looking up at the Melcassar Comet, Blackwell looked down, watching Scandinavia slide 240km below GENIE and NOVAD, MAYFLOWER and COLUMBUS and PILGRIM, wondering why a secret that would kill millions was important if the comet had the potential to wipe out most life on Earth anyway.

All reports put it as enormous, capable of either massive ocean displacement or a dust cloud that would ruin climates and cool the earth for years. Despite government assurances, the suicide rate dropped dramatically as Earlies hoped to lose their lives under the most dramatic weapon ever.

But Blackwell was constantly struck by the sheer surreal fantasy of life as he sat in a concrete bunker deep under the ground and the weight of night, listening to Carl's operatic hummings and speaking as little as was politely allowable while the world waited for potential catastrophe.

And the terrible irony was that the comet, should it hit, was predicted to destroy hope on the single day of hope for the year.

Father Nick's Day.

Two

Trigger

Father Nick's Day minus fifteen days
The home of Zack and Liz Smith
Perth, Western Australia

Zack was sure the comet was going to hit.

Even though governments were saying it would just sail on by, Zack just knew it was going to slam into their precious planet, ruining axial tilts, climates, civilizations, and more lives than a cold and random chunk of rock had a right to do. The universe just shouldn't hurl such things around.

Zack and Liz watched the news without speaking. With a four year old autistic boy, they were used to silence. Shaped by years of hope that her boy would eventually emerge from the iron box of his brain, Liz had become a stubborn and unyielding fortress. Someday her son would speak. Some day he would fall in love and have kids. Some day he would *shine*.

But now he was sitting in his room with paintbrushes clutched in his fists, gently rocking back and forward, staring at the wall.

Some day.

If the comet didn't rip the life out of him first.

Zack turned the TV off and stood there in silence. Liz went to check on John.

Zack thought he should trim the edges of his lawn. Yes, that Melcassar Comet might just hit Earth and blast him, his pathetic lawn and civilization into the Stone Age. But perhaps governments were right, for once. So if he fertilized his lawn now with a good sprinkle of Baileys 3:1:1, he might just catch the rain that was forecast for later in the week. Nice dark, green lawn. Pride of the neighborhood.

He filled up his bucket with fertilizer and started, walking end to end across his front lawn in grim determination, refusing to look up at the sky. So quiet was it that when Liz cried out from inside, he dropped his spade and ran. It just wasn't worth delaying with a four-year-old autistic son. Anything could go wrong, and many times had. Some had been no more dangerous than John chewing furiously on lipstick, but spending a night in Princess Margaret Hospital with John after he had swallowed turpentine had been a harrowing time.

On the porch, Zack toed off his work boots and slid open the screen door. The smell of paint surprised him.

House paint.

He followed the smell into the garage and stopped dead. In a corner of the garage, someone—not Liz from the shock in her eyes—had cleared a neat area and lined it with paint tins and equipment. It could not possibly have been John, nor the faint image of an old man Zack thought he saw standing next to John with a look of defiance on his face. Though when he blinked and looked again, the man had gone.

Liz's expression was gorgeously bewildered. She raised a finger to her lips, but Zack had no intention of speaking. Seeing his son doing *anything* other than rocking back and forward with paintbrushes clutched in his pink fists was incomparably priceless. But John's hands were moving in a way Zack had never before seen. Rather than splashing paint all over the walls with uncontrolled movements, he was carefully dipping brushes into tins of Tuscan Sun yellow, cream and white, holding them as steady as a surgeon, and creating on the wall a picture.

No, not just a picture, Zack realized in complete disbelief. A blazing re-creation—as though the gods of space were breathing—of something millions of kilometers away from Earth. Somehow his son, autistic and silent, who had never read a book or newspaper or watched the increasingly grim news on TV, was painting the Melcassar Comet.

Zack stared, as though somehow the passage of the image along his optic nerves would translate it from sheer impossible to reasonable.

Prickles began on his neck and would not cease.

He said to Liz, "But how?" and then again, stupidly, dumbly, "How?"

John continued painting, which just made it more incomprehensible.

Zack said, "John?" almost expecting his son to turn and smile and calmly explain how he was able to do such a thing. And then, realizing it was his task to make meaning, he said, "We have to tell someone."

Liz nodded, though it could have meant anything.

"That doctor psychologist bloke—what's his name—Raja something."

"Rajanayagam," she said.

Zack's fingers prickled as he ran a quick search for the number and keyed it in. He felt such a strong wrongness about such an action, but it was beyond his merely mortal ability to leave such strangeness untold. Doctors should know these things, he reasoned.

The doctor was quickly interested. Zack recounted the story with as much neutrality as he was capable, hoping he was doing the right thing, but all the while knowing—just *knowing*—that he was not.

The doctor hung up. There was a finance committee meeting to attend and an anniversary present to buy his wife. None of which would mean anything at all should the comet hit Earth.

But he—and many others of his fraternal association—had been promised a great sum of money by an anonymous source for any unusual information about the comet, and the story he had just heard fitted well. All he needed do was report it, exactly as he had heard it.

Nothing more.

Easy money, he thought, and keyed in the London number.

Father Nick's Day minus fourteen days
London, UK

The Thames stank.

Before she began, Mantell slipped off her right glove and looked at her right hand, at that thing on her palm she had never shown anyone.

That she would *never* show anyone. Not after the recent disaster, not since the annihilation of her hope. Hope, she thought, as the martial armoring around the remnants of her heart quivered briefly—she could have had everything!—then locked again.

Hardness, she told herself instead. Life without hope.

She slipped the glove back on.

Then she triggered the protectives on her suit—night vision, hearing augmentor, helmet laser, exo-armor, threat detector—and set off across the rough wooden structure that made the long-collapsed Tower Bridge crossable. The wailings of plague survivors huddled in their nests among the rubble almost slowed her—she could so easily have been one. So easily alone in the City of the Dead. London the wasteland since the Kent Plague and the massive nationwide riots. Britain the Alone. The Disunited Kingdom. Though Europe was scarcely better with its suicide parties and unenforceable anti-suicide laws. A continent without hope.

With the Second's summons in her secure pouch alongside her dead mother's bottle of perfume, she passed through the twisted metal and collapsed granite and stagnant pools where the Thames had backwatered.

On the muddy southern bank, near the abandoned docks, she drew her laser and set out through the empty streets of Southwark, watching for the violently territorial gangs that made the Borough impassable by night. Shielded as she was by the best body armor in her cell leader's armory, she made her passage through Southwark rapid and silent.

The day coughed up the last of its light. A leprous silence followed Mantell through the streets like the abandoned child she was. Rain spattered. Viscous discharges scummed the surface of puddles. She panted shallow breaths and ran on. The smell of ozone accelerated her stride when she detected and shot several gang sentries, brought a hungry, adrenal charge to her throat. The taste of war, she mused with a strong, iron thrill, brutal and beautiful.

Come, provoke this lost child, this once-lover. Name your armaments. Show me your wounds, for all mine are within.

She turned the last corner puzzling, as she had received the message. *Why did the Second summon me?* The greatly-feared Second of the mighty Cabal. He to whom much was owed, but nothing taken. Why *me?*

The Second summoned so *few*. His orders appeared in cheap

brown envelopes on doorsteps in mornings. Hurricanes did not shift them; storms did not wet them. No-one could open them but the person for whom they were intended. Inside, the orders were written in red ink on cheap lined paper in a child's awkward script, and in some places, the pressure of the pen had torn the paper. Some were stained with substances that no-one dared analyze.

Nevertheless, those who received such an envelope and fulfilled their orders well were accorded the highest esteem in the Cabal. Those who failed in their tasks, even the hardest soldiers, were left to live a few paranoid weeks waiting for punishment until their own terror guided their hands to a suitable weapon.

Mantell's summons simply read 'Come to me' above a scribbled map. Her few friends had warned: *there's strange things happening across the Channel. Be careful, soldier.* She had heard through Cabal sources of the strange boy and his baffling painting of the comet and wondered what the Second thought.

And the closed faces of her friends had made the message very clear: *How much of your soul are you prepared to lose?*

Lose? she thought. She had already lost everything—mother, father, lover, all gone. And since that terrible night a month ago, she had sometimes considered how best she might stop the meaninglessness of her pulse, most often with a knife.

All that prevented her was her mother's bottle of perfume. Deep in her secure pouch, it still offered the hope that one day she would be attractive to a man. Perfume to bring love, her mother used to say. Faint hope better than none, she thought. And war beat love most times.

So why summon her? Perhaps it involved preparations for the Melcassar Comet. *Comet and curse are coming together,* her fellow assassins told her. The social media was full of its approach to Earth. Some predicted a Pacific impact that would obliterate most coastal Rim cities, others an African landfall that would rival Tunguska, while others proclaimed it would obliterate all life on Earth. Mantell almost hoped for devastation, either with her at the blast center or watching the tsunami it caused bear down on her on an isolated coast somewhere. How loud would her scream be as an ocean advanced on her? The laws of physics had no love for her. One last kiss of a billion tonnes of seawater hardly counted.

If not that, she thought, and in the absence of anything sensible, the Second must have summoned her on an impulsive desire for nothing more than a cup of tea and a chat about ballistics or entry wounds, her favorite topics of conversation.

The building surprised her when she reached it. Windowless. Like a prisoner whose eyes had been cut out, whose mouth had been fused shut. Ungraffitied, though the buildings to both sides shrieked with ragged scrawls. A single door was two meters above ground level, with no steps to reach it. She leaped up, grabbed the sill and, just as she pulled herself up, her right threat-sensor pinged. She jerked left and a bullet embedded itself into the door next to her neck. She whirled, sighted the sniper and shot him. Then she drew careful breath and pushed open the door, remembering the message: *Come to me*. Lover or hunter? Parts of her wanted both.

The door behind closed her into darkness. A latch clicked. Her pulse accelerated, calibrating seconds like a bomb timer. She stowed her laser in her thigh-sheath. In the half-second before her night-vision goggles kicked in, she smelled new concrete. Then a light came on above her, a single dim globe, illuminating stairs and nothing else. She climbed two flights with no landings and no doors. At the top, the staircase ended with a plain wooden door.

Come to me.

Lover or hunter?

There's strange things happening. How much of your soul are you prepared to lose?

Everything. I have nothing.

A voice said, "Enter" even before Mantell knocked.

The light went off.

Mantell removed her goggles as she entered, careful to keep her eyes forward. For the Second of the mighty Cabal, the room he occupied was scarcely appropriate. The furniture had its own brown misery that the single dull lamp and the curtained, late afternoon London gloom did nothing to dispel. And there was a *window* on the wall? She kept the surprise from her face. No windows showed from the outside. Faded wallpaper peeled and drooped in places, a forgettable and much-stained coffee table was propped up with bricks in the place of a missing leg and a sofa appeared once to have been olive green and now looked as though too many drunks had emptied their stomachs onto it. The Second occupied one end of it, and the other was draped with a rank clutter of browned newspapers, rags, and objects that appeared never to have had names.

The room stank of cigarettes and other odours Mantell did not want to consider.

She bowed her head in respect, breathing shallow. This was the place of the Second, after all, however much it resembled a lowly hovel. Although, having seen the blank wall from the outside and the window from the inside, she was sure that the room was disconnected from the bleak reality of London and the world.

On the sofa, hunched in a drab dressing gown that made his hands look cancerous, the Second sat, surrounded by smoke as dark and ugly as industrial pollution. Mantell could not see his face. Yellowed toenails protruded from tattered slippers beneath the frayed gown's hem.

"Thank you for coming," said the Second in a voice like a python choking. "Please sit." He gestured to the coffee table. There were no other chairs.

Mantell sat, her back straight so as keep her legs from quivering visibly. The body armor would not lock except under impact.

Without any movement from the Second, the cloud around him thinned, and Mantell caught a brief terrifying glimpse of a clean-shaven jaw and a single colorless eye. She was an assassin without compassion, but merely being in the presence of the Second excited her in strange, ghoulish ways.

"Are you happy, soldier? In spite of this comet, are you happy?"

She was so shocked she could barely speak, although the analytic part of her assassin's brain registered the mention of the comet and linked it with the boy's painting. "Yes, sir," she stammered, sure he could see into the place in her heart where she hungered for stillness and an end to killing.

"I will take you into my confidence then, soldier, as I have with O'Roarke."

Mantell flinched. The Second took no-one into his confidence. All his lieutenants perished within months. The longest serving had lasted nine. No-one had ever seen his face. Indeed, no-one had ever seen him outside this room. No-one brought him food. He was sustained by nothing more than smoke.

Within the cloud, unseen, the Second sucked his tongue, and strangely, it reminded Mantell of her sniper training, how she had loved the moments readying for the shot, positioning her tongue behind her teeth in the half-eternity before the bullet. Though she knew that no-one ever—*ever!*—questioned the Second, the question was out before she realized.

"Sir…is this because of the boy's painting?"

"If the boy knows anything, he is not revealing it. We will watch him, but I have other plans for you." The Second raised two gowned arms in a ghoulish benediction and his voice lowered in conspiratorial quietness. "You are to go with O'Roarke to Finland to destroy the Brotherhood's main distribution base."

"Sir." Mantell almost laughed. This was the mission for which every Cabal member had long dreamed. A cup of tea and a chat, indeed.

"But…sir…but how?"

"How did I know? Because I placed a sleeper among them years ago."

Mantell leaned forward. Her warlike heart leapt to readiness. "Sir!" Though it still made no sense why the Second had chosen her. There were better assassins, surely!

The Second lowered his arms and chuckled like a father to a well-loved daughter. "Yes, it is good news indeed. Our mole told us that it is deep under the northern fells of Finland. Finland, of all places! After all those years that we thought they were operating out of the Egyptian pyramids. And so…our secret war will soon come to an end." He leaned back and the sound of his sneer rattled off walls. "Hasn't it been a long time? Seventeen hundred years, and all the people on this planet have gone about their hopeless threescore years and ten of existence, completely unaware of the Cabal and Brotherhood warring around their very ears." He paused. "Anderson was to be your leader, but he was killed in a laboratory incident. The Mother kissed him." He chuckled, a soft, private chuckle such as a torturer might make. "She is a jealous lover, that one." A finger jabbed at Mantell from the cloud. "Have you met the Mother yet?"

Mantell hesitated, trying to remember Anderson. "I have not had the pleasure, sir." And neither did she know what the Mother was.

"You might know it as Incendiary Device A. Or a variety of other names, mostly foul, to denominate its cruelties. Eleven scientists burned to nothing and two laboratories destroyed. No maternal softness in *our* Mother." He paused. "Our lion to the Brotherhood's lamb, you might say. And did you know for which mission Anderson was training?"

Mantell hid her frown. *Lion?* An odd choice of metaphor. The Second was afraid of lions, so the rumors went. "I did not, sir."

"I am told," said the Second,"our scientists have devised a way to contain the Mother in a bomb, and our mole has told us how we might conceal it in a cargo shipment into their base. Once the Mother is inside, O'Roarke will detonate it remotely, and then the Mother will kiss the Poor Men and put an end to their seventeen hundred years of noble and selfless charity. All of it." He lifted his arms in a ragged gesture of humour. "Gone," he cackled, and his shoulders rocked a little. "Gone within the time a cigarette takes to burn down, the time a mouse takes to drown."

"Sir," said Mantell, keeping her back straight.

"And you shall assist O'Roarke. You will witness the Mother's kiss from a distance and record it for my later pleasure. What a shame that we cannot see it close at hand: the beauty of its burning, the way her kiss will convert the Poor Men's flesh into nothing but heat. Ah, there will be a certain symmetry to the conflagration—Finnish snow counterbalancing the passion of the Mother's kiss. I only wish I could witness it with you."

"Sir," said Mantell. What an incredible honor! Without thinking, she made to stand, believing the audience complete.

"There is another task, soldier," said the Second in a deadly whisper.

And Mantell sat fast, hoping her offence to the Second would not be fatal.

"Destroying the base will slow them, but not defeat them. They will still try to continue their pathetic Father Nick's Day. So our technicians will shortly be sending unpleasant electronic messages to all the Brotherhood Scout IDs on the list the mole gave us." His chuckle was like the sound of entrails spilling. "A plague, you might call it. Within an hour or so, almost every Poor Man on the planet will be permanently comatose. But not all. So when the burning is done and the plague is sent, you will go to the small town in Turkey where the Brotherhood began—Patara, it is called—and rendezvous with the mole, who will tell you where you might find…a *certain* Poor Man. As soon as O'Roarke has completed the task I have given him, you are to kill this Poor Man. And then you will receive all the wealth, adoration and fame you could possibly want."

Mantell dared not ask why one Poor Man was so significant if almost all his fellows were comatose. "Sir." It could not have become any more bizarre.

"When you have completed your task, you shall return here to this very room—oh, do not fear! I shall not stray far—and bring to me images of this dead Poor Man. I am told you delight in such things."

"Sir!" said Mantell with feeling.

The Second's cloud swirled as he leaned forward. "Do you only have the one word?" he asked quietly, dangerously.

Mantell's heart went skidding along, and she swallowed bile. *Be calm, soldier.* "I am honored to serve you, my Second."

The Second leaned back and the smoke sucked back around his head. "So you are." Without lifting his cigarette to his mouth, he blew out a continuous foul yellow gust, more than his lungs could possibly hold. His form seemed to dissolve behind the cloud. "And would you be honored to perish thereafter? To serve your beloved Second unto death? Not that it would matter much. Life without hope now, death without hope after."

"Sir, I would." She hoped he would release her, both to end this meeting, and so she could start preparing.

Instead, though, he extended a finger from the cloud and wagged it once, like a conductor. His voice became gentle, almost seductive. "You were a girl, once."

Mantell's heart missed an echo.

"And you had a kitten, before you were abandoned. A white creature it was, pure of blood, clean of character. I believe you called it Matilda. One of its feet was brown."

"Sir." It was only her strict discipline that kept Mantell upright, that forced the surprised word out. She had told no-one in the Cabal of her childhood—and only—pet. *No-one!* All her memories nestled in pillowed spaces well away from her heart, so that no one could see and steal them. For a moment, she remembered with affection and guilt the way Matilda had slept on her bed in the clean nights of her girlhood, its way of leaping sideways when surprised. Or upside down in the crook of her arm, marking its drift into catsleep with a soft purring contentedness.

"You loved the kitten."

Mantell nodded, suddenly deeply troubled, aware that there were no maps for this territory. This conversation was like an enemy-held minefield, muddy and heavily mined, and she was entering it unarmed and blind. She feared for many things at that moment, her own life not the least.

"Yet you found one day on returning from an errand that the kitten had not been let out and had soiled your bed."

Mantell dared not reach up to wipe at the violent shock and shame that welled in her eyes. *How could you know this?*

"And in your childish anger, you killed your own pet. Regret and shame came later, but neither have the capacity to restore life. Your heart hardened. You buried the kitten away from where your fellows could see it. You spoke of this to no-one." His voice had not wavered once from its gentle tone, not once, and Mantell wondered if her heart was still within her, or whether it had been drilled out. The Second pointed his finger directly at her eyes, and held it there, unwavering, as precise as a chronometer. "I have not lied, have I?"

"The Second is incapable of untruth," whispered Mantell automatically. The old words of the Cabal litany. The Third Principle. Red shame burned on her tongue, in her eyes. *Why say this? How did he know? How did he know?* Cold terror etched acid in her throat and every other chamber. *And does he know what happened two months ago?* That would be a far worse shame. The Second lowered his finger. "All things end. The kitten's life ended. And if you fail, I should like to kill you, just as you killed Matilda."

"I would be honored to die for you, my Second." Mantell kept her heart and back stiff, wondering if this whole meeting were nothing but a pretence and she would die immediately. *Life without hope now, death without hope after.*

The Second breathed out a factoryful of brown fume, as though his lungs were rotting. "Get out, then," he said tiredly. "Go and blow them all up. Blow up the world for all I care."

As Mantell stood, the gangrenous cloud around the Second continued to grow in both volume and density until it occupied most of the room. Mantell retreated to the door, which opened before she reached it, and closed when she passed through.

On the other side, she was grateful for the smell of new concrete in the stairwell, the sight of plain grey concrete, and the stupid but honest beat of her heart. She saw darkened rubbery smears on the floor, then threw up violently and added her own.

Father Nick's Day minus thirteen days
NASAD
Walton, USA

Expecting disaster on every one of the old man's fourteen days, Blackwell viewed every event with suspicion, though the two weeks unwound without any drama at all.

But as he and Carl passed through midnight into the fourteenth day, on a freezing night when Scandinavia seemed buried ten meters under permafrost, every flashpoint was quiet and generals had withdrawn their border patrols, when the Diplomatic Lists were two grades better than 'watchful,' and European armed forces were stood down, everything changed. Fifteen minutes before the end of their Watch, Carl peered at the door. "Where's Watch One? They should be here by now."

Blackwell kept his eyes on the screen, watching as the NOVAD satellite passed out of range and the GENIE orbit began transmitting images of the northern Finnish fells. In fourteen and a half minutes, he would lean back and count the lumipanels on the ceiling, his Watch-end ritual to signal his mind to stop sucking in data.

Carl yawned. "Europe safe for another night. Any plans for the weekend?"

Blackwell thought how strange it was that people were still discussing ordinary daily routines only a fortnight or so away from potential terrible destruction. "No," he said automatically. "How about your weekend?"

The GENIE images of the northern fells of Finland appeared on Blackwell's thermal register, cold white and blue.

"Family mainly. Jilly's started ballet on Saturday mornings, Ben's got his basketball final on Saturday afternoon, though he's not hopeful of winning. One of my old school buddies shot himself last week, so I'm going to his funeral Saturday evening…it's been a pretty full year for Earlies. I think when I go—if that comet don't get me first—I'm going to jump out of a plane without a parachute—the Great Last Fall is the way the suicide agents are advertising it. It's been pretty popular apparently—hey, you still doing that counseling thing?"

Blackwell nodded.

"Had any success?"

"None." They had all suicided, even one of the counselors. Nothing anyone had said or done changed anything.

"But there's always hope, yes?"

"Yes." Although the statistics said otherwise, there was always hope. His stubborn defiance had taken him by surprise. Perhaps his DNA was different. Perhaps his reconfigured brain had something to do with it.

"I might get out to the river for some fishing Sunday morning," Carl said. "Hey, wanna come? All your good thoughts might inspire those fishies to jump on my hook. You can just sit and watch if you don't want to fish."

"River?" said Blackwell...*a cobbled courtyard, the smell of a muddy river, the far-off noise of a freeway and city, and closer at hand the sounds of engines firing up and taking off and landing.* "What kind of river?"

"Fishing river, buddy, nothing special."

At that moment, though, something registered yellow on his thermal monitor. Yellow for *warmth*. That was strange; the thaw was slower at those higher altitudes. He gridded the shape and zoomed in. "There's something unusual here," he said, but Carl had left his chair and was staring out the door. "Watch One is late," he called back. "They should have been here twenty minutes ago."

Size of a missile, Blackwell thought, scrolling through his mental register of weaponry and cross-checking it with local armories and missile caches. Nothing matched. Neither did body temperatures of the local fauna. The image, under maximum magnification, revealed itself to be *two* figures, side by side, well below normal human body temperature. Campers? No, the register showed no tent or sleeping bags. The object in front of one of the figures, though, showed heat traces suspiciously like those of a detonator.

The phone chirped, startling him. The caller screen was blank. Carl puffed back from the door and clicked on the voice link. "Randall, Dungeon."

"Lieutenant Winston, Mission Room. Captain Wenders wants to see you in the Pulpit immediately. Bring Corporal Blackwell, your watchcards and all your personals with you."

"Sir."

The line clicked off.

Northern Finland

Mantell adjusted her goggles against the glare of the afternoon sun and shivered. Even so, this was better than endless training and drills. The promise of beautiful conflagration had illuminated her thoughts since her audience with the Second.

She elevated her scope until she could see the marker in the crosshairs. Even five hundred meters distant, it showed clearly.

"Two minutes until detonation," O'Roarke said.

"Scope ready, sir," said Mantell. "Recording on your mark."

"Mark."

Mantell thumbed the scope on, wincing as she pictured the Second in his miasmic room. Apart from the briefing, she had been called in for a routine dental check that had somehow stretched into two hours under general anesthetic. It was strange, but she had more important things to think about than fillings.

The Brotherhood base was old, so it wouldn't take much of a blast to start the cave-in. Any Poor Men who survived would find the escape routes blocked. The dead would be lucky to miss the kiss of the Mother, the compound that sought out organic material, attached and burned slowly and evenly, leaving not even ash. Nearly inextinguishable, its fires would last for days.

"One minute." O'Roarke pulled down his hood over his ginger hair and drew out a small lancet from a pocket. "Can't come soon enough." He started whistling an Irish jig. He knew dozens of them, and liked to whistle them as he prepared for the kill. Mantell knew that orbiting satcams would pick up the blast, and that white-faced Poor Men across the world would be flashing frantic messages to their leaders—

Kavonatur is destroyed.

She did not understand why the mission was so important if the comet was going to destroy so much, but perhaps she did not have all the facts. In any case, on the next Father Nick's Day, when gifts did not appear, hundreds of millions would suicide, and the world would degenerate into permanent hopeless darkness.

Let it be. Seventeen hundred years is a long time to wait.

"Focus!" snapped O'Roarke. Mantell focused. Bare seconds after O'Roarke dripped a drop of blood from his pricked thumb onto the detonation panel, and the DNA circuit closed, the explosion turned the twilight sky a brief incandescent white, and the last of the winter snow cascaded in muddy slowness into the enormous pit. The flash illumined O'Roarke's leer, and Mantell knew she would never forget the beauty of the moment. The faint crump of the blast reached her seconds later, then the terrible groan of collapsing ground. The seismic tremors rolled under her, though the boffins had assured them both they would not be in any danger. Localised vertical displacement, they had termed it. A cave-in. Mantell thought of the decaliters of screaming Brotherhood blood even now converting into heat in their devastated underground base, as the Mother went roaming, spreading her corrosive kisses. A caress unto death.

Mantell wished she were there, watching them die. She would be very quiet. She would not make a sound.

O'Roarke grunted. "Movement on the ground."

Mantell zoomed out her scope to show snow sliding off three truck-sized domes that appeared several hundred meters from the edge of the blast site and rose up through the ground, revealing scurrying figures and compact vehicles, ugly and stub-winged, for all the world like a child's drawing of a submarine. She whistled as the domes rose about twenty meters before stopping.

"Watch closely," O'Roarke said, his breath a mist. "You're seeing some of the last Brotherhood sleds in history. You ever felt the timeslip?"

"No."

"Feels like your heart stops for a moment. It's quite a jolt, though at this distance, we might be outside the zone of influence."

One of the sleds lifted off in a vertical jump. O'Roarke grunted. "Never seen *that* before. They normally engage the timeslip before lift-off and just disappear. Maybe the blast damaged the timeslip controllers inside the base." He began keying in coordinates on his scope for a Tracer attack. Mantell watched his fingers on the screen and…

then…

…time skidded a short way without her. Her heart thudded. Her arms flailed, nearly knocking over her scope. O'Roarke's fingers slewed over his scope's screen.

And both the sky and snow around the three domes were empty.

"We've lost them?"

O'Roarke thumbed his panel, smearing blood. "Not yet. The Second's plague will be hitting them soon. But we've got other business."

"Sir, may I ask the details of our mission? The Second said you would provide further information." He hadn't, but Mantell hoped invoking his name would convince O'Roarke.

O'Roarke peered at her, his slightly open mouth revealing yellow smokers' teeth. "You know everything you need," he snapped. "Patara, further instructions from the mole, kill the target. What else do you need to know?" He clicked off his scope and began disassembling it.

What is in that unmarked metal case you loaded earlier into the jumpship, and what it's for. She loaded her cameras, sure there was more to the mission than she had been told.

NASAD
Walton, USA

Carl whistled. "Wenders? What's he want us for? Come on, he don't like to be kept waiting."

"Now?" said Blackwell, alarmed at both the strangeness of the data and the timing of Wenders' call. This was not right. Well into the old man's fourteenth day, it seemed a good opportunity for Carl to extract his secret.

"Now, buddy," said Carl. "You don't keep Wenders waiting. You got everything?" He started moving towards the door.

Blackwell did not move. There was the unusual fact of two human-sized figures lying prone and emitting heat on a northern Finnish fell.

You must not lose a single moment of data. And when you see anything unusual in Scandinavia…

"I should stay. Something is happening in Scandinavia. I should—"

Carl spun. "Didn't you hear the man? You can't just *stay!*"

Whoever is in the Pulpit will try to prevent you. "I won't be a moment. This is important."

Carl waved his arms. "There ain't *nothing* more important than getting your butt up to the Pulpit before Wenders sends a squad down here to drag you up!"

But Ed's command weighed against Blackwell—*You must not lose a single moment of data. And when you see anything unusual in Scandinavia, use the tile and Scout as I instructed you.*

Blackwell pulled the data tile from his rucksack, and his Scout from his pocket. "I have to."

Carl eyed him, swung around to the door, then turned back. "Yeah, but what the—? What is that thing? The monitors are firewalled. You can't tile that stuff! It's classified—"

Blackwell found it difficult to breathe, to move at all. He knew he would physically shut down if he was not careful. "I have to," he said, as much for himself as for Carl.

He used the Scout to instruct the tile to record thermal, visual and seismic data from the monitors. Then he stood on the chair and slipped the tile into its usual spot on top of the central pillar where none of the other Watch staffers would see it.

Carl's forehead was rampant with sweat. "Where'd you get that?

I've never seen a Scout like it!" He held up both hands. "No, I don't want to know."

Blackwell grabbed his rucksack. They carded out of the Dungeon, crossed the hallway and took the elevator to the Mission Room, an enormous chamber that hummed of trade craft and secrets and a million things the dark and worried world would never know. Blackwell smelled tightly controlled airflow and suspicion. A bank of TVs near him were tuned to suicide groups across the world, where thousands were hoping to go Early if they could get themselves into what they hoped was the Melcassar Comet's impact zone. Others monitored the near-daily speculation on the comet's course. Some were showing the collapse of the Beijing global warming summit, and others, like succubi, followed the never-ending conflicts of ambassadors and generals and governments.

Blackwell followed Carl to the shift captain's central Pulpit. From a station on the railing that overlooked their approach lane, one of the Pulpit aides turned to them with a look of polite disdain. Carl had told him what that curl of the lip represented.

"Blackwell? Randall?"

"Reporting as ordered, sir." Both men offered a smart salute.

"Captain Wenders will see you shortly."

Blackwell put down his rucksack, aware of other eyes watching him. Wenders was in the command chair, a VR headset obscuring his eyes. The bulbous black headset made him look like a beetle. *Something secret's going on,* thought Blackwell, though he knew well not to express interest. Only Factor 3 events and higher were channelled into VR headsets, isolated from the main monitors. And only a few in NASAD ranked high enough to see them: those who occupied the Pulpit command chair and the generals hidden behind the dark grey windows of the Nest, ten meters above their heads.

Carl wiped his forehead with his hand, and wiped his hand on his trousers. Wenders swung up the faceplate. As he took off the headset, he gestured for Blackwell and Carl to ascend the Pulpit. He glanced at a clock as they approached. "Gentlemen." He smiled, though Blackwell thought it looked purple and spiky. "Anything interesting?"

"On our shift, sir?" said Carl. "No sir, everything is…no, sir."

Wenders paused a moment and glanced at the clock again. "Staff sergeant Humphries would have told you the good news, but he has been called away."

Purple and spiky, thought Blackwell.

"You've both earned three day leave passes effective immediately." Wenders smiled. "Furthermore, you're leaving the Scandinavia desk with promotions to the Asian desk, Watch One for an immediate start, though you will retain your three days leave. Hand in your watchcards now. You'll get them back encoded with your new access rights when you report for your next shift. The guards on the outer Gate are waiting for you. They have my orders to let you out without cards."

Blackwell unclipped his card from his pocket and handed it to Wenders, careful not to show surprise. Carl opened his mouth and closed it again.

"You've got three days leave, soldiers," Wenders said, as an aide palmed open a secure box and dropped the cards inside. "I'd make the most of it if I were you."

Carl hesitated. "Thank you, sir. But, sir, Watch One hasn't arrived, sir."

Wenders eyed him for a moment. "Unusual," he said, and gestured to an aide. "Get a watch crew down there now."

He turned back, his professional smile well in place. The headset had indented his forehead. "Gentlemen, good hunting on the Asian desk and good day to you."

The aide spoke into an headset. Blackwell and Carl saluted and left. At the elevator, Blackwell looked back and saw Wenders watching and a second figure there as well.

Sullivan.

It fitted, he thought with a kind of grim resolve. He had wondered when Sullivan would turn up again, and it was too much of a coincidence that Carl was with him as well.

Carl grabbed his arm. "Don't turn around!" he hissed. "Do you want to lose your promotion and leave pass?"

At the main level, where the access tunnel led out to the office buildings that housed the entry Gates, Carl left the elevator but Blackwell remained inside. If he could get rid of Carl, he could get the information to Ed. Surely his secret was tied in with the Finnish images. Fourteen days into the old man's fourteen...everything fitted. "I have to go back and get my tile," he said, and pressed the Dungeon button.

"You can't!" called Carl through the closing doors. "We handed in our cards, remember?" He jammed a hand between the doors. "Hey, wait!"

The doors opened.

"I have to," Blackwell said.

"Why?"

"There was something strange on my screen. I can't leave the data."

Carl confronted him. "Waddya mean, strange? How strange?" He paused. "What exactly did you see?"

Blackwell was immediately suspicious, but could neither refuse a direct question or lie. "Two heat sources on the Finnish fells. Human-sized. Motionless. Maybe people recently dead, still cooling. But please go. It doesn't concern you."

Carl's eyes widened. He stepped into the elevator and punched the 'Close' button. "Damn right it concerns me. I can't let you go down there alone, especially..." He glanced around the elevator ceiling. "Especially with Wenders acting so strange; it's too much of a coincidence, no? You see something strange, then Wenders—no, then *Sarge* gets called away on *other duties,* then Wenders calls us out precisely when your bodies appear, and Watch One doesn't show. No—and then we have to hand in our watchcards as well! So it's pretty clear—you saw something you weren't meant to see, and Wenders tried to prevent you from seeing it." He whistled softly. "It's too much of a coincidence—something classified, F3 or higher—but it doesn't make any difference—we still can't get in without watchcards."

"I have to."

"Yeah, yeah, but *have to* doesn't translate into *able to*. How are we going to break into a secure room without watchcards, assuming Wenders' watch crew hasn't already shown up and found your illegal tile?" He paused. "Ah. With that Scout of yours, right? It hacks into secure NASAD computers, defeats door access codes—" He hesitated. "Who are you working for?"

Something dropped out the bottom of Blackwell's heart. He wondered with a vague unease why Ed had never mentioned the old man, or if they were on the same side. "I don't know," he whispered, then more loudly, "I have to."

The elevator stopped. The doors opened.

"OK." Carl breathed deeply. "How long will you take?"

Blackwell calculated. "Forty-five seconds. Maybe fifty."

"Make it quick." He stepped out, looked up and down the corridor, then gestured for Blackwell to follow. "We're clear. Go! I'll hold the lifts."

Silence walked the corridor instead of Wenders' watch crew. A black subterranean silence, so unlike the quiet watchful hum of the Dungeon. The image of Wenders and Sullivan in the Pulpit troubled him.

Purple and spiky.

At the Dungeon door, he aligned the Scout's beamer with the door panel as Ed had shown him, thumbed a little-used icon on the screen and waited until the Scout located and decrypted the door's access sequence. The door slid open and Blackwell crossed to the monitors. His monitor was off. That was odd.

"Get it and let's get out of here!" hissed Carl from the elevator..

So was the screen next to it and the one next to that. In fact, *all* the monitors were off.

"Someone coming!" gritted Carl. "Go go go!"

Power failure? Blackwell wondered as he climbed up on a chair, but immediately rejected it. The overhead lumipanels lit up the tile where he had left it. *Strange.* He slid the tile into his pocket and left, beaming the door closed as he did. Carl was half out of the elevator, gesturing frantically. The level indicator showed the second lift descending.

Carl punched the 'Close' button as Blackwell hurried in. The elevator moved upwards. Carl let out a whoosh of air. "We're not clear yet. When we get to the access tunnel, don't run." His work blues were dark with sweat. "If they find we've been down here, they'll seal the place off. Look casual."

In the echo of the access tunnel, Carl walked alongside Blackwell. "Stay close," he hissed. "In case they've got cameras, we're talking. I'll say something, and you'll nod and say something back. Don't look anywhere except forward, not back, up, down, sideways." He continued to talk about insignificances as Blackwell counted seconds, and shapes purple and spiky thrummed panic in his skull.

Fifty meters from the outer Gate, Carl slowed. "Don't speak when we get there. You'll only tell the truth—you can't help yourself. They should just let us through unless the watch crew has discovered your break and enter. Don't do the panic act on me now, buddy. Stay cool. Think of something sweet and happy like...like data. Pretend you're in the library."

At the Gate, the sentry was speaking into his headset. "Corporals Blackwell and Randall?

"Yes?" Carl's voice was so calm, Blackwell thought. His own teeth were clamped tight.

"Is there any reason for your tardiness?"

I had to get my tile. Blackwell's teeth ached with the effort of holding in the truth.

"Restroom break." Carl chuckled. "Sitting down watching monitors for six hours. Pressure builds up—you know how it is."

The sentry considered them with all the affection a hovering hawk might have for a mouse. He made a note on his Scout and waved them through.

Outside, without turning, Carl said, "We're not clear yet. If that magic box of yours leaves traces, we're shot. Walk quickly now; car's this way." Carl pulled out his carcom and triggered off the safeties. About forty meters away, an engine started, doorlocks clicked, and the car's impact zone generator hummed into existence and the doors flicked open.

As they reached the car, Blackwell was plotting escape. Synapses were igniting, firing, recoiling, recharging. He felt crisp, heady with charge. He could overpower Carl, steal the car and get out of town quickly. His job was lost, his apartment would be watched, so he could only hope that Ed or the old man would find him before Sullivan. "Sullivan and Wenders ordered you to get my secret." It seemed so horribly clear. "This was all a setup."

To his surprise, Carl barked a short laugh. "Get in the car, Tower. This is no setup, and this is not about your secret. It's complex. I'll explain later."

Demolition fuses ignited under Blackwell's careful foundations. "Tower? You *knew?* But Sullivan—"

"You want proof? Old man with the beagle's name is Michael. Funny ability to stop time. Do that for you, did he? Knows everything about everything. Deceived everyone to get me into NASAD to watch over you. Couldn't tell you because you can't lie." Carl checked the mirror for movement at the outer Gate. "Nothing." He slipped into the driver's seat. "They would have locked the place down by now. Get in."

The seat's personal field zone tightened across Blackwell's shoulders and waist, locking in his bewilderment.

Carl reversed out. "Check that tile. We may not have long."

The tile powered up far quicker than commercial units, and its small screen opened with the last recorded image and time. *0710* the screen read, but it was the image that accelerated Blackwell's pulse. He shuttled back a frame or two to check it wasn't an error, and put the tile back into his pocket.

Carl glanced over. "Dead bodies like you thought?"

"Worse."

Blackwell ran up the stairs to his apartment, flung open the front door and raced in. They hadn't seen anyone following them, but still, this was not good. He remembered with green prickly excitement the stranger named Ed standing in his living room.

And when you see anything unusual in Scandinavia, any military escalation, any unexplained combat activity…

He shivered. Still, this wasn't that. Yet. Nor, if Carl was correct, was it anything to do with his secret. Just two motionless yellow figures in a place where they shouldn't be and an object with the signatures of a detonator.

Blackwell shoved the tile into his homehub and stood there, staring at it, Carl arrived five minutes later, breathless. "No-one's watching us," he puffed.

Except Wenders. The image of Wenders under the bulbous VR headset disturbed him. Purple and spiky. Carl pulled out his shirt and wiped his face with it, then his glasses, smearing them. "Not unless they're scoping us from a distance." His white belly heaved.

Blackwell nodded, only partly relieved. "I've transferred thermal, visual and seismic registers to both my Scout and home homehub and—"

"You got tracking software on your homehub? NASAD software? Michael didn't tell me about that."

Tell no-one of this meeting. Why had neither Ed nor the old man spoken of each other?

Blackwell could barely interpret Carl's words for the alarm rising in his throat. "I've wired the seismic register on the tile to my Scout." He handed over the palm-sized device carefully.

"The magic Scout," Carl breathed. "I didn't know Michael had this sort of thing."

"I've synched the registers to start together. I've only seen the last image, so I'm not sure what started it yet." Blackwell thumbed the 'Execute' icon on the homehub remote, and the slightly grainy satellite image appeared. He focused on the two yellow figures. "Those are the two bodies I told you about. You can see the detonator in front of one of them. They don't appear on the visual register, so they must have been camouflaged."

Carl muttered something in Italian. "But what's there to hide in Finland? Nothing there but miles of snow. Who lies around in an arctic wasteland?"

"I don't know."

Carl snorted. "I'm taking you to Michael's place as soon as we've checked this out."

There are more than two players in this game, Tower—how to get the information to Ed?—Ed and Michael working together?

But the bodies remained still, and Carl glanced across at Blackwell with a raised eyebrow that Blackwell understood very well indeed.

Nothing changed for a minute or so.

"Still watching," said Carl. "Watching and waiting. Looking at some seriously gripping images of snow. I'm transfixed." But when the flash bloomed brighter than snow across the homehub screen, momentarily blinding the satcam iris, Carl leaped, almost dropping the Scout. "What the—hey, Pete, you see this? Got a geo collapse in—you seeing this, Pete? Tremors vectoring out about two—three thousand meters, non-radial, no fault line impact. What's visual showing?"

"Thermal and visual both Factor Two—no, Three...Factor *Four* initial, then subsiding. Subterranean origin—"

"Volcanic?"

"No, Finland is geologically stable—no volcanoes, no fault lines. I'd say non-natural origin—the detonator would indicate that—high yield..." He peered at the screen. "Unusual..." He paused the image sequence. "The heat levels are constant, which would mean..." He paused and scratched his nose. "Something burning down there, but there's nothing but *rock*, nothing flammable."

"Residual heat from the blast?"

"Too much snow. I doubt it. And this heat is—"

"Some government running bomb testing? Anything on the Dip Lists?"

Blackwell shook his head. "No, nothing."

And when you see anything unusual in Scandinavia, any military escalation, any unexplained combat activity not covered by the Diplomatic Lists, anything unusual at all, use the Scout as I instructed you. Immediately.

But was this that? Or related to the old man's warning? Or both?

Carl ran a distracted hand through his hair. "This is F3 at least! This is VR material! This is what Wenders didn't want us to see." He groaned. "But why? Who's blowing up stuff in Finland—what *is* there to blow up in Finland?"

Immediately.

A flicker near the edge of the blast distracted Blackwell. "Wait. There's something odd with this." He zoomed out so that the red pulsing shape of the blast area filled the screen.

Carl wiped at the screen. "Your monitor's pixellating, Pete. Better get that looked at."

Blackwell wiped at the monitor, but the flickering continued. He zoomed in, peered at the screen. The flickering was in the image. "There. See the displacement at B plus 1.45? See the shadows appear behind that spot…there?" He advanced the monitor a minute, and split the screen into two 'Compare' modules. "See the difference? Something has risen out of the ground, throwing the shadow behind. Whatever is under that dome is invisible to the sats, but—"

Carl looked closer. "Size?"

Blackwell overlaid a screen grid, boxed in the shape. "About ten meters diameter."

"Sounds like a cargo elevator like on aircraft carriers, only smaller. Missile launchers? Go to real-time and compare."

Blackwell jabbed at the red RT icon, studied the spot as the screen moved forward to real-time and then zoomed in again. "No movement. Nothing left that elevator or entered it." He leaned back, thinking, though Carl was still staring at the homehub, adjusting the resolution and zooming in and out on various sections. "There's three domes. All rose at about the same time, and all have a strange ripple at about the same time. Look, there." He pointed. "See how the edge of the dome blurs, then re-clarifies? Like a mirage blur. They all do it, see, there at B plus 2.30?"

Without warning, the image cleared and the screen blanked. Carl whooshed out surprised air and sat back heavily.

"Must be the time of the power outage," said Blackwell. "Must have been Wenders. Yes, the flicker is non-natural, no doubt about it. But that's not the problem. We've got an explosive incident in northern Finland. Cause unknown, but the heat sigs make it a non-nuclear—a non *standard*—munition, geo displacement, no subsequent events save for the three strange elevators, no visible human movement. It's definitely F3. Concur?"

"Definitely. Underground blast of some kind. Someone tried to escape via the elevators but failed."

"Either that or the blast triggered the elevator mechanisms, and they rose automatically. That would explain why no-one got out."

And when you see anything unusual in Scandinavia…use the Scout as I instructed you.

Carl waved his arms. "Yeah yeah, but why? What's important enough for Wenders to twist himself into knots trying to hide it?

He woulda succeeded too but for your magic Scout and tile. We're way over our security clearance for this—*stratospherically* over—but what's underground in Finland worth destroying? Waste dumps maybe? No, but those woulda been on the Dip lists—the greenies woulda screamed otherwise."

We need you to keep a watch on our interests in Scandinavia. "The Finnish government had three old pre-nuclear bases, but these coordinates don't match any of them."

"Ya sure? No chance the Finns built others on the sly?"

"No, I would have seen it."

"Yeah, but you ain't been there 24/7 to watch every moment. Ya gotta sleep, buddy, gotta shower, talk to people and eat and do stuff." He paused, and even Blackwell's juvenile face-reading abilities interpreted Carl's stare correctly. "Sweet mothers of the unborn! Ya not saying you tiled—? Ya not serious? What…where…how do you make time? How many lives ya got hidden away?"

"I tile all the data from Watches One to Three, and bring it here. Then I watch it at eight speed so as not to waste time."

Carl's hand was in his hair. "Waste time? Serious?" He breathed out slowly, half-smiled and jabbed an accusing finger. "No wonder you don't understand women. You got a stratospheric problem, buddy! You are *soooooo* afflicted! And what do you do with all this data? What would Michael want with this?"

Not Michael. Ed. "I don't know. I remember it." Though it felt like being naked, this inability to withhold the truth.

Carl snorted. "Yeah, and I'm the—" He waved his hands as though swatting away missiles. "OK, don't matter whether I believe you or not. Question is: does Wenders know this?"

"I don't think so. He hasn't asked."

"But you'd tell him if he did, right?"

"Yes. I have to."

Carl tugged at his hair as he walked around. "OK, that makes no difference to anything. We seen something we shouldn't have seen." Carl jabbed a pudgy finger at him. His shirt flapped, creased below the waistline. "Michael's given you classified software from who knows where. You been tiling classified data. *You* got a Scout that don't even *look* legal." He laid it on the carpet as though surrendering weapons, then stood back. "If Wenders' watch crew discovers any glitch in the monitor logs, we're shot. How secure is your Scout? Will it leave any traces?"

"No."

Carl made several distracted attempts to stuff his shirt back in, all unsuccessful. His hairy white navel showed between buttons. He wiped his forehead on his sleeve, looked at the hub screen, then at Blackwell. "Well, seems like we're safe from Wenders and Sullivan for the moment, and I got no idea why Michael would need all that data, but doesn't matter—gotta get you to him now." He grabbed his carcom out of his pocket. "I can't leave you here. Sullivan will come looking, and you'll get a laser through the head. Get a change of clothes, something warm. Wipe your hub memory, get your Scout, any tiles, any evidence they can use against you."

The alarm in Blackwell's throat rose like a poisoned well. Carl hadn't mentioned Ed once. He knew nothing of Ed's command or the heavily-modified Scout. The realisations and consequences banked up against Blackwell: Ed and Carl could be on opposing sides. Either one of them could even now be leading him into danger. And Wenders was almost certainly after him.

But Blackwell had to signal Ed as he had promised.

You'll know when men start firing at you.

The message was only a few words, but as Blackwell began to move, his links with reality began to disengage. He realized Carl was speaking, but it sounded blurry—voices under water. He felt himself fading.

A hand on his shoulder. Shaking him. A voice through layers of opaque rubber. "Buddy! Hey Pete—come back to me! Come on, Mystery Man, this is no time for—!"

Blackwell's vision cleared enough to see Carl's sweaty forehead, ridged with concern, his brown Italian eyes wide. "Ya with me, buddy? What happened there?"

"I panicked," croaked Blackwell with a disembodied voice. "Don't cope well with unpredictable situations...black out a bit... sorry."

Carl stared. "Well, I got some of your clothes and that tile stuff in your rucksack—hope it's OK. Here's your Scout. I wiped the home-hub memory—come on, we gotta go. Get you outa here—"

The phone chimed, and Blackwell reached for it without thinking.

...use the Scout as I instructed you. Immediately.

Carl was blinking, his mouth working. "Hey, *no no no no NO!*"

But Blackwell's hand was already on the cool white handset with no reason or logic in his head.

Carl was staring at the ID screen on the phone unit. "Sweet mothers!" he hissed, reaching for the handset. "It's Wenders! Hang up! Hang up!"

Disoriented illogical colors and tastes flared in Blackwell's head. Dimly aware he was doing something very wrong, but completely unable to stop himself, he lifted the handset to his ear.

Carl jabbed at the phone pad, turning - *Speaker* - on and - *Visual* - off. He muttered something with passion and urgency in another language, then listened, his teeth bared, one hand in his hair. He spun around, stalked a few paces towards the door, waving his arms, and extended a finger to the doorpanel before stepping back.

Blackwell leaned against a wall for balance. "Blackwell."

"Record begins. This is Captain Wenders, Corporal." The voice took presence in the room, armed and armored, purple and spiky. Blackwell had to draw in two breaths. Weights like planetary orbits shifted above him, preparing to fall. He had the Scout in his palm. It would only take a few seconds to key in the emergency code. Not untenable yet, but close.

Carl's took two handfuls of his own hair and tugged.

Menace coiled in Wenders' voice. "Understand that this conversation is being recorded, and that your testimony will stand as a verifiable record of your actions in any subsequent court-martial. Do you understand and acknowledge this?"

Court-martial? Muscles in his legs destabilised. "Yes, sir."

"The guard at the main Gate reported that you and Corporal Randall were late leaving after the conclusion of your Watch earlier today. Surprising, since you had just been promoted and given three day leave passes, effective immediately." He paused like the half-second before bulletstrike, and the manic pound of Blackwell's pulse measured the silence. "Is this true?"

Carl snatched up the rucksack and headed for the door.

Blackwell's heart iced. *I cannot lie to a direct question.* "Yes, sir."

"Furthermore, the guard at the Gate reported that Corporal Randall claimed you had visited the men's room, though the hall cams disprove this. So Corporal Randall lied, did he not?"

The door opened, and closed quietly a moment later.

"Yes, sir." The words came out with a ghastly fluency that sickened Blackwell. He pulled out his Scout and laid it on the table. With a shaking finger, he began slowly keying the emergency sequence.

M.U.C.H...

"Is Corporal Randall with you now?"

Blackwell looked around, hoping wildly Carl was not there. "No, sir."

With the deliberate slowness of a predator circling, Wenders said, "Ah."

Blackwell's knees locked, then released. His foot began tapping on the floor. His wildly mobile tongue slewed around his mouth, nearly choking him. To his surprise, the line went silent except for the sounds of Wenders' muffled orders and acknowledgements from aides. Blackwell's vision hazed. M.U.C.H. A.N.D...he tapped, though the keys swerved.

The line cleared. "Why were you late, soldier?"

Blackwell hated himself. *I cannot lie.*"We went back to the Dungeon, sir."

Circling. "For what purpose, soldier?"

"To retrieve a personal item, sir."

Wenders whistled. His voice took on a curious softness. "You are aware that you are incriminating yourself, soldier? Do you have anything to say in your defense?"

"No, sir." Blackwell looked anxiously around to the still-closed door, but something else caught his attention, something that rocked him backwards as sharply as any blow. On a small subscreen in the corner of the main homehub screen, four small, blue, diamond-shaped icons began flashing. Centered, in bold red characters were the words 'Origin: NASAD,' 'Type: termination team,' and "Time since activation: 0 min 24 sec.' The threat detection software Ed had installed on his homehub. Blackwell had never used it, but he knew the icons represented the surveillance pings NASAD used to establish the location of terrorist groups before they sent in the body-armored termination teams.

Why? Why was this so important to set up such an elaborate deception? What does Wenders want hidden?

Blackwell wrenched back control of his foot. *24 seconds*. About the time Wenders established that Blackwell was alone. Blackwell knew Wenders was now monitoring every call he made, every connection through his hub to the Net, although Wenders could not possibly know that Blackwell was aware of the surveillance. With shaking fingers, he tapped. M.U.C.H. A.N.D. N.O.T.H...

The predator returned—jaws snapping, circle closing. "Then you have two charges to answer. For the first, how you entered the

Dungeon without a watchcard. For the second, what personal item you retrieved that was worth your certain court-martial."

"A data tile, sir."

There was no humour in Wenders' barking laugh. "I would hardly credit you with such foolishness, soldier! Not unless…not unless there was something on this tile…something you wanted preserved. Is that the case?"

Blackwell desperately wanted for it not to be the case, but his mouth was open and the truth was escaping.

0.58

"Yes, sir." He looked around frantically for Carl, but the door remained closed. *We have to get out of here!*

M.U.C.H. A.N.D. N.O.T.H.I.N…

"And what was on this tile?"

"The seismic, thermal and visual data from Watch Four."

Wenders paused. The sound of him sucking in breath sounded like a suicide toppling from a bridge. "All of it?"

"No, sir, just the last fourteen minutes."

Wenders paused. The diamond icons flicked on—off—on—off. "And what did you see?"

1.14.

Blackwell calculated furiously. Twenty-three minutes from NASAD to his apartment by bus, Carl had done it in ten, less again by official vehicle with sirens. Perhaps seven minutes. Six minutes to get out. "Sir, I saw the beginnings of an F3 incident in northern Finland, sir."

The doorpanel chimed softly. The door handle rattled. From outside, Carl tapped insistently on the door.

"F3?" said Wenders. "Soldier, you are in serious violation of… wait." Wenders covered the handset and issued a whispered order. A moment later, his voice tightened in the hollowness of the VR headset. "I am in the data now. Stay on the line."

"Yes, sir." Blackwell tapped frantically, hit incorrect keys twice, and started again. M.U.C.H. A.N.D. N.O.T.H.I.N.G. He keyed the last character and hit 'TRANSMIT.' He could barely hold in his breath of relief. Violent colorshocks rimmed his vision.

1.36.

Wenders drew in breath. "Where is this?" he demanded. For an odd moment, calculating how he could escape, Blackwell didn't register that the question was directed at him.

"Northern Finland, sir." His voice was down to a croak. His legs threatened collapse. He clutched the sofa as he slumped to the floor.

For the next thirty seconds, Blackwell heard nothing but Wenders' breathing. His vision swirled in and out of focus.

2.11

Then, to Blackwell's utter astonishment, Wenders laughed. "Finland, ah, yes. The old pre-nuclear bases. Yes, this would fit. The Finns have been planning to retire those for a while now, remove all the toxics and then collapse them to keep out hikers and idiots. They built three bases, I think, back in '05, before the White Sea Crisis. This will be one of those."

Blackwell would rather have cut out his tongue and left it there to babble as he fled—

2.34

—but the words came out anyway in rags and scraps. "The coordinates don't match, sir."

"No, it's a minor waste dump attached to one of the sites, soldier, which makes the charges of treason against you more ironic. Remain in your apartment until NASAD officials arrive. Do not attempt to make contact with anyone. You will be permitted legal representation under the terms of the Kaufmann Act. Record ends."

The line clicked off.

2.51

Blackwell knew he had to flee, but haze crowded his vision. He sat heavily on the floor, cold bile swirling in a light murderous ballet in his throat. Warm dampness flooded his crotch.

From outside, Carl whispered loudly, though at a great distance, "Pete. Pete! The door's locked, the doorpanel's showing an internal security barring. I got your gear in the car ready. Hey, let me in!"

"Get out," Blackwell said with all the volume of a drowner. So brief a friend. "They're coming. Go. Go."

Speech unfastens itself from Blackwell, and a strange hollow wind comes sweeping, erasing all his maps. Blackwell sags as Carl thuds.

"Let. Me. In!"

But Blackwell is three degrees off-center to reality and fading fast. His Scout is still clutched in his hand, though it looks like another's hand. Digits below four blue flashing diamonds on his homehub screen read—4.05.

A loud crash startles him. Glass tinkling. Grunts, cursing, footsteps. Blackwell tries to turn, but his major muscle groups have abandoned him. It could be either Carl or Ed, he thinks, but the smell of garlic tells him.

"What happened to you? Pete, you OK? Can you move? What's happening, Reconfigured Man, what did Wenders want? Did he do this to you?"

Two minutes until the termination team gets here! Blackwell wants to say. Get out of here while you can! But his tongue is just a random muscle in his mouth. He cannot move his arm, his hand, his finger to point and warn Carl.

But he can move his eyes. He flicks his glance back to the threat detection subscreen, hoping to catch Carl's eye—look, he commands. Look. LOOK!

And Carl looks, sees the blue diamonds, and reads off the time notations with surprise that becomes anger that becomes frantic action. "What have you done?" He grabs Blackwell's limp body—hands under his armpits—and pulls him towards a window. "Never mind, never mind, got a minute, maybe two." He says other words, none of which Blackwell understands, but Carl is very fluent in Italian maledictions.

And in Blackwell, something stirs with physical contact. Synapses connect. Neurons fire, skin sense points activate. Saliva lubricates his tongue. He chokes, dribbles, and croaks.

"What's that?" Carl hoists Blackwell to his shoulders as though he is as light as a flapping sail, kicks out the shards of glass and begins levering them both out of the broken window. The world is big and sudden with wind and sun on Blackwell's face, but neither his tongue nor his body are working. "Car's ready," grunts Carl as he carries Blackwell across the yard. "Glad you're on the ground floor." Carl eases Blackwell into the car, straps him in, and there's a fierce energy in Carl's touch that gives Blackwell strength. His head straightens. He looks around, no longer the limp sack.

Carl leaps in—the engine is running—and maxes the impact zone generator. "For all the good it will do if the shooters are after us. Michael, hope you got your gates open."

Blackwell manages a grunt that completely lacks the meaning he intends.

Carl floors it.

Blackwell watched in his side mirror the street behind them, though the street remained quiet, empty. Carl swerved around a corner into a suburban street lined with trees. "Anyone following?"

Intending to say no and angry at himself for his condition, Blackwell grunted.

"You are in a bad way. OK, help me here—one grunt yes, two for no—does this lead to George St?"

Blackwell grunted.

Carl hesitated, then punched the phone button on the dash. "Home," he muttered, and when Jilly came on-speaker, he said, "Something's come up, babe...friend in trouble...No, not me, but—no, I haven't done anything stupid, believe me! Just get the kids and get out of the house. Don't pack, don't call anyone, just go. No, not your mother's...No, I'll be fine...No, can't tell ya...Take your Scout and set the house security from the car. Wait till I call...Gotta go."

We have to stay close to the apartment! Ed won't be able to find us! Blackwell moved his tongue around his mouth, trying to gather air to protest.

Carl bit his nails. "Now, Mister Reconfigured Man, we're on our own."

No! We have to turn back! But before he could form the word, Carl spoke again.

"Any chance ya got police tracking software on your magic Scout? Any chance you can—"

The word came out, though he knew it was one question too late. "Ngaaaooaah!"

Carl glanced at Blackwell. "That was no? OK..." He turned back to the road. "I'm taking you to Michael's house, lay low for a while till we can work this out."

How? Does he have a fortress and armed guards? Blackwell struggled to speak, to shake his head, anything. *We have to turn back!*

Carl pulled out his Scout and keyed a number. "Michael? There's trouble. Bringing Peter to you. Ten minutes away. Open the gates and let us in."

Then he turned onto Ashland Road, the main street through the center of Walton, past fast food outlets, the main supermarket, the largest of the four suicide agencies, past the furthest limit of Blackwell's walks. He slowed, checked for pursuit in every direction, and accelerated. "Might be clear," he muttered. "Hope there's no cops around." He glanced across at Blackwell and grasped his shoulder, and inside Blackwell, at the touch of Carl's hand, cords and ligaments tightened. He lifted his arms. Thirty percent good, he thought, though he still could not speak.

Carl has to turn back.

"You OK?" Carl said. "Ya had me scared there for a minute—what's with the sack of potatoes thing? How come you can't move?"

Unpredictable situations lead to panic, sometimes physical, sometimes mental, sometimes both. Desperate but unable to speak intelligibly, he merely grunted.

Carl reached over and shook his shoulder. "Sometimes, buddy, that says it as eloquently as any speech. Stay cool and I'll help you out when we get to Michael's."

With all his strength, Blackwell croaked his protest, though it sounded no more defiant than a bleat.

Carl turned. "Don't worry, buddy! We'll be safe there. He's got… ah, some *unusual* things going on. It's just an old lumberjack's shack out in Northcott—nothin' special—you'd walk past it and not see it if you wasn't looking."

"How far?"

"About three miles away. Old logging camp. Strange place—clocks don't work inside it. Cameras see right through it. Strange… but good for us."

They passed through the central town area and out into the steep roads that wound through the hilly region that bordered Walton to the west. Carl was humming something operatic, but he stopped abruptly when he checked the rear-vision mirror. "That car's been there for a while."

Blackwell looked in the mirror. A white vehicle was following about seventy meters back, jacked high, with something circular mounted on the roof under higher-than-normal ski racks. A termination team. A man and woman in the front seats wore sunglasses, looking around with the careful precision of snipers. For a brief moment, Blackwell hoped the man was Ed, but he knew full well who would be following him. Sullivan. *Where are you, Ed?* thought Blackwell darkly, desperate to break out of his silence and tell Carl. *How will Ed know where I am? We have to turn back.*

"Maybe they don't know it's us," Carl muttered. "Maybe they didn't see us leave." Swinging tight around a sharp bend, Carl held his arm out to brace Blackwell, and his touch jolted energy into Blackwell's bones. Fifty percent body, Blackwell calculated. Twenty percent voice. *They're tracking us at the American Desk with PILGRIM and HYDRA.* He did his best to form words. "Pi…Pil . . Hei…Hy… sat…cam."

"You're talking! Yeah, I thought so too. I dunno the orbits, but Wenders got 'em tracking us for sure. We need to get undercover soon—" He glanced around as the NASAD vehicle took the bend without slowing.

"Turn back!" croaked Blackwell. "It's Sullivan!"

"No way, they'll shoot as we turn! And PILGRIM's tracking the car's heat sigs as well." He accelerated; the NASAD vehicle dropped back for a second or two, then caught up. "He's waiting for a deserted spot, then he'll move in for the kill, so we'll have to go down the logging track to Michael's shack, drop the car and run. And—hey! That rucksack of yours—did you realize it's braced with titanium panels? Some of the stitching tore. You had it specially made or what?"

"No." Though he remembered Ed's words. *If the situation becomes untenable, the Scout and rucksack will keep you alive until we get you out.* A cold jolt circuited up Blackwell's nervous system. *He knew this was going to happen.* "It was a gift."

"Yeah, well, stick it on your back when you get out, and hope they don't aim for head or legs." Carl glanced in the mirror, gritting an operatic aria with venom and desperation. When Blackwell looked, the NASAD vehicle was forty meters behind, and the woman in the passenger's seat was intent on something on the dash. Underneath the ski racks, the circular object began rotating until Blackwell realized what it was. A high-grade sniper laser. Powerful enough to penetrate Carl's impact zone shield and the thin sheetmetal of the car. Sullivan was going to disable the car, kill Carl then capture him. Interrogation certainly, and this time Sullivan wouldn't be kind.

Carl must have seen it too. "Hang on," he gritted. "Can't wait for the track. Let's see how well he drives off-road." Soon after the road swung hard to the left. Carl swung harder, and the SUV dived over the narrow gutter and downslope through undergrowth towards denser knots of trees.

Blackwell knew he would not be strong enough to flee the NASAD laser. *Touch equals strength,* he realized, and unclicked his PFZ.

"Hey!" yelled Carl. Blackwell bounced, hitting his head on the car roof and windows until Carl held out an arm to steady him, and Blackwell leaned into the touch, extracting its energy until he felt muscular control return.

Seventy percent body, he thought, reaching out to clutch Carl's shoulder. Not perfect, but enough. He swivelled to scan the trees, hoping he had enough strength to run.

"Yale River," said Carl. "Michael's shack is on this bank a bit further downstream. He'll have the gates open."

Ed's leaving it late, wherever he is. "Gates?"

"You won't see 'em but you'll know. Just run."

"And you?"

"Tell Michael to get the coffee hot. I'll lose these sickos and get back soon."

Blackwell glanced in the rear-vision mirror and saw that the NASAD vehicle had dropped about a hundred meters behind.

"He's no good off-road," said Carl. "Here's your chance, buddy—where these trees get thick. I'll veer left to shield you. Jump wide, get your rucksack on, get under cover behind the riverbank trees and bolt right. You'll know you're inside the gates when your heart goes crazy. He won't let you miss it. Got me?"

Blackwell felt the first clenches of panic in his chest. "Yes." He opened the door, and the alarm triggered in a steady whine.

Carl accelerated, narrowly missing trees. "Four," he muttered, "Three...two...wait till we're past that boulder...*Now!*" He braked hard and reached over and pushed Blackwell out.

Two impacts jolt Blackwell as he hits the ground. The first is pleasant: the sensories of leaf-fall and dirtsmell, the sound of the river, and the quiet otherness of the forest, busy with its own secrets. Then second impact is his right arm breaking under him as he hits the ground at an angle that jolts breath and hope out, and pain comes sweeping through him. The rucksack slips off a shoulder. Blackwell bites down a scream as blood pumps out near the white bone that cannot possibly be sticking out of his forearm.

A scream comes anyway—or maybe that is enginescream—and then shouts and doorslam as stupid blaring colors shriek nausea around his vision. They are pursuing him, he realizes, not Carl. His percentages unravel. One voice is Sullivan's. "Peter! Stop!" He rises to the run—treecover within nine seconds, maybe ten—he calculates with a speed that startles him. His arm hangs like the victim he will be if he stops for Sullivan. Nine long seconds. The titanium panel in the rucksack might deflect a beam once, but not twice. He cannot run to Michael's house with a broken arm. He runs anyway.

Three seconds.

Keeping low, expecting the brief sting-before-obliteration of Sullivan's laser, his brain screaming, Why Ed why NASAD why Wenders why pursuit?

Five seconds.

The trees—he sees a gap in the bushes and veers right a degree or two, lowering his stride again—the gate the gate where is the gate the gate the gate? His arm screams.

Six seconds.

Now reality disintegrates: the white shriek of laser hisses, to his left and high, and foliage flares, a tree branch cracks and falls.

Seven seconds.

A second hiss, closer but still high, the air tangs hot and acrid. Shouts behind him. A third shot misses wildly. Branches crack and tumble. He nears the tree shadows and his mental clock reaches eight seconds but the fourth shot takes him in the shoulder, above the titanium panel. Fabric and muscle burn as he screams, and his pulse quickens stupidly, erratically, loses contact with his musculature. Ed! he thinks at the last, hopelessly. He stumbles, veering right towards an open gate and a bright wizened face.

A fifth shot blooms black, violent pain in his left elbow.

A sixth and seventh rip skin, muscle and lungs.

Strength and sense disconnect.

His seeing blurs, falls into shadow…

…a dog yelps…

his heart trips madly and…

…light opens above him.

Three

Purpose

Father Nick's Day minus three hundred and sixty-seven days
Murdoch Hospital
Murdoch, Perth
Australia

Ten steps from where Harker Brown stands in the corridor of a Perth hospital, his beloved Ruth is fading down through the last degrees of cancer to the death he cannot prevent. Even their forty-four married years of good memories are not enough to stop Ruth's cells being devoured. It still angers him that they have become apart: she lying there in her hospital bed, and he in full health in the corridor outside. He's still wishing they were on the verandah at home, planning their trek to Cradle Mountain in northern Tasmania, though there's no hope of that now. The Australian sun outside is strong, just as he must be for her.

He listens to the doctors—he stands taller than most of them—as they tell him, this will be her last Father Nick's Day, Mr Brown. We've done all we can. *They shake his hand, and he notices how slender their hands are, how cool.*

How useless.

He goes back into her ward, with several volumes of protests banging around inside his heart, though he will speak none of them in her presence.

"Come on, Mrs Brown," he says, putting on the smile he knows she will understand. "I'm taking you home." With two days left before Father Nick's Day and not many more for Ruth Louise Brown, Harker leads her out through the fixed faces and bouquets of the grieving and stoic and bewildered, past the Father Nick's Registration office in the lobby where new parents are registering their newborns for that one magical day of the year, past the pictures on the wall he's never really looked at. He thinks it's strange that they are leaving the place as though she is better. She is far too thin, Harker thinks. She's got as much sun in her as flesh. She's full of light; he sees it in her skin.

The wind is a furrowed broom across the wide expanses of the Swan River as they drive north along the Kwinana Freeway towards the city center, and the sails of tacking Sunday yachts collapse and expand like marathoners' lungs. Bagnecked pelicans sit on the steel light poles like fat magistrates.

"I'd like to go sailing again," says Ruth with that cheerful defiance that Harker has so long loved, and overwhelmed Harker just drives, unable to bring anything to the silence but his own grim lostness. He is a man without any maps, like Burke and Wills dragging their fishing boat across the endless blister of the Australian outback in search of the great inland sea.

It's the daily processes he fears most. Reading without her, taking off his walking boots alone, turning in the night to find her pillow vacant. Nine months of cancer is no way to end forty-four years of companionship. Once or twice, when the anger rises, he's almost hoped she would go Early and take her own life, though that thought just disgusts him now.

On the morning of Father Nick's Day, with the old lemon eucalyptus scratching against the gutters outside and magpies squawking like manic woodwinds, Harker wakes to the promise of death and gifts, not sure which will come first. His beloved Ruth is only sixty-two! She should have years left!

He slips out of bed without waking her. In the kitchen, he cooks bacon and eggs with Worcestershire sauce, with ginger marmalade on toast and herbal tea to follow, all the while afraid he'll go in and find she's already gone.

When he hears her tread along the corridor, though, a sharp, hopeless happiness quivers his chin. She is wearing a dusty plum sweater and jeans and her old walking boots, just as though they were about to head off for a weekend climbing Bluff Knoll or tramping along the Walpole coast. Or sitting under the blackfrosted night sky at the Leeuwin lighthouse as they had on that youth camp decades ago when everyone had noticed the way she laughed at his jokes and leaned towards him, and then wisely left them alone. Harker remembers one arm around Ruth, and the two of them watching shooting stars making strange maps across the heavens, pointing to places well beyond the future's horizon. One hundred and eleven they counted, their own private record, and Harker remembers clambering in the dark over rocks back to the carpark, giggling at anything, unbelievably drunk with the smell of her and the way she laughed.

Now, four decades later, she takes the herbal tea, but only picks at her breakfast.

"Come on, love," he says, and takes her into the lounge room where they sit and wait on the floral lounge suite that Ruth has always loved. The smell of gardenia drifts in through the open windows, but behind the gentle fragrance is the vast hot weight of the Australian desert wind bearing down on him like the cancer that has overwhelmed his wife.

"I'd love to know how they do it," says Ruth. Her face is far too thin. The sweater hangs from her shoulders.

"The gifts, do you mean?" asks Harker, though he knows full well. He chooses his words carefully. "I've often wondered how they organize the making and delivering. It seems like a huge job. My dad told me when I was a boy that there are thousands of workers in Father Nick's secret gift-making workshop under the Himalayas. Maybe that's why I became a postie."

She tries to chuckle, though her throat sounded like it was lined with rotting cloth. "Do you think you could put in a good word for me so I can go? What an adventure that would be." She coughs again, straining the gaunt tendons of her neck.

"I didn't mean— " says Harker.

"Sweetheart, I'm going to die soon." Her words are difficult and whisperous. "Turn to dust or join in with Father Nick's gift-making workshop—either one is fine with me. I've been a good"—she coughs—"girl, so maybe that counts for something. Even if there's no-one on the other side with a Good and Bad list, ticking people off when they come in"—Her coughing is like dust—"it's been a wonderful life with you. I'm not hoping for anything much afterwards."

"I vote for the workshop thing then," says Harker, with the dull realisation that she will be starting on the afterlife without him. Whatever that *means, he thinks dully. He's got no plans to get himself mummified in a ludicrously expensive mausoleum, as some celebs and royalty have after their suicides. Nor does he want the Gaians to go dancing around his silk-wrapped body in a woodland grove, with all their chants and pale candles, and beseecheries for a fair go to whoever runs the afterlife. Or the Zodiac folk either. He doesn't want to be laid out on a stone floor, and their grand master bloke to align all the brass circles in the floor until all the*

metaphysical doors are open for him to enter the afterlife.

No thanks, he thinks. He'll take his chances with the local magistrate presiding over his cremation, then doing him the symbolic favor of mingling his and Ruth's ashes and flinging them to the wind over Ocean Beach.

And he'll be happy if there's nothing after death. The world's a pretty sick and sorry place, though the idea of becoming an Early revolts him. So many of his peers have killed themselves, and he's been to the funerals where a body was present, or the simple court ceremonies where one wasn't. Drownings at sea were popular among the wealthy a few years ago, with the major suicide agents arranging forty foot yachts and string quartets on the foredeck. At least it was dignified, better than the snipers' bullets some young people were choosing from that Cable Co. that organized such things.

He's told himself many times that there's only body and soul, though he wonders sometimes whether there's another part to people, something secret hidden deep in an unmapped part of the body. He thought he glimpsed it once down on Ocean Beach in Denmark an hour before sunrise on a bitterly cold winter's morning. Ruth was still asleep in their caravan, but the sound of the waves breaking woke him with a deep yearning. For a moment of wonderful clarity as he stood alone on the sand, he resonated with something outside himself. Something pinged on his radar. All the lamps in his heart lit up at the same time.

He never quite forgot it.

Now he looks at the clock to distract himself. "It's about time."

A few minutes later, as they sit watching, three beautifully wrapped boxes appear on the coffee table from out of the still air. No warning, no lights, no nothing. Year after year it's been the same, for them and families all across the world. Kids and their parents open their gifts with not the faintest clue how the presents get there. Not all the scientists and sociologists, the writers and journoes, the pollies and celebs with all their cleverness put together have ever worked it out. There's magic somewhere in this universe, thinks Harker, wondering why it won't work for his wife's cancer.

Why are there three boxes, though? He stares blankly as Ruth reaches for her gift. One gift for every person, it should be. One for him and one for her. Just like everyone in the world gets one magical gift each, perfectly suited to that person, unique, unbuyable, irreplaceable. A gift to keep suicide at bay. But Ruth squeals with delight, a sound which still thrills Harker, and makes to gets up.

"No, let me," says Harker, but she pushes herself out of her chair anyway. Harker, helping her up, thinks she is made entirely of last breaths

and porcelain. Just for a moment, he believes her well and whole, uncancered, so the next moment nearly breaks him.

"It's my last time," coughs Ruth as Harker keeps a strong forearm behind her back. "So what if I can't breathe?"

Her box is wrapped in jade green paper. She sits down and when she tugs gently at the cord, it falls off the paper by itself, against all the laws of thermodynamics. Harker has always loved the way she gasps in surprise, as she does now, and she looks up at him with an innocent smile as she folds the paper. "Saving it for later," she says. Her face is made of old and quite lovely petals.

Harker chuckles in a moment of happy grief.

Inside the box is a pair of new leather walking boots.

Oh, thinks Harker, disappointed at the plainness of the boots, thinking she deserves more, and then the strangeness of the gift hits. What good are walking boots, he thinks in a moment he will never tell Ruth, if she will never do any more hiking?

It makes him think. He knows these boots are significant, but he can't for the life of him figure out why. Every *Father Nick's Day gift is significant—the good Father always gets it right. So how does he know whether the receiver will even be alive when the gifts arrive? That's always made him wonder. And how is it that he got this gift so completely wrong?*

But something even more curious presents itself. He expects the smell of leather, but it's another smell entirely that comes stealing into his defenseless heart. The smell of the wind over Ocean Beach, of him alone in the world, of the waves washing their feet before him. There is something more about these boots, he realizes, something disconnected from reality. He takes stock. He knows what magical means. He and millions around the world every year have been delighted, overwhelmed, ecstatic with their Father Nick's Day gifts. One perfect day every year. One day that keeps the walls of hope high against the siege of suicide. One day to believe that someone beyond normal life knows you, cherishes you.

But these boots are something different altogether. This is a stratum above magical. This is light spilling through a door never before opened. This is being alone on a midnight beach among nothing but stars. He shivers a little. He never expected it here. This is transcendence.

But Ruth is as happy as a postie with a payrise. She pulls the boots out, still squealing, and tries them on. Harker helps her. The laces slip together into neat knots without any help from Ruth's papery fingers. The boots fit perfectly, of course, and she stands up like a tottery boxer. "Look, Harks! Aren't they wonderful?"

Harker doesn't quite believe what he sees next. Maybe Ruth doesn't see the leather become a diaphanous silk, soft as a dancer's slippers, light as a baby dreaming. But as Harker watches, too stunned to speak, her feet become pink and smooth, and the silk shifts around her toes, her heels, her ankles, forming up perfectly, adjusting to every contour.

Getting her measure, he thinks and, as light spills through his door, as his height and width gain depth, he realizes that the boots are a leaving gift, a dying gift. A gift for Ruth to walk through that door. Alone. He knows he's staring, but realizes as she follows his gaze down, then back up, that she hasn't seen anything.

She laughs. "Don't look so worried! It's a good sign, Mister Brown. It's Father Nick himself wishing me well on my next journey. Look! You've got two! Father Nick must think you're special this year!"

And that makes him wonder. The leather remains silk, but his attention turns to the table. Why are there two gifts? Anyone who received two would make headline news. The two boxes sit there on the table. There aren't words for his fright.

The first is wrapped in silver paper with a strange shimmery pattern. And it's empty. His heart goes off like the Australia Day fireworks. He shakes his head: leather that becomes silk, two boxes instead of one, and one box empty. This isn't happening, he thinks as he puts the lid back on. There's a borderless wind blowing clean through his skull, and he knows he's the only one feeling it.

Ruth peers in. "Oh, darling," she whispers, "Father Nick made a mistake!" She giggles, and manages to give the soft sound whole continents of joy. "Come on, dear, don't bother with that one—you've got another box! Quick, open it up!"

He hesitates, worried and curious and a little angry, then opens the box. Inside is a book. There is no title, though both the cover and the pages are made of exquisite parchment.

Ruth is saying, "A book! What kind—crime, thriller, suspense?"

Harker is bewildered. The first page is blank, and the second. There is no chapter one, nor a chapter two, nor anything. Every page is blank. He turns back to the first page, wondering if he has missed something, but it is as blank as his future.

"I don't know. It's a mystery," says Harker Brown.

"Who by? Christie, Outhwaite, Branniff? Is it that Cornwell you haven't read yet?"

But Harker is too amazed to speak because, on the top of the first page, in beautifully serifed characters, words are appearing. They read:

This is a mystery.

Father Nick's Day minus thirteen days
A local community hall
Perth, Western Australia
Australia

Widowed, Harker Brown sat. The hall, an hour before his retirement party was due to start, was empty. His Father Nick's Day book lay on his lap, still as unfathomable as when he had first seen it almost a year earlier.

A car pulled up outside. A few minutes later, the door next to Harker opened and a large, trousered bottom entered backwards.

"Harker?" said the bottom's owner, looking over his shoulder. "You're here early, old son. Thought you were going to make a grand entrance later."

Harker looked up to see George Wilkins, his Post Office tie askew and a few too many latitudes of belly drifting south over his equatorial waistline. In his arms, a Post Office crate looked ready to overbalance. Harker closed the book, perhaps a little too loudly, stood up and put the book on his chair. "Need a hand with that?"

"Thanks." George's deodorant wafted at Harker as he offloaded the crate. As Harker set it on the floor and eased its contents back into place, he heard George's sudden silence.

George was flicking through the book. "What's this?"

"Diary. It's a diary."

George stared. "Pretty fancy paper. Where'd you get it?"

Harker looked at it. It had been worrying him for months. Since Ruth's death, he had carried it with him at all times, but it remained blank except for the four words on the first page. What mystery? he pondered. Nothing in his life was mysterious apart from being the only person he knew of to receive two Father Nick's Day gifts. It was as though the book itself was its own mystery, a self-referential enigma. "It was a gift."

George frowned. "You told me you got an empty box for Father Nick's Day."

Harker felt surprisingly calm. "I got two gifts."

George's frown took on global war proportions. "Two? *Two?* No-one ever gets two."

"Three boxes on the table, mate. One for her, two for me."

"Maybe Ruth gave you something?"

"Nup. Not unless she can do the appear-out-of-thin-air thing. She was as surprised as me."

George's stare flicked from the book to Harker and back. "It's not a diary, is it?"

"Don't know yet."

George considered that, his eyes narrowing. "What do you mean, you don't know?"

Harker showed him the four words.

George's eyes glazed. "That's it? What did you write that for? What kind of life you living, Harks?"

"I didn't write it."

"Don't believe you."

"Watch this then." Harker took George's pen from his top pocket and scrawled vigorously all over the page without leaving any mark or imprint on the paper.

"Pen's not working," George said.

"Really?" Harker pulled a paper scrap from his own pocket and scribbled visible scrawls with the same pen.

George took the pen, shook it, wrote on the scrap, then tried to write on the page underneath the four words. The paper remained blank, pure. *This is a mystery*, it declared. "What kind of flamin' book is this?" George whispered.

"Kind of book you'll keep to yourself," said Harker, putting George's pen back. "You're my oldest mate still alive, and mates keep secrets." He put the book into his pocket.

George looked troubled. "I'll do me best." He glanced around. "You reported this?"

"What would I say? Father Nick made a mistake? I'm going to hang onto it, and wait and see. The words wrote themselves. Maybe something else will appear."

George tried unsuccessfully to hitch up his trousers over his belly. "You're dealing with darkness, mate. I don't like it."

"Mystery, George, not darkness. These Father Nick's Day people know what they're doing. There must be a reason for it. Just gotta wait and see."

George considered. "Fair enough." He transferred sweat from his forehead to his sleeve, and new ranks broke out immediately. "I'll keep me mouth shut. Look, we didn't expect you to be here, but now you are, you want a job? Frank's got some young blokes for the set up—"

"There are only two ages, mate. Young and dead," and the memory of Ruth inhabited his smile. "I'm still on the right side of that ledger."

"Yeah," said George. "Sorry. Well then, young 'un, how about giving me a hand with getting these trestle tables organized? I promised we would get the setup done before the caterers arrive."

Harker gave a hand until, an hour later, with a hall full of people crowding around Harker and wishing him well, bald and fat Frank puffed his way up to the front of the hall with a wad of crumpled notes in his fist and tried to straighten one page on his thigh. George looked around for the keg, and Harker took the moment to slip back in the crowd, well away from the stage. When he turned back, Frank was tapping the microphone. "Is this on?" He peered across assembled heads to the back of the room where Harry monitored the PA and slide projector. "Harry? I can't hear anything."

"It's on, Frank."

"Hate these things." Frank prodded at it as though it had teeth, then looked up and smiled uncertainly. "Ladies and gentlemen," he whispered into the microphone, then covered it with one hand. "Am I too loud, Harry?" he bellowed, bringing a fresh sweat to his face.

"You're fine, Frank. Just talk normally."

George gestured with an empty beer glass, caught too far away from the keg and too close to the front. "Get on with it, Frank."

Frank gave George a glare of supreme condescension and got on with it. "Well, then, for the sake of those…um…um. Well, ladies and gentlemen, distinguished…um, guests, I'd like to introduce a bloke who…um…really doesn't need any introductions, who's been with us, faithful servant an' all…" He covered the microphone again and bellowed, "How long's he been with us, Harry?"

Chuckles from everyone except George. "Fifty years!"

"Well, right. Fifty years, and we'll be sad to see him go. He's won so many Postie of the Year awards over the years I've lost count, listening to all the kids with their gift lists. Mums and kids reckon he's got a direct line to Father Nick. Anyways, I've got a few notes here, put together by me and some of his mates—though they might not be his mates after tonight."

Chuckles and nudges among the crowd, and grumbles over a spilled beer.

"Some of us've got homes to go to, ya great ditherer."

Fully in charge of the microphone, Frank smiled. "Right, then. Here we go. Harker Lucas Brown started—"

"Lucas?" blurted someone. "Izzat your middle name, Harks? Kept that well-hidden all these years, dintcha?"

Frank waved his notes at the blurter. "You're a peasant is what you are, interrupting like that. Now kindly keep it down, or I'll dock your next pay. As I was saying before I was so rudely interrupted, Harker Lucas Brown started his working life at the Post Office when he was fifteen, sweeping floors and running errands out at Merredin. In the mornings, so he useter tell me, he set his rabbit traps in the fields down the road, and skinned the rabbits at night to make a coupla extra bob. Later on, he moved to York, where he met Ruth at the local dance—Harry, you got that projector sorted out yet?"

"No need to shout, Frank," grumbled George, a finger inserted theatrically in an ear.

Frank grinned. "C'n someone here give George some happy pills? Or another beer? Shut him up and let me finish?"

He adjusted his notes, though he was still only on his first page. The lights went out, and a large white oblong appeared on the wall behind, over the space where the ghastly painting of an Aussie bush sunset had earlier hung, complete with flaming reds and silhouetted kangaroos. Frank did his best to remove the microphone from the stand, failed, so bellowed at the crowd, "This one's when Harker was doing his army stint. About twenty, he reckons."

An image appeared of Harker and three mates in jungle greens, half-turned to the camera, rifles slung, on patrol among scrubby bush and ghost gums. Harker looked faintly lost, as though homesick without knowing it.

"This was about the time that Harker blew up the sarge."

Snorks of beery laughter, choking sounds. "You did what? I never heard that one, Harks."

Frank held up his pointer. "Not only that. He also fixed up a stone-dead engine when the squad was out the back of nowhere on exercises. Up Meekatharra way, wasn't it? Got everyone home safe and well or they'd still be stuck out there. And jury-rigged the radio with bits of wire and a ration tin after some dill dropped it in a creek. Bit of a hero, our Harks. Next, Harry."

The projector whirred and shunted and a group of six or so young people appeared, lounging in monochrome laziness against the bonnet of an ancient ute, the men's hair Brylcreemed and shiny under the country sun, and the women holding tennis rackets like they would later hold the hands of snotty-nosed five-year-olds looking wide-eyed on their first days at school, and possibly later their instruments of suicide.

Shouts of approval. "You *were* a skinny one, Harks!"

"Still is."

"Is that Jack Riley on the right? Y' know, the one that played footy for the Dugites?"

Amid discussion, Frank walked over to the image, a long pointer in his hand. For a blinding moment, as he walked through the dusty projector beam, his head became a forty-five year old image of Dunlop-clad feet. "Harks here on the left," he said, pointing, "Ruth next to him, then Bob Cowan that went into politics, then Ruth's sister who married that crooked businessman, Pat you all know, and…um…"

"No! That's not you, izzit Frank?" boomed George.

"It is!"

"You're twice the man now, Frank! Did scales go out of fashion, or were you solely responsible for the fast food boom?"

Guffaws. Frank reddened. "Pat's a fine cook. Anyway, some of you were at Harks' and Ruth's wedding, and I'm sure you'll all agree that Ruth was the finest of wives, a great companion for Harker. They tramped around India on their long service—" The projector slotted in a picture of a lean bare-chested Harker wearing a sarong in a tea plantation somewhere, his arm around Ruth, looking very pleased with himself. The sight of the healthy Ruth quietened everyone. Many had admired her for refusing to go Early, or accept the death pills the doctors had often offered her. Standing there looking at her, they took sips of beer, not slugs. George kept his wisecracks to himself.

"Coupla years later," croaked Frank, "off they went—got that next slide ready, Harry?—off to Canada…"

The next slide blinded some. An adult Harker with a statuesque Ruth standing on a cruise liner and backgrounded by a glacier. Their sunglasses were off, yellow Goretex collars high around their necks, and they looked excited enough to burst into the national anthem. Harker with three days of contented stubble, and the Arctic wind forever adoring Ruth's hair. The sun bright around their happiness.

Frank joined the gathering in staring. Just staring. "Right pair of travellers they were," he said eventually. "We haven't got any photos of their trip to Hawaii—Harks wouldn't let me see those ones—but they were off every Father Nick's holidays. They'd save all year, then while we're all opening what we got on Father Nick's morning, Harks and Ruth are on a plane to somewhere. And how many of you got postcards from Harks from China or Brazil or Tan-gan-flamin'-yika marked 'Having a good time. See ya later'? Man of few words, our Harks. Hobart was their next trip, but…unfortunately, we…we lost Ruth."

For a moment or two, only the projector hum marked time, then Frank cleared his throat. "Anyways, this is Harker's retirement party, so let's all welcome him up to say a few words."

Back in the crowd, Harker put down a still-full beer glass someone had given him, adjusted his collar, then moved forward. Hands patted his shoulders as he went. An aisle formed for him.

"Harks," someone said.

"Only a few words, now, Harks."

George was absently rubbing at his face with his beer glass hand, leaving foam on his forehead. "Where'd ya get to? Turned round 'n' you were gone."

When Harker reached the front, he ignored the microphone. Instead, he stood under the image of Ruth, gazing up at her like a climber worshipping a mountain. Frank could easily have been invisible. Then he went to the microphone. "Turn the pictures off, Harry," he said gently. The projector whirred and ticked. The room went dark and quiet and full of memories until someone found the lights. "Thanks," said Harker Brown, looked out over the crowd for a moment, then made to turn away.

"A few words," grumbled George loudly. "You promised us a few words, Frank, and he's given us only one."

Hoots. Harker smiled, though it was clear his mouth was only in it for appearances.

"Come on, Harks," said an encouraging voice.

Harker hesitated, looked down, and turned his wedding ring around his finger with his thumb. Frank sidled away. A fluoro flickered nervously. "She would have enjoyed tonight," said Harker in a voice that carried forty-four years of companionship. "She was a great woman." He looked down, then over at the curtained windows, then at the far end of the hall. Wetness glimmered in one eye, and he let it stay there. "But…well. Thanks to all of you. It's been great working with you all. You've all pitched in with dinners and visits and helping out. Thanks Frank for the extra time off work." He waved an inclusive hand. "Thanks to you all." And for the second time, he made to move away.

"Got any plans, Harks?" called someone hastily.

"Retirement plans, yeah!"

Harker's smile amped up a few notches. "Not much. A week or so on Ocean Beach. Clean out my head. Do some fishing. Then I've got a few little things to take care of: get my photos in order now you lot've been rummaging through 'em. My reticulation needs a bit of work," and many groaned. Harker's lawn varied between brown and dead, even at the best of times. "I want to spend more time with John." Those who knew Harker's four year old autistic godson nodded. "And I'm going to buy a computer and learn how to play the stock market online. Oh, and learn Russian."

"How many languages will that be, Harks?" grumbled George. "Seven?"

Laughter, good-natured.

"We were going to learn it together," said Harker Brown quietly. "Me and Ruth. Then go off on the Trans-Siberian Railway and practise."

"Bloo-dy," said George with feeling. "I'd be lucky if the wife wanted to go to Perth on the train and practise her *English*."

"I'll tell her that," said Frank, back in charge of the microphone. "Thanks, Harker. Don't nick off again, we've got a little something for you. Maggie, where are you?" He gazed around the room. "Can you bring it up here, thanks?" A young postie with arms like footballs appeared, carrying an enormous packing box wrapped with gold paper and tied up with flourishes of red ribbons.

George's eyes widened. "Did you wrap this, Jean? That's the annual budget in ribbons right there! Didn't anyone ever teach you the difference between centimeters and kilometers?"

"Frank approved it, Mister Grizzleguts!" said Jean with a voice like a dirt bike on a gravel road. "It's for Harker, in case you hadn't noticed."

Harker's expression oscillated between a prudent frown and delight when he took it. "You…you shouldn't…well, thank you." He put it on the floor, unwrapped it and opened the flaps. His chuckle was muffled from inside. "I bet George had a hand in this," he laughed as he took out a cricket bat, emblazoned with an engraved plaque and signed by Harker's every living colleague. "By my grandmother's grave," he whispered and turned the bat over. "This must have taken ages!" He peered closer. "Tubby? You found Tubby Holmes? I thought he'd gone to New Zealand!"

"He did. We had to send the bat in the overnight bag to get it back here on time. You'll see we got old Robinson to add his scrawl as well."

"You didn't!" Old Robinson was the grumpiest Director of Post ever. "And here's Robert Jones, Stinky Rhodes, Mabel the tea lady…" Harker looked up, unusually bright-eyed. "Well, this will be going up over the mantlepiece. Thank you to you all. You've made an old bloke very happy."

For a moment, after the three cheers, one or two in the crowd reckoned they saw a younger Harks standing there, his comfortable check shirt and cords transformed into a bare chest and sarong, his silvery hair a youthful brown, and his arm around a woman that no cancer could ever touch.

Frank said, "Supper's on at the back. Make sure George has got a beer, someone, willya?"

But George was among the first to embrace Harker, ruffling the older man's hair and holding the hug a moment or two or three longer than his many years of teasing Harker seemed to warrant. "Y'old dog," he muttered affectionately. "Place won't be the same without ya. Come on, let's get something to eat."

At the back, George stared at the catering people behind the laden trestle tables. "You're not the normal people," he said, reaching for a plate.

"They were called out to an urgent job." The man had an unusual accent and looked excited about something. "We're replacing for them."

"Fair enough." George piled his plate full of canapes and pizza slices. "I'll get you a beer, Harks," he said, and headed off.

The caterer watched George go and leaned forward a little to Harker, "If you could, by your actions, give hope to many, would you?"

"Excuse me?" said Harker. "Not sure I follow you, mate. You are the caterers, right?"

The man's smile was secretive. "If you could, by your actions, end the hopelessness in the world so that people no longer took their own lives, would you?"

Harker chuckled. "This is some kind of joke, yes? You've got TV cameras somewhere. George set you up for it."

The man did not even blink. "Would you?"

Harker stopped laughing. The bloke was serious, although it was a bizarre question to be asking a new-retired postie. "Yes, of course." Though it would do nothing to bring back Ruth, and sometimes he wondered about George's emotional well-being. "But there's not much one bloke can do. This a survey or something?"

But before the man could answer, Harker's heart tripped. When he opened his eyes, the noise was somehow different and George was somehow at his side, explaining the relative benefits of a sniper's bullet as his preferred suicide method.

And the strange caterer was gone.

Standing in the carpark after the last of the guests had gone, George said, "Wanna lift home?"

"Thanks," said Harker. "But I reckon a walk'd do me good. It's only a mile or so."

"Fair enough." George got into his car. "See ya, mate."

Harker turned to go, but it had to be spoken. "Hang on a minute."

George's personal field zone shimmered a little as he clicked on the car's automatics. The engine started. The radio came on with the news of a strange explosion in Finland. "Yeah?"

"Don't go Early on me, mate."

George's laugh wasn't convincing. The red brake light glowed on a tree. "What brought that up?"

"Just don't."

George looked away, let the engine idle. "Wasn't planning to." His hands were fixed on the steering wheel like it would save his life. "Things get a little hard sometimes, though. Nothing like what you've been through, but…sometimes I can't see the point in things."

It hit Harker like a cricket ball in the belly. He thought for a moment about hugging his oldest friend to remind them both of the great sturdy ramshackle structure of their friendship, but the distance between them stalled him.

"You can't stop it," said George. "It comes, it comes. You know that." The glow on the tree dimmed a little as the car eased back. "I'll let you know when it does. I won't go without a last beer together."

It did little to reassure Harker.

As George drove off, though, Harker's heart kicked and looped like a grandkid having a tantrum, then settled like nothing had happened.

Odd, he thought. He was fit as they came, but the body did strange things the older you got. He glanced up once, and thought it was a little strange how the moon and the bright streak of the comet hadn't moved much. The streets were oddly silent. George must have changed the muffler on his car, it was that quiet. He jumped over the low fence in front of the community hall and got into his long easy stride, practising cricket strokes with his bat.

Behind him, an engine started.

Lights flicked on.

Shadows aimed at Harker.

Four

Vows

Father Nick's Day minus twelve days
Unknown location

Blackwell surfaced into darkness, then dull pain in his shoulder and chest. Someone was holding him down…some thing. A plastic strap around his wrist. His head, when he tried to lift it, was restrained with a band across his forehead. Ankles also, his thighs, and his chest. No personal field zone, this. Fear came ripping cold and sick up his throat.

Careful.

He breathed out. Slow. Methodical. Felt the calm return. Minutes glaciated past his taut heart as he counted. After three hundred seconds, as his breathing became easier, he tugged at where his left hand should have joined his arm. Nothing. Not the feel of plastic, or pressure or any pain at all. He licked his mouth slowly, breathed out, flexed his left bicep and its pressure against the cloth of his shirt relieved him. But when he commanded his wrist to pull back, no sensation came from below his elbow. As though nothing was there.

Nothing. Laserfire blasting foliage, black fire blasting through his arm…He forced calmness with difficulty. *Where is this?*

No hospital. The wall next to him was metal. Rivets rose to where release bolts lined the ceiling, and the room was vibrating. *How did I know about release bolts?* Disoriented, he struggled to remember.

Careful, careful, he warned himself, keeping his eyes closed, remembering, though it was a crazy blur: the Dungeon…old man…tile…Wenders…the diamond-blue icons…pursuit… running towards trees, laserfire blasting foliage, black fire blasting through his shoulder. NASAD! Alarm iced his veins. Air-conditioning. No windows. Interrogation room. Strapped down. They must have caught him. Although a memory lingered—a dog yelping, a light bursting around a wizened face. Michael?

He listened for movement, footsteps, anything. The room was too quiet. His stomach growled. He couldn't remember his last meal. He could remember Carl, though. Carl of the garlic and operatic maledictions, his only buddy. He twisted his head, but the strap restrained his arc of movement. All he saw was a canister on a nearby trolley. From it, through two clear tubes, a fluid pulsed into needles inserted in his left shoulder. Sedated, he realized. Though his senses had none of the porridgy numbness of anesthetic. And the familiar weight of his Scout and jasmine perfume bottle in his pockets surprised him. Why hadn't they taken them?

He analyzed. If Wenders had the power to order the termination team and the interrogation, he could court-martial Blackwell, or erase all records of him from NASAD. Blackwell had no friends other than Carl, no family he knew of. no imprint on society; he could disappear without much disturbance at all. NASAD owned him, his apartment, his income, his only friend. There would be no government inquiry into his disappearance, interrogation and then death. If he leaked information slowly enough, he might determine from their questions who had caused the explosion, and why NASAD wanted it kept secret. What his ninth planet was. And how Ed and the old man were involved.

Footsteps. He kept his eyes closed, though his captors would certainly know when the anesthetic had worn off. Expecting Wenders, he tensed, made a fist of the only hand he could feel and prepared himself for interrogation and the sight of half his arm missing. He knew he had broken it; perhaps they had amputated. The footsteps approached. Blackwell kept his head still, his eyes closed.

"What did you see?" a voice demanded.

That wasn't Wenders. He relaxed fractionally, cautious. It could have been a NASAD interrogator, though it sounded familiar. Blackwell slowed his breathing, still suspicious. His fingers locked wiretight.

"No need to pretend," said the voice. "NASAD didn't get you, if that's what you were thinking. But what did you see? Quickly, why did you beacon us?"

Blackwell opened his eyes, memory sudden and total: the voice, the tall figure standing in his living room, the drift and float of Ed's fine and wispy hair.

"Ed? You came! But where were you? I thought—Where's Carl? He was driving when I jumped out."

Ed appeared at the side of the bed, connected something with a faint click that Blackwell could not see, and appeared intent on some instrument on his wrist—a chronometer? He was clutching wires connected to the silver canister. He seemed thinner. "We saw no-one except you and the NASAD pursuit vehicle."

"No-one? How? Carl was only fifty meters away! Surely—"

"You were seriously injured with a broken arm and under fire, so our focus was solely on you. Perhaps your friend escaped. But you beaconed us with the emergency code 'MUCH AND NOTHING.' Why? What did you see?"

Escaped. Blackwell doubted it. There was too much of Carl to escape, especially if NASAD had immobilized his vehicle and left him to flee on foot.

"A strange detonation in northern Finland—underground, localised collapse, non-nuclear, non-seismic, non-volcanic. It didn't match any known bases or installations—what's going on? How are you and Michael—?"

Ed glanced around quickly and leaned forward. "Michael?" he hissed. "The old man with the beagle? What did he tell you?"

"You know him?"

Ed laughed softly. "Oh yes, we know him. And he told you not to remember things, right? I'm just glad we got you before he did. And did he tell you there were more than two players in this game?"

Blackwell tried to nod, surprised.

Ed leaned back, smiling. "He's been saying that for years, crazy old fool, full of mad conspiracy ideas, but he's harmless enough and we've got real business to attend to. Like the location of this explosion you saw."

Blackwell recited the coordinates. "NASAD tried to hide it. When they found out, they sent out the termination team after Carl and me. What kind of hospital is this place? How long till you release me?"

"No hospital," Ed tapped something on his palm, a Scout, Blackwell realized, not a chronometer. A woman's voice acknowledged the connection. "Val, they've destroyed Kavonatur." He listened for a moment. "No, he verified the coordinates. Tell Book." Checked something on the canister attached to Blackwell's arm. "About nine minutes left." Then, "OK," and clicked off the link.

Questions tumbled through Blackwell: *Kavonatur? Nine minutes? Where is this? Who is Book?* Much as he wanted desperately to be released from his bonds, he still remembered Ed's clear instructions on that strange night. "I'm sorry. I should have contacted you earlier."

Ed shook his head slowly. "You did well in the circumstances, precisely as we asked."

"But I didn't contact you in time! This is what you wanted me to warn you about, this Kavonatur place."

"It wouldn't have made any difference," said Ed. "Kavonatur is—was our main European base—our second oldest base—so we knew something was wrong when it went offline. Your beacon came in shortly after, but we were on high alert anyway trying to get a link to Kavonatur. We were hoping it was a simple comms failure, but the longer they were offline, the less chance there was of it being something simple. They had backup generators; they could have used the old landline, sent out a sled—anything!" He turned away and swore violently. "A thousand men!" He fell silent for a moment. "It wouldn't have mattered anyway," he muttered. "We had no warning, so your beacon wouldn't have helped even if it had been on time. So don't punish yourself. Now tell me everything you remember in exact detail."

Blackwell wondered how the destruction of a European base and loss of a thousand men connected with his ninth planet. He paused. One question at a time. "Book is a person?"

"Book is a *Patron*. Now tell me."

So Blackwell related the entire sequence, complete with time counters, heat signatures, temperature gradients, everything, all the while hoping that something would become clear in the whirling constellations of unknown data around him. "Just before the tile vision ended, we saw three unusual elevators rising out of the ground. It might have been someone trying to escape."

Ed hesitated. "Escape?" he said softly, then a strange note entered his voice. "Did you see anyone? "Any vehicles, aircraft? They would have looked like planes with short wings."

"No, the vision ended at that point."

"Do you have the tile here?"

"In my rucksack. Let me up and I'll get it."

"Not yet. You were badly shot up." He released the head strap. "You can move your head now, but not the rest of your body yet." Ed strode over to the far side of the room where he rummaged through the rucksack. "Your arm's fine, but no-one's ever survived the kind of injuries you sustained. Or this rucksack, for that matter. It served its purpose, though. You took wounds to the bones and muscles of your upper chest, shoulders, left arm, part of your lung. Luckily they missed your heart."

"You knew this was going to happen?"

"We suspected it might. I'm sorry we couldn't prepare you more, but the more you knew, the more chance there was of Sullivan extracting it from you. I nearly ran out of nanotubes and gel trying to glue you back together again. You're lucky your pursuers were only trying to stop or disable you, or no amount of nanos would have saved you. You've still got about seven minutes left. Stay calm. I know it's not pleasant." He pulled out the tile and clicked it on. Then there was a long period of quiet as he watched. On three occasions, he sucked in air sharply.

Eventually, he coughed. "This is it," he whispered. "A thousand dead, the European operation devastated. Everything…gone in a night. This tile is all that's left. There won't be any other record. If not for you, there would be nothing at all. Even with all our preparations, safeguards and fallbacks, our campaigns of deception, putting you at NASAD, they…" His voice cracked.

"A thousand dead? I don't understand."

But then Ed muttered something in excitement, strode over and shoved the tile in Blackwell's face. His hand was shaking. "This tile shouldn't pixellate like that. What's the image resolution?"

Blackwell told him.

Ed cycled the vision back and restarted it. "But the blurring only occurs here, then clears again briefly before the vision ends." He put the tile down and tapped at something out of Blackwell's vision. "Book, there's a chance that three sleds escaped Kavonatur… No, no vision, but the blurring on Tower's tile seems to indicate timeslip before they lifted off… Well yes, if they followed emergency procs, but…but there are a lot of ifs. If the Kavonatur timeslip wasn't compromised, if the sleds weren't damaged in the blast, if the sled launchers were intact. Can you scan for Kavonatur sled IDs? They might be trying to beacon." None of it made the slightest bit of sense to Blackwell. Ed checked something on the trolley next to Blackwell's bed and said, "About six minutes. Yes, I'll bring him up then." He clicked off his Scout.

"Bring me where?" Blackwell demanded. "You promised I would learn everything after my extraction. Right now, I don't understand anything! What just happened in Finland—"

"You want to know?"

"Everything. Especially what my nine planets mean."

Ed paused a second. "Planets?"

"Memory fragments. They're all I have left of my past life."

"OK. But Book and Valentina should be in on this discussion, so let's start at the beginning first. We've got a few minutes. Have you ever wanted to go Early? Felt hopeless and decided to take your own life?"

The question jolted Blackwell a little. The image of the man killing himself in the alley smelled bitter in his memory. "No," he said carefully. "Never."

"What about Father Nick's Day?"

"Of course." The answer was easy, though the question puzzled him. "Magical gifts every December sixth. No-one knows how they get there."

"We put them there." He paused. "*You* put them there."

"I do?" Blackwell snorted in disbelief. "I don't re—"

"You're a Poor Man, Peter." Ed smiled. "You're one of us. For seventeen hundred years, the Brotherhood of Poor Men have given gifts and kept the Cabal's suicide curse at bay. You and I and thousands of Poor Men around the world are all that stops suicide. Now that the Cabal has destroyed Kavonatur, the whole operation is under serious threat. Can you imagine the disaster if Father Nick's Day was lost? Instead of thousands dying every year, there would be millions! Whole nations would perish!"

Blackwell could only think of Carl, though, and his talk of jumping out of a plane, and the awful grief of that pathetic plummet angered him more than he had ever known. Inside Corporal Peter Blackwell, who owned nothing but nine planets, enormous armored mechanisms geared into place in his heart and musculature, locked down, bulked out. War declared itself. "What are you doing to fight the Cabal?" he demanded hotly. "You can't...gifts won't stop them!"

Ed smiled softly. "That's all we have. Poor Men bear gifts, not weapons. No massed armies or navies or orbital laser attack platforms. Just small boxes on living room tables once a year." He paused. "It's a fragile line we walk, Tower."

Blackwell's mind raced. "It doesn't make sense," he muttered.

"It makes all the sense in the world," said Ed, smiling. "Gifts given in grace, not greed. Given for the benefit of the receiver, not the ego of the giver. For generosity, not for profit. People still love their families and life, but everyone knows the time might come when the Black Despair hits and there's no more point in waking up every day. For millions of people, Father Nick's Day is the only time, that single solitary day of the year, that gives them hope against despair. Hope is a wonderful thing, Tower. Hope that someone out there—us—cares for them. Hope in the extra-ordinary, in something more than they can see. We're only human, but to them, we're the red-suited Santas that dandle kids on their knees in supermarkets—"

"Santas?" blurted Blackwell, feeling the stupid yawning chasm between listening and understanding grow wider. "But how can you keep secret?"

Ed's Scout buzzed. "One minute, Valentina," he said into it without looking at the screen. He grinned. "Because they can't see us. Because this world has two streams of time, side by side. The one that the Cabal and most of humanity live in goes at normal speed, but we're in the other stream, where time moves faster, where mysteries happen, where the Fay folk and monsters live. We share the same planet, but the timeslip keeps us separate. That's why Peter Blackwell didn't have a wallet or any evidence of identity when he was brought into NASAD. That's why you remember so little. That's why you're not on any government records or censuses, no birth certificates, no nothing. You don't exist."

"But..." A hollow wind gusted chill through Blackwell's skull. He reached out and gripped Ed's arm, clutched it as the strength slowly returned. "But...this...room! You, me! This...we...everything...it's all invisible?"

Ed grinned broadly, all his teeth neat and straight. "One of the strangest things you'll see is a real world jogger. In his perception of reality, each step takes a second, but in timeslipped reality—our reality—that step takes a hour, sometimes two. It's the oddest thing to come back from deliveries and find him only a few feet further along than where he was in the morning."

Blackwell just shook his head.

"Poor Men are the warm current within a cold ocean," said Ed. "We're sunlight in winter. We're the Santas that kids the world over wait up for. We're the sweet shadows that warm you in a chill world. We've made the sacrifice of service, Tower. We can leave the Brotherhood at any time and rejoin humanity, but no-one ever has. Does any of this resonate?"

Only one point of it did, and Blackwell was grateful for it. Internally, the planet named gifts dimmed and winked out. "I remember gifts. But what about my other memories?"

Ed glanced up at the closed hatch, then at Blackwell, then at his chrono. "There'll be time for that after we go up to the bridge, meet Book and Valentina—"

"Who's Book?"

"Patron of the North American continental enclave, one of the top men in the Brotherhood. After that, we'll insert into Patara, supervise your vows, then work out how to reorganize and set our defences."

Blackwell lifted his head to see cables plugged into Ed's wrist. Blood roared in his ears. "Vows? I'm not taking any vows!"

"You wanted to fight the Cabal a minute ago. You'll be no good to anyone as a novice. You have to take your vows. We've got work to do, and we'll need every Poor Man."

"That's it? No other choices?"

"Only three. Go back to NASAD and get shot. Make your vows at Patara and come back to the only family you've ever had. Or fall."

"Fall?"

"If you want to go Early, this would be a pretty dramatic way to go." He pointed up at the explosive release bolts. "It will be a quick death." He smiled faintly. "Not much of a choice, I'm sorry." He stepped back.

"This is a plane?"

"Not a plane." Ed tapped something on his Scout. "A sled." Something whirred. The walls and floor irised open, endless blue sky opened around and below Blackwell, and he clutched the straps and screamed, certain of an imminent plummet.

After a moment, he realized he was not falling. The straps still restrained him. He looked down through a clear but solid floor past clouds to Earth far below him.

"You're in the cargo hold of a Brotherhood command sled," Ed said. "Fifteen thousand meters up, over Portugal, eastbound, one hour from insertion into the Patara timeslip. We're not only timeslipped, but also invisible to all detectors: visual, thermal, IR, accelerator." Ed was moving away to a control panel near the ladder. Blackwell's abdominals tensed, ready for the brief explosive jolt of the bolts detonating, half a second of grinding metal and weightlessness, and an eternity of plunging. "Vows?" said Ed.

"Just close this window!"

"Done." The walls irised closed. Blackwell's retinas flared with afterburn, and his heart with shock. "I'm sorry to do that to you. But this is war, no place for the undecided. Now let's get you up and mobile." Blackwell felt faint sensation in his left arm, and his chest ached. Ed tapped his palm, though Blackwell could not see his Scout. His palm looked empty. Then Ed pulled two cables out of his wrist, moved to the table and started releasing restraints. Blackwell lifted his arm gingerly, but it felt strong, stronger perhaps than his right arm.

"Slowly," Ed warned as Blackwell sat up. After a moment of dizziness, Blackwell moved his arm around. His shoulder twinged, though in stiffness rather than pain. He tensed it, swung a cautious full circle as Ed picked up Blackwell's rucksack from against the wall. New sensations pulsed in Blackwell's chest, as though he inhabited someone else's body. He rubbed his shoulder, probed his thumb into the muscles, feeling for tightness and finding none. Ed gave him a cloth. "Clean yourself first," he said, and gave Blackwell a cloth and a bottle. "Your sugars were quite low. You had an intravenous drip earlier, but this drink will keep you going until you get some real food."

Blackwell drank and wiped his face vigorously. "You're a doctor?"

"More a plumber. I fix things: sleds, people, Scouts, computers. Pipes are pipes whether they carry fuel or blood or data."

Blackwell stood.

"Any dizziness?"

"No, I'm fine."

"Good." Ed's Scout buzzed again. He snatched it up. His face tightened. "When?" he demanded. "Converging? Yes, coming now." He clicked it off. "Time to go." He grabbed Blackwell's arm. "Listen! This is important. When we go up to the bridge, for your own safety, stay silent. However Book questions you, whatever happens, you must not speak of Book's daughter."

"I knew her?"

Ed raised his hand. "There's no time to give you all the details. Just know this. A few weeks ago, just before you were to take your vows, you got into some…ah, trouble. You were brought to me with serious head injuries, comatose, near death. Nothing was clear, and the Patrons suppressed the report, but the word was that four men had to pull Book off you. He was trying to crush your skull with a hammer."

It took all Blackwell's will not to shout out. "What did I do?"

"You killed her."

Perth, Western Australia

The phone woke George. When he rolled over into a band of light from between the blinds, Louise's side of the bed was empty. He smelled coffee as he picked up the phone. "H'lo?"

"George, it's Frank." He sounded strained. "Is Harker there with you?"

George croaked out a chuckle. "I'm in bed, mate, so I don't really think so."

Frank didn't laugh. "No, really. Is he?"

George rubbed his eyes and levered himself up. Frank's voice was three semitones above 'trouble.' "What's wrong?"

"He's not home. I went round this morning to invite him over for lunch, knocked on the door, went round the back—nothing. His paper's still on the front lawn."

"Gone out for a walk maybe?"

"Not without his walking shoes. They're still on the doorstep. Car's in the garage."

"Strange. Neighbors' house, maybe?"

"Checked. How did he seem last night? Did he say anything about going to Denmark?"

"He's going Monday. He seemed happy enough last night when I left him in the carpark."

"He walked home?"

"He walks everywhere, Frank. Nothing unusual about that. D'ya reckon someone did him in, an old bloke of sixty-odd? To steal his bat?"

"Don't joke. I've driven all along Cardan St this morning, up and down three times. I looked in every driveway, every alley..."

"You worried or something? He's a postie for goodness sake—he's strong as a bull, knows every street and family for miles, everyone loves the bloke, not the sort that someone would—"

"There're some strange people out there, George. It only takes one idiot."

George snorted. "What—kill Harker?"

Frank's brief silence jabbed at George. "I just hope he hasn't gone Early, y'know, retirement and losing Ruth an' all."

"Doubt it. Look, stay where you are. I'm coming over."

It was a neighbor who told them. Barely ten houses from the community hall, they knocked on a door and were greeted by an overweight mother in a dull green dressing gown and a piercing in her nose. Behind her, like a besieging army, the permanent smells of burnt bacon, ashtrays and damp washing were dug in for the long haul. Kids were already plugged into VR gamesets on their homehubs. George wondered if his own carpet smelled of Worcestershire sauce and failed plumbing like this one.

"He was such a good postie," she sniffled. "Collected all our gift lists—I reckon he had a direct line to Father Nick, the way the kids got just about everything they asked for. We voted for him every year in that Father Nick's Postie contest you people ran—the man was a genius."

George gagged. "Was?" She showed them the skidmarks behind the front fence. Frank stared at the flattened grevillea while a couple of kids watched silently like refugees from the front porch. "Where did they take him?"

She told him, and George took the keys from Frank's hands and helped his mate into the passenger's side, overwhelmed with a kind of hopeless anger that he realized had always comprised at least forty percent of his demeanour. He said nothing as he drove. Frank stared out the window, swore at just about everything, and muttered questions for which George could only say, "It'll be alright, Frank. He'll be fine." The car's satnav guided him to the hospital he hated, the one he had long secretly believed he would die in.

A news channel was covering speculation on the path of the Melcassar Comet, but there was no angle on global destruction that would bring a smile to Frank's face. A Torino Level 7 comet blasting through space with the potential to eradicate humanity had very little humour, he realized.

He had seen the weekly TV panel shows where professors and astronomers argued strategies and contingencies should the thing break up: weapon launches, spacecraft landings, mass population movements; and possibilities: climate radicalisation, coastal devastation, survival rates. It left him so dead-hearted that he sat there for an hour after he had turned off the TV, wondering what the blue blazes was the point of living if it was only half a breath before dying.

He knew what people were thinking, though. The world was closing up shop, and focusing on the things that meant most to it. Family. Pleasure. Love, or whatever came close. Most of the mail these days was to family: cards, parcels, perfumed letters, though new parents left right and center were registering their newborns at the new www.fathernicksday.com so they could get one last Father Nick's Day. Hardly any bill payments passed through the mail any more. Colin the accountant, two months shy of retirement, had left one day and not come back. Painfully shy backroom Ted had proposed to Elaine, and to George's muted delight, she had agreed. Wayne the postie, always a revhead, had bought the biggest vroomiest V8 from his old man's dealership with little more than a handshake, and set out to drive across Australia in less than a day, traffic cops be damned.

George parked and gave the keys to Frank, and they walked through the carpark towards the vast hospital complex that always reminded George of a moon base with its numbered buildings. A receptionist with a practised smile told them where they could find Harker, and it was at that point that the last of George's hope dribbled out. Just the mention of his friend's name cancered into his courage like nothing had a right to do. He jammed his teeth together to stop his jaw from quivering.

Harker Brown, Ward Nineteen. Along the corridor, turn right at the end. Harks in hospital when he should be getting ready for Denmark.

"Intensive care?" George asked, hating the question. It wasn't him, surely, who was standing in a hospital on a perfectly good Saturday morning when kids were mucking around, blokes grizzling about gardening and mums setting course through the weekend with all their sails full. Disease inside, sunshine outside, comet approaching. Hopeless, he thought. Might as well go Early and be done with it all.

The receptionist smiled with genuine compassion. "No, but he's unconscious. Are you next of kin? We tried to find his family, but he didn't have a Scout or anything with him."

Frank groaned and turned away.

The green carpet tiles that stretched away down the corridor behind the reception desk stung George's eyes. No amount of pastel paint could cover the smell of illness in the place. "No, friends. Work colleagues. He retired yesterday. We gave him a cricket b— No, we're not."

"There'll be a doctor on the ward," said the receptionist. She checked her list. "Doctor Powell. She'll help you."

Harker was lying in bed when they got there. His eyes were closed. Frank swore softly and with feeling. Various tubings and drips invaded Harker's nostrils and wrist like parasites. A doctor was checking something. The sheets on the bed were white."Are you next of kin?" asked the doctor.

"No, just work friends," said George. Frank was already sitting in the chair next to the bed, holding Harker's hand. "His wife died recently, and he doesn't have much family. How is he?"

"Pretty badly injured. Both legs broken, fractured skull, kidney damage, possible internal bleeding. We've operated to reduce the cranial pressure and pin his legs, but he isn't responding as we would like."

"Responding?" croaked Frank.

"He's in a coma. He might not come out of it. I'm sorry."

In the car, George Wilkins turned on the radio to add some noise to the silence he was getting from Frank in the passenger's seat. He wanted some mindless talk to deaden the blow of seeing Harker there in the hospital bed, a human voice to tell him that things were well elsewhere in the world, that everything would be alright. Harker Brown, the most well-loved postie he had ever known, was critically injured, comatose, and not expected to rise above a vegetative state, but things must be better elsewhere.

And he had to take the news to Zack and Liz Smith, the parents of Harker's autistic godson John. There should be laws against the sun being so bright on such a day, he thought. It wasn't right that the weather was so beautiful when the task was so grim.

He flicked through music channels, but nothing was stirring Frank, who sat, staring out the window at nothing. George could have ticked off the thoughts in his friend's mind: the time he and Harker had first met, their many barbecues, fishing trips, trying to fix Harker's reticulation, dinner and cards, watching Test matches at the WACA, sharing a quiet beer after work on a Friday afternoon. "It'll be OK," he murmured, as much reassurance to himself as to Frank.

Frank didn't move.

George didn't feel like talking, but Frank was likely to walk into the ocean if George didn't say something, so he pressed on. "Doctors are amazing these days. Got all sorts of nano-thingies to stick things back together. Couple of weeks—he'll be up and around."

"You know he won't." Frank's voice was as flat and dull as an industrial machine.

"He's got a lifetime ahead of him still! Thirty comet-free years at least! He's too strong to let it get the better of him." Though George wondered. Sixty-five, and the body was getting low on reserves. Maybe Harker was fitter than the average bloke. Maybe he had an extra couple of years on men his own age. George hoped so, though no amount of hoping would reverse the bleak sight of Harker in that hospital bed with tubes sticking into places any normal man would kick up a stink at.

"He's in a coma, George. You heard what the doctor said. He might not come out of it."

Unknown location

Harker Brown opened his eyes to darkness, aware of strangeness, like waking in a strange hotel room at 3AM and not remembering his name.

No. Not a hotel room. He couldn't remember checking in anywhere, and Ruth was…He blinked in the dark. Ruth was deep in memory, forever his wife, never anything but healthy. Grinning on a mountain somewhere, or asleep on a plane next to him with the light of thirty thousand feet on her face. So where was he? He moved his hand and felt a long handle, wrapped in a soft plastic substance—his cricket bat! The weight of his Father Nick's book in his pocket pressed against his leg. Memory washed over him:

his retirement party...George...walking home wondering how he was going to keep George from suicide...car lights approaching...the screech of brakes and tyres...car doors slamming...someone grabbing his arm...two men pinning his arms...a body on the ground...shoving him into a van...shouting...struggling...swinging the bat...

He clutched the bat, worried.

Kidnapped? Why would anyone want to kidnap a retired postie? He doubted he was worth much to anyone, with Ruth gone. Thoughts of his four-year-old autistic godson John snapped clear and painful in his mind. Now *he* was precious, well worth a ransom, although it was doubtful if he recognized anything outside the immoveable shutter of his dark brown eyes. But no-one would want a retired postman, widowed, lonely and alone. When he tried to sit up, something was holding him down, though he could feel no straps or braces around his limbs. He heard voices close by in careful but unintelligible speech, but they were out of sight. "Hey!" he shouted. His voice echoed around a small space. "Hey! Who are you?" Harker tried to free his elbows so he could tug at the restraints. "Hey, is anyone there?"

A voice chuckled, and said in faintly accented English, "We are here."

The familiarity of the voice shocked him. "You ... the caterers!"

"Indeed. I am Altan, and with me are Haru and Gumer."

Altan. Haru. Gumer. He couldn't place the first name, but the second one could have been Japanese, the third possibly Spanish or South American. But if they were a multinational kidnapping ring, why tell him their names? He could hear the faint humming of movement, so he was in a vehicle of some kind. It didn't sound like a train and it was too smooth for a small boat, so he was being taken somewhere on a plane or ship. And if he was being kidnapped, how would anyone raise the ransom money? Chook raffles? Sausage sizzles once a week on the footpath outside the post office? A bit of a whip-around of the postie union in the hope of solidarity for a kidnapped comrade? An appeal to the current affairs shows? He put the thought aside. It made no sense.

An elaborate send-off for his retirement? He grinned at the thought. The buggers. It would be just like his post office mates to arrange for some loonies to take him for a wild ride somewhere and scare the living daylights out of him. Probably payback for all the times he had missed their birthdays because he and Ruth had been gallivanting off somewhere. And the man who had chuckled—Altan—seemed friendly enough, unlike a kidnapper. "So," said Harker carefully. "George and Frank hired you? This is all a setup?"

A man came into view. He had oiled hair, dark brown eyes and a calm suntanned face. About mid-thirties, Harker thought. Fit. Strong. Plenty of time working outdoors. "Your friends?" the man said. "No."

Harker recognized the voice as Altan's. "Then what do you want with me?"

Altan's face remained calm and reasonable. "We have need of you, Harker Brown."

Harker tried calm reason as well, though his pulse was pounding. "Mate, no-one needs old posties. Especially when all his postie mates are out looking for him."

"Your friends? They believe you injured in a hit and run accident." The voice sounded calm, and Harker gripped his cricket bat with the great desire to lash out. "Even now, they most certainly know you are in hospital. One of our fellows has assumed your face and form and will appear to remain comatose for the time you serve with us. The illusion is complete, even to your doctors and their machines. Everyone will believe the man in the hospital bed is you."

"Serve? Who the blazes are you?"

"I am the one who asked you if you would, by your actions, end the hopelessness in the world so that people no longer took their own lives. And you were the one who agreed."

Harker remembered it all with swelling anger. "So you kidnapped me?" he shouted. "In this world, you ask people to do jobs, not flamin' kidnap them!"

"We are no longer in your world, Harker Brown," said Altan. "I am sorry for the deception, but there was no time for discussion. Do not fear; we will not harm you in any way, and when your task is done, you may choose to return to your home."

"Choose?" demanded Harker. "You're not giving me any choice!"

Altan leaned across, his smile diminishing into a sorry wistfulness, and touched Harker's forehead with a finger.

The gesture surprised Harker, even more so when he realized that his anger was receding, and a pleasant warmth settling in all the places of his body that had not been warm for a fair while. A single touch to the forehead? All Harker's boundaries kept shifting, and nothing he did or thought recalibrated things back to normal.

As the touchpoint of Altan's finger glowed warm on his forehead, Harker leaned back with suddenly heavy eyes, and sleep came wandering up like a lost child. He dreamed of primary school lunchtimes, hearing the sodden thump of the waterlogged footy being kicked around on the oval, and smelling wet woollen school jumpers and oiled timber floorboards and Vegemite sandwiches as the rain came down on the tin roof.

He woke after an undetermined time, disoriented. His eyes scratched when he opened them, remembering the time when he had seen Ruth's coffin slide along the cremation rails, and the meaningless sunlight watching over it. He knew with a sad heartslide that he was alone, that Ruth was aloft in a different reality perhaps, or just vanished from all existence altogether. The thought of her there on the verandah in her garden chair on that last morning together, her boots turning to silk, left him bereft.

He understood then, though he had known it since Ruth's death, why George couldn't see the point in things. There was such a granite futility to existence if separation and nothingness was the end of it. Why finish school if there were no exams? Why play out the football season if there was no grand final? Death was so impenetrable, so obscure, such a random punishment for life. On many occasions on watch around a desert campfire while his squad mates slept, Harker used to think he could have planned the whole life thing better.

Brotherhood command sled

Blackwell followed Ed up the steep ladder out of the hold and into an open area where passages led off fore and aft. "Why did I kill her?"

Motion-sensitive lights flicked on briefly as he followed Ed along a corridor towards a second steep ladder.

"The only man who knows is you. The report was suppressed. None of the Patrons will tell you."

Blackwell gritted his teeth. "Is that why I was moved to NASAD?"

Ed hesitated and Blackwell wondered why he wasn't sure about something so obvious. "Yes." Ed nodded up the ladder. "When we get to the bridge, keep silent!" he whispered, and started climbing.

Blackwell thought of Carl, and quickly saw the irony of the situation: his only two friends in life were in the habit of keeping him from death at the hands of others. With a sharp anger that surprised him, Blackwell wondered when he would be free enough to protect himself.

As he followed Ed up the ladder, a schematic of the sled's fire escape routes on the wall caught his attention. In the seconds while Ed keyed in an access code, he absorbed the information instantly: a sled was an aircraft of sorts, though one lacking any semblance of aerodynamic grace. The main fuselage extended fore and aft like a commercial airliner, but strange cylindrical pods clustered around the tail, and the cargo hold bulged out belowdecks like an afterthought. A conning tower midships made the sled look like a child's drawing of a submarine, and the bridge comprised the topmost of the sled's three levels, jutting out over the main hull like the bowsprit of an ancient windjammer.

"What's the emergency?"

Ed kept climbing. "Possible Cabal jumpship converging with us. We've got to jettison the hold to increase speed, and insert into Patara before he does."

"One of the Kavonatur sleds?"

"Possible, though it's not responding to our signals. Wrong ID as well. But good. You're thinking like you used to. Keep alert; you might see something we've missed." The hatch hissed open into a soft white haze. Ed climbed up but Blackwell waited, only his head and shoulders above the floor, his pulse triggering in readiness for battle and flight. With a careful breath, he looked around for the man who would kill him.

All he saw, though, as Ed disappeared around a bulkhead to his right, was a diminutive and slender woman in white shirt and brown trousers—Valentina, he realized—leaning over a raised circular platform in the center of the bridge. Her olive skin and nondescript wavy brown hair made her seem unimportant, mousy.

Voices to the right. Ed and another man. Book. Blackwell climbed up and stood, assessing distances and angles. The hatch retracted with a soft hiss near his feet. Valentina glanced at him but said nothing.

Forward of the platform was a command chair with a small screen attached to the right arm. A single clear vertical dome, the foremost structure on the sled, comprised the forward end of the bridge, and arcane symbols marked its circumference.

Ed and the second man appeared. Book. *So that's him,* Blackwell thought. The man whose daughter he had killed. Grief had done damage to Book's face, and he wore his age poorly. Blackwell thought he was about sixty. His hair was mostly gone, his eyes pouched and heavy, his forehead a war-zone. Even so, he had clearly kept the flab from his frame, his chin jutted defiantly, and command was compassed in the broad musculature of his chest.

Book looked over to Blackwell. "Stay silent," he growled softly. "Stay away from me. One word and I'll kill you."

He and Ed strode over to where Valentina was pointing at something near one edge of the platform, and Blackwell thought he saw an illuminated panel on the back of her hand. Her other hand, encased in a control mitt, described incomprehensible figures in the air. Book asked about reactor IDs and vector convergences, and Valentina read off data from what seemed to be a hidden screen on the platform.

She point to something on the illuminated platform surface. "We'll be visible! As soon as the hold detaches from our 'slip field, the unknown will have our bearing and speed, if it hasn't already!"

"If we don't," Book growled, "He'll get to Patara before us. If he's Cabal, and they've penetrated the timeslip—"

"That's not possible!"

"They destroyed Kavonatur, so anything's possible. Set the destruct timer on the hold for immediate detonation and detach now by my order."

Valentina reached down below the surface of the platform, and tugged at something unseen. Below Blackwell's feet, the sled shuddered for a moment, then accelerated.

"Speed increased by eleven percent," Valentina said in a flat voice. "Descending. Automatic pilot, sir?"

"Yes, but keep the mitt on and the override ready until we land. I'm taking Tower under the 'slip with me to the Door, but I want you and Ed to remain here to monitor things and extract us if we need it."

Valentina's voice only wavered a fraction. "Sir."

"Full preparation. Shunt into the Core. Link to the sled's defensives, comms, drives, life support and the reactor. Override all the automatics. Reactor at full power, ready for emergency extraction. Max the auxiliary drive, close off all outbound comms from the sled, set inbound ping receipts to silent, and initiate a closed comm circle between the three…four of us. Full encryption."

Valentina nodded. "Sir." From under the Chair, she took a cable from which black assemblies flared at both ends, and laid it on the Chair's arm. She keyed something on a datapad on the Chair's arm, and a small silvery panel near it slid back. Inside it was a shadowed socket. She inserted one end of the cable into the socket. Unseen motors hummed and clicked. Then, with one hand, she pushed up the hair at the back of her head. With the other, she clicked the second flared black fitting into a hidden port at the base of her skull. Blackwell winced as surfaces rotated, hummed and engaged in what he thought was a ghastly preparation for her own execution, though Valentina seemed unaffected. As her mitted hands described figures in the air, elegant and abrupt, slow and irregular, the vertical dome in front of her flashed with symbols, arcane data and graphics completely unreadable to Blackwell.

"Ed," said Book, "get Tower ready. Update his Scout, get him suited and briefed. If this rogue sled has penetrated the Patara 'slip, we won't have much time for him to make his vows."

Ed nodded, and gestured for Blackwell to join him at the platform.

Book strode over to where Blackwell waited near the hatch and held out a hand. "Not yet. A word with you first. Who are you?" his voice was harsh, like concrete crumbling. "Do you remember that?"

"A Poor Man now. Before that, Blackwell, at least when I was at NASAD."

"Before that?"

"I don't remember."

"You don't remember what happened a month ago?"

"No."

"Nothing else of that time?"

"Nothing but nine fragments of memory."

"That's all? Nothing else? No places, people, things?"

"Nothing but those fragments."

Book's stare was unblinking, unsmiling. "Follow orders. You'll hear me in full later."

"We have to get ready," said Ed. "Patara insertion in twenty-four minutes, and we have to be suited up and strapped in. It's going to be faster than normal, a little rushed, but we're ahead of the rogue and we want to stay that way." Blackwell looked up, but Book was gone. Ed pointed to a burgundy icon in the constant center of the display and just within a pulsing circle around a bright yellow triangle.

"That's us. We're at the outer limits of the Patara zone now." He indicated a silver icon to the south-east and outside the circle. "That's our unknown. We'll beat him into Patara, and see who he is then."

Blackwell nodded. The sled icon continued to move eastward."Give me your Scout. You're going to get the sled's non-command data in case you need it later. It'll take about five minutes to load, and probably the same time to memorise, with your memory as strong as it is. I'll brief you while it's loading."

Blackwell gave it to him, and Ed connected it to a port on the platform with a cable. "This will also recharge your Scout powercell and upgrade your system matrix."

Blackwell looked around. "What about yours? Where's your Scout?"

"We don't use Scouts anymore. We decided on physical incorporation about a year ago to make them more integral. The technology was there, so it seemed sensible." He touched finger and thumb together, and showed Blackwell the back of his hand.

"This is my Scout."

Blackwell wasn't watching his face, but he was sure Ed had half a smile at his astonishment. Blackwell couldn't help but blink, hoping stupidly that reality would kick in, that he wasn't really seeing something on the back of Ed's hand slide back and become a screen.

"You built your Scout into your hand? Is this some kind of joke?"

Ed rolled up his sleeve and touched his elbow. "The Scout starts here. My whole forearm is artificial, though the internal framework is pretty similiar to your bone structure. I have pretty much the same range of movement and muscular control as a flesh limb, and the nano-sensors take the place of nerves, though the wetware linkages are still under development."

Blackwell barely heard him. "They cut off your arm ? You lost it in a fight? Injury? Leprosy maybe?..." It annoyed him that Ed chuckled. "You agreed to it?"

"It's pretty impressive hardware." Ed touched something and the screen slid closed so neatly that the outline was invisible. "It has all the tools of your Scout, as well as a tightline data beam—it's tightlining the sled data across to Book and me as we speak—cortical link, parallel biocell drive, a defensive unit, medical diagnostics, satcom link to any timeslip reactor within a thousand meters, full Earth maps down to a one meter grid, all fully real-time, fully upgradable."

Blackwell flinched. "Tell me yours are the only ones."

Ed's smile irritated Blackwell. "Thousands of Poor Men have them. Ninety-nine percent, actually. We'll do your surgery after you take your vows. "

Blackwell leaned against the hold wall, terrible gravities weighing down his chest. "What is this?" he demanded, closing his eyes to control the swirl of new information, though it felt no better. Data were good, but not this data.

"This is staying ahead of the Cabal, Poor Man. This is protecting our heritage, strengthening our future."

Blackwell heard in the quietness of his voice the pressure of something relentless and unavoidable, like headlights approaching over a hill. "But…but…" Ed jabbed a finger at Blackwell's face, and pronounced each word separately. "This is. Not. Your. Choice. You take your vows, we give you a new forearm."

Blackwell leaned against the platform, all his senses and understanding unbalanced. At the thought of spinning saws slicing through his arm, a hollow wind gusted inside his skull. Closing his eyes against it made no difference, nor biting hard into the coppery blood of his tongue. A sharp blow to his stomach. He retched dry winded air, found himself on his knees. Ed was pulling him up. Stupid screaming colors eased. Sound returned. He gulped, locked his knees, clutched at the edge of the platform.

Ed held his shoulders until he could stand. "You go into physical shutdown when you panic? Let's hope your vows fix that."

But Blackwell was furious. "This is your Brotherhood?" he choked. "You cut off arms but give gifts in secret, your enemies want to kill you but you carry no weapons—who are you?"

"Who are *we*." Ed's expressionless face worried Blackwell. "You are one of us, whether you remember or not. Let me remind you, so that a blow to your flesh does not seem so troubling." He spoke slowly, and and Blackwell realized that Ed was teaching him, fathering him. "We've just lost our European distribution base. Since we are all that stands against the curse, there is one massive *must*." He narrowed his eyes. "Understand this well. We must finish all our deliveries before Father Nick's Day."

"How long have we got?"

"Twelve days. If we don't, the curse will prevail and millions will kill themselves. Society will basically shut down, and it will never recover. Ever. It's that simple. So is the hope of humanity worth the loss of your arm?" Though Ed was smiling, Blackwell knew it wasn't humour.

"The world will never recover?"

"Never." Ed smiled. "But we've had many crises over the years, and we've always recovered. Not a single Father Nick's Day has come that all gifts weren't delivered on time. Not one. So even with the Kavonatur disaster, we can still finish."

"But what would happen if the Cabal cracked through the timeslip?" Blackwell's arm still prickled with the ghastly promise of amputation.

Ed studied him closely. "Same answer. Mass suicides. The curse prevails."

A beeper pinged.

Blackwell looked over at the platform, but what he saw made him gasp for breath. In a dizzying shift, the grey faulty screen in the platform slid north, then vanished.

Blackwell stared. There was no bottom to the well. No screen, faulty or not. And below that, there was no hull, nothing apparently between him and Earth but air. A long, vertiginous plummet. He could see the Greek Islands, and a breeze circulating up from within the well ruffled his hair. "What?" he shouted. Vertigo flared wildly in him.

A hand grabbed him, righted him. "You're not going to fall," said Ed. "It was just cloud. We're clear of it now."

"No no!" He breathed a shaky breath. "Sorry. I thought there was no hull there."

"There's not," said Ed. "But the sled has a strong repulsor shield, so it'd just push you back up if you fell in. Don't worry, you're safe." Ed disconnected Blackwell's Scout. "Transfer's complete. Come on, let's go."

Still in stunned disbelief, Blackwell had one foot on the ladder when Valentina started screaming.

Ed brushed past Blackwell and stood by Valentina at the command chair.

"Report! Are we under attack?"

"Poor Man beacons!" she shouted, her head jerking from side to side. "Going out everywhere—started in Boston, then down the eastern seaboard, then..."

Attack? Blackwell imagined the sled exploding and going down. Ed, however, strode over to the dome screen. "Show the Net," he commanded.

Valentina pulled her mitted hand back and a world map appeared, marked with clusters of tiny blue lights around the main population centers. Along the North American eastern seaboard, from Boston down to Florida, lights were going out in a rapid topple, whole clusters dimming from a vibrant blue to a dull grey. As Blackwell watched in vacant horror, Chicago greyed, the Dakotas and Midwest, then New Mexico and Texas like a massive outbreak of plague.

"Refresh!" commanded Ed. The screen blanked and refreshed instantly, but the US mainland remained almost entirely grey, with only tiny individual lights showing in random regional centers, away from the main cities. "Hardware glitch?"

Valentina's voice was calmer, though still tight. "Maintenance ran a full ops cycle two days ago."

"Software? Dammit, Valentina, get the cause now! Run diags, check the feeds, interference from the rogue, anything!"

Val moved her mitted hand. "Sequencing now, sir."

Book entered behind them and strode over. "Command is mine," he said. "Set status to Extreme. Raise all Patrons on visual. Open the comms logs. Time to insertion?"

Quiet as Book's entrance had been, Valentina didn't flinch. She wrapped her mitted hand around an unseen VR control and twisted. "Eighteen minutes thirteen seconds. Status set." A red ring appeared around the circumference of the dome. "Patron beacons sent." Around the red ring, randomly spaced double circles appeared and began flashing, each marked with the name of the Patron and the city. Blackwell read them off: Hand, Sigil and Tree in Boston, Wing in San Francisco, Banner and Eagle in Cairo, and others in Paris, Munich and Bern, Singapore, Brasilia, Lagos, Petersburg.

"Comms log open." Valentina's even voice steadied Blackwell's wavering confidence a degree or two. On the lower left of the dome, a panel opened.

"Your time frame is two watches before the Kavonatur incident to now." Book's voice was low and firm. "Interrogate for emergency beacons, intruder pings, power spikes, infiltrators, anything non-standard."

The screen flashed. Valentina's fingers flicked the entries forward and back, then clicked a VR control. It only required two or three seconds for a blank node window to open. "Nothing, sir."

"Go back then." Book pointed at the screen. "Three watches, four if you have to!" He stared at the screen as Valentina set the markers and executed the interrogation, but even Blackwell could see the blank results screen and Book's expression of surprise. "We can't lose contact with the whole Brotherhood just like that. There's got to be a fault in the Net somewhere. Have you run diags on the sled receiver?"

"Twice, sir. Same results."

"Do it again! This can't be happening. How can a hundred thousand Scouts malfunction simultaneously worldwide?"

Ed was tapping on his own Scout-hand. "Ours haven't. Check yours, sir."

Book hesitated, considered Ed with a cocked head for a second, then tapped on the back of his hand. "Full function," he muttered after a moment. "Strange. Val?"

"The same, sir."

"No way this could be accidental hardware failure across the Net, so it must be something else… something common to all Scouts or…what could have caused this?"

"Net failure?" Ed muttered.

Book's hesitation was only slight, but Blackwell noticed it. "Ed, I want solutions, and quickly! Valentina, how long?"

"About seventeen thirty bef—"

Book jabbed a finger at Ed. "And you've written half the code for the Net and the Scouts, so you'll see any errors or faults. Shunt into the Core and get me answers. Leave the Chair for Valentina in case she needs to get in quickly. Use the main screen."

"Sir."

"Listen. I want this under control before we insert into Patara. That Cabal jumpship doesn't fill me with confidence. I want my own house in order before I deal with him. Work fast."

Valentina's hair was sweat-damp, her eyes dark and narrowed as she slipped out the cables and handed both to Ed, who nodded as he slotted them in and stood in front of the command table, facing the main screen. As he did, Blackwell tasted something like purple and spiky suspicion as he listened to the three of them, and he wondered where amongst the three of them the distrust lay.

Though the cables in Ed's skull disgusted him, Blackwell trusted him deeply. Already, Ed was describing intricate figures in the air with his control mitt, and a panel on the main screen showed his deft VR movements, probing into code sequences, analyzing command blocks, manipulating objects, tagging some, discarding many. If anyone could find reasons for the worldwide Scout failure, Blackwell thought,

Ed could. Ed the Plumber, equally skilled with pipes or arteries or code. Give him a roll of duct tape, a scalpel or a VR mitt and watch him fix blockages, haemorrhages or shutdowns. No mistrust there.

So perhaps it was Valentina's errors or incompetence that had caused the shutdown.

Or perhaps the deception and treachery lay with Book, the very same man who would kill him for a wrong word. Or perhaps the rot was in Blackwell himself, cancered deep into places visible to everyone but him.

You killed Book's daughter.

But as he listened, something about the Scout shutdown brought the taste of limes and the sound of gentle rain falling on trees in his head. He understood things, the sequencing in the attack, the patterns. He wanted to tell Book, but Valentina was speaking.

"Permission to offer an opinion?"

"Speak." Book glanced over at Ed's node window.

"Sir, this can't be coincidence, not after Kavonatur and the Cabal jumpship."

Ed slipped out the shunt cables from his skull and turned. "Nothing. I could do a full search, but it would take—"

Book raised his hand. "Leave it. This is no coincidence. We're under attack. Someone's betrayed us."

Valentina's eyes were wide. "Someone? Sir, this could only be someone who's got all the access codes, a...a...Patron." She shook her head with snapping motions. "That can't be possible—"

"But only the Patrons have got that kind of access," said Book, "and it's not me."

"No no, of course not. But sir, it doesn't make any sense—a Patron gone mad and betrayed us? Sold out to the Cabal?"

"How else?" Book bared his teeth as Blackwell tried to keep from looking. "This looks like massive sabotage—"

"A detonator command?" said Valentina. "To blow up every Poor Man? That's impossible! Someone would have had to plant individual bombs on a hundred thousand Poor Men worldwide!"

Blackwell opened his mouth. "No, it's an electronic bug," he said, "a neural virus." For a single silent moment, everyone just stared, and Blackwell could not read whether it was surprise or anger in their eyes. Was this the Tower he had been, who saw underlying patterns in events?

"Instant Scout shutdown," whispered Book with a nod that Blackwell chose to interpret as agreement or respect. "Everyone with the new Scouts will be out of communication, out of—"

"Instant *brain* shutdown," said Ed grimly. "They wouldn't be able to filter out the virus from other incoming signals—we hadn't perfected that mechanism. So this virus would have hit their brains within seconds...milliseconds." He knuckled his eyes, turned away. "They wouldn't have known what hit them," he whispered. "If they're not dead, they'll be brain-dead, comatose at best."

Valentina cried out. Her eyes widened, rimmed in white.

An insistent loud beeping sounded from the main screen. Valentina turned to it. Ed muttered a curse. Book clutched the Chair. On the screen, the node of Hand the Patron was blank.

"Refresh," Book choked, but the grey uniformity of the screen remained. "Get the others! Tree, Sigil, anyone!" But before Valentina could manipulate anything, every double-circled node began flashing, then went blank.

All across the world.

Blank. "The Patrons gone too?" Valentina cried. "Sir, the virus?"

Book strode forward and stood an arm's length from the main screen, his fists clenched like a sea captain watching a torpedo approach.

"Sir?"

Book didn't turn to Valentina, but stared at Ed instead, for much longer than Blackwell thought necessary. On the screen, the blankness remained.

"Sir?" repeated Valentina. "Awaiting your instructions."

After a long pause, Book turned to Ed. "Get Tower suited up and down to the Door to take his vows. Get headsets, activated and on. I want to hear everything that goes on down there."

Ed stiffened. "Sir? Only Patrons can administer the vows. With your permission, I will stay here while you take Tower to the Door."

Book smiled, which surprised Blackwell. "Things have changed, old friend. With all the Patrons gone, I am making you a Patron. Take Tower to the Door. Administer his vows and get back quickly. There have to be some Poor Men left. We'll have to be careful, but we'll find them, regroup and continue. This is not the end. Understood?"

Ed hesitated. "Yes, sir."

"Eight minutes till touchdown," said Book. "Get ready, Poor Men."

When Blackwell and Ed returned two minutes later, Blackwell felt strong. The black suit he had zipped on firmed up his courage, tightened his rigging like a galleon under full sail.

"Altitude?" said Book.

"Five thousand." Valentina's voice was calm.

"Cabal?"

"No closer."

The altimeter unwound, though Blackwell felt was not aware of any noticeable signs of descent, heard no fuselage windrush, felt no hydraulic movements of wings and wheels locking. "This doesn't feel like we're going down," he said.

"You won't feel anything at all," said Ed. "We're entering the Patara timeslip, biggest and strongest 'slip zone in the world, completely impenetrable to the Cabal, offscope to all detection instruments, locked out of the weather. Sailing on silk, the Poor Men call it. Most of the town is within it without realizing."

Blackwell grabbed his moment while he had the chance. "Town? Is there a freeway close by? A muddy river?"

It was disconcerting how all three answered at almost exactly the same time. "Why?"

Blackwell hesitated a moment, hopeful but cautious. "I have nine...planets—memories. Fragments from my life before my coma. I know eight of them, but all I know of the ninth one is that it tastes like a muddy river, a cobbled courtyard, a freeway and city, and an airstrip. Walton had none of these, so it must be somewhere else. Maybe here in Patara. Maybe somewhere else."

Only Book answered. "Who told you this?"

But Ed said, "Sounds like Boston. It's got all those...uhm, except the airstrip, unless he's remembering...wait. How do you know it's an airstrip? Can you see it?"

"No, it's more like tasting, hearing, smelling. It's difficult to explain."

"So you could be hearing the sounds of sleds taking off and landing?"

"I suppose so. They sound like engines—"

Ed nodded. "Boston. It must be."

"We have to get there immediately!" demanded Blackwell.

"Why?"

"Because that's where the secret is!"

"What secret?"

"My ninth planet—it's locked, armored. If the Cabal get it, they'll destroy all hope for humanity forever. But—"

"They've already done that," Ed snapped. "But how are they going to get a secret if it's locked? Do you know how to unlock it?"

"Unlocking the first eight will unlock the ninth. And if I can do that before the Cabal find me, we can break the curse forever."

And Book shook his head. "How? How is it possible that I lived at Boston House all my life—a Patron, no less!—and never found anything, never heard anything, never even the slightest hint of a secret. And nothing of this earth will stop the curse."

"But why then all these disasters?" Valentina's voice was tight, urgent. "Listen to me. Tell me if this makes sense. The comet is announced and Tower wakes up with a secret hidden in his memory. I can't see the link there, but there must be one. And what happens? The Second destroys Kavonatur and wipes out the Poor Men. Coincidence? No, Tower's right. Tower's got the Second scared. He knows that whatever is in Tower's head could wipe him out. Even with the comet and Poor Man massacre, he still wants that secret. So if we find it first, we've still got a chance."

"How?" Book scoffed. "How could he possibly know what's in a Poor Man's head, especially if Tower himself doesn't know? And how can anyone be scared of a secret if the comet might wipe out half the life on Earth? He won't need a curse if a natural disaster's going to do it for him!"

The altimeter pinged.

"One thousand," Valentina said. "The Second knows everything."

Book said, "Put us down one hundred meters from the Door, Valentina, no more."

"Confirmed."

"Time to landing?"

"One hundred seconds."

"But why wait until now? If the comet hits, nothing will matter."

"The Second does nothing without a reason," said Ed. "And look what happened at Moscow."

"Moscow?" said Blackwell, as the planet of that name pulsed with light. "What happened there?" But then the sled shuddered. Valentina cried out. Blackwell grabbed the edge of the Chair for support. Book stared at the screen. "What was that? Valentina?"

Valentina reached up with the mitt, grabbed invisible objects and manipulated them. "Undefined detection activity just outside the northern 'slip boundary. Someone is pulsing an aggressive search signal across a wide band...maybe the jumpship looking for us. I've heightened our dampening, locked us down from all inbound signalling."

"But the Cabal know we're here?"

Valentina hesitated. "It can't be, sir."

"But the Second knows everything," Ed said. "You said so."

Valentina paused. "Yes, he does," she said softly. "Yes, he does." Then her voice became flat. "Five hundred," she said. "Lock in, Poor Men."

Blackwell glanced up to where the altimeter was shedding height. "Moscow?" he demanded. "What happened in Moscow?"

"Later," said Book.

A hard object nudged Blackwell's thigh, and he turned to see a chair rising up from the floor. Ed was already in his, activating a PFZ over his shoulders and across his chest.

Valentina said, "Jumpship closing."

"How far?" Book asked.

"At its current speed, you'll have four minutes ten before he lands."

"Can you get us closer than one hundred meters?"

"Sir, the pulsing is strongest near the Door. If the jumpship has penetrated the 'slip, Ed and Tower will be entering a firezone...I can't be sure. I'll put down about two hundred away where the signal is weaker."

"Do it."

"Seventy seconds to landing."

Book turned to Blackwell. "Follow Ed. Do exactly as he says, no more, no less."

"Yes, sir," said Blackwell, a dark brown courage rich in his blood. He wanted not only to find the Boston secret, but to take up arms and wade into combat, fight off all-comers, rescue the Brotherhood.

"While we've got a moment, you need to know this. We'll be entering Father Nikolas' cottage soon where everything began. The part above ground is for tourists. We moved the Door underground into a chamber behind multiple secure gates. You'll be touching the very same Door that Nikolas touched seventeen hundred years ago on that first night. The beginning of the Brotherhood and modern history. And now it's your time. Swear the vows after me, lay your hand on the Door, receive the power to command the timeslip, and you'll become a Poor Man in full. I'll do your surgery later, we'll re-form, and fight off this evil. Got it?"

"I have." Something stabilised inside Blackwell. *Fight off this evil.*

A slight pressure on Blackwell's thighs marked the landing. Ed was already standing and clipping on an earpiece, though Blackwell was surprised to see him at the command platform, not sliding down the stairs towards what Blackwell thought would be the main hatch.

Valentina flicked a mitted finger. "Repulsor shield off." The luminous glow from the command platform dimmed. Ed climbed up on the edge.

"Get up here," he ordered. "It's a three meter drop, but faster than the main hatch. Hang from the edge, and roll on landing. Time, Valentina?"

"Three minutes fifty-six."

Blackwell's internal chronometer started as Ed dropped into a brief silence and a faint thump.

He unlocked his PFZ and followed before fear could catch up. *Three fifty-two,* he counted, as he hit the ground.

He swivelled around to see Ed standing behind him in a narrow and dark alley marked by silence and an unearthly luminescence. Wooden crates were stacked against walls, some opened and spilling undefined cargoes onto the ground. Under the timeslip, a dog was caught gracelessly cocking his leg against a wall, and its stream hung icelike under a moon that did not move.

"This way," said Ed and, as he turned, he knocked over a can on the ground with a loud clatter. "Don't worry. "No-one can hear a thing. We're in the 'slip—we've got ten thousand heartbeats to their one."

Ed led him past several apartment buildings, running strongly. Blackwell was surprised to find himself mapping out defense positions and weapon requirements.

Poor Men bear gifts, not weapons.

At the next corner, Ed stopped, his hand against his earpiece. His eyes widened, his mouth tight. "Already? Where? Confirm." He paused. "The jumpship's penetrated the 'slip," he whispered to Blackwell. "There was some sort of anomaly in Valentina's tracking—he vanished off the screens three minutes out of the Patara 'slip, and reappeared a second later within it. He's on the ground now, but Valentina can't locate him. So now they can hear us."

Panic gripped Blackwell's ankles. "Inside? You told me the Patara timeslip was impenetrable."

Ed thumbed a panel on his Scout. A red light glowed and faded. Something whirred and engaged. "Until thirty seconds ago, it was," he gritted. "Don't worry, we'll fight our way out if we need to."

Blackwell grabbed Ed's arm. "Fight? How? Your Scout's a gun?"

"Low calibre, defensive response only. The hand has a detachable explosive unit. Last resort only. Better handless than dead." He scanned the street ahead, his eyes narrowed. "Don't give out on me now, Tower. Fifty meters, just around that corner, across an open space. Inside the cottage, down the stairs, make your vows, then we're out of here."

Ed's warm skin pulsed strength into Blackwell's limbs. "What about the jumpship?"

Ed activated something on his Scout. "Just stay behind me. Come on."

Blackwell followed him into the street, assembling his courage as he did, shoving fear down into the back reaches of his belly, holding on to a single word. *Fight.* No more panic.

At the opening of the alley, Ed made the signal for Blackwell to get behind him. Ahead, across the street, people were captured mid-stride, their hearts beating with gelled blood and sluggish fluids, their coats flicking with movements they would never remember. Blackwell scanned each one, half expecting one of them to move, draw a weapon and fire.

"Come on," hissed Ed. "We're clear for the moment."

"Do they know we're coming?"

"Impossible to say. Valentina will signal us if she sees anything. From now on, whispers only." As Ed and Blackwell sprinted across the street, Blackwell wondered if the figures he passed would remember him as nothing more than a fleeting chill between heartbeats, a shiver across their shoulders.

The street was clear as they approached a low-roofed cottage whose bricks appeared held together by no more than ancient gravity. A signboard, paved path and roped off front yard marked it as a tourist attraction. Ed raced along the well-trodden path without apparent concern. The front door appeared newer than the rest of the building. Ed pushed at it, pulled Blackwell in and eased it closed behind him. They were in a moderately-sized room. Furniture was partitioned off from the central walkway with royal blue cord looped through gold stands. Signboards were labelled in several languages, and a dark blue carpet led through to a hallway.

Instead of the old timber and musty smells that Blackwell expected, the air quivered tight around his ears, crisp and anticipatory as an electric storm. Light was everywhere, luminous and deep as coin-glow.

Take my vows, fight this evil, find the Boston secret. "The unknowns are in here?" he whispered.

Ed thumbed his Scout, and the cover slid back. He consulted the screen, looked around, and looked back at the screen. "Odd," he said slowly. "They're a hundred meters from us, but Valentina can't get a bearing. It's not clear where they are. Stay behind me. I don't want you killed."

"What if you are?"

"Leave me and get back to the sled. Alert Book. You must take your vows, but you'll need Book to assist you. Clear?"

"Acknowledged." Battle was assembling in Blackwell's limbs, setting gunposts around him. *This is war,* he thought. *This is justice for the Poor Men killed. This is recompense for losing memory and life.* Blackwell trailed Ed across the room, moved aside a partition and stood before a blank wall. There, Ed uttered five clear words. Blackwell's heart tripped a little, but he was intent on the wall, where the outline of a door appeared and faded rapidly. A panel marked with unintelligible icons appeared about halfway up the door, all glowing a pale blue. Ed held his finger above the panel for a few seconds, looked around once, and looked at his Scout screen.

"Anything wrong?"

Ed said nothing. He touched an icon on the panel with a Scout-finger and held it there. Blackwell peered around his shoulder and saw the icon change to black. Ed pulled back quickly. "They're inside," he muttered.

"The unknowns?"

Ed hesitated, shook his head. "Can't be," he said softly. "How could anyone...?"

"They blew up Kavonatur and penetrated the timeslip," said Blackwell. "Nothing's safe now." But Ed was not moving. "Sir?"

"It shouldn't be possible," Ed whispered, and Blackwell knew enough to recognize the shock, the disbelief.

"Sir, the unknowns are—"

"Yes, yes!" Ed jabbed at an icon. The door swung open without noise. Ed scanned the room behind him, then slipped through, pointing his Scout as he did. They were in a low concrete corridor that sloped down to the right. The door closed without sound, the warm light behind them dimmed, and cool white striplights came on above them.

Blackwell thought he could smell books. "Are they getting closer?"

Ed glanced at his Scout. "Seventy meters. Still no bearing."

Two minutes and twenty-nine seconds, Blackwell thought, though the counter was meaningless now.

"Either they're closing in," Ed whispered, "or they've set an ambush and we're moving towards them. Stay behind." Ed led him down the corridor. Where it ended in a blank wall, Ed stepped up, placed his hand on it, and whispered something. The wall vanished. Ed glanced behind them, and Blackwell saw over his shoulder a wooden staircase that led down into the darkness, winding away through hewn walls.

Ed activated something on his Scout, and a tiny red panel on a knuckle glowed. He touched his earpiece. "Valentina," he whispered. "Weaponry is live. We're through the second barrier. Going down."

Blackwell heard the slight fizz in his earbuds, then her steady voice. "Take care, Poor Men."

They stepped across the threshold.

Something—the door?—hummed behind them, then silence. And utter blackness. The air became colder. Blackwell heard water dripping on lightless rock, but saw nothing. *Fight,* he told himself.

"Slide your feet, don't thump," whispered Ed. "Grab my shoulder. No speaking."

Blackwell concentrated on his feet as he followed Ed down the wooden staircase, down through darkness, his hand on Ed's shoulder. The physical touch from his hand on Ed's skin calmed him a little. He tightened his teeth, stared into the unknown.

Dim light appeared ahead of them as they descended, illuminating the right side of Ed's face. Blackwell thought he heard voices, though Ed showed no signs of either of noticing or stopping to check. He worried about it, and for the first time doubted Ed's ability.

The light opened out into a chamber, floored with concrete, walled with rock. A third door waited on the far side. Ed slowed, shook off Blackwell's hand, raised his Scout-hand. Blackwell halted. From the roof of the chamber, a dim lamp hung, shedding a wavering yellow light. Ed scanned the chamber carefully, beckoned Blackwell forward. At the door, he listened, checked his Scout, whispered something to Valentina. And as he stood there,

Blackwell heard it again, voices on the other side of the door. He couldn't make out any words, though the accents sounded foreign. Ed was listening intently. The red indicator on his Scout-knuckle glowed. Blackwell breathed in. Out. Bit hard on his tongue.

He was surprised a few moments later when the voices faded. Ed had not moved. Blackwell released his fists, eased his stance. Ed turned a little, raised a warning hand, then turned back to the door. He listened there for a moment, and when Blackwell had counted fifty two seconds of silence, Ed grabbed his arm. "Come on! Follow my instructions precisely. We won't get a second chance at this." He whispered something, eased open the door, and slipped inside.

Blackwell followed him as he stood against a wall, scanning the room inside. Within three seconds, he realized he had automatically calculated manpower, armament requirements and crossfire angles to lead an assault force against it.

Poor Men don't carry weapons. Did NASAD train me in that?

It was much larger than Blackwell had imagined, about fifty meters in diameter and illuminated by glowing strips around the walls. Several doors stood closed. Above their heads, a low ceiling domed up to where a lantern hung. A flame flickered there, but Blackwell thought it was decorative, as it cast little light. Under it, a wide circular platform stood at the center of the chamber, and on the platform was a door, supported by a simple metallic frame. Even from where he stood, Blackwell was surprised. The door seemed new, brown and grained.

His secret door? Blackwell leaned towards it, hopeful, expectant.

Ed tapped his shoulder. "We have to be quick. I don't know when the unknowns will be back, who they are, if they're armed, what they're doing here. They're forty meters away and stationary, so they've given us a few moments. It's all we'll need. If they get closer than twenty meters, we'll have to run, finished or not. If I'm killed or disabled before you take your vows, get back to the sled as quick as you can. Ready?"

Start work. Take your vows. Find the Poor Men. Fight off this evil. "Yes."

Ed gave him a faint smile. "Good. Let's go." He led Blackwell across the smooth floor and leapt up onto the platform. All the doors around the chamber, when Ed scanned around, remained closed. Ed checked his Scout. "Forty meters," he muttered. The silence was absolute. He took Blackwell's hand, laid it on the Door, and placed his own alongside it, one eye on his Scout. "Repeat these wor—"

he whispered, then choked a strangled cry. "They're coming!" he hissed. "Quick! Repeat after me."

The five words, when Blackwell spoke them, seemed insignificant.

Avein en deisum senkudis neim.

Although two of his planets winked out and substance massed in him, no power jolted through his arm, no ghostly brotherhood appeared in witness, time did not halt.

Instead, Ed gritted, "Twenty-five meters! Run!"

They ran. Behind Blackwell, as they neared the door, a door opened, and voices grew louder, shouted in shock. Blackwell staggered, then charged ahead. They drew closer to the door. Ed held his arm thrust forward to pull the door open. His Scout arm was raised; the knuckle glowed red. Blackwell expected a blast like the one in the forest near Walton, but there was no crackling laser fire in his shoulder, no sound of pursuing footsteps, no searing burst of laser impact. He knew he shouldn't, but he needed to scan the chamber, evaluate. The silence behind them in the chamber puzzled him. Against all common sense, he slowed. Ed pulled open the door and tugged at Blackwell's arm, but Blackwell shook it free and turned. At the center of the platform, at the place where he had just been standing, Blackwell saw something astonishing.

Two men had their hands on the Door, as though taking vows. Blackwell found himself scanning, analyzing, remembering. One was tall and dressed in check shirt and cords. Late fifties, Blackwell noted, fit and strong, about six two. The other: about five ten, early thirties, wearing a sand-cloured tunic, brown hair, olive complexion, powerful upper body, could run a hundred in eleven seconds if pushed. Two other men in sand-colored tunics stood nearby. All were staring wide-eyed at Ed and Blackwell, who only had a second to complete his analysis—as dangerous as goldfish, no visible weapons, out of knife throwing range, response time too slow for fighters—before Ed pulled him away. *It didn't make any sense!* He was expecting armed fighters.

As Ed and Blackwell raced up the stairs, Ed pressed his earpiece in and panted, "Vows complete. We're returning. Prepare for extraction."

And Blackwell, excited, pressed his own earbud. "Book! Valentina! There were Poor Men there, taking their vows!" Though the difference in their clothing styles puzzled him.

His earbud was silent. "Book!" he hissed. "Valentina!"

Ed held up a hand as he sprinted. "Audio's been penetrated," he gritted as they passed through the second door. "Quick!" They passed through the second and third doors, and Ed glanced back and grunted. "No pursuit. Good. A quick run now back to the sled." Out in the open air, Ed immediately sprinted off ahead of Blackwell, across the street and into the alley.

"Why so fast?" Blackwell panted to his back. "The intruders are..." He couldn't think of a word. "They're...harmless! They're not following, check your Scout!" But Ed checked nothing and did not slow. The dog was still mid-stream as they passed through the alley, the moon still mid-orbit. But as Blackwell passed a dark doorway, a strong hand clamped tight over his mouth and nose. Another pulled him back into a shadowed recess. He choked, twisted his head, struggled against the restraint, trying to breathe, but the hand gripped harder. Other hands were wrapped around his chest, pinning his arms. Ed's footsteps faded. Whatever air he had whooshed out. Yellow icy alarm flashed around his vision, confusing him. The grip around his chest tightened.

"Keep still!" a voice hissed.

Blackwell could not hear Ed's footsteps. Apart from the sound of someone wheezing close by as though winded, the silence was absolute."Nod to show you understand," the voice whispered, "and I'll let you breathe. Do anything stupid and you're dead."

Blackwell thought frantically. He had no weaponry, no skill in unarmed combat. And the Cabal wouldn't let him live, he was sure of that. They had destroyed Kavonatur, eliminated thousands of Poor Men and penetrated the timeslip, so one frantic Poor Man would not slow them down.

And he could not breathe.

He nodded.

The grip eased. Air rushed into his lungs. He coughed, choked, breathed again. The voice whispered, "Keep silent!" And the hands spun him around. Instead of the masked or hostile face he expected, he found himself staring into Valentina's grim eyes. Behind her, Book was checking something on his Scout. Blackwell gasped. "You!" he whispered before Valentina clamped a tight hand over his mouth. She smelled of plastics and circuitry and hard work. "What are you doing—?"

"Silent!" Her sleeves were rucked up around her elbows. Even in shadow, muscle corded her natural arm. The screen on her Scout arm glimmered faintly.

"Rogues haven't moved," said Book behind her.

"But Ed's gone ahead!" Blackwell whispered, realizing that something was wrong. Terribly wrong. Book and Valentina should be in the sled!

Valentina held up a hand. Her mouth was tight. "Have you taken your vows?"

"Yes, but—"

"There's not much time. Book will speak to you before we go."

"Good! We need to get to Boston immediately!"

Valentina shook her head. "Not Boston. You can't come where we're going. You don't want to. Now listen." She stepped aside.

Uncertain weights shifted in Blackwell's belly.

Book's face was haggard. "You're a Poor Man now. Listen. We're—Valentina and I—we're dead. The neural virus will strike soon. You have to go on alone."

It took a moment for the word to have any impact. Alone? Blackwell shook his head frantically, clamped down on his tongue. This couldn't be right! "What about Ed?"

"The Brotherhood is decimated. Father Nick's Day and our work of centuries is all but finished. There may be some Poor Men remaining, though I don't know where. Those without the new Scouts and any novices—they'll be protected from the neural virus—"

Blackwell waved his hands to keep back the onrushing insanity. "Wait wait! Ed's gone on just ahead. Why are you ignoring him?"

Book winced. "Ed the Plumber? Arteries, pipes, code?"

But Blackwell knew that something was missing, the mathematics were wrong. Ed was gone, they weren't speaking of him, and he didn't understand. He smelled the anger rising in his bones like rotting flesh, stronger than anything he had ever felt before. "He knows more than me, he can work out the neural virus and bring the Poor Men back, he can fix things!"

"He's the traitor!" Book snapped. "He set up Kavonatur and the neural virus, he killed thousands of Poor Men, he betrayed us! He now knows about your Boston secret, so he's gone on to meet up with his Cabal buddies, get armed and hostile, and then they'll hunt you down to get the secret out of you. You've got to get back to Boston House immediately and change the codes on the artificial timeslip there. That will lock out the Cabal and keep you safe until the survivors arrive. Then you must unlock this secret of yours—if it's real—and restore Father Nick's Day before—"

Mad incomprehension swirled around Blackwell. "Restore what? Before when?"

Valentina kept her gaze steady. "Father Nick's Day. In twelve days."

"Twelve?" demanded Blackwell, incredulous. "That's impossible! By myself? Are you kidding?"

He was amazed at how Valentina held his gaze without wavering. "No." She was shorter than him, but even in that moment, he felt the power shift. Any strength he had felt earlier vanished. "Acknowledge that you understand the command," said Valentina, squeezing his arm.

"I acknowledge it," he snapped, "but even if I find the Boston secret—"

Valentina struck his face with her open palm. "Acknowledge you will obey."

"Obey?" Blackwell's face stung. "Yes, but how do I restore seventeen centuries of tradition in twelve days with the Brotherhood wiped out?"

"If this secret of yours is genuine, you will know," said Book. "And if you don't, no-one else will." He checked his Scout and stepped out of the doorway. "We have to get you back to the sled before the virus hits. I know you can remember everything, so Val's going to tell you how to drive the sled, operate the Core, reset the Boston 'slip. You're all we have. Enough talk. Come. Listen."

And those words stirred something strange and foreign and sweet tasting in Blackwell. All we have. *Courage,* he thought. It smelled of rain approaching, of the promise of harvest, and he was vaguely surprised.

Book straightened. "Valentina," he said. "Lead. Tell him. We don't have much time." His irregular footsteps tracked behind her soft tread as he followed her along the alley.

Valentina described the sled's Core computer, the bridge controls, navigation, VR linkages, piloting, threat detection and evasion. Blackwell listened, remembering everything. Valentina was midway through Core access procotols when they turned a corner. She stopped dead. Book slammed into her, muttering, grabbing at air for balance, staggering until Blackwell caught him.

When Blackwell looked up, they were out of cover, standing in a wide street between low buildings.

But it was not the cars that had halted Valentina. Nothing moved. The comatose moon hung, drugged. A few cars and taxis comprised an oddly still late night traffic, their drivers ten thousand timeslip heartbeats behind Blackwell's. It was when Blackwell steadied Book, then looked up to see, that he heard Valentina mutter words he did not understand and saw her face turn the color of a weak fluorescent tube. Ahead of them were two figures, both battle-clad and helmeted, holding ferocious looking weaponry that Blackwell recognized as Cabal assault lasers, and around them stood four Cabal figures facing away, scanning.

On the ground in front of them lay a twisted figure with a dark red stain blossoming over his chest and his face blown away.

Valentina was already running, grabbing Book and screaming as Blackwell realized who it was.

Ed.

They sprinted for the corner, Blackwell a sure target for the same weapons that had killed Ed. Seventeen steps, he counted, his certain death scoped on every one. But when no bullets or lasers tore him apart, when the shock of Ed's lifeless body grimed his heart, a deep dread weighted him instead of relief.

"This way!" commanded Valentina as they reached the corner and ran past. "They're between us and the sled. We'll have to use back streets."

As they ran, Blackwell calculated fire angles and response times, expecting blasts to rip apart their hearts, but apart from their footsteps, there was only silence. No gunshots. No crackling air from hissing lasers. After fifty meters, with Valentina a few paces ahead, Book scanned the road around, checked his Scout, and pulled Blackwell and Valentina into an alley. A timeslipped drunk was slumped against a nearby wall, a bottle on the ground nearby.

Sweat flicked off Book's forehead. "They're not following, so they must have flanked us and gone ahead."

Blackwell almost hoped Ed would come jogging up grinning, muttering about failed batteries or signal strength. "He's not the traitor."

"Not if they killed him, but it hardly matters now."

The screen on Book's Scout flashed red. His Scout pinged. "Five hundred meters away!" he hissed. "Follow." And he led Blackwell and Valentina at a run down a side street, ducking through times-lipped cars and vagrants, scanning shadows and dark spaces for the assassins. "Now swear that you will do these things: get to Boston as soon as you can, warn the survivors there and get to safety—"

"Survivors?"

"Some haven't had the surgery for the new Scouts, so the virus won't affect them. Find them. They'll help you hunt for your secret. But stay alert! We've been betrayed, and the traitor is still out there, maybe in Boston. Whatever this secret is, if there is one at all, you have to find it before the traitor finds you. Remember, you were one of a kind, afraid of nothing, accepted every challenge, backed down from nothing. Single minded, a mean streak if challenged, highly intelligent. There's part of him still in you, but you just have to find it. You need to be that man again."

Fierce anger erupted in Blackwell. "I can't! My brain has been reconfigured. I'll never be him again!"

Book hit him, a sharp fist to the belly that found gaps through muscle into lungs. "You're alive!" he snapped as Blackwell recoiled, winded. "Soon they're going to find Valentina and me and we won't be. Now listen!"

"But we've been betrayed! The Cabal must know the five words now! Nothing's safe anymore!"

To his surprise, Book laughed. "As the old Tower would have said! But what are you worried about? The Cabal don't know you exist! You have an old Scout—you're not on the Brotherhood network—so the virus can't reach you."

"Four hundred meters," Valentina gritted.

"I can't coerce you," said Book, "but we're not going to die hopeless! I need your agreement!"

"But what about the four men at the Door as I was taking my vows? Can't they help?" The image of the strangers in the chamber of the Door reflected off everything Blackwell imagined. On Book's harsh creased countenance, out of shadows, Blackwell only saw the surprised face of the man in the check shirt. "One had his hand on the Door. I tried to tell you but the line was dead."

Book grabbed Blackwell's arm so suddenly that Blackwell thought he had been shot. "The unknowns!" He started running again. "How were they dressed?"

"One in casual clothes, three in sand-colored tunics."

"Not Poor Men, then. Not with those clothes. Sand-colored!"

Book was silent for a moment, then, "It was the Arcadans in there! Who else would know how to get to the Door?"

"You know them?"

"They're the Poor Men who prepare the gifts and deliver them to our bases, but their timeslip is different to ours. We've never seen them, we've had no contact with them for five hundred years, we don't know where they operate from. It was safer that way."

"Three hundred meters," said Valentina.

Blackwell said, "Maybe they found out what happened here and they're coming with thousands to help! We've got to get back there!"

But Book shook his head. "We're forbidden to contact each other, even if we knew how. If the Cabal penetrated us, they would penetrate the Arcadans as well, and that would be an end to everything. No. Coming to our aid would be a terrible risk. I don't know what they're doing, but it's not important now. Now I need your agreement!"

Blackwell's engine was firing on strange fuel, generating energy faster than he thought possible. He wanted to engage with the world, to fight. "You have it."

"Good." Book scanned for the sled. 'The sled is eighty-five meters along this street. We'll draw them off here while you run for it. I've locked down the sled, so you'll need to speak the five words at the secondary hatch to get in." But then his Scout pinged. "There's one thing you must know." His voice was steel hard. His jaw jutted. He grabbed Blackwell's shoulder in his great fist. "You don't deserve it, not after what you did, but before you lost your memory, you were one of the brightest Brotherhood novices we had seen for generations, for centuries." His Scout flashed yellow and emitted a whining sound. "But then you wrecked everything. You started this whole disaster, at—" His voice cracked, "at Moscow—"

Every one of Blackwell's alarms klaxoned wild, white and frantic. Moscow. "What? Where? Tell me!"

But both Book and Valentina collapsed in an awful limb-heavy thud. Skull and bones cracked as they hit the pavement, although, their brains shut down by the virus, they uttered no sound. Blackwell whirled, reached down to lift and drag them to safety, but approaching footsteps stopped him. Instantly, all thoughts of Moscow vanished. With a dispassioned precision, Blackwell turned away from them and scanned the street, measured distances, plotted his escape. He was unarmed and pursued. Eighty-five meters to safety.

Twelve seconds.

He reached the sled in eleven, the increments ticking off inside his head. Valentina had landed it at the front of a public carpark that Blackwell had not seen when they landed. A timeslipped businessman, his tie loosened, was standing next to his car, his car keys in one hand, his briefcase on the ground next to him.

Near the sled hatch, the signifier 'Book: E1. The Black Dash' brought a picture to mind: Ed, Book and Valentina sprinting across the cobbled yard to Book's flagship sled, then blasting upwards through the timeslip and westwards towards Walton. *The Black Dash of mercy*, he thought, still unable to imagine the world without them.

He spoke the five words, and the hatch slid open with a wash of light. Grateful for safety, with the strange tastes of alarm and relief on his tongue, he clambered up the ladder, and the entry sensors triggered the hatch closed. At the top, in the central gangway, he grabbed a handrail for support, realizing how crazy it was to consider such an ungainly, bulbous, unlovely vehicle as the sled as wonderful. But he was safe.

Listening for the sounds of attack, he climbed the forward ladder, and raced to the Chair. It only took seconds to sequence the engines from *Idle* to *Ascent*, listening to Valentina's instructions as they played inside his mind. On the main screen as he pushed the virtual throttle forward, the reactor icon swelled to capacity and the thruster icons on the screen pulsed rapidly. Patara sank below him as the sled rose to five thousand meters, then blasted westward to where a secret waited in Boston.

Five

Search

Father Nick's Day minus twelve days
Arcada

Harker woke to a change in sound and vibration. It took him a moment to realize he was in an aircraft his captors called a sled, after going underground somewhere in Turkey and speaking five peculiar words while watching two strange black-clad men charge out like Olympic sprinters. All of which while stuck in some Hollywood science fiction movie set where time appeared to have stopped. Pretty good with the special effects, these blokes. And now he was back on the same sled, heading for somewhere south, as far as had made out before he fell asleep. "Where are we?" he asked.

Haru pointed out the window. "Look."

Out of the porthole near Harker, images appeared of landscape, of low evening-shadowed hills, dry creekbeds, scrubby trees, the bleached white of salt lakes, now blood-pink in the late afternoon sun. Only one country in the world looked like that. The Australian outback.

And a pale white streak a couple of handspans above the horizon caught his attention: the Melcassar Comet blasting through space millions of kilometers away. And then his heart kicked like an infantryman on a tripwire, the way it had when they had touched down in Turkey.

"Landing," said Altan from the front of the cabin, and a slight pressure on Harker's thighs confirmed it. "Come, let me show you Arcada."

Night, and its geometrically pure moon, fell fully on Harker as Altan led him out of the sled and up to a slight sandy rise. Around them, the desert was big enough to be measured in lifetimes: mulga, saltbush and low scrub scattered over wide silent land that looked as though it would forget itself if the moon wasn't watching. It reminded him of army exercises out in the desert where the darkness was deep and pure enough to make you think, to draw thoughts out over days. *Good days,* he thought. Satisfying, challenging, rich with mateship. But what sort of challenge would this be? No weapons training with these blokes, he was sure of that, though he still had no idea what this hopelessness caper was that he had agreed to. He looked around for a base or building but, apart from a line of hills nearby, the desert was empty. Apart from a million million stars at all points across the heavens, so too, he realized, was the space in the sky where the comet should have been. He blinked, as if blinking would change reality, thinking stupidly that Altan and his boys had kidnapped the comet as well as him. How could a bloody comet disappear? It wasn't as if one of those TV illusionists was trying to pull a swifty on him. Or the moon or city lights were blocking its light. It had to be there somewhere.

"What the blazes is this?" he demanded, though he knew he was on a different page to the annoyingly pleasant Altan. "How can you hide a comet?"

"Did you see it as we flew south in the sled?"

Harker frowned. This was not making any sense. This was surreal, all the laws of flamin' everything twisted and bent out of shape. "Yes."

"But you cannot see it now."

"No." Maybe this bloke had a learning difficulty. "So. How. Did. You. Hide it?"

Altan laughed, a desert-filling sound. "What a feat that would be, to conceal a comet! I doubt even the gods could achieve such a thing! No, the comet will indeed approach. Your eyes are not deceivers." He gripped Harker's arm, and Harker felt his internal gears slip a little. The man worried him with his eyes as steady as a night watchman.

"Mate, you're making as much sense as George with a six pack inside him. Let's get this clear. We're in the Australian desert. The comet's out there, but it's slowed down somehow. How'm I going so far?"

Altan nodded. "Good. For now, though, know this. Arcada is safe from the comet now, and will be so for many years yet. For we are not in your time, Harker Brown. We—"

"Too right," snorted Harker. "I don't think you know where you are."

The way Altan chuckled softly worried Harker. It reminded him of getting in trouble when he smashed windows with a cricket ball as a boy. Sergeant major trouble. Comets falling out of the sky trouble. Soft voices were never good.

"I know where we are," said Altan. "But we have shifted ourselves sideways outside of space a little. There is a boundary around our city that shields us from both the world and from comets. It was not always so. When we first arrived, I fear the local tribesmen took fright at our pale skin and height." He smiled.

Harker realized with a shock of ghastly disbelief. "Those strange Aboriginal cave paintings of blokes with helmets and spaceships? That was you?" The rush of realisation was stronger in him than a tidal surge. "We always thought they were aliens! UFOs and all!"

Altan smiled. "Poor Men in their sleds must have appeared so." He gestured to a nearby hill. "Now come. You can sleep out here in the desert if you choose, but Arcada is much more comfortable. I spent a night out here once, but it is very cold."

Harker looked around, baffled. "Sorry mate, but I can't see any Arcada here."

"Neither will you. We have hidden much more than a mere comet, Harker Brown. There is an entire city beneath your feet that will never be found by your folk."

Harker dug at the sand with his toe. "Fair enough," he said carefully. "Under—bloody—ground. Makes sense. Now tell me this. I'm happy to help you blokes out with getting rid of world hopelessness, unless this is all a great joke at my expense, but I'd appreciate it if you could just fill me in a bit. What have you got in mind?"

"In your pocket is a book."

Harker kept his eyes level, though his pulse went suddenly seismic. *How did he know about the book?*

"You received it on the last Father Nick's Day."

It struck Harker as distinctly surreal to be standing in the Gibson Desert discussing presents with a kidnapper while an Earth-threatening comet had just…*vanished*. He laughed, glad to be able to release some of the tension. "Yeah mate, I got it. Don't know what it's for, though. Oddest Father Nick's Day prezzie I've ever received. I don't reckon those blokes did their jobs very well."

That chuckle again. Harker wished he would just not chuckle. It didn't help things one bit. "And you know the words on the first page very well."

Harker found it almost impossible to speak. "I've read them once or twice." The sweat on his forehead smelled like panic.

"Then come with me," said Altan, "and let me show you the mystery."

As Altan led Harker up to the top of the nearby sandy rise, light poured out of the ground, straight up, a twenty meter wide beam, like a shuttle taking off. Harker leaped backwards, but Altan only chuckled. "Come, he is waiting."

Harker didn't even want to ask who. He was still trying to work out how Altan knew about the book.

As Altan walked into the light, it dimmed down into a pearly glow that illuminated an empty circular basin reached by a wide flight of stone stairs. Harker followed cautiously, assessing his options, both troubled and intrigued. As Altan led him down, Harker wondered where the enormous lantern was that had powered the vertical beam of light. The walls seemed to be a honey-colored stone, and the floor either a well-packed pale sand or some kind of rough carpet. But apart from the man at its center, the basin was otherwise bare.

Harker stared at him, until he realized that the light was coming from the man, from his face, from his clothes. His own portable generator, thought Harker in a moment of the plain-headed practicality his army days had drilled into him. Useful on a dark night in the bush trying to fix the squad jeep with nothing but fading torchlight and wire. He didn't even want to think how a single bloke could generate that much light.

"Harker Brown," the man said.

"You're the boss around here?"

The man inclined his head. His eyes and Altan's had the same quiet steadiness. Harker could not imagine either of them getting angry. "My name is Jacob. You have questions."

Harker just peered at him. "Bloody right I do! Who are you people?"

"A suicide society devoid of hope? You once raged against such a thought. A guerrilla army plotting violent revolution? You most fervently hope not, though your training was once in war.

A polygamous cult? It is doubtful whether you have considered this, though it would be abhorrent for one so devoted in marriage as you once were."

Harker waited a moment. "Alright," he said slowly, establishing the ground carefully. "You've told me who you're not. Enough of riddles. Who are you people? What have I let myself in for?"

"How often, on Father Nick's Day, have you thanked the person who prepared the gifts you have received?"

Harker shook his head, bemused. "I don't know who was responsible, mate! Can't thank him if I've never met him."

"We did them, Harker Brown. Perhaps it was one of the thousands of Arcadans who are at work even now preparing gifts." He paused for a faint smile. "Perhaps even me."

Well, thought Harker, *that just takes the cake*. Without any idea what he should say or do to such an outlandish claim, he laughed. "Oh, that's great! I'm really glad you explained that—now it all makes sense! And I suppose you—"

"Only last year," said Jacob calmly, "we made walking boots for your wife that turned to silk that only you could see, that she wore when she died, sitting on the garden chair that she loved. In the year before that, in her last full year of life, we gave her the series of hand-drawn pictures, both of her mother that she adored as well as all her female ancestors back to the first of her family to arrive in Australia in 1797. On your thirty-fourth Father Nick's Day, deeply in debt with the repairs to your house that was uninsured when it burned, you woke on Father Nick's Day to find it had been repaired around you as you slept."

"Hang on hang on hangonhangonhangon! That was you? How—?"

"On your eighteenth, your Father Nick's Day box contained a map of York with the town hall circled, and you had the good sense to move there and find your beloved Ruth serving tea and biscuits at the local dance. She was wearing a yellow frock on that night, I am told." He paused. "Need I continue?"

Harker stared at him, angrier than he cared to admit. "And what about the last? What was in the box then? Was that you who made the mistake?" Although it just didn't bear thinking about how wrong he knew he was going to be.

"Yes," said Altan calmly. "But it was no mistake."

Chills took hold in the places of Harker's body where anesthetic would never reach. "Why was it empty then?" he demanded. "Was this some sort of message? Some kind of symbolic thing?"

Jacob nodded slightly. "Well done. Yes, symbolic. To represent all those who will wake on the next Father Nick's Day and find nothing, all those for whom hope will die."

Things started to make sense then for Harker Brown. "The Earlies, you mean?"

"Those who take their own lives before their natural time, yes. Humanity is under a curse of hopelessness, Harker Brown, and all that prevents them from sinking into a permanent suicidal darkness are the gifts that we prepare and our brothers deliver. For seventeen hundred years it has been so."

Harker snorted. "A curse? Not sure I'm following you, mate."

"Then would you say that suicide is a normal part of life?"

"It's been that way for as long as I can remember, mate. Seventeen hundred years, as you say. Mental illness, maybe, bad genes, toxins in the air, who knows?"

Harker hated it when Jacob smiled.

"And what would you do, my friend, if you could change that? If, by your actions, the curse of suicide would end, and people would live in hope and fulfilment until they died peacefully in their beds, having seen eighty or ninety or a hundred years?"

"That's what Altan asked when he kidnapped me. There's not much one bloke can do, though, mate."

Jacob smiled again. "Not one man, Harker Brown."

Not all the words in Harker's head put together had any chance of even getting close to expressing his bafflement. "Who then?" he croaked.

"The Brotherhood of Poor Men, who have for seventeen hundred years shielded humanity from the curse, is no more. Without them, on the next Father Nick's Day in twelve days, the world will descend into a permanent suicidal darkness from which it will never emerge. On this Father Nick's Day, we want that everyone will receive his due gift."

Harker struggled for both words and the breath to speak them. "And you…ah, and you need help in…ah…making these…box… ah, gifts?"

Jacob's smile had all his teeth lined up and glowing. His whole face had enough candlepower to bring a ship safely into port. And there Harker stood, dimfaced and bewildered as the light swirled around Jacob like a galaxy expanding, creating a well of radiance around Harker and beaming upwards towards the desert night so pure and strong that Harker thought for a moment mere bodyweight would not be enough to hold him down."No, Harker Brown," said Jacob, grinning. "We need a leader."

Harker nearly choked. "You...what? A leader? Mate, I think you've got the wrong bloke. I'm not a leader!"

"You're a Poor Man now."

Harker laughed a disbelieving snort. "Mate, I'm a postie! Posties have always been poor. Nothing new there. But I'm not your leader. Let me go, put an ad in the papers, I'm sure you'll get the man you need. You've got a big job ahead of you, by the sounds of it."

"An impossible job if you do not agree. Let me explain."

Harker folded his arms. "Hang on—didn't you say you've got a city here? With lots of people? Surely you've got someone who could help out. Some trainees, apprentices?"

"Not for this work. No Arcadan is suitable for what you will do. Neither would I permit it."

Harker frowned at that statement, but let it pass.

"And we know who you are. We of all people should, since we have known you for many years through the letters of hope we have written and the pictures we have drawn of your future. You are retired now, and after the sad death of your wife, little remains to you but a quiet descent to the grave, if you do not take your own life first."

"I'm no Early, mate!"

"The curse falls where it will."

This was getting surreal. "Mate, even so, you've got a crazy selection process if you ended up with a sixty-five year old retired postie. There's younger blokes and women around who'd do a good job. Much quicker too than these creaky old bones."

From out of the air, Jacob produced a slip of paper.

"Outback survival," he read, "from your army training, mechanical expertise, calmness in crisis, fluency in six languages, extensive travel experience, ability to improvise under pressure, courage under fire, gentleness, compassion, simple humanity." He looked up. "And skills in leadership." Jacob folded the paper and the air took it away.

"You've done your homework," he said quietly, "but the army days are long past. But what does this leader's job involve, though? And is it a...permanent position?"

Jacob smiled. "Consider your situation. We have neither threatened nor harmed you, bringing you to this place and time in the best way we knew how, and I apologise that we could not tell you before now but we thought this way was best. But tell me this. What do you hope for?"

Harker stared. "In general terms, you mean? Travel around a bit, do a bit of fishing off Rottnest, watch a Test match in the West Indies—always wanted to go to Trinidad and Tobago…"

"Yet these are all only for your benefit. What do you hope for in the greater scheme of things?"

"Like world peace and all that? Hadn't given it too much thought, to tell the truth. I'd hate for George—he's my best mate—to go Early, but there's not much I can do about that now."

Jacob smiled. "Then here is the grand adventure that combines both. We will train and equip you, and you can lead us in restoring…this Father Nick's Day around the world."

Harker caught the slight pause before the word. "Only this one?"

"Then you can reconsider."

"You still haven't told me what the job involves? You called me a leader, but it seems like you're doing the leadership thing pretty well already."

"Of Arcada, yes. But our adversary has wiped out our brothers who deliver the gifts we make. He believes his job done. So we will make him believe otherwise and take over the deliveries until Father Nick's Day. Your work comprises two tasks, the first much larger, the second smaller but vitally important. The first is this. After your training, you will lead a squad of Poor Men in delivering gifts."

"Sounds straightforward enough. What about the second?"

"I cannot tell you. Not yet."

Harker prickled, though it was clear Jacob had thought this through already. "Not very good staffing policy to keep the job description secret."

Jacob smiled. "I'm sorry, but you must wait. Now come. There is much to see."

Harker was greeted by name by everyone as Jacob took him through Arcada, passing through amazement to a kind of celebrity chuckling amusement and then to calm smiling steadiness, none of which, he thought, were really him. Harker the postie, the husband, the traveller, yes. But Harker the leader? Of a bunch of people who lived underground, and made presents? He could not help but wonder what Ruth would have thought of it all. *Come on, Harks,* she would have said. *It'll do you good. You'll turn into a grumpy old bugger otherwise.*

The refectory was unlike any army mess he had seen. Instead, people were gathered around open fires, cooking their own meals on skewers and spits and in pots. Bulbous brick ovens stood in places, vegetable gardens were scattered around, and pigs were scooting around underfoot. He couldn't see a ceiling, but there was light everywhere.

A young man smiled at him and and put a slice of some kind of bread in his hand.

"Thank you, Joe," said Jacob and Harker nodded at him. Harker tasted it...spicy. Pizza maybe? Though the base was different and Harker wolfed it down, realizing he hadn't eaten anything substantial for hours. Days? He thanked Joe, who smiled, inclined his head and waved to others. Within a minute, the wide wooden bowl that Joe had placed in Harker's hands was full of fruit, cheese, nuts, bread, something that looked like flaky feta, a sausage of some kind. He balanced it carefully and started with the cheese first but Jacob wouldn't let him stop.

One of the—apparently many—libraries was next, a vast humming chamber the size of the Melbourne Cricket Ground, with enough room for a hundred thousand fans watching the first ball of a Test match. But instead of cricket fans, it was filled with a fabulous steepled architecture of wooden platforms at different levels and linked with staircases and ladders. On each were tables and workbenches, shelves and cupboards, boxes and toolkits, and everything was strewn with fabrics and paper and brushes, nibs, paintpots, inkpots, pencils, palettes, bits of wood, saws, nails, hammers, frames. Everywhere, hundreds of people moved, talked, wrote, cut, assembled, painted, laughed, carried, stored and filled the chamber with the orderly voices of quiet steady production. Harker stood there in disbelief. Light everywhere, though Harker couldn't see any fluoros or giant spotlights or anything.

"You prepare all the gifts here? What do you...how?"

Jacob just smiled. "Most gifts are simple, as you know. We draw pictures or write letters of a person's future. Imagine seeing an image of your future where you are alive and happy, where you have not submitted to the curse. Would that not give hope?"

Harker had received many such letters and hand-drawn pictures. "It would."

"Some are different, but every person who receives them is unique, so every gift is also unique. Everyone deserves hope."

Harker followed in a daze as Jacob showed him one of the residential districts—"You need a public transport system," he muttered as he saw the wide underground avenues.

In the hangars, where rows upon rows upon rows of sleds stood, Harker leaned back at Jacob's gesture and saw the moon through vast raised doors. "I saw something like this on an aircraft carrier once," Harker said, barely able to recognize the sound of his own voice, "but even the US Navy hasn't got to this level, and they rule the waves, pretty much. You ever thought of taking over the world?"

"We'll leave that for someone else," said Jacob with a smile. "Come. One last place before your night is over. You meet your squad and start your training at first light."

Jacob's command chambers were surprisingly small. "Everyone has his task here, but only one person can keep the predators and searchers from finding us. So it is here that I guard Arcada."

The chamber was small and windowless, only about five meters square. In one corner was a small bed and low table, In another a simple desk and chair. A door on the further wall was closed. And in the middle was a raised structure that looked like a well. Harker was intrigued.

"The Sentry," said Jacob.

Harker peered in, not knowing what to expect. Jacob guarded Arcada with cool mossy walls and dark water at the bottom?

"Look closely," said Jacob, placing his hands on the rim and leaning slightly over. Harker did the same, and was surprised to see a globe inside the well, blue and green, rotating on an axis he could not see.

The planet Earth, revolving slowly, with the sun rising and moving around it, and clouds darkening its face, and the movements of cold fronts and storms clear and orderly. Earth, with the depths of its oceans darker, and white coasts like continental crowns, and mountains white, breathed over by close clouds.

Harker sucked in shocked air. "How did you do that?" he breathed. "Is it real?"

"Come, look." Jacob flicked his hand across the globe and started it spinning, then slowed and stopped it, then pushed down. The globe enlarged and then Australia swelled out, narrowing down down to the Western Australian desert.

Harker stared. "This is where we are now?"

"This is where we are." Jacob swung the globe around, rotating oceans fast enough for massive tidal waves, until it came to rest on the United Kingdom. The rank stink of industrial pollution rose up from the image in the well so powerfully that Harker stepped back, his hand over his nose, more than a little afraid.

"And this is where our adversary is."

"England?" said Harker. "That's a dead country—there's only iceheads and Earlies left!"

"And the adversary," said Jacob quietly. "He has been in London since the Kent Plagues. No, he caused the Kent Plagues so that his preparations would be unseen and unhindered. He has been searching for us for hundreds of years, and since the announcement of the comet, his gaze has been wide and powerful, unsleeping. He will not be denied for long now. He is building his strength, assembling his weaponry."

"What's holding him back?"

"I am."

Harker stared. "How?"

Jacob pulled his hand back. The gaseous stink vanished. "It works. We have kept secret for nearly seventeen hundred years with no more protection than sleepless vigilance and the timeslip." He must have seen Harker's baffled expression. "Have you heard of Hanging Rock, Harker Brown? Or Loch Ness? The Bermuda Triangle?"

"That's you?"

"No, just places where the timeslip is strong, where wanderers lose their way and fall into the cracks between time and place. Here in Arcada, the timeslip is very powerful, and requires little help from me to resist probes. Yet it is not all-powerful, and so I must remain watchful, especially with this unrelenting attention from London. You have seen what the other Arcadans do. This is my job." He smiled faintly, grim but calm. "Tomorrow you begin yours." He gestured to the door. "Your chambers are close by."

"Hang on a minute," said Harker. "I'm sure you've hired lots of great people committed to making this work for you, but I reckon some of them have got families to go back to. I'm wondering how many have signed on for the long term, and how you're going to keep replacing people year after year. It's just going to get impossible."

"Indeed. But what else but gifts will stop the curse, Harker Brown?"

What else indeed?

Harker woke in the night from strange, mad dreams. The bed was comfortable, the room plain and adequate, but he barely noticed. He got out of bed, still not used to the absence of Ruth, and walked around his room until he was certain he was not dreaming. Finally, certain he would not sleep, he got out of bed, dressed in the sand-colored tunic left by his bed and went to the surface.

There, huddled against the cold, he watched the desert light slip out of the ground like the Earth breathing, and thought how beautiful Ruth would have looked under that light. Even in her last years, she had still aroused him. Wrinkles didn't hide beauty; they *translated* it. The fall of her hair, the way she sang quietly to herself while ironing, the plant of her boots as she climbed mountain trails ahead of him…

Well. There had been a time for tears, and an abundance of them. But that time was not now. Whatever this Jacob had in mind, he would have to give it his full focus.

At breakfast, Joe brought Harker a plate of food he hardly noticed, and then led him through a cool and fresh vegetable garden where lettuce grew alongside strawberries and broccoli and a fine mist hung in the air. The sight of green produce in desert caves astonished him.

At the end of the tunnel, he heard low voices. They walked down a ramp and entered an enormous circular chamber just under the surface where a massive crowd of men and women in sand-colored clothing was standing around an Arcadan sled. On top of the sled, a tall lean man was watching them enter. The tall man nodded at Harker. "Welcome. We are about to begin."

Joe left, and Harker took his place with the others. A pale bearded man to his left whispered, "Ivan," and reached out a hand. "From Russia." Ivan had arms capable of uprooting forests.

"Harker. Australia." He looked up at Ivan's wide blue eyes. "Russia, eh? They've spread their net wide, then."

"Poor Men!" said the tall man, now next to the sled. "Your attention, please. My name is Beo. I will train you. The Poor Men worldwide have been wiped out, and our main European distribution base at Kavonatur has been destroyed. We have eleven days before Father Nick's Day to set things right. We know what the Poor Men have already delivered, so we will not waste our efforts, and our makers are working without halt to reproduce the gifts lost at Kavonatur. All our calculations show that we can complete the task if all Arcadans work together, though it will be extremely difficult. We cannot afford to waste a day."

He looked around. The chamber was silent. Ivan's bearded chin was raised, his Arctic Circle eyes cold and determined. *Ruth would have liked him,* Harker thought. She had always had a soft spot for tall men, the more bearlike the better.

"This is one of twenty such gatherings this morning." Beo paused. "Twenty thousand of you to replace the Poor Men. For your training, you will remain in hundreds, each one led by an experienced Arcadan and several assistants. Deliveries begin tomorrow, or earlier if your leader so deems. At that time, you will be divided into Delivery Groups of twenty each. Training begins now."

Within minutes, Harker found himself number fifty-three in a group of a hundred men and women, led by a young Arcadan woman named Maria. It was only when she turned to one side that Harker realized she was pregnant, and pretty well advanced, too. "Poor Men," she said. "Our training area is this room, Chamber Forty-seven, and you are Training Group Forty-seven." All Harker's team-mates were regarding Maria with serious attention. *Like being back in the army,* Harker thought wryly, though this was no weapons training for a war that might or might not happen. *Never mind that,* he thought. Stopping the curse of suicide forever thrilled him with a deep excitement in a way the army never had. He was fit, reasonably young, and intelligent. *Bring it on.*

Maria's voice never rose above a conversational level, even when she had to speak above others, but she was never drowned out. Her sand-colored tunic glowed faintly. "Poor Men," she said, "Let's begin."

When Maria announced lunch, Harker looked up, surprised, having barely noticed the passage of time. He ate with the team on the sandy chamber floor, discussing piloting and navigation, timeslip insertion and extraction, the intricacies of ground level flying. Ivan was in his team, as well as young Ryan from Cairns, Anna from Ballarat, the middle-aged bachelor brothers Martin and Graeme from Darwin, Frances from Albany, Jacqueline from Perth, Wayne from Sydney.

After lunch, when Ryan accidentally broke the sled hatch couplings, a young pale-faced girl appeared among Team Forty-Seven even before Ryan had time to apologise. Unlike the others, she was wearing a black tunic and a leather headset to which was attached a set of brass goggles and a succession of lenses like a watchmaker.

She couldn't have been older that fourteen.

Maria stood back, Harker thought in deference, and the girl took off her outer smock, revealing a toolbelt fixed around her waist, and a shirt comprising pockets loaded with strange brass and wooden tools. She flipped down several lenses, inspected the damage and set to work. Even with the full Team around her, she did not look up from her task, ask for help or even notice them. She brushed aside her black hair once, and the Team stood there like acolytes, even Maria. The hatch was fixed within minutes, and when the girl had left, Ryan examined it with a mix of awe and suspicion. "New bolts," he said, "new seals, new joins—hey, did she have a welder?"

Wayne looked baffled. "What did she have in that toolbelt?"

Maria said, in an awed tone, "The Spanner," and when asked for more details, would not answer.

They practised sled piloting, navigation, communications, weaponless defense, outback survival, Cabal methodology. Harker found timeslip insertion and extraction the most exciting, and wondered if he could patent it. It was fascinating to advance in time to the morning of Father Nick's Day and leave gifts there so that people would see gifts magically appearing when normal Earth time caught up. He wished Ruth could have been there to share it with him.

When three bells rang and Maria declared training over for the day, Harker and most of his teammates had flown a sled on a short training flight, entered a simulated timeslip, practised cruising one meter above ground level while a delivery crew of ten ran alongside, taking standard-sized boxes from the loadmaster and delivering them to doorpanel mockups. Sitting with his teammates on the desert under a violet twilight sky, he felt good. The training had absorbed him, and the only thing missing was Ruth. *How she would have loved this*, he thought—the adventure of it, a project that would occupy her fully. When the moon came up full and round and much larger than Harker thought it could possibly be, even out here in the clear air, they all lay on their backs on saltbush and warm red sand, feeling the desert wind kiss their faces.

"Gonna be cold tonight," said Martin.

"Won't even notice," said Graeme, and laughed. "This is harder than concreting. Never learned so much since high school."

"My oath. Keepin' that sled on the straight and narrow while you blokes were delivering—kept wondering when I was gunna prang it."

"Any of you blokes play cricket?" Harker said. Above him, a million million stars formed up into galactic divisions, the Southern Cross and all its allies.

"More a football man," said Bill.

"Rugby union," said Anna.

Wayne was just silent, and Ryan was asleep.

But Ivan said, "I play cricket."

"You? What do Russians know about cricket?"

"In Petersburg, we have ice cricket club."

"Cricket on *ice*? Sorry, but that must be very dangerous."

"Only losing is dangerous."

And Harker was so astonished he sat up, leaned on his hands, and looked across at Ivan's Arctic Circle eyes reflecting the Southern Cross. "Got a ball?"

Ivan rolled over, his pale face awash with moonlight. "Got bat?"

"You're on."

Harker slept very well that night.

Before sunrise, when they gathered in Chamber Forty-seven, Maria said, "You start deliveries today." Eighty of them, including Ryan, were taken off to join other Groups. The training sled appeared to have been painted black overnight. Joe, the young man Harker had met on his first day, appeared at the hatch with a weary look, a paint-spattered shirt and a beltful of tools. He kissed Maria lightly on her cheek and left.

"First child?" Harker asked.

Maria nodded.

"Delivery Group Forty-Seven," Anna said.

"Sounds boring," said Wayne. "Sounds like some concrete truck-drivers I know."

Graeme chuckled. "What d'ya suggest then?"

"Dunno. I never got married because I knew I couldn't think of any decent kids' names."

Graeme snorted. "You never got married because you're uglier than the north end of a dog going south."

Harker laughed. "I'm happy with the name they gave us."

"The Curse Breakers," said Ivan in a voice without the slightest trace of humour and a face like a stone.

Graeme said, "Breakers for short."

When Maria opened the hatch, the Spanner-fixed couplings moved as sweetly as oiled seals. The hold was now filled with colorfully wrapped boxes, and the loadmaster's table had been moved to make room for the strapped-in cargo, and the manifests in holders on the hold walls. "This is it?" whispered Frances. "We're really starting?"

"These are your tasks for today, though you each know every one and should be able to switch without difficulty. Wayne will be the loadmaster, Frances and Martin on piloting duties, Jacqui navigator, Graeme communications. Your zone is Queensland, and the run is a one day turnaround. Supplies have been loaded. Your sled knows the route, so the navigator's job should be little more than oversight. Questions?"

Martin was swinging the sled door open and closed. "Can we have the Spanner as well? For emergencies and repairs? She did a great job on this door."

Maria nodded. "She's on board already. The Spanner chooses her own team, and you must have impressed her."

"What about the leader?"

"Harker." Maria turned and smiled at him. "The postman comes out of retirement."

Harker wondered what Ruth would have thought. *Old bloke makes good*. Even so, he wondered when Jacob would reveal the second task.

Perth, Western Australia

The newsreader on George's car radio was speaking in an animated voice, the kind they reserved for Aussie Test cricket victories and lottery wins by ninety year old pensioners.

"...police are now reporting something that has them completely mystified—the unexplained appearance of thousands of unconscious men and women across America, many dressed in leather aprons. Local police stations have been flooded with calls from residents, who have reported finding these people on doorsteps, in streets and gardens and even in living rooms. Police have discounted initial speculation of organized crime, though they admit to being puzzled at the absence of any signs of forced entry..."

"Hey, Frank, have a listen to this!" It seemed better than comet news, none of which was new anyway.

"...dressed identically in white shirts, brown trousers and black leather aprons, none appears to be carrying any form of identification. Hospitals and ambulance services have been overloaded, though none of the John and Jane Does appear to be injured in any way and what's stranger, none appear to show any signs of regaining consciousness and explaining their mysterious circumstances. We're now crossing to Jeff Stanley in Columbia, South Carolina, who has further developments on the FBI involvement in the case."

George slapped the steering wheel in an attempt at lightening the mood, though Frank's face was so resolute and ugly it could have blasted concrete in half. "What do you think, mate, terrorists?"

"We're all doomed," said Frank.

Brotherhood command sled

Twenty minutes out of Boston, Blackwell checked the sled's threat screens, looking for the traitor's Cabal jumpship.

Most of the traffic was routine—shuttles, commercial airliners, cargo planes, military aircraft patrolling borders—but a single icon distracted him. The flight path of a green cube matched his exactly, although it trailed him by some distance. He stared at it for a few seconds with increasing suspicion—the Cabal jumpship, surely—marked it with a red circle as a possible threat, but withdrew his hand without revealing its ID. Breathing carefully, he walked around the platform, considered all the traffic from every angle.

It did no good; he only noticed the green cube. And how it eroded that small nugget of courage in his belly! He reached out his hand several times towards it. It would only take a second, he thought, to touch it and see it was nothing but an innocent plane.

Innocent indeed. He reached out his finger and touched the icon, and the data rose above it in clear shimmering letters.

Corporate jumpship. Registration: Metron Corp, Hamburg. Holiday charter.

Cabal? The jumpship ID passed all the deceptor checks down to about seven verification levels, though he still didn't trust it. He would watch it and see.

With a cautious relief, he did a thorough check of the screens as Valentina had instructed him, mildly surprised he was still alive, that the great stub-winged sled was aloft, held there in space by powers and principles too complex for him. All indicators were green. The Poor Man status screen showed Book and Valentina still alive, though Ed's icon had greyed. The sled hummed faintly.

Blackwell breathed out, aware for the first time of many things, even stronger than the deep memory of Moscow. His heart flexing, taking the load. His command of the situation. A clear purpose. The faint presence on the bridge of Book and Ed and Valentina, resonating softly off walls, continuing with him. The pulsing sense of obligation to make good their sacrifice.

And a secret hidden in Boston.

After a foodcell from the galley and a brief but satisfying wash and shave, he nudged the VR control into autopilot and set the sled on its final approach to the Brotherhood base in the Back Bay Fens.

The screens showed other aircraft—passenger liners, cargo planes, merchant and company jumpships—although their flight paths showed a slight change as they vectored in towards Logan International, and the jumpship followed him exactly.

So, he thought, not surprised.

Cabal. They're following me.

At a thousand meters, with the sled in vertical descent, he unbuckled himself from the chair and leaned over the edge of the command platform to watch the ground rise up to meet him. An eight-lane freeway lay to the north, its lights both red and white, rows of dark-roofed buildings like townhouses to the south-east, and the lights of a city's tall buildings to the east. He scanned the terrain like a minesweeper, trying to remember, though all he saw at the center of his field of vision was a dark pocket of marshy land through which a moonlit river bent like an arthritic snake.

The muddy river, freeway and city. His ninth planet pulsed faintly and, although he could not see the cobbled courtyard, and his was the only engine ascending or descending, he knew he would see everything as soon as he passed into the timeslip zone. He sat down and clicked into his PFZ, waiting for his heart to jolt.

The sled descended through five hundred meters without so much as a flutter, and he was starting to worry when, three hundred and ninety meters above the ground, his pulse jolted like a sparrow frightened.

The sled touched down with barely a shudder, its hydraulics settling. As the faint whine of the reactor slowed and deepened, he saw that the sled's safeties—reactor, shields, navigation—were green.

But now the red threat circle of the Cabal jumpship was flashing as it grew nearer to his stationary sled, the diminishing seconds ticking down inside his head.

At one hour fifty seven and eight seconds, he stepped out of the sled into the smell of cool marsh night.

On the timeslipped Patara street, Mantell and O'Roarke took their final orders from the mole.

We have begun the sequence of destruction, the mole said. *We have penetrated the timeslip, destroyed the Finnish distribution base, and now disabled almost all of the Poor Men. Now finish it all by finding and killing the target.*

How one solitary Poor Man, possibly the last, could present a threat to the Second was inconceivable to Mantell, but she had her orders. As she climbed the ladder into the jumpship, intent on her mission, she heard fragments of conversation.

Change in plans, the mole told O'Roarke. *Pursue and kill…target… before, but…is…no need to extract…*

Extract what? Mantell eased back to the hatch, eager to hear.

No need? The Second…approved this?

…wouldn't…telling you otherwise, sol… target is in the…sled. Just track…kill…have…ID. Kill all…

Mantell fronted him when he climbed up into the cockpit. "What was that about?"

"Restricted information, soldier," he snapped. "Get aloft. I'm keen for killin'."

Mantell strapped into the navigator's seat in the small Cabal jumpship and keyed the identifiers for the Brotherhood sled that the mole had given them.

O'Roarke was whistling an Irish jig. His broad stubby fingers were manipulating controls, preparing the jumpship for ascent. Mantell said nothing, focusing on her own tasks.

Kill missions were usually straightforward affairs: transit, set up, wait, kill, return. But this one had a strangely forthright Second, a secretive O'Roarke, changes in plans, and most peculiar of all, no apparent point.

Why send them out to kill this Poor Man when almost the entire Brotherhood was comatose, and the comet might just shroud half of humanity in apocalyptic darkness anyway?

The timing was so...peculiar. So *pointless*. Much as she pondered, she couldn't think of any reason for the mission, although the Second was nothing if not endlessly cunning, insanely malicious.

Still, she was an assassin, not an interrogator. Her weapons were disruptors and lasers, not questions, and the black thrill of murder was delicious on her tongue.

She had to complete her mission and when her laser blasted the last remaining Poor Man, the Brotherhood and their infuriating gifts—the only antidote to the Cabal curse—would be eliminated forever. Shocked when no gifts appeared on Father Nick's Day, people would buy anything, and the Cabal, immune to the curse, would rake in the unending profit. What matter that Western civilization would degenerate into a suicidal chaotic shambles?

Thoughts of glory prickled her with dark excitement: when she killed the target, she would earn great Cabal honor, recognition from the Second, and wealth forever.

But there was work to be done. She reset her focus.

Who is the target? She had his Scout ID from the mole, but she needed to see his face, so she flicked on her helmet cam. The image was fuzzy, but something about the image seemed oddly familiar.

"Going up," said O'Roarke, startling her. Her fingers stuttered across controls.

O'Roarke glanced across with lightless eyes like a shark's, opened his mouth but said nothing. Mantell concentrated on her tasks.

The jumpship burners lifted them a hundred meters before the thrusters ignited and pushed them back in their seats. The screens showed the lights of Patara fading rapidly behind them. Ten seconds later, Mantell's heart leaped as they passed through the timeslip zone. Time disconnected from her for a moment. She shook the strangeness out of her head and wondered how the Poor Men ever got used to it.

O'Roarke turned to her. "Deceptors?"

Mantell hesitated, unready. "Ah...we're—"

"Deceptors, soldier!" O'Roarke snapped.

"Private corporate jumpship, Metron Corp, German registry, holiday charter. These new deceptors have about ten levels of verification, so he won't ID us."

"Target bearing?"

"Westward. He's going to Boston."

"Locked on?"

"Affirmative."

"Any evasive measures?"

"None apparent."

O'Roarke chuckled, a grim sound like an iceberg ripping a hull. "Distance?"

"Three hundred kilometers. He's faster than we are, though."

He snickered. "But I've got a nasty surprise for him he won't be expecting." He turned to her, though she was careful not to meet the ugliness in his face. "Are you alert yet, soldier?"

She twitched a little at that. Her wrist laser was still charged and ready. She could so easily slit his throat with a hissing red line and watch the last light leak from his eyes. It would be so easy. "Affirmative."

He thumbed a control. "Autopilot on," he said slowly. "I'm going aft. You have the con."

"Before you go," she said, "I need the target's face. My cam didn't focus."

"Later," he grumbled and, as he passed through the narrow hatchway, he started whistling again, out of key with the faint whine of the jumpship engines. Mantell wished he would just stop. It was the most grotesque sound.

In the jumpship's tiny galley, made smaller by the long range fuel tanks, O'Roarke made muttering sounds of annoyance as he selected a foodcell, and Mantell smelled goulash. She hoped he would have a nap as well to give her time to think. When she heard the quiet effort of O'Roarke toeing off his boots and easing into the narrow bunk, she sat back and waited. A few minutes later, O'Roarke grunted and turned, snuffled and snorted. She waited for snoring, but was happy with the slow regular breathing that would have been hard to fake.

The jumpship engines hummed. Her comms screen flashed red with an incoming message.

'Further geological breakup makes the Melcassar Comet's trajectory uncertain. Details to follow.'

Well, she thought. That would make things more interesting, though she still didn't understand why there was any point in hunting and killing one of the last Poor Men when all his brethren were permanently comatose and the world was possibly heading for catastrophe anyway.

Still, whatever insanely twisted reason the Second had for this Poor Man's death would make little difference to her. She looked out to where a thousand stars glimmered, none with names she knew or cared about. Reality ended on the flat human dirt of the planet. There was nothing beyond what she could sense or kill. She was an assassin, after all, nothing more than a human gunsight, and when she had killed the target, a very wealthy gunsight.

Alone at ten thousand meters, she checked her screens, but the Poor Man's sled was still three hundred kilometers west, still tracking across the Mediterranean as oblivious as a kitten.

She smiled, a secret assassin's smile, then reached inside her body armor and removed the kill photos from her secure pouch. She laid the pictures out on a screen, carefully straightening those that were bent or ragged. Her precious images, so often gazed upon, particularly the close-ups of entry wounds, so good to prepare for a mission. This time was no different. Her mind and muscles focused. Her pulse slowed, her breathing calmed. And in a few minutes, she was battle-ready. For the Poor Man or anyone, it didn't matter. Her sniper's eye was still, blinking only when necessary. She had fastened her imaginary gunsights to the bony ridge between the Poor Man's eyes, whoever he was.

A laser, she decided. A blistering white hole through his brain, and then she would get the images for proof. Leave the corpses for the police, if they were discovered at all. Let them think they were some of the suicides they would bundle off to the morgue every day.

An hour later, in the rear compartment, O'Roarke snorted.

She jumped. Her pulse skipped an echo. She worked fast and checked her screens. The target indicator still showed the Poor Man's sled still three hundred kilometers ahead, though the new stealth device especially fitted to this jumpship alone would soon obliterate her from his screens. The status board showed all systems optimal. Good, then.

Fabric shifted in the aft cabin as O'Roarke stirred.

Come, provoke me, she thought darkly as he came through the hatchway stretching. *Name your armaments, for all mine are internal. If I am to be broken, I will slay many first.*

"Status?" he yawned. His breath stank.

"Cruising altitude ten thousand meters. Operational systems normal."

O'Roarke snapped out of his yawn, and Mantell hoped the crack of his jaw would be permanent. "That's all? Has he seen us?"

She paused to annoy him. "No," she said lightly.

O'Roarke glanced at her, though her sniper preparation kept her vision steady, unwavering. "Been a good navigator, have we, soldier?" he sneered.

"The cam vision," she said. "If you would."

"You don't need it," he snapped. "The ID's enough."

She glared at him for a moment then turned away, imagining a sweet clean hole between his eyes and the lovely scent of burned flesh.

Boston House

Uncertain about surveillance, or even the reception he would get from surviving Poor Men, Blackwell stood in the hatchway of the sled for a few careful minutes, scanning the nightbound landscape and checking his options. There was no-one moving around, and the ancient but huge red brick building about fifty yards away seemed abandoned. Two if its wide wooden doors stood open, though others were closed, and shadow prevented Blackwell from seeing inside. He scanned, measured, planned possible escape routes and places where he could find cover.

But something about the building was familiar, and it was all he could do to stop himself running across the yard and going in.

Something deeply familiar. His armored planet pulsed slightly, brightly. His chest loaded up with excited air; this was home, he realized, more home than his sterile NASAD apartment. This was where he would find the Boston secret, he was sure of that, although he had to ensure his safety first. *The traitor's still out there.*

He took a step out of the sled, half expecting gunfire, though it was only the wind and the smells of rivermud and marshy pools that brushed his cheeks as he ran across the cobbled yard. Flanking the yard was a line of red maples and elms, and beyond it, the river, the muddy river!

But that could wait. He had first to reset the House timeslip reactor, find and warn any survivors of the Cabal jumpship only two hours away, avoid the probes of the Cabal and traitor searching for him, and all the while search for the meanings of his planets.

He hoped he could achieve everything within two hours, but he knew it would take longer. Much longer.

On the far side of the sled, he saw a second building, obscured to him when he landed. It was smaller than the hangar but taller and more imposing, a building of substance that seemed to declare: *the people and activities of this place are important*. He found it difficult to determine how many levels it had: no straight rows of windows for this building. Instead, leaded dormer windows poked like inquisitive birds from the steep shingle roof, and brick spired towers and chimneys reached heavenwards from various points in the roof line. Blackwell thought the Poor Men must have added to the building several times—much of the wall was brick, but other sections were a black timber.

In the middle of the House, under a roofed and gabled porch, stood a wide wooden door, closed, ancient and red.

Boston House, he thought with grinning delight, running towards it, memories tightening, both giddy and dark. Laughter, noise, hundreds of Poor Men passing through the doorway at all hours. Crossing over a rainy courtyard, as a downpour drummed across the cobbles, misting the trees and darkening the river. Or waiting for the jasmine woman. Or another, more disturbing memory that he couldn't quite name. Arriving here on the doorstep from…*somewhere*. He tried to remember, but the thought eluded him.

It didn't matter. If that was his door, then this was home. Where the secrets to his nine planets lay. Surely the surviving Poor Men had seen his sled descend through the 'slip shield and would be waiting for him inside.

The door didn't creak as he swung it open slowly. He wanted to run in, his internal clock unwinding the minutes of his two hours, but the cascade of lamplit memory from the smells of polish and the ancient timber of the floor and furniture halted him. The enormous Turkish carpet spread out over the floor—the gift from the Emin Pasha after the Antivari Crisis, he remembered.

The far wall bore the number '12' in glowing blue letters. Twelve days before Father Nick's Day. Before it stood a small desk, and he remembered the times he had been assigned the cherished front desk duty, where he witnessed much of daily Brotherhood life, often with sleep racking up its debt behind his eyes: Poor Men standing in the sunlight of the front door that was never closed in the warmer months, bursts of greetings and jests, the sound of sleds lifting off and landing in the courtyard outside, transits of Patrons marked by sudden hushes and cautious resumptions, and overall the steady hum of purpose. No-one complained, no-one asked for praise or encouragement though much was given, everyone worked, and as every year folded in its petals down to the winter blossoms of Father Nick's Day, life was strong with purpose and meaning.

But somewhere, deeper than sight, darker than taste, Blackwell smelled shadows, a quiet wrongness.

Behind the desk, through a doorway, a wide hall stretched away into the shadowed distance, far further than the House appeared on the outside, and a grand staircase rose up towards a shadowed gallery. He knew what was up those stairs—the Patrons' rooms.

Book's rooms.

The two thoughts connected with a strong warm taste. Book. The jasmine woman. His daughter. Not the one Blackwell had killed, but his other daughter.

Excited, he strode across the room, through the doorway and down the hall towards the staircase.

Behind him, the floor creaked.

He turned, but just as quickly remembered. The much-trodden floorboards always creaked.

At the foot of the stairs, he paused. That was Patron territory up there. Ordinary Poor Men never ventured up the stairs except by invitation. He had only been once to be interviewed by Hand in an upstairs room, with its arrays of unusual Father Nick's Day gifts on shelves and tables, and views of the Muddy River outside the mullioned window.

The creak sounded again, closer this time, though he could not place it.

It jolted him out of his dreamings though. He had to reset the House timeslip reactor, find the survivors and start the search for his secret. This was no time for delays.

But as he set off along the hall, with his internal clock at one hour, fifty-two minutes and fifty-seven seconds until the Cabal arrived, he saw sudden movement in the corner of his vision, and a sharp blow to the back of his head brought spinning darkness.

Father Nick's Day minus eleven days
Boston House

The smell of soup and a hard surface beneath him woke Blackwell, though the blazing ache in the back of his head kept his eyes closed in caution as he tried to calculate how long he had been unconscious. Oddly, the smell of soup reminded him of Carl's garlic arias in the deeps of Watch Four nights. But this was not that.

He frowned as his memory skipped across tracks: Ed, Book, the Cabal neural virus—the man in the chamber of the Door had been so strange!—the Boston secret—the sled—the rogue—landing in Boston with two hours before the Cabal arrived.

The unknown traitor, he thought. *Careful.*

He was on a timber floor in a bare room, unbound, he realized as he moved his wrists and ankles slightly. A single lamp in a corner flickered orange. Standing in front of him were three men, clean-shaven, strong as weightlifters and unsmiling, all wearing plain brown trousers, white buttoned shirts and leather boots. Two were wearing black aprons. Their hair was either cut short or oiled. It didn't matter, though. He recognized the traditional Poor Men working clothes from Book's description. He moved slightly.

"He stirs," said one of the men.

"He does," said another, this one behind him, *an older voice,* Blackwell thought. *Perhaps their leader.*

Blackwell sucked in breath and determination. "I do." He made to sit up, but a strong hand on the back of his neck pushed him back down. The ache in his head blazed like an argument turned feral. "Why are you welcoming a Poor Man with violence?"

The voice behind him spoke again in a deep growl. "When they are strangers, it's always violence."

Blackwell turned, counting, evaluating. His head thumped. There were ten men, not three. One was shorter and stooped and goblin-like, though no less muscular. None appeared to be armed, though they were all strong enough to do him serious injury. The door was closed, and Blackwell had no doubt there were others waiting outside. The room was windowless, unfurnished. Not even a chair, and from the dust in the corners of the room, not often used. A lever on a wall told him everything. He knew which room he was in.

The interrogation room, and under him was the trapdoor that opened into one of the soundproof steel chambers into which Cabal spies were dumped to live out their lives in silence and darkness. The Pits.

His internal clock startled him. "Let me go! We have"—he calculated times furiously—"forty-seven minutes to reset the House timeslip reactor before a Cabal jumpship arrives!"

The man sneered. "You seem very precise about that time, stranger. As though you planned it. We were in some doubt about your identity, but now you have kindly removed that doubt. So you will enter the Pit shortly unless you can convince us otherwise."

"Convince you?" demanded Blackwell. "Why should I need to? We've been betrayed and there's a Cabal jumpship closing in! We have to reset the timeslip reactor before they reach us!"

"Or you are the traitor, sent here to turn it off and let in the entire Cabal with the Second at their head. Oh yes, a fine ploy, stranger."

"Then what will convince you? The five words?"

The man paused. "There have been Cabal spies in the past who have learned the five words and tried to infiltrate us, but have failed other tests." He nodded at the floor under Blackwell. "If you know the five words, speak them."

"Avein en deisum senkudis neim."

The old man's mouth tightened. "Poor Men have Patrons, though. Who is yours?" he said softly, and Blackwell recognized the same quiet menace that Wenders had once used.

"Book. Have you no Patron here?"

"None. All perished."

None. So the traitor is not among them. "You're wasting time! You have to reset the access codes on the 'slip reactor immediately!"

Murmurs around the room, though the old man's face was unchanged. "If you are a Poor Man, tell me this. How do we deal with spies and…traitors?"

The challenge caught Blackwell. But something else surprised him even more. He realized with considerable surprise that there were colors in his mind, colors that sounded like soft rain falling on trees and tasted of limes. *Truth,* he thought, tasting it. He could not read faces, but the touch of the man's hand on the back of his neck tasted of order and truth. Blackwell almost chuckled. Skin contact as his own private code-breaker.

"Silence is no reply," the man growled. "Answer me."

Blackwell found words in his mouth he had not placed there, and as he blurted them, he realized they were old memories, tightening like hawsers below his skin and muscling upwards. "Sealed in steel chambers deep below the House." He saw in enormous relief that the man was nodding. "Without light or sound, alone until death." He breathed hard as the man stared at him.

"If you know that," the man whispered, "you would also know the interrogation questions."

"I was a novice then," Blackwell said quickly. "I was not permitted to interrogate." Though he had seen white-faced Cabal spies taken down into the interrogation rooms, never to emerge, and had heard the stories.

"All Poor Men know these things," the man snapped, "whether they interrogated spies or not! Answer this. How many doors must you open to reach the Chamber of the Door?"

"Four." He did know. Though the man who opened them, he thought with bitter loss, is brain-dead.

The old man's upper lip curled, and he gestured to someone behind Blackwell, though Blackwell didn't dare turn. Four men surrounded him. They smelled of leather and sweat. "You defeat yourself at the first turn," the man sneered. "There are only three."

Blackwell kept his gaze forward as a hollow wind gusted through his consciousness. The men were silent. They breathed slow. "The door into Nikolas' cottage, the blank door on the back wall of the cottage, the door at the end of the short sloping corridor with the strip-lights on the ceiling above, and the door into the chamber itself."

The man paused for a few seconds then laughed suddenly, startling Blackwell. "What does it matter? You are a Poor Man certainly, you have taken your vows, lived among us, walked alongside us, eaten with us—but you have betrayed us! Let me imagine the process of your betrayal aloud: you had doubts about your vows, doubted the Brotherhood could continue their work. You spoke of it to no-one, sought no guidance for your disbelief, but decided to—" He waved his hands. "No, none of it matters a whit! You went across to the Cabal, accepted blood money and handed across the five words and all our secrets to them! They destroyed Kavonatur, massacred the Poor Men and sent you here to slaughter the last of us."

Blackwell scrambled to his feet, but the four men stepped forward and grabbed his arms. In their skin, despite his panic, he tasted their individual characters: one was porridgy hard work, another sly acidic humour, the third sour disappointment and the last a soft salty gentleness, though none of that mattered now.

The floor below him sounded hollow.

He was on the rope bridge across the chasm, and his friends at both ends were pulling at the ropes, swaying it from side to side. Like a child locked in a nightmare, he was clutching at the ropes, screaming for them to stop, though they only rocked the bridge further and further, laughing, and the chasm opened its maw and bared its teeth, ready for his plunge. "No no no! I'm no spy!" He struggled without effect. "I came back to reset the access codes, find the survivors and—"

"So you say. But it does not counterbalance the evidence against you. Shall I list them?" He lifted his fingers one by one. "You are not dressed as a Poor Man. You made no contact on your approach, as standard practice requires. Neither does your face appear anywhere on any of the record screens. Is that enough?"

"Release me and I will explain every one."

The old man snorted. "Release you and you will kill us all." He gestured to a man. "The trapdoor lever, if you please, Nicholas."

Blackwell wondered if his four captors realized that he didn't want them to release him. The strength he was drawing from their skin amazed him, made him think he could fight them off and escape. "I would not have come in so openly if I were a spy!" he shouted. "And I would have been carrying weapons. Did you find any when you searched me?"

"Cabal assassins need no weapons," the old man said, though in a lower voice. "You would have needed none when you killed Book and any who were with him."

"I didn't kill anyone! The Cabal assassins killed Ed and Book."

Someone behind him cried out. The old man raised a silencing finger. "Grieve later. For now, sojourner, you claim to be a Poor Man, but why can we not find your face in records? Who are you?"

Blackwell knew enough from his voice to guess the old man was wavering. "I don't know," Blackwell said. "I lost my memory a few weeks ago. I remembered some things when I returned here—standing guard in the hangar, the Turkish rug, the day counter—but a lot is still missing."

The old man's eyes narrowed. "How much? The things of which you speak would be clear to anyone. But do you recall important Brotherhood matters, things that only Poor Men would know? Let me ask you. The events of three years ago when fifty sleds broke down twenty days prior to Father Nick's Day? Do you remember how the Patrons solved that problem?"

"I'm sorry, I don't—"

"Or the monstrous Cabal threat in the twenty-third year of Bridge the Second? How far did we pursue the Cabal agent and where did we trap her?"

"No, I don't, but—"

"Nicholas." The man gestured to the trapdoor release, then jabbed a finger at Blackwell. "Something more recent then. The latest Brotherhood base in China. When was it opened?"

Blackwell just shook his head.

"No? Very well. The first lesson of all Brotherhood children. How did the Poor Men come to America? Surely you know that. You will certainly plummet if you do not."

Blackwell closed his eyes. He didn't know any of this. All his courage and hope shuddered down into a glutinous mess. This was the end. All that remained was a sudden drop, then silence and darkness until he died. Not even the growing strength in his arms would be enough to shake off his four captors. He opened his eyes to see Nicholas' hand on the release. The old man chuckled. "And you claim to be one of Book's Poor Men?"

Blackwell looked up, furious that the jasmine woman would return and find him dead. "He called me Tower before he died!" he shouted.

The old man's eyes ceilinged fast, the whites like vast vaults of astonishment. His fellows around the room murmured, though the four men holding him did not loosen their grips. "Tower?" the old man whispered. "How do you know that name?"

One of his captors, blond in hair and beard, said softly, "The rumors."

Almost instantly, Blackwell isolated which man it was, and remembered the taste of soft salty gentleness. "Book said it was my name," he said cautiously.

"Be careful, stranger," said the old man. "The ice is very thin under that name."

"Thin?" He recalled Ed telling him in the sled long ago.

"Where have you been since you left?" the old man asked.

"At…at NASAD, monitoring live satellite feeds on the Scandinavian Desk."

The old man raised an eyebrow. "Who placed you there?"

"Ed."

The blond said, "The stories were true then."

"What stories?"

"There was talk a month or so ago of a Boston novice vanishing under strange circumstances," the old man said softly, "and no-one would explain it. Ed had spirited him away from Book's wrath, so the rumors went. He became rather a legend across America. It was whispered that he had been chosen for a vital covert operation only a few of the Patrons knew about." He nodded at the four men, who released Blackwell and stepped back. "We thought it exceeding strange when we searched you that you were carrying a Patron Scout forbidden to novices."

"How did you know I was a novice?"

"Your ankle tattoo. Poor Men have a second tattoo above the first. Patrons have three. But strangest of all is that Tower is a Patron's name. None have ever been assigned this name. There have been many Books, Hands, Banners, but you are the first Tower. Book must have thought highly of you to accord you such an honor." He held out a hand. "I am Paul. Three of us are from Albuquerque House: Timothy, Benedict and me. Philip, Antonius, Frederick, and the brothers William, Henry and Calvin are from New York, Nathanael, Thomas and his son Arthur are from Michigan."

"None of you are Patrons? You are all that's left?"

"We are."

No traitor here then. "We have to reset the access codes. The Cabal jumpship is"—he consulted his internal clock—"less than thirty-six minutes away."

"What good will it do?" demanded the old man. "The Cabal has all but destroyed us."

To which Blackwell grinned. "But not completely. I have a weapon, and both sides of it are very sharp. Now take me to the reactor immediately."

The four men looked at the old man, who nodded. "Benedict, you have been here before, yes?"

"I have." The man Blackwell had identified with the soft, salty gentleness led Blackwell out of the room at a run and down flights of wooden stairs to a room walled entirely of concrete and humming faintly. A closed wooden door stood at one end. The reactor stood in the center with a console and screen built into it, where Blackwell saw the red threat circle of the Cabal jumpship closing in on Boston House.

Blackwell ran to the reactor, playing Valentina's instructions across the inside of his eyes. He followed each one carefully and precisely, and his internal clock registered thirty-four minutes and eight seconds as he changed the final access code. He breathed out with enormous relief when the safety icon changed to green.

"Done?" said Benedict.

"Done," said Blackwell. "He won't be able to see us now." But when he looked up at the screen to verify, the red threat circle flashed twice and disappeared.

Benedict sucked in breath. "It shouldn't do that. What class jumpship is it?"

"Sorry, but I didn't check."

"Did you get its deceptor settings?"

"Corporate registry, on holiday charter, Metron Corp out of Hamburg."

"Metron?" gritted Benedict. "Mothers of the unborn! Come on!" He yanked Blackwell to his feet. "It's the Cabal's fastest light attack vessel, Probe class, heavily armed, crew of three—pilot, navigator, shooter—and using their latest stealth cloaking."

"But we're safe now! The codes have been set!"

Benedict yelled over his shoulder as he bolted up the stairs two at a time. "And he saw you do it! That's why he turned on his stealth! He must have the access codes already. Now we're visible, and we've got...how long?"

"Thirty-three minutes."

Benedict reached the top of the stairs, yelling, "Paul! Poor Men! Cabal intrusion! To the sleds!" The Poor Men tumbled out of the door and across the early morning courtyard.

The sight of his sled—Book's sled—triggered something in his brain. Events and consequences slid across each other, then fitted neatly and locked into place, and he knew what he had to do. "Go!" he called to Benedict, waving him on. "Give me a minute." And he turned on every light he could, wedged the House door open behind him and sprinted to his own sled, where he initiated the startup sequences: reactor, engine and the deeper resonances of the hydraulics a minute later. Then he leapt out, latched the hatch closed and sprinted into the hangar. It was dark and cool when he entered, with only a few high windows letting in the dawn. Ranks upon ranks of sleds stretched back into the shadows amid the smells of machinery and oiled timber and old settled dust. Under the cockpit windows of each one, the identifying markings signified Patron and region. *Hand: SW23* read one in block letters, and underneath it, someone had carefully painted 'The Blitz.'

The group or division of Hand the Patron. South-west. Region 23. Others read *Sigil: C07, The Red Dance. Banner: E212, The White Comet.* The world all neatly divided up into delivery zones. Centuries of service to the unknowing people of the world. Devotion to hope in the face of the curse of hopelessness. Blackwell wondered how much louder the place would have been with hundreds of Poor Men loading, trolleying sleds out into the pads for take-off, sled engines ticking and whirring, collaborative laughter, discussions, orders. And here he was with probably the last twelve Poor Men. The entire worldwide Brotherhood shrunk to a dozen plus one as the Cabal closed in.

Thirty minutes and eleven seconds.

Up ahead, Benedict was waiting near a sled's open hold bay doors. The bridge and running lights were on. The old man—Paul, Blackwell realized—yelled through the external speaker, "Ten seconds!" Blackwell leaped in, Benedict pulled the hatch closed and they both scrambled up the ladder.

Up on the bridge almost identical to Book's flagship, Paul thumbed the Drive icon. "Ascending," he said. The screen graphic indicated a fast and straight ascent, though Blackwell felt no evidence of speed. He stood there with one hand on the Chair where Antonius sat, watching the altimeter wind up to two thousand feet.

"Timothy, Henry," Paul said, "get to the reactor. Timothy, I want to know of any faults, small or large. Henry, tune the detector sensors to maximum, all outbound signals off. I want to know if that jumpship gets within ten miles. Thomas, William, Calvin, secure the load. Frederick, the con, if you please. Antonius, where was this sled bound tonight?"

"Two zones. Northwest 21 first. North Adams. Then Southeast 5 second. Worcester."

A second later, the map appeared on the main screen and shaded itself: Boston city center and suburbs first, then the north-eastern districts and islands, south along the coast, then the northern inland regions until most of Massachusetts was complete. Antonius whistled. "Ninety-six percent complete!"

"Nice radials, Book," said Calvin, running his finger along the shaded completion zones before racing down the gangway after Thomas and William. "You ran a tight House."

"Transit altitude reached," said Antonius.

"Mark," Paul said. "Set course for North Adams."

But Blackwell, seeing patterns align and lock, saw his moment and grabbed it. "No. Set ghosting deceptors for public air taxi, course New York, maximum verification depth. Then amend course for Worcester."

"Worcester?" snarled Paul. "Denied! What are you thinking, Poor Man?"

"He's after me, not you. Fortunately, he thinks I'm still in my sled, or at worst, close by."

"How can you know that? He's under stealth—you can't be sure!"

"Either way, he won't be able to resist the temptation of being the first Cabal assassin ever to break into the timeslip. So he'll hunt for me first at the House, and I've bought us some time by making it look like the House is occupied or I'm still in the sled. If he doesn't buy that, he'll check for sled movement, and if he's got the House access codes, then it's possible he'll see through our deceptors as well, no matter how deep. Which means he'll come after us, and North Adams is too far away to be still in the air when he realizes. We need to set down as soon as possible, rig for minimal 'slip and stay still and silent so that when he realizes he's been fooled, he won't be able to find us."

"It makes sense," Benedict said.

Paul frowned, his eyes narrow and dark. "Nothing makes sense," he growled. "Least of all a stranger who says he's a Poor Man but who brings the Cabal with him."

"Set deceptors and course for Worcester," Blackwell repeated. "Maximum speed, all outbound signalling off."

But Paul wasn't finished. "So why are the Cabal pursuing you?" He stared at Blackwell. "They've wiped out almost the entire Brotherhood worldwide, destroyed Kavonatur, penetrated the timeslip, and yet they're coming after you?"

"I have something they want."

Paul's laugh was short and hostile. "What could they possibly want? They've got everything they've wanted for seventeen hundred years! All that's left are thirteen unprotected Poor Men!"

"I know how to break the curse."

"Nothing of this earth will break the curse," said Benedict.

Paul snorted, "Then do it, for all that is decent! Break it now and be done with it!"

"I can't. At least not yet. I lost all my memory apart from nine fragments. I've remembered eight of them—at least the names of them—

but the ninth is locked, and that's where the key to the curse is. I have to decipher the first eight to unlock the ninth."

"And? And? Tell us the eight, damn you!"

"Gifts, five secret words, a secret door, a jasmine woman, ice, Moscow, the smell of planes, stars. Two I know already."

Paul waved his arms. "Yes, yes, gifts and the five secret words. The secret door was Father Nikolas' door."

"Yes. And the ninth memory—tasted of Boston, so the curse-breaker must be there."

"So we have to get back to Boston somehow and search," Benedict said. "Are you sure of this, Poor Man?"

"We don't have the luxury of certainty. The Brotherhood has been destroyed, and we have eleven days to restore hope to the world, or there's mass suicide and the Cabal wins."

Benedict grinned broadly. "But if we break the curse, we don't need to worry about not finishing deliveries! We won't need gifts at all! Hope at last!"

A sudden movement startled Blackwell. He turned to see Frederick sitting forward in the Chair and the screens flaring. "Explosion at the House!" shouted Frederick.

Blackwell strode over to the screen. "Report!"

"Tower's sled! Simultaneous comms and reactor failure—controlled explosion—could have been—"

Blackwell hesitated a moment. The roaring wind raced cold and hollow through his ears, unbuckling his courage. He grabbed Benedict's arm for support, and the moment geared back into focus. He realigned himself, clamped down on panic. He knew what had happened."Command is mine," he declared, remembering Ed. "They're early. They must have increased speed when they went under stealth."

But Paul's face turned white, his hands balled into fists. "You knew all the time, traitor!" he shouted, whirling to face Blackwell. "You're Cabal! I should have put you into the pit!"

"He's not Cabal," snapped Benedict. "And you are out of line. Step off the bridge, Poor Man."

"We will all die!" Paul snarled. "He's opened the door to them, and now he wants to lead us all back into their arms!"

Benedict smiled with his soft salty gentleness. "Break the curse and renew hope or give up now and die in despair? Choose, Poor Man." His hands were very still. "Choose now."

Paul flinched, but said nothing and stepped back to the rear of the bridge.

"Time to arrival?" said Blackwell, fixing his focus on the screen.

"One minute, sir. Same course?"

Sir. The sound rang like a sweet bell. "Same course." And with words that barely seemed his, with memories he *hadn't* received from Valentina—he said, "Get a visual line to the House. No outbound signals, reception only."

With his VR mitt, Frederick manipulated unseen controls, his mouth tight, his eyes narrowed. Blackwell was aware of footsteps receding behind him, then intense silence. Frederick made a noise of disgust."They're at the House."

"Engine status?"

"Throttled down. They're in no hurry to leave."

"So they think I'm still there. If we can get to Worcester and shut down before they realize, we'll be safe."

"For the moment," muttered Paul from the back.

"This moment is all we are granted," said Benedict loudly.

"Frederick, how do we stand?" asked Blackwell.

"'Slip integrity high. No pings."

Benedict cocked his head. "None? He's alone? No other Cabal vessels nearby? No-one's tracking us?"

"None."

Blackwell checked off his mental list. "Timothy, reactor?"

"Ninety-nine percent. Twenty percent emergency reserve."

"Rig for minimal 'slip immediately on landing."

"Sir."

"Thomas, is that load secure?"

"Secure."

He keyed on the intercom. "Poor Men, prepare for possible evacuation in threes on my order. Set Scouts for Emergency mode, receipt only." He keyed off. "Well, strangely enough, we're safe." He smiled a crooked smile. "For the moment."

Benedict smiled. "And then? Sit and wait for how long?"

"As long as it takes. We have to get back to Boston eventually. We'll walk back if we need to. But I'm hoping they'll destroy my sled, think they've killed me and leave. It would be good if they were that stupid."

"You don't think so?"

"No, but there's a faint chance they'll be so excited about breaking into the Boston timeslip that they'll neglect basic procedures. Have they ever penetrated the slip before?"

"Oh, they're always snooping around. Their analysts are always trying to work out our delivery routes and when they think they've pinned one down, they send out a jumpship along that route, waiting, just waiting for a slip. All they'd need is a sled reactor to hiccup, and within twelve seconds they'd have a fix." He frowned.

"But it's never happened," said Blackwell.

Benedict hesitated and looked away. "Only once," he said. "Only once. But that story's for another time. At worst, they'll destroy the House and the hangars." He paused. "And the sleeping Poor Men."

Blackwell looked away. "They're not after the Poor Men. It's me they want. So we'll wait until they leave, then slip back quietly. We'll have to sweep the House meticulously for tracers and get an emergency evacuation plan in place in case they return."

The sun was warm with rural New England light when Frederick brought the sled down on the corner of two streets. Blackwell saw the sun out of the window like a rich coin of promise and plenty, and he made promises by it, fixed all his hope to it. Safety for the Poor Men. The jasmine woman alive and well. His remaining planets decoded. The curse broken. And most of all, in the still place in his heart where hope and suicide rested in equal balance, a future. A future with as much promise and plenty as the moon had. Hope for humanity against the relentless tide of suicides.

"Rig for minimal 'slip," he whispered into the intercom, and a moment later, the hydraulics settled and quietened, the reactor whirred down to nothing but a faint hum, and the bridge's secondary screens dimmed. The screen showing the visual feed to the House faded to black.

"Now we're both invisible and blind," said Benedict. "Like one of those old subs sitting on the bottom of the ocean while enemy surface ships prowled above. Safe up to the point where the jumpship realizes he's been tricked and comes looking then we won't even be able to see him coming. We'll have to evacuate the sled in a hurry."

Blackwell was considering setting a physical watch when the thought occurred to him. It was so wildly, wonderfully defiant that he almost laughed. He thought for a moment, then keyed the intercom. "Timothy, what radius does the reactor have under minimal slip settings?"

"One mile."

Blackwell keyed off to Benedict's quizzical look. "What are you thinking?"

"That one mile is enough. We've got a full load here. Rather than sit around waiting for the Cabal to find us, let's deliver. If he does come looking, we'll be gone."

Benedict chuckled. "Brilliant with a hint of sheer insanity. The last thirteen Poor Men in the whole world, under threat of death, thumb their noses at their enemies and deliver instead. Led by a Poor Men who remembers nothing of delivery processes, I'm guessing, since you were a novice. Am I right?"

"I'm sorry."

Benedict considered him for a moment, nodded slightly. "Very well. Would you mind if I lead this one?"

"Of course not. Why do you ask?"

Benedict chuckled. "Because as the only one among us with the name of a Patron, you should. You're our leader. All the men know that." He called everyone into the bridge. "We're going out delivering, Poor Men." He looked out over them. "The Cabal are looking for us, and if they find us, seventeen hundred years of Brotherhood service may end tonight." He grinned. "But if we're to die, let it be in service, as we were born. Agreed?"

To Blackwell's surprise, every single Poor Man's head snapped up, even Paul's. "Agreed," they declared.

"Good. We're at Roxbury and William Streets, so finish those streets first, note crossing or joining streets as you go, then come back for those. We're going to run things the old way: parallel support grid, with bilateral separations at street-end. No crossovers. No Scout use except under threat to life. We've got a mile protection under minimal 'slip, so don't go wandering too far. There's a Cabal shark out there somewhere, and he might appear without warning. Questions?"

"Single man deliveries?" said Arthur, his eyes wide.

"You'll be unlocking your own doors today, Poor Man," said Benedict. "But you're young and fit, so it shouldn't bother you." From across the bridge, his father Thomas nodded, and Blackwell remembered the grey gaunt determination of his character: *Do what's right, son, even though it hurts.*

Benedict looked across at Thomas. "Loadmaster, if you would, Thomas. Manual recording, I'm sorry."

Thomas nodded and left.

"Paul, I'd like you to handle oversight."

Blackwell was watching the old man carefully while Benedict was speaking, and he was surprised to see Paul shake his head. The old man's face was even. "With respect," he said quietly. "Tower runs with me today. I'll mentor him so he can do it alone in the future."

The future. Blackwell was more grateful for those words than he could say.

Benedict opened his mouth, then closed it. Blackwell thought he would argue, but he had the grace to nod."Very well," he said. "Get down to the hold. Run hard."

In the hold, Thomas had made ten piles of boxes, each box in a plastic bag with a cardboard label inside a pouch. When all the Poor Men had gone, he gave Blackwell and Paul their bags last. "Keep them in the right order to save time," he told Blackwell. "Check the label on the flimsy, make the delivery and keep the flimsy for next year. Don't leave it behind." He grinned. "Looks unprofessional."

Over the next hour, Blackwell followed Paul, whose stooped frame belied a long loping stride that seemed to be able to keep him going forever. Either the Cabal jumpship had given up and left, or their minimal 'slip settings had kept them invisible because the sled was there every time Blackwell and Paul ran back and the sky clear. For the first twenty minutes, Blackwell thought his lungs were going to implode, so he concentrated on his breathing and the slap of the pack straps against his thighs. After half an hour, though, as Paul slipped quietly into a house, Blackwell felt warm and easy. He had to admit it, he was enjoying himself. With every gift placed on a living room table eleven days into the future, he was adding another brick to the wall of hope he was building around Massachusetts. *One less suicide*, he told himself. One more person who believed that someone out there cared. And if he could unlock his ninth planet and break the curse, it would all be worth it.

The level of gift boxes in the hold dropped steadily. While Thomas did not smile often, he always had the right pile of boxes ready when Blackwell jogged back to the sled to refill his pack. Dover Street. Hack Field Road. Elmhorn, Trowbridge, Schussler. The long stretch of Highland with its cars and trucks caught midway between piston strokes, their drivers still another four hours away from the next heartbeat. He and Paul completed every street as the sun promised them everything.

Boston House

It was quite bizarre, Mantell thought, that it could have been so easy. She had practised the five words many times, fearing she would mispronounce or forget one, or her voice would crack. To her surprise, though, the jumpship slid easily through the timeslip barrier, and buildings, ascent pads and paved areas appeared suddenly where before she had only seen marshes, muddy ground and a brown sluggish river. It was so amazing that she thought she must have missed something. but there they were in the Boston base, within the timeslip shield, in the courtyard of their enemies, between the massive hangar and the old brick building with the red door.

She climbed out of the jumpship, weapons ready, hoping the kill would be over quick, and that she could take her money and go. Live out the rest of her life—however long it might be—in oceanic quiet.

Yet the thought would not die. What was so significant about this solitary Poor Man? And why did it coincide with the announcement of the comet? What macabre logic compelled the Second to hunt down one man when almost all his brothers were almost irreversibly comatose?And extract what? For an awful moment, suspicion soured her gut. What if it was all a massive fraud, and the Second was lying to her, tormenting her for some perverse reason of his own? There was no contesting the Second.

O'Roarke glanced across at her, silencing her thoughts.

The timeslipped Brotherhood base was silent and empty. Mantell was hardly expecting squadrons of heavily armed Poor Men waiting, but even so, the flat silence of the place disquieted her. Perhaps the target had escaped, she thought doubtfully. It hardly mattered. Now that they could penetrate the timeslip, nothing would stop them.

O'Roarke scanned the surroundings—the large red brick base behind them, a line of trees to the east and the river beyond it, brick sheds and low buildings to the west, and the hangar and ascent pads in front of them. Mantell thought the base building looked comfortable and elegant under the morning sun. Cabal buildings were almost always ugly grey concrete. A single sled stood before them, marked just under the cockpit windows with the words *Book: E1. The Black Dash*. The Book, the renowned Patron, high up on the list of Brotherhood targets. The one whose limp body they had seen slumped against a wall in Patara.

O'Roarke gave her one of the biothermal and movement detectors and nodded at the base. "Perimeter sweep first, then enter with caution. Lasers inside, no disruptors. Blast canisters at ten meter intervals around the collapse points, armed for concurrent detonation, set to frequency K, one hundred minutes from my mark. I'll do the hangar, and watch his sled in case he comes out."

"You think he's still in there?"

"Looks like it, girlie. If this is our target, we've got him cornered."

"Aye." It was the only word that carried both the required military obedience and the disgust she felt for him.

O'Roarke checked his chrono. "Mark."

She zeroed her chrono. "Mark."

"Kill them all."

She watched him stride towards the hangar, swinging his laser with an almost sexual arrogance, then turned to the base building, where she hoped the target was hiding. She wanted to be the one who killed him, not the vile O'Roarke.

Inside the base building, she found instead hundreds of Poor Men laid out on their beds. She thought at first they were the off-shift, but they were all in exactly the same positions, and it was a moment before she realized someone must have put them there. The victims of the Cabal plague. And a moment more to realize that somewhere, there would have to be the survivors who had carried them in, the target among them. Her pulse accelerating, she checked her scanners every minute or so, but the place seemed empty of movement or bodyheat. They were hiding, then.

So she checked every room, observing detail with an assassin's eye. Rooms decorated and furnished plainly but honestly. Timber tables and chairs, simple white bedspreads, herbs and flowers hung to dry, flowers in hand-turned ceramic pots, pencil sketches on walls. The smells of soap, herbs, timber oil and leather. With a stubborn defiance, she walked among the victims, faintly amused by the notion of a heavily armed killer not slaughtering her unprotected enemies. She was glad the Second was not there with her, though he would surely know sooner or later. Their hands folded on their chests, the Poor Men slept, serene in their soft breathings, dreaming of whatever the plague wasn't blocking.

When she returned to the jumpship twenty minutes later, thoughtful, O'Roarke was standing in front of the sled. She nodded at the sled. "Any movement?" If the target was inside, he was as good as dead.

"Reckon he's sleeping. He probably arrived, locked down and stayed put. Can't get in but it won't matter. I've mined the hangar, so any Poor Men who return won't last long. Any survivors in the base?"

"None." Not quite true, she admitted to herself in mild surprise.

"Set the mines then?"

"Of course." And that surprised her more. Not only had she not placed the blast canisters according to his orders, or armed them, but she had actually sat on a victim's bed and touched his hand, feeling his cool skin and watched his neck pulse beat slowly. An assassin with compassion? These Poor Men were not the unyielding fanatics the Second had warned them against, and she had surprised herself by deciding that they were not going to perish at her hands at any rate. Not today anyway. If the Second was betraying her, she would rebel.

O'Roarke stared with the same menacing suspicion she had used many times herself. "Sure and certain, girlie?"

Assassins were liars, all of them, but he must have believed more in her greed than her humanity. "Sure and certain." She caught herself. *Compassion? Humanity?* She was an assassin, and there was a job to be done.

"Well, then." He flicked on his helmet cam. "Who's it to be?"

She had her disruptor charged and ready, but she nodded to him, oddly reluctant to fire. "Kill him good," she said, and did not mean a word.

O'Roarke raised his disruptor. "Watch me get rich." He turned the weapon on the sled and fired.

The sled burned with the disruptor's eerie green flame, sucking out air and weakening atomic bonds until the structure started to collapse in on itself with a ghoulish violence. Mantell always loved watching disruptor flames. But this time, she turned away from the sight, back to where the base building stood like a testament to her deceit. "That's it," said O'Roarke, lowering his weapon, and Mantell knew an Irish jig would follow within seconds. "One dead target." He chuckled. "I'm a millionaire."

After Mantell had checked her helmet cam and taken careful pictures of the wreckage, they walked back to the jumpship and strapped in. O'Roarke was actually singing his jig this time, a song about someone called Mary, and waiting at the fair, and a love since childhood. "Status?" laughed O'Roarke. "Not that I'm too worried. I've got me a hankering for riches beyond countin'."

She checked the board: deceptors, altitude, bearing, threats. "Clear." A yellow light winked on. "No, wait. Something's—" And then she realized with a strange shock what it was."You're not a millionaire yet," she said, holding down a surprised laugh. "The target you just killed? Well, you didn't. He's fooled us both. He's still alive, or at least his marker is."

"You sure, girlie? That's his sled burning there."

"It just came on. Thirty-eight miles west of here. He's changed sleds."

O'Roarke swore viciously, then took the jumpship up sharply to a thousand meters, rotated out of hover, and blasted westwards. "Lock on," he growled. "Arm everything. Check twice." He started whistling.

And then Mantell knew. What kind of man would the Second fear, even when all his enemies lay comatose and defenseless? What kind of man could defy the Second, the Predominant, to whom much was owed and nothing taken?

What man had something the Second wanted?

And then, at last, she knew.

She covered her mouth with her gloved hand so O'Roarke would not see her faint smile.

Boston

Hours after they began, out beyond the quiet cool breathings of Salisbury Pond, with the afternoon sun splintering its promises between bare trees and darkening clouds, Paul and Blackwell were running along Waconah Road with empty packs towards the waiting sled. Sweat cooled Blackwell's back under his pack. He was ready for soup first, and sleep soon after. If the Cabal had left the House, he would set about unlocking his planets tomorrow. If they were coming to kill him, he would not go easily. He would kill as many as he could before they got him. Weary as he was, it seemed such a waste to lose everything so close to Boston.

"We must be just about done," Paul said without so much as breathing hard. "How do you feel after your first run?"

"I'll sleep well." He could barely stand. "Any sight of the Cabal?"

"None," said Thomas from the hold.

Where were they? Blackwell couldn't believe they had not pursued him further. He could only think that they were waiting for him back at the House. But before he could speak, Thomas held out one last bundle. Blackwell was too weary to accept, although he knew he should.

"I'll do it," said Paul quickly. "You've done enough, Tower. That's more than most Poor Men do on their first run."

Blackwell was too exhausted for the encouragement and perhaps the grimace around his mouth translated as a smile. Paul chuckled when Blackwell raised a weary hand but as Paul reached for the pack, his Scout dropped to the ground. Paul made an annoyed sound and reached for it, but only bunted it further. It rolled several times and then slid into a roadside drain. Blackwell heard it splash.

"Don't worry," said Thomas from the hold. "I've lost four that way."

"Take my Scout." Blackwell turned it on and gave it to him. "It's a little different to yours, but it has the same functions, I think. I've opened doors with it, anyway, the same as yours."

When Paul had gone, Blackwell unslung his pack, gave it to Thomas and sat down on the ground. After a few minutes, as gravity caught up with his eyelids, Thomas came up behind him and gave him an apple. "The first run is always hardest, Tower," he said.

The brothers arrived together, grinning at something, then Arthur, sweating like a racehorse coming in from the track, then the others in twos and threes. They loaded their packs and flimsies into the hold and stood around. Benedict came down from the bridge and welcomed them back. Every time they moved, a warm pungent brotherhood of sweat and fraternity surrounded Blackwell, and he loved it. He counted them off. "Eleven. Where's Paul?" He counted again.

Benedict stared down the street. "Thomas, how big was that last load?"

"Eighteen boxes."

"That shouldn't take any more than twenty minutes."

"He should be back soon," said Thomas, tightening straps around the packs. But he wasn't. Nor after twenty-five.

Benedict called Blackwell's Scout. No answer. Nor after thirty minutes.

"I'm going to look for him," said Blackwell, though his legs had all the strength of bedposts. "He's my partner. It won't take long. He's probably just fallen and needs to be carried back." Though several other reasons were lining up in his mind, and none of them were pleasant.

Arthur stepped forward. "I'll come with you. There's Cabal out there."

They found Paul on Pratt Street under a bare tree. His dropped bag lay at his feet, and boxes spilled from it, silver and turquoise and emerald. Paul was standing behind his bag, his arms raised, his face an ugly mix of terror and fury. And in front of him stood two armored figures, both with disruptors. The shorter of them, a woman, was holding Blackwell's Scout. Her left hand was gloved. Her visor was down.

Cabal assassins. And the taller one had his disruptor aimed at Paul.

Realizing without understanding that he had three seconds before the disruptor became active, Blackwell pushed Arthur back behind him and started running at the taller of the two, planning to dive under the weapon, take out his legs, knock the weapon clear. Someone was screaming—the woman?—but everything was directionless noise in Blackwell's head. The assassin raised his weapon, clicked the activator and a wisp of cold gas flared from the muzzle.

Two seconds.

The assassin aimed the weapon at Blackwell's head.

The Poor Man charged towards them.

It's him, thought Mantell with a wild furious elation. *It's him!* Shocked as she was, and even as a swarm of angry thoughts snarled through her—Moscow—vanished for four weeks—Second's cruel morbid joke!—the target!—Mantell knew exactly what to do.

O'Roarke clicked the activator. The Poor Man was about fifteen feet away.

With blazing murderous liberty, Mantell turned her weapon and swept O'Roarke with green hissing fire. In delicious, violent justice, she watched his astonished eyes glaze hard, his mouth snap closed, his skin shrivel black, his clothes and flesh form an unbreakable chemical bond. As his hardened corpse fell and his unfired weapon clattered away, she heard the Poor Men shouting in terror. The running man—the target, she realized—had halted and was staring first at O'Roarke's corpse, then at her. Sweat sheened his forehead. The other two were standing together, their mouths open in shock, though the younger one was spitting out a slag of fluid at the sight of steam wisping from O'Roarke's eye sockets.

She kept her weapon aimed at the Poor Men, her pulse pounding, her breath coming in short astonished gasps. *The Second will know soon enough, but consequences be damned!* "Get back!" she ordered, and the Poor Man target raised his hands and stepped back, his eyes on her weapon. His fellows pulled him back and shielded him.

Her visor was down, she realized. Sheer good luck. Once he recognized her, he'd kill her for sure. *But ah! What if he didn't?* She thought fast, amazed at the possibilities. Maybe she could deceive the Second...disable the target's Scout...disrupt one of the Poor Men similar in appearance to the target...it could be done! All that she would leave would be a shrunken effigy for the Poor Men to find, cold and dense and still flickering with green smoke. She could then make the short hop back to London, show the Second her—false—images of the kill, and claim her reward.

But...no. She breathed out slowly, smiling a little. This new future was better than that. She had the target alive. Standing right in front of her. And whatever joke the Second was playing, he would have to contend with her first. Lion and lamb indeed.

She ordered the Poor Man back to their sled, but motioned for the target to wait.

He stared at her, his glance flicking down to her disruptor, his face surprisingly calm. Behind her visor, she treasured the moment. She held out his Scout. "This is yours, I believe. It's how we found you, in case you were wondering."

On board the sled, she herded the Poor Men into the cockpit and scanned the layout, making sure she was between everyone and the hatch. She kept her visor down and swept her disruptor around. "You saw what it did back there," she said as the last one climbed up, watching her disruptor carefully.

"You killed your own partner!" shouted a Poor Man. "What kind of—?"

She swung it around on him, admiring the way he kept his position, did not recoil. "And now it's on you, Poor Man. Listen closely. Here are my conditions. I am not interested in anything you say or think or want to say. You will remain silent, and you may carry out whatever tasks are necessary in returning me to your Boston base, where I will remain with you until further notice. If you speak, I will disrupt you, and your comrades may dispose of your body however they choose. I will speak only with your leader."

"You're Cabal! What do—!" shouted another before his fellow clamped a hand over his mouth.

Mantell aimed the disruptor at him. "I am only sorry I cannot merely wound you with this weapon. I will...*forgive* you"—the word sat strangely on her tongue—"this once, but not again. Those are my conditions, and this is my warning. Any attempt on my life will result in the immediate death of one of you, chosen at random." She was watching the target—they called him Tower—as she said it, and saw the way his brow furrowed at that. "Be grateful I have not killed you all," she said. "Now go."

The old Poor Man turned away, though his fellow regarded Mantell with mingled disgust and fear. Several glared at her as they pulled down seats from the cockpit walls and sat. The way they scanned the situation impressed her: the position of her disruptor, Tower's location, their escape paths to the hatch. *Resourceful,* she thought. No wonder that they had stayed hidden for seventeen hundred years.

She settled back into the corner, checked she had a good line on every man, though none of the Poor Men were even watching her. One of them, blond and bearded, spoke quietly to Tower, and then took the pilot's chair and took the sled up. None of the Poor Men moved around or spoke. She let the silence extend, let her pulse settle. She moved the disruptor in random arcs. She had almost forgotten murdering O'Roarke. Vulgar Irishmen like him were not worth remembering. Instead, she watched Tower in silence as he moved among the Poor Men, calming them, this quiet man with his messy hair and still eyes who considered everything. His serious face resonated with her as it had on that terrible night, but now he was here in front of her, with only her visor between them.

London

The mole entered the Second's room, closed the door, and eased the satcom pack onto the floor where the Second could not see it. The Second sat forward in a foul swirl of darkening pollution, and the sofa beneath him groaned like a trapped beast. Afraid of the stillness and the noxious blackness of the smoke, the mole delivered the report.

"What does this mean?" The Second whispered with a pleasantness the mole knew not to trust.

"O'Roarke's communicator failed, sir. The evidence from the audio record immediately preceding the failure indicates that he came under fire."

The Second laughed like a suicide choking. "Poor Men do not carry weapons."

"Disruptor fire, sir. We believe it was Mantell."

The Second was quiet for a long time. The cloud around him shivered in and out in ragged pulses. Eventually, he leaned back on the sofa, dragging back smoke with him. "She has…turned?" he breathed.

He gave the word such menace that the mole stood straight automatically, as though posture was guard against such things. "It appears so, sir."

The Second was silent for a few moments, then chuckled again, a deathly rattle. Dense ugly fumes gusted out. He clapped his hands together, beautiful hands, slim and elegant like a woman's. "Ah," he said softly. "Good, good."

The mole shuddered, desperate to get out, fly to Boston and kill the target. "I'll send a team immediately, sir! Kill her and the target before she reveals your secrets!"

But the Second only pointed a long finger. "It is *your* secrets she will reveal, my dear traitor, and that in good time, be in no doubt. But she is still doing my bidding, whether she knows it or not. She sat in the dentist's chair before she left, and in one tooth is a device through which we might both listen and transmit signals that she will believe are her own thoughts and desires, even over-riding the orders you wrongfully issued. Very soon, now that they both believe she has slipped my leash, she will assist him in unlocking the curse-breaking secret before the comet strikes, if it does. With it, we can destroy all human hope forever. And you will remain here to hear it with me. I will sustain you. All you need is here."

"Yes, sir." The mole stood very still, hardly blinking, waiting and planning. *The target had to die,* that much was clear. It should not be too hard to transmit the necessary message.

An hour passed, maybe two. The Second sat without moving or sound. Smoke pulsed in and out with long crocodilian breaths.

After three hours, the mole thought the cloud of smoke around the Second was dense enough to hide movement, and slipped the receiver out slowly, without noise. It took about ten minutes. The keypad was thankfully exposed.

The Second had not moved.

The mole's heart pounded. Carefully, with teeth clamped and fingers shaking slightly, the mole keyed the message, "Kill him now," and pressed 'Transmit.'

Boston House

Paul put the sled down into a soaking evening rain, between the blackened hulk of Book's sled and the House, and the assassin ordered the Poor Men down into the cargo hold, sweeping her weapon back and forth. In the hold, Blackwell found himself standing alongside the assassin."Open the hatch," she ordered, but no-one moved. "Open it!" she demanded, pointed the disruptor at Thomas, clicked something and a thin wisp of green gas flared from the muzzle.

Blackwell thought the tightening of her fingers on the weapon was going to preface a blast, and was preparing to launch himself at her, pin her arms or knock the weapon from her hands. He knew instinctively he could do it. Her reaction time would not be fast enough. Neither would she have time to draw other weapons from the bulges in her pockets and thigh-holsters that he knew were not Scouts or purses. But something deeper than common sense held him back.

Thomas looked at him. "Tower?"

"Do it."

Thomas opened the hatch to the roar of the rain and the intermittent waft of charred metal and burning chemicals.

The assassin gestured at the hatch with her weapon. "Get out," she said. "All of you. Tower, stay here." Someone gasped. None of the Poor Men moved. Blackwell wondered how well the weapon would work in rain.

Benedict glanced at Blackwell, then back at the assassin. "Why?" he demanded. "What do you want with him?"

"I am going to speak with your leader about certain matters," she said quietly.

Certain matters. Why *talk* when she should have killed all of them? Blackwell analyzed patterns and probabilities, laying out events in their order. *Why had it taken seventeen hundred years for the*

Second to act? His destruction of the Brotherhood had been so decisive, swift and complete that Blackwell found it impossible to believe he had not had the ability to do it before.

The comet must have triggered it.

And unlikely as it was that something that would bring about the almost-complete destruction of Western civilization could possibly make things worse, it had got the Second worried enough not only to destroy the main European distribution base at Kavonatur and eliminate almost every Poor Man on the planet, but then send out assassins to track him to Boston, to extract from him the key to either catastrophe or hope. Up to that moment of confrontation in Worcester, the Second had everything he wanted.

But then the woman had turned her weapon on her own partner in one of the most bizarre acts Blackwell had ever witnessed. Little as he knew of Cabal battle tactics, murdering one's allies wasn't part of it. So she had something else in mind. And although he couldn't trust a Cabal assassin, he wanted to know it.

Benedict took a step forward, his fists clenched at his side. "One Cabal scum against twelve," he snarled. "You may get one of us, but we'll pin you, carry you into the House and drop you into a pit. Be sure of it."

"Benedict, *no!*" He grabbed Benedict's arm, pulled him back.

"Do not provoke me into more violence, Poor Man." The assassin scanned the hold, turned toward Blackwell, though her visor still covered her face. "This is not war. I don't have much to say, but it must be in private. Get out and don't try anything stupid. There are other weapons trained on you that I control through this helmet."

Blackwell nodded at them, and the Poor Men glanced at the disruptor then slipped out into the downpour. Benedict waited until the assassin threatened him with the disruptor, then glanced back at Blackwell with an unreadable expression, and left.

The rain drummed down, lightless and solid, a vertical force, but Blackwell heard a different sound out there, something large enough to separate the downpour, create a rainshadow beneath it. An aircraft? Blackwell thought madly at first it was a Brotherhood sled, the first of many loaded with Poor Men, but the assassin just nodded at the sound. Turning, Blackwell glanced out and saw a jumpship descending slowly, a blast of rain steaming away from its undercarriage.

"You're with others?" He could think of nothing worse than another of these women.

"It has a remote tracking function," she said. "No, I'm alone." she said quietly. "I set it to follow me. The external lasers are trained on your comrades. Now sit down over there, facing me." She gestured with the weapon.

He moved, uncomfortable at the distance between them and leaned back against the hold wall, watching as she slid carefully down the opposite wall, easing her feet forward. The hold light cast shadows on the wall fixing points behind her. He kept his voice as even as possible. "What do you want to say?"

"Don't worry," she said. "I'm not going to hurt you."

He snorted his disbelief, watching her closely. It was strange talking to a mouth without eyes. "Not before you extract my secret and kill me, anyway. That's why you've come, isn't it?"

"Perhaps, but I'm not going to kill you, Poor Man. I just saved your life. O'Roarke was a vicious murderer at the best of times, but we were an effective partnership. Now the people of Worcester will put him in a body bag, the police will issue a suicide notice 104 that no-one will care about, and everyone will shake their heads at the bizarre ways some Earlies will choose. Is that not proof enough?"

The tumble of disbelief came faster than Blackwell could control. "Saved my…why didn't you just extract the secret and kill us all? You had the chance." The thought of death made him glance quickly at the snout of the weapon, a brutish, ugly beast that looked terribly heavy. It disturbed him that she had checked her chrono twice, about ninety seconds apart.

"Because I want you to…" The horizon of her gaze wavered. She looked down at the disruptor. It was only a brief blip on the seismograph of her head, but Blackwell noticed it. "I want you to look at me," she whispered.

Her slow, deliberate gravity unnerved Blackwell deeply. "I can see you already," he said, sure it was the wrong answer. *You don't want my secret?*

"At my face." Her voice was barely more than a whisper. She lifted the weapon slightly, and for a moment, Blackwell was ready to leap up, fearing the green fire. Instead, though, she laid it on her knees with a quiet delicate softness that he found both repulsive and curiously attractive.

Her fingers twitched. Then she fumbled with something on her helmet and swore under her breath. Blackwell leaned forward a little, despite himself. *What was this all about?* She took the corners of her visor in both hands, lifted it a little, then paused and lowered it again.

Blackwell stared, puzzled. "I don't understand," he said, noticing that the weapon still lay on her knees, untouched.

"You will," she said quietly and breathed out a long exhalation. Then, with a quick decisive movement, she lifted the helmet fully from her head, lay it on the floor and looked at him.

Blackwell stared, not quite sure what he was meant to understand. She was unremarkable, though perhaps that was desirable for an assassin. Shoulder length brown hair. Brown eyes that rarely blinked, steady as lines of latitude. Two scars, one he thought at first a wrinkle just below her left eye, and the other a shadowed line below her left ear. But why was she looking away? He knew it signified nervousness, but didn't she have a weapon within reach? What was there to be nervous about? "I don't understand," he said, sure it was the wrong thing to say, but he was just so...*baffled*.

She gazed at him. The corners of her mouth turned up a fraction. "You don't recognize me?"

He hesitated. This made no sense. "No."

She chuckled, a soft sound that scratched his vulnerable heart. "You're serious?"

He shook his head carefully, frowning. This was almost too bizarre for words.

"Two months ago we met on a frozen river outside Moscow," she said. Her hands lay on the disruptor, but not near the trigger. "Do you remember that night?"

Moscow. Every hair, every nerve, every cell bristled at the word. Shock and warning prickled on the back of his neck. His planets shuddered in their orbits. He gaped. *How did she know?* The terror in ice. The smell of planes. Stars. Maybe she also knew of these things. Although she was not the jasmine woman; he knew that much.

"So you do," she said, glancing down at his hand. Her smile lifted a few degrees."What do you remember of that night?"

"Ice scares me," he jerked out, though he desperately wanted to say nothing. Three planets glimmered, but did not disappear.

"Is that all?" Her voice never lifted from its calm plateau. "What do you remember *before* that night?"

He frowned, deeply troubled, almost wishing that it would be better to lose his secret than this exquisite unravelling of his life. "Nothing." It felt like defeat, that single word. "I was in a coma for two weeks. I lost my memory. I don't remember anything."

She smiled widely, which unhinged him in a way only Wenders had done, and it remained there between them, that uplift of her mouth, like a balancing point. The rain fell like a slaughtered army. On the Cabal jumpship, a small running light flicked on and off slowly, misted white through the rain. He didn't know what to make of the sight of the Poor Men huddled beneath the jumpship.

"But I do," she said. "And I can tell you who you were."

"I'm Tower," he said defiantly, glad for that small rallying point to hold her smile at bay, though the building darkness in his belly told him it would not be enough. "I was Blackwell for a while but before that I was Tower. I was always Tower."

She gazed at him for a while. "That's what they call you now. But I know your real name, and I can tell you what you did on that night. I can tell you how you got your head injury."

"How do you know that?" he demanded. "How could you possibly know anything about me?" *None of this made any sense!* The terrain of the conversation shifted under his feet. This woman unbalanced him with her eyes and voice so levelly anchored.

"I know more about you than you do yourself. Your story and mine are bound deep and dark, Tower. Deep and dark."

"Who was I, then?" He was angry now, at powerlessness, at the hollow globe of his history, and at this woman who tantalised him, intrigued him, disgusted him all at once.

She leaned forward and lay the weapon to one side. "You were the best Cabal agent ever."

Blackwell laughed, it was so stupid. "Cabal? That...that's impossible! I was a Poor Man here in Boston!"

"The Second planted you here. A year ago."

He snorted. "The Brotherhood is impenetrable."

"Not any more. Do you remember the Second?"

"No!" But her insistence unsettled him. "All you're saying is impossible! It's just—"

"The Second is the Cabal leader, my—our—master. Surely you remember this."

He shook his head in anger. "No! Of course not!"

"Listen then. You have to hear this. For—"

Unable to read the grimace on her face, though he desperately wanted to, Blackwell shook his head. "Why are you telling me this? You've already wiped out the whole Brotherhood except for us."

And the jasmine woman, who is still to return. "None of this matters any more."

She held up a hand, and her voice was soft when she continued. "All of it matters, or I wouldn't have killed my partner, and I wouldn't be here telling you." She paused, touched the weapon with one hand and drew away.

It occurred to Blackwell that she was not telling him everything. He wanted to touch her then and taste her character on his tongue.

"Do you remember how the Brotherhood came into existence?"

"What? How will that explain what you just did?"

Her smile was faint, but it disturbed Blackwell. "It will, don't worry. Seventeen hundred years ago, the Second laid a curse of hopelessness—"

"Yes, yes, I know all that. Despair first and then suicide. Untreatable. But the Brotherhood had the timeslip and protected humanity behind it for seventeen centuries, unseen, unthanked, unrewarded."

"The greatest and longest sacrifice in human history. No-one could get past the timeslip, not even the Second—no-one except those who knew the five words. It didn't stop him, though. He tried to get agents into the Brotherhood with all kinds of ploys and ruses, but none got past their defences."

Blackwell didn't interrupt. A strange woman, this, and surely crazy, but she was leading to a point, and a ghoulish fascination in him wanted to hear it.

"When the Poor Men uncovered our agents, they dropped them in ten foot square steel boxes thirty meters below ground and left them there. We lost hundreds that way. But then the Second got scared. We found out later he somehow knew about the comet months before it was publicly announced—"

"But why is he so afraid of it? Even if the timeslip protected the Brotherhood from it, it would cause huge devastation. Surely that would be good for the Second."

"No-one knows. It makes no sense at all, but the Second is never wrong. The speculation was that the Brotherhood had—has—something that he wants. What it was, no-one knows, although there was furious debate, and most agreed it was something that would wipe out the Brotherhood forever. A map or a physical item of some kind, a piece of information, or some code hidden in seventeen hundred years of intense secrecy and hatred? Who knows? Why did he wait so long before he decided he wanted it? Most Cabal think that the appearance of the comet was some kind of trigger, unlikely as it sounds. So, anyway, the Second set up an amazingly elaborate insertion to place his best agent into the Brotherhood to hunt down this thing."

"So how did you know this if all your spies were killed?" He was furious, fighting hard just to understand, though one part of the mystery was already frighteningly in place.

"We had a mole."

"Who?"

"That's not important. Just listen." She pointed at him. "*You* were that agent. The best assassin for centuries, the best at everything, far better than anyone except the Second. Complete lack of compassion or mercy for almost everyone, extraordinary ability with weapons, incisive analytic mind, frighteningly good leadership skills, you had it all. Do you remember any of this?"

Blackwell could only stare dumbly, remembering the way he had been able to analyze situations with Book, Ed and Valentina, recognize Cabal weapons, plan tactics and assaults.

"The Second trusted you with so much," she said. "Did you know he had named you as his Third, his most trusted lieutenant? If you failed, he would fail, but if you succeeded and found this secret, the Brotherhood would be destroyed totally."

At that point, though, the assassin's fists clenched. She looked away once and then back, and Blackwell realized something was very wrong with her when he saw her right hand stroke the stock of her weapon, seemingly without her knowing.

"Then all the Second's plans went bad."

And all of mine as well, Mantell thought bitterly. Tower's face was surprisingly calm, as though he had little control over his facial muscles. She could see the moment ahead when he would be faced with the truth, and wondered how he would react. She forced herself back to her task. "It became clear to the Second within seven months or so that his agent was not following orders."

"This would be fascinating if it were true."

"You'll remember. Things changed, all of them around you. You were meant to stay out of sight, but you drew attention. The Patrons started treating you with enormous respect. They said you would one day lead the worldwide Brotherhood. Not only did they give you a Patron's name, which was unheard of for a novice, but they also called you Tower. No-one had ever been called that before. It was enough to enrage and terrify the Second. He became violent, killed his assistants—"

Tower snorted. "That's stupid! How could the top Cabal assassin become the Brotherhood leader?"

How indeed? She had slashed herself many times wondering how such a vile thing could have happened. "Because you were so...so confident. A natural leader, and you hid your violence well. People listened to you. And because your...your heart changed. You...you fell in love with a Brotherhood woman."

Ah. That drew a reaction. His eyes focused. He frowned. His fists bunched, then relaxed. "What was her name?" he said carefully.

"Caroline. The jasmine woman, you called her—"

His head jerked up. "Say it again," he said. His eyes had gone wandering. His right hand twitched, and he didn't seem to notice.

"Caroline."

He paused a moment, as though unable to believe things, then breathed out a long sigh. Mantell, little that she knew of hope, thought all of his hope was in that breath. "Tell me about her." His voice shook.

"She was the daughter of the Patron Book, your mentor. You mentioned her often enough in your reports for the Second to become at first suspicious, then angry, and when your reports began to arrive less frequently, and with less information, and then not at all, he became so furious no-one dared speak to him or enter his presence."

"We stood guard together," murmured Tower absently. His eyes were in different orbits altogether. His whole arm was twitching, and now his leg as well, and Mantell, so unskilled in friendship, felt a great useless hole open inside her. She was so close to achieving what she had so long wanted, but it felt so empty. "The mole wanted to kill you immediately, but the Second stopped him. He ordered an enormous Cabal force to Boston to watch and wait, looking for a security lapse to extract you, but the Brotherhood had closed ranks around you. In the end, it was only luck that turned things. Caroline was assisting in a delivery run two months ago when the sled reactor failed, and a nearby Cabal jumpship swooped. They kidnapped Caroline, unable to believe their fortune, and left a message with the shocked Poor Men to deliver to Book. An agent swap. You for her."

Tower's hand still twitched. He looked like an old man who dribbled, whose lack of muscular control had left him unlovely. His head shook slowly side to side. For a moment, with the rain so massive outside, so formidable in its noise, she feared he would walk out into it, and it would crush him. Then he stood, surprising her for a moment, and although she half-expected him to snatch up a weapon and aim it at her, he held out his hand. "Touch me," he said. His leg jerked like a disabled marionette. She saw his eyes roll back in his head. He staggered a little, regained his footing. She knew he was fighting something and losing badly. "My hand," he whispered. "Please."

Without understanding anything at all, she did. It was smooth, a writer's hand, she thought. It both warmed and repulsed her. Assassins did not touch. They were a breed separate, a cold people. He closed his eyes.

"Are you alright?" She wanted so much to shake him free.

He nodded. "No." He sat down next to her, and his grip on her wrist strengthened, though it was still weak as an infant's.

She watched the twitching in his hand slow, then stop, felt her own heart beat endlessly like a stupid thing, as if it had no grasp on compassion.

His leg stilled. "The trade was in Moscow," he whispered with a quiet firmness. "On a frozen river."

"You know?" The man had steel and depth even in his weakness. He was a different man to the calculating Cabal prodigy she remembered. No longer the arrogant assassin convinced of his own supremacy, the plotter and schemer, the man for whom murder was just work. He had become a man more capable of dealing with difficulties, a leader of note, a man comfortable with himself. His guileless resilience and innocent strength was nothing like the darkness of the bleak spirit that once so polluted her. He had strength he hadn't named yet.

"Ice terrifies me. And…I could smell something about planes. What does that mean?"

She nodded, too amazed to speak for a moment. "The smell… yes, there was an airfield close by. You could smell aviation fuel."

"Tell me what happened."

She could barely hear him over the ferocity of the rain. His presence shielded her from the freezing gusts that blasted in at her legs. She wanted so much to kill him, and didn't know why. His hand became warm in hers. He showed no sign of releasing the pressure on her fingers. "The trade was to take place on the middle of the Moscow River." The truth was easier broken into shorter sentences. She hated every word. The moment was coming, she knew, when he would know the truth, and she hated to think how he would react.

"The Second ordered a sniper perimeter. I was permitted to be in the guard detail on the ice. The Brotherhood sled landed on the ice, turned off the timeslip, and became visible. There was you, Book, three other Patrons, some Poor Men. We had Caroline on our side. The two sides approached. Book was very agitated when he saw his daughter. You stood to one side with two Poor Men. Caroline stood opposite you. You could barely keep your eyes off her. You wanted her, but everyone there knew you weren't going to get her." She knew her next words would be vomit, and wondered where the hope was. "You refused to return. Everyone got edgy. Caroline stood very straight. Cabal fingers on triggers." She settled a little. No future if she could not speak. His hand had warmed, though his grip had lessened a fraction. The rain was planning flood. Though Tower was taking most of the cold gusts, he didn't flinch or move. "The leaders of both sides came to an agreement, and you and Caroline were brought forward for the trade." *Oh, she could see it so clearly!* The strongest of all her memories—breath misting, the Poor Men like chess pieces, the moon cold as a suicide's drowned face, the voice of the Cabal leader sharper than ice splinters. "But then you pulled away. You panicked."

He looked up at that, his face alert though darkened. His grip tightened again. "I panicked." And then, "Blood on the ice," he said quietly, naming the names of his agony. "*Caroline's* blood. A stray Cabal bullet. The smell of planes. Blood on the ice."

"I'm sorry," she said. It surprised her that she was. His hand, so warm against her skin, no longer repulsed her. Even the Second's command eased.

"It was you," he whispered. " You killed Caroline. Not me."

"I killed her." And because she knew so much depended on this moment, she plunged ahead. "It was the only time I…" But she could not bring herself to speak that awful truth.

He let go of her hand and stood. His sweat on her hand cooled. A great, useless hole chasmed inside her, and an angry loss as well. Gusts swept at him. He stumbled to the hatch without shivering. The wind blew back his hair and beyond him, she could see the Poor Men huddled under the jumpship. Pathetic as they were, she barely noticed them.

Tower stood there a very long time. She sat in silence, accepting the cold as due punishment, realizing how much she missed the touch of his hand.

She glanced up at the weapons once, expecting the cool metallic precision of barrels and triggers and gunsights to settle her, as they always had. But her mind was still, balanced, in a way that felt foreign to her. There had been no balance for months for Mantell the assassin. Perilous slopes instead, and all her thoughts since Matilda the kitten had rolled down into a cold granite pit. But now her heart had opened a degree.

Tower turned. His hair blew across his eyes. The dim hold lights made him look old, yellow. "Why are you telling me all this?" he said at last in a voice tight with anguish. "Why did you kill her? What do you get out of this?"

And there it was. Mantell's turning point. It was much worse than she had hoped, but she had to tell him anyway. "We were lovers," she said, feeling the agony of all the old passion and tenderness surfacing alongside the guilt. "Before you entered the Brotherhood. Your name was Robert."

"Lovers!" Blackwell shouted. His laugh was a crazy, abrasive noise. His wet hair flung in wild strands across his face. "Impossible! I loved the jasmine woman—Caroline! You're crazy! This is just ridiculous!" But when he looked inside, hoping to see Caroline's planet still orbiting, it was gone, together with those marked for the smell of planes and ice. Only his ninth armored planet remained.

"Look on your right hand," the woman said quietly.

He held his hand up and glanced at it. "There's nothing on it!" he snapped, but in the hold's dim light, the outline of the patch of darker skin was clearly visible.

She must have seen him looking. "There's a skin graft on it. Under that—and I hope one day you'll remember—was my name. Rebecca. We scarred them together, against all Cabal laws. Romance is forbidden among assassins. When you were inserted into the Brotherhood, we had to get yours removed fast."

"And I suppose you have my name on your hand!" he shouted. Truth or not, he was still furious that she controlled so much, and he was left only to follow.

"I do," she said quietly, removing her glove and extending her hand. "We scarred our names on our palms as a permanent marker of our love."

There it was, inexpertly done, but there nevertheless.

Robert.

Blackwell knew it was true. *Robert.* He had been Robert Tyzach, Cabal assassin. He struggled to keep his feet. A hollow wind screamed through his skull. Reality separated, degree by degree, sight and sound and smell. He staggered, felt sense fade from his nerves, control from his limbs. He fell.

She caught him with arms strong and sure, and eased him down into a sitting position. She touched his face, kissed his cheek, and the touch both restored and sickened him.

"Get away from me!" he grated, his voice a weak defenseless thing. The world contracted down to the cold metal of the hold and the primal rain.

Mantell squeezed her eyes closed. How was it that the urge to kill had become so ferociously urgent, a throbbing compulsion in her head? She had been so clear on trying to get Peter to return. She couldn't call him Robert anymore. There he was in her arms—all she had hoped for, so what obscure part of her brain was rebelling now?

He pulled away from her, stood. That was bad enough, that loss of touch. She blinked. His hand…how she had missed him taking her firmly, the strength in his grip. He used to have such control of life, of people, and a small part of her—hidden deeply with the memory of Matilda, no doubt—just wanted the strength he offered. A shield around her. She had been her own shield since he had been gone, and it just wasn't enough.

He took a step outside into the rain. Within a second, his clothes were dark, his hair slicked down over his face. He didn't wipe it away. Two Poor Men under the jumpship stood and stepped out into the deluge, but Peter waved them back.

He was shivering. She wanted to go out and pull him in, wrap him up and keep him warm, but there was pity in that, and she wanted him to become again the strong man she had known. It was selfish, she knew, all about her needs and desires, but she knew with her assassin patience that she would wait for him. There was nothing for him with the Poor Men. He had to come back.

"How would I have any feelings for a killer?" he said suddenly, with such sharp violence that she flinched. "You even killed your own partner. I can remember Caroline. I have no memories of you."

"But this is your chance!" she snapped, annoyed for losing her temper so easily. *Control,* she told herself, although this needed a much different control to everyday killing.

"Chance for what?" he demanded.

Control be damned! He needed to hear this. "You are not your own man! Can't you see that? You've been controlled, manipulated, lied to! This is your opportunity to get your life back." She stood and threw the disruptor across the hold. Peter might wonder at it, but it would keep quiet the murderous voice in her head that she thought to be either a vengeful and spiritous O'Roarke demonising her or the onset of madness. She did not want to kill Peter, but the urges were strong. *So strong!*

He was focused on her now, she saw. His arms were folded, his face steady. "Keep talking," he said.

So she did, trying to drown out the voice inside. "After the plague hit, you were made to believe that you were the only one remaining, so—"

"I *was* the only one remaining. Ed was killed—you killed him, and the neural virus hit Book and Valentina."

She laughed. "How well you were deceived! It's fortunate for you that I'm here now, or you would never have known." She saw anger and bafflement on his face. "Didn't you wonder why Ed, Valentina and Book were the only three Poor Men whose Scouts weren't hit by the plague?" He nodded carefully, frowning. "Who would have rescued you otherwise? How else would the mole have escaped? We were sure Book would work it out in the end, and maybe he did, but it didn't really matter."

"Betrayed by the mole," he snapped. "But who was it?"

"Ed."

"You killed him!"

"He faked it well."

"His beacon was greyed!"

"Ed the Plumber. Didn't he use that title with you? Good with arteries, pipes or code?" She edged closer, admiring his innocent courage, yet angry at his trust and loyalty and wishing she had it herself.

"He was jealous of your position as Third, and devised most of the plan to eliminate you so he could claim it for himself. He still wants you dead, so much he went against the Second's orders."

Peter stared, his mouth gaping slightly. "Ed?"

"It was Ed who set you up at the Scandinavia Desk at NASAD so you would see the Kavonatur explosion, Ed who got us the Kavonatur access codes and set up the Kavonatur crisis to start things off, Ed who developed the new Scouts and the network that joined them all so that the plague would work, Ed who wrote the signal blocker that convinced you of his death." She smiled, hating herself but wanting his trust and alliance desperately. He shook his head, but she knew he believed her. She could see his anger was gone as he worked it all out.

"And so your master destroys a Brotherhood base, makes almost every Poor Man permanently comatose, and then sends you out to kill me."

She smiled, hoping for warmth rather than a sneer. "No. There was something else we had to do first. Before you fell in love, you found the secret, and the Second wanted it desperately. The trade was intended to get you and the secret back, but Book was furious at the death of his daughter, and tried to kill you. His attack gave you brain damage, but when Ed tried to extract the secret with the new technology he was developing at the time, he made things worse. So O'Roarke was tasked first to extract the secret with Ed's improved device and then kill you."

"But then you recognized me and killed him." He glanced at the disruptor. "So now you can extract the secret, kill me and claim the bounty."

But no, she thought, *that was not it at all.* She almost buckled as she pictured it.

Dreams revealed weakness. But oh, this one was close. So close!

A bungalow on a remote Californian coast somewhere. That would be a good start.

Rows of vegetables in pots, for the dune sand would lack nutrients.

Two bicycles leaned against the wall.

Storms approaching across the gunmetal ocean.

A ginger cat brushing soft figures about their legs. Toby for a male, or Matilda for a female.

Silence as salvation.

And Peter.

Peter as she had imagined him since he had been gone: quiet, as steady as sunrise, whose thoughts occupied whole days, who knew the names of stars and clouds, to whom cats came when called. For him she would unstopper her mother's perfume and dab some on her wrists.

For him, she would abandon her weaponry.

Although, should the Melcassar Comet hit, it would not really matter. Then they would both stand on the dunes and watch the horizon for a vertical pillar of fire come punishing the sky one otherwise clear day, stripping it of color and air. And then she would resist tears, gather up the kitten, and they would go down to the water together, watching for the billion tonnes of seawater to immerse their tears. One last kiss for Mantell.

"I don't care for the secret, whatever it is. I've had enough of killing. But if we can fool the Second, we can claim the bounty—"

"We?"

And there it was. One last chance for Mantell the assassin. "I want you to come back to me. You loved me once. Maybe you will again. We could have it all." But then, before he could reply, a sudden and overwhelming urge clamored violent and loud in her head.

Kill the target.

Much as she tried to silence it, this time there was no escaping its power. How had she ever believed she could have him back? She was an assassin—it seemed so clear! Kill the Poor Man now, and get her rewards. A place in Cabal legend, for certain. The unending awe of her peers. She grimaced and glanced down at the weapons. Kill the target now.

But killing him would rob her of so much! She bit hard on her tongue, hoping for the sharp slash of pain to silence the awful compulsion.

Kill him. Kill him now.

She clamped her eyes closed—this made no sense. She moved to kick the disruptor away, but instead saw her hand, like a wild creature, grabbing it. The metal felt cool and wonderful and right under her fingers…

Blackwell's pulse raced. The assassin's eyes were squinched shut, her mouth a tightly wound spring, her weapon-reaching fingers fisted, clutched to her side.

Disease or madness. Either would be enough to swing her hand onto the disruptor and aim it at him. Whatever she had said, she was clearly insane, and he was only two steps from the hatch. Enough, he thought, to bolt, hoping he could outrun the green hissing fire, warn the Poor Men, and get them all safely inside the House.

The ridged grip of the disruptor almost made Mantell cry out with pleasure. Oh, it was so good to become the sniper, so right! The unseen killer on a rooftop, on a hill, in a hide. The power of it! One sweep to end this fool's life and get what was hers by right. Wealth beyond measure. All that pathetic nonsense about getting him back was nothing more than fantasy. She was Mantell of the Cabal. 5614 kills. No-one would ever come back to her. No point in even asking. *Kill him now.*

The Poor Man was scrambling to his feet as she swung the disruptor around towards him and thumbed on the fuel activator. The weapon vibrated like a rousing hound. She sighted and aimed, all her senses cold and precise.

Blackwell was already leaping towards the hatch when Paul came blundering into the hold, yelling like a maniac, rain spitting off him, smelling like wet wool and leather and great masculine courage. It was enough to put the assassin off her shot. As Blackwell tried to shove Paul out of the path of the disruptor, Paul leaped on top of the assassin, arms swinging like blunderbusses, and knocked the disruptor out of her grip. She collapsed under his weight as Benedict and the other Poor Men charged into the hold. The disruptor clattered onto the hold floor, unfired.

Without concern for her, Paul and Benedict tied the assassin spread-eagled to the hold fixing points, facing the grey steel wall. Blood stood out from her wrists where the rope bit, but she made no sound. She turned her cheek to the wall, her unblinking eyes steady.

"Thank you," said Blackwell to Paul and Benedict. Panic would have been so easy, but he was not that man anymore. There was not only the debt of honor to Book, but also, he realized, to himself. To the man he once was.

"What happened?" yelled Thomas, his gaze flicking from the assassin to Blackwell to the disruptor. Rain puddled off the Poor Men on the bare metal floor.

"She tried to kill Tower," gritted Paul, tying the last knot around her booted ankle.

"Then why tie her up?" Thomas demanded. Blackwell saw him glancing at the disruptor and realized that Thomas was only two steps to the weapon to his four. No-one else stood nearby, and though Poor Men did not bear weapons, Blackwell realized, neither had they been in such a situation as this.

"Seal her!" Thomas' yelled, his voice cracking. "Leave her to rot!"

"No." Blackwell took two steps to stand between Thomas and the assassin. "She stays alive."

The assassin's eyes closed at that and her shoulders relaxed a little, as much as was possible with the ropes holding her up. The Poor Men made no sound at all.

"Then why did she try to kill you?" Thomas's face was red in the dim glow."You're making as much sense as her!"

"Don't doubt the word of a Poor Man," said Paul, shaking his head slowly. He still had a length of rope dangling from one hand.

"It's not his word I'm doubting!" snapped Thomas. "It's hers, and his wisdom for believing it. She tried to kill you, Tower!" Thomas clenched his fists. "Set her free and she'll kill us all!"

Blackwell held his position. "She stays tied. But she's not going into a chamber. She knows something we need."

"She knows nothing!" Thomas snapped. "Whose dream is this?"

"The Second." When they hesitated, he jabbed a finger at them and yelled, "Your enemy, Poor Men! Your enemy is afraid of us! He thinks I can break the curse!"

"Nothing of this earth can break the curse!" Paul snarled. "And how could the Second be afraid of anything? He has everything—an unbreakable curse, incredible riches, enormous control over so much. How could he possibly be afraid of a few Poor Men? He's not even human…he's a level outside humanity. He's untouchable! There's no fighting that sort of power. Not in this world, anyway. And that's not even the point! All he has to do is wait! In eleven days, when the Father Nick's Day gifts don't arrive, the curse will prevail, and millions—hundreds of millions—will kill themselves. Whatever he's wanted all these centuries, he'll get. The story ends."

"So why send..." Blackwell couldn't bring himself to say her name, "her and her partner out after us to kill us all?"

"After *you*, Poor Man," said Benedict. "I'd like to point out that I'm not on the Second's screens."

"Because, whatever the Second has, there's something he still hasn't got. And we have it. So she won't get sealed until we know what that is. We'll leave her here for the night under guard. I'll stand the first watch." Not that he wanted to. He did not want to speak to her or hear anything she would say, and the thought of three hours seeing the assassin spread out on the wall like a sacrifice disturbed him deeply. But he had spoken.

The rain drummed, its own loud silence. Benedict adjusted his collar with quick movements. In the dim hold light, shadows stood watch on his face. "I'll stand the second."

Paul coiled rope with snapping actions. "The third."

Benedict nodded toward the hatch, his face expressionless. "Poor Men, you are dismissed."

Thomas stared, though his stare flicked at least once to the disruptor. "Dismissed? That's it?" Benedict gestured to the hatch, but the voice that spoke next was not his.

"No," said the assassin, her voice muffled partly by the metal wall. "That's not it. Everyone stay here. I'm not done yet."

"Done?" echoed Thomas in a mad snort. "How could you not be done?"

"I will need a blanket soon," said the assassin softly. "Would one of you be so kind as to fetch one?"

"What for?" demanded Thomas, but on a nod from Blackwell, Benedict ran up and fetched one while the Poor Men stared in silence.

"Could you please lay it on the floor near my feet?" she asked, and Benedict did, then stepped back. "Thank you. Now, Tower, would you come here, please?"

Without looking at anyone, Blackwell went to her quickly, scanning the ropes around her hands and feet for any signs of loosening. All four were tight. The Poor Men certainly knew their knots. He wished fervently he could read the grimaces on her face. He wondered what colors and shapes were in her head.

She waited until he had moved close and whispered, "Don't trust me. I think I'm going mad. I wanted to kill you before, but now I don't. Before the madness hits again, I..." She closed her eyes. "Listen, I...the Second has betrayed us both. I...I want to join you."

She grimaced as though in pain, but then her eyes cleared, her face relaxed, and light opened out of tight darkness. Her smile was so gentle Blackwell almost trusted it.

"So you can betray us from within?" he hissed in frightened astonishment.

"We have to find out why the Second is afraid of you and this comet!" Her breath smelled of old strangely sweet fruit. "Help me here. No-one's going to like what happens next." Her voice strengthened. "Poor Men, I have left the Cabal, and I wish to become one of you."

"Lies!" Thomas shouted.

"As a sign of my goodwill," said the assassin slowly, "I am going to show you how to disable the disruptor. Bring it to me, please."

Blackwell glanced back. Thomas was a step closer to the disruptor, though Benedict was standing next to him, watching him. Blackwell strode over, grabbed the weapon and moved back, watching Thomas. The tight grit of his mouth and his narrow stare was clear and obvious, even to someone who could not read faces. He took the disruptor back to the assassin. Thomas muttered. The Poor Men were silent.

The assassin's voice was clear. "Place the stock in my right hand."

Instantly, Thomas stepped forward. "No! She will kill us all!"

"I cannot even see you, Poor Man," she said loudly, "let alone aim with only one hand and facing away. But the disruptor is keyed to me alone to prevent tampering, so you will not be able to disable it unless I am holding it."

Blackwell placed it in her hand. This was crazy, although he realized that everything since the explosion in Finland had been crazy, a mad, unrelenting distortion of reality.

The assassin gripped the stock tightly. The tendons in her wrist stood out. Blackwell kept the weapon pointing to the ceiling and away from anyone. Her voice was calm. "Just forward of the trigger housing on the underside of the barrel is a recessed panel. Find that first."

Even in the dim hold light, it was easy to see. "Got it."

"On the left and right of the panel are two sliders. One moves front to back, the other the reverse. Place your fingers on them."

"Done."

"Move and click them into position at the same time. Keep your palm under the panel."

Blackwell moved the sliders until some internal mechanism clicked and disengaged. A small metallic cylinder dropped neatly into his hand, cool and light and silver. "What next?"

"Get it out of my sight," said the assassin, releasing her grip and slumping a little in her restraints.

Blackwell dropped it into a pocket and took the weapon from her now-loose hand. "What is this part?"

"The fuel activator. Without it, the weapon's only good for bludgeoning you to death." She raised her voice. "Poor Men, to prove that I have renounced killing forever, there is one more thing you must do. Leader, I do not know your name, but I must ask you to swear on everything that is sacred to the Brotherhood that you will do what I say."

Blackwell leaned forward slightly. "Without telling me first what it is?"

"You must. I will not harm you, I swear it."

"You will have to offer more sureties than that, assassin. You can't expect us to believe someone with your history."

"O'Roarke placed blast canisters in the hangar while we were here. If you remove my chrono, you will see how much time remains of the hundred minutes they were set for. My guess is about four minutes. If you do not do what I say, we will all die."

Blackwell gestured to Benedict, who removed the chrono from the assassin's wrist. "Three minutes fourteen," he said.

The mental chronometer behind Blackwell's eyes began incrementing. Without hesitating, he said, "Very well. What do you want?"

Standing as he was near the assassin, Blackwell saw the way her eyes slumped closed, her breathing quickened, and the soft shapes of her faces became grey and pained. He wished he knew what she was thinking. Children read faces better than him.

"Strip me," she said in little more than a whisper, her eyes closed.

Blackwell stared stupidly. "Strip you? Remove your…your clothes?"

"Everything. I am an assassin. I want to join you, but you will not trust me unless I surrender everything. Neither will I have any bargaining power if I tell you first where the blast canisters are. Take all my weapons from me, then search me thoroughly, then toss my weapons into one of your pits."

Benedict laughed. "We shall do no such thing! You are a woman—such actions are unseemly at best and vile at worst!"

It was like walking along a cliff at night for Blackwell, screamed at by fierce relentless ghosts and the banshee wind. He felt his mind retreat into his head, counting two minutes fifty-seven, fifty-six, fifty-five and smelling the bright pink of swirling madness. He breathed to regain steadiness and heard the assassin's voice again.

"As was the Cabal's destruction of your Finnish base and the shutdown of almost your entire Brotherhood." She was as calm as when she began. "These are vile times, Poor Man. Adjust."

Benedict took a step forward. "And if we do not, you will allow your explosive devices to detonate?"

"Yes."

Benedict shook his head. "You want to be humiliated?"

"These are vile times, Poor Man."

Blackwell said aloud, desperately, "Two minutes forty-seven."

"How long to defuse your devices?"

"A second, maybe two."

Blackwell flicked both hands as though shaking off blood. "Very well," he said and stepped forward.

He worked alone for the most part. None of the Poor Men moved, not even Thomas. Most of them closed their eyes. The rain quietened. Blackwell's motions were sharp and efficient. He removed her glove, boots, sheaths and holsters. With a knife he found in one, he cut along the seams of her jumpsuit, nicking the skin below her ribs. Blood welled and dripped. She flinched, but her eyes remained open. Benedict counted aloud until Blackwell commanded silence.

An array of weaponry grew on the floor: a mid-sized Stewart laser, three knives, two stubby pistols, six blast canisters and other smaller hand-made objects, personal favorites, Blackwell guessed. From pockets on the inside lining of her jumpsuit came two stilettos, a coil of wire and two flat barbed disks.

"Thirty one seconds," he told himself. The assassin had not moved. Her eyes were open, unblinking, and fixed on the hold ceiling, like a child waiting for the dentist's drill.

"It's done," said Blackwell loudly, turning away from her. "Defuse your devices."

"Press the top right and bottom left buttons on my chrono simultaneously," the assassin said.

The chrono. Benedict fumbled for it in his pocket, could not find it.

Blackwell gritted, "Benedict!"

It was on the floor, next to the helmet. Benedict grabbed it, aligned it as Blackwell counted, "Nine eight seven…"

And pressed both buttons.

And in the lovely silence after zero, Rebecca closed her eyes.

London

Without a chair or anywhere to sit, Ed stood, oddly sustained by nothing more than smoke and the presence of the Second. Without warning or sound, and in a swirl of smoke and industrial stink, the Second stood up next to him.

Ed bit down a cry, sure death was imminent. No-one had ever seen the Second stand. It had the feel of urgent violence. Smoke billowed, then sucked in towards him in a tight vortex, as dense and perilous as a gas planet. His heart thudding, Ed dared not look at the space on the sofa where the Second had sat for as long as anyone could remember. It was sacrilegious to be standing next to the Second, almost as though they were *equals*. He held his breath and his words, deeply disturbed, and waited, either for a tortuous death or his next command.

"Good, good," the Second whispered, in a tone of quiet, almost-thoughtful malice. "She has gained his trust now. Time for the jumpships."

Ed realized the Second was facing Boston, almost as though he could see across the wasted British fields and Atlantic. "She will surely kill him now, sir."

The Second paused for a moment, then turned and stretched out his hand in a graceless motion, all snakelike limbs, seemingly without joints. "Ah, my beloved and disobedient traitor," he said, in a voice that Ed almost thought gentle. "Come here, that I may punish you."

"Punish?" croaked Ed. One did not escape the room of the Second, once in.

"Did you doubt it? There could only be punishment for your treachery and desire to kill. I cannot trust you now, and you cannot remain here to watch my victory in Boston." He beckoned. "So come. I have something to give you."

Ed could only think, strangely, since he had not remembered his family for many years, of his father, a mean-spirited alcoholic whose favorite pastime had been abuse. Alien though the Second was, as far from humanity as it was possible to be, Ed took a step towards him, feeling both relief and a ghastly hollow affection. Someone was surgically extracting his conscience, and he almost welcomed it.

Under the hand of the Second, he halted. It rested above his head. No-one had ever been touched by the Second and lived, he was sure of it.

"You will need this," said the Second, softly, almost regretfully. And lowered his fingers to rest upon the head of Edward Harrison, once, but no longer, human.

Boston House

"Dump all her weapons in a pit," Blackwell ordered Arthur and Thomas. "Leave the laser. And check the screens for any jumpship movement." He showed Benedict how to use the laser in case her killing urge struck again, then draped the blanket over her nakedness, trying not to look at her. Her legs were pale. He looked no higher, sure that he had at one point. What kind of man had he been? What had he done with or to her?

Benedict was standing in the hatchway. The other Poor Men had gone into the House. He cut her bonds and helped her down, holding the blanket in place. She seemed placid enough, though he had no doubt her insanity would strike whether she was naked or not.

He placed the pillow on the metal floor, next to the pile of blankets the Poor Men had made up. She lay down on it, the blanket wrapped tightly. He wasn't sure how he felt about it—he certainly felt no intimacy for her in that moment, not even a hint of feeling. He realized that he had never thought about his own emotions. Apart from his awkward boyish feelings for Kay the librarian, he might as well have been alone in the world. Not that any of Rebecca's talk of love matterered. Almost everything he had hoped for was gone.

"You'll sleep on the floor tonight, locked in here alone," he told her. "I'll be on watch outside."

When he stepped out and locked the hatch, though, Benedict said, "Sleep, Tower. Poor Men will take your watches. You've done enough. I'll see you in the morning."

Blackwell was too tired to argue, but he had one task before sleep.

The downpour was heavy enough, as a weary Blackwell walked through it, to float the House loose of its moorings and drift it off into a private universe somewhere. He wondered what the Poor Men would do if they were forced into the world, how any of them would survive. Inside the House, he found and lit a lantern and climbed the staircase to where he knew Book's room would be. It was empty but neat, and there on a low wooden table, alongside a candle and book and some folded white linen, were two hand-painted pictures. One was a thin-faced though smiling woman, her greying hair swept back. Book's wife. He did not know her name, though he realized she was either a victim of the neural virus or had died earlier. Grief either way. But the second picture showed two younger women. Blackwell picked it up and studied it closely. One woman was dark-haired and Blackwell didn't recognize her. The other, though, had auburn hair, and her blue eyes were radiant. Blackwell's heart stumbled in strange lovely ways.

The jasmine woman. She who had loved him. His scant store of images swelled—standing guard with her, smelling her perfume, and then more!—touching her face, stroking her hair, laughing with her. But she was dead at the hands of a Cabal assassin. In Moscow. He didn't even know where she had been buried. He sucked in a great, shuddering, hopeless breath.

With careful loving movements, he replaced the portrait on the table. Then he took out his jar of jasmine oil, carried across oceans and continents, and opened it. The scent, so rich with memory and once-hope, nearly buckled his knees. He took some on his finger and gently dabbed it on her mouth. One last kiss for Caroline, the jasmine woman.

And Robert the Cabal assassin, the novice Poor Man, Blackwell the NASAD watcher, and Tower the leader of few, wept for what he could never have.

Then he closed the jar, placed it on the table next to her picture and went out. He shut the door and leaned on it. "Enough," he said.

When he went downstairs and into the common room, the smell of stew and coffee was too rich for the abandonment and loss he felt. Surely it was another universe he was in. A bed had been prepared for him in a corner. He barely smelled lavender in the pillow before sleep overwhelmed him.

Father Nick's Day minus ten days
Boston House

Blackwell woke to urgent voices. "Tower, Cabal jumpships on their way! Ten of them just left London on a direct route for the House!" It was Benedict, with Calvin and William carrying lanterns.

Still night, Blackwell thought.

"How long?" Blackwell recognized Benedict's voice.

"Seven hours! Everyone's in the sled."

Blackwell came to instant alertness, and was aligning patterns, possibilities and events even as he sat up. "Where's Rebecca?" he said.

Benedict raised an eyebrow. "You're on first name terms already?"

We were lovers. We killed every day and laughed about it afterwards. There was no justice with love, memory or weaponry. "Where?"

"Still locked up in the cargo hold. Come on, we have to leave now!"

"Not yet. There's still time to escape, don't worry, but I've got something to do first."

Benedict flung up his hands. "You're insane! The Cabal have the access codes and five words—they've penetrated the timeslip—Father Nick's Day is history! Ten jumpships are on their way. So—"

"So we have to find and crack the secret in my head now."

"Haven't you heard? Nothing of this earth can stop the curse! Get into the sled!"

"Listen—if we leave, we'll stay alive, but then the jumpships will arrive and destroy the House and the secret inside it, and we'll lose everything." Blackwell paused. It was a terrible risk, but the other option was worse. "Get Rebecca some clothes and bring her here. I need Rebecca now."

"What for?"

"She's got the machine to get the secret out."

William frowned. "What machine?"

"The Second gave her partner orders to extract the secret with a machine and then kill me. The equipment is still in the jumpship." He started for the door, his stomach groaning with hunger, and found an apple on the way.

Calvin hesitated. "You've thought this through?"

"I have. Tell the Poor Men what's happening. We'll be with you soon. Benedict, come with me. Get the laser. If she threatens in any way, take out her legs first. I don't want her dead yet."

Inside the jumpship, the device contained cables, something that looked like an ugly audio headset without speakers and a control box. By lamplight, Blackwell considered them while Benedict kept the laser trained on Rebecca's legs. She ran her fingers carefully across the control box until she found a recessed panel. Benedict waved the laser. "Know how to use it?"

"I can try. I've never seen anything like this before, though." She took the components carefully from the case and laid them on the floor. Benedict moved his hand to the Power button, but Rebecca pushed him roughly away. "Not yet! For someone who's been hidden for seventeen hundred years, you're amazingly stupid. Stand back!" Benedict stood back, his face even while Rebecca glared.

"OK," she said, looking back to the device. "OK." For the next few minutes, she examined every part carefully, laying out cables near their sockets, inspecting the helmet, checking every indicator and switch on the control box.

Benedict shuffled his feet. "Yes? Is it safe to use?"

She was silent for a moment. Her hair fell across her eyes. "Should be," she said slowly, "if it's disconnected from the jumpship systems. The Second knows everything about every jumpship; it's as though he's hardwired in. So we'll stay clear of that." She sat back. "Power supply here for field operations away from the jumpship, good for ten hours standby, two hours full usage, headset connects to the control box here." She pointed. "Audio recorder and storage here for later transmission back to base. Compact, efficient, unique. Could be the only one of its kind."

"Can we disable the recorder," asked Blackwell, "in case it ever gets back to the Second?"

"Not without recircuiting. But this won't get back."

"That's a Cabal assassin speaking?" asked Benedict.

"A defector," she said carefully. "And as soon as you have your curse-breaking secret, it won't matter anyway. The war will be over, the curse broken, the Second's power ended."

And you'll have the man you always wanted. Though Blackwell wasn't sure what he felt about that.

"So when you're ready, Tower, we'll start." She slipped the headset on Blackwell, clicked in the cables from the headset to the control box, and rested her finger on the power button. "OK?"

"Wait," said Blackwell.

"What?" said Benedict. "This was your idea, so what's the delay?"

Blackwell ripped off the headset. "You said that this was for use in the field."

"So?"

"And if you were in the field, at some distance from the jumpship on a critically important mission—such as this one—I doubt that the Second would want to wait for you to get back to the jumpship to transfer the information and send it."

"So?"

"So there has to be a transmitter built in. As soon as you power up, any data it produces will be automatically sent to the Second. Even if we powered it up to see how it worked, it would send a signal. And there's also a failsafe or tamper alert somewhere, so we won't even be able to disable it."

Benedict leaned across and pulled out the cables. "And you knew it was there, assassin. Nice try. You were right. As soon as you have our curse-breaking secret, it won't matter at all."

Blackwell reached out a hand. "Let it go, Benedict. She didn't know anything about this."

"And you believe her?" demanded Benedict. "You believe the word of a Cabal assassin?"

I was Cabal myself once. "She's telling the truth."

"You're very sure of that."

"I can taste character when I touch skin. She tastes of limes for telling the truth. You taste salty for gentleness."

Benedict just stared and shook his head slowly. "I'm not even going to take that thought any further. Alright. I'll accept that, for the moment, though this box is going to be sealed in the Pit. So. The world is balancing on something in your skull that you don't remember. If the Second gets it, disaster. If we get it, we can restore hope, even if Father Nick's Day is gone forever. But the device that would allow us to extract it is rigged. The jumpships are on their way. We have ten days before Father Nick's Day, a comet is heading for possible Earth impact, and we have no timeslip, no protection, no weapons, thirteen men and an assassin who tastes of limes." He stood. "Sleds are waiting, Poor Man."

They left the extraction device in the jumpship, locked it down and headed across the cobbled courtyard to the waiting sled.

"How much time?" said Benedict.

"Six hours thirty-nine."

"Paul is thinking we should put down somewhere close by, go to minimal 'slip, like you did before, and wait. He wants to set watchers along the river inside the boundary in case the jumpships penetrate, and some outside as well."

Something stirred in Blackwell's head. "River."

"We need to see what they're planning. We can't go too far away or it will be impossible to get back in."

"Muddy river," said Blackwell, with rising realisation, "cobbled courtyard, city and freeway, sounds of sleds taking off and landing." He halted, scanned around. "Stop! It's here."

"Jumpships are coming, Poor Man."

"No, no, this is the place! This is the ninth planet!"

Benedict hesitated. "More detail, please, and quickly."

"I first thought these symbols were pointing me to Boston, where I would find the curse-breaker. When I got here, I recognized them, and realized I was in the right place. But I misread them! They were more than pointers—they were showing me where to start looking for the curse-breaker!"

Benedict stared. "Here? In this courtyard?"

"This is the start point!" He pointed out to the jumpship hatch to the pre-dawn courtyard. "River, courtyard, freeway, city—I just need to hear a sled taking off to complete the picture. Get the Poor Men to lift off, quickly!"

Benedict was already running for the hangar.

A few moments later, a hatch slammed and reactor swelled into full power. Benedict raised an acknowledging hand from the cockpit.

Blackwell pulled Rebecca back from the ascent zone and blast of air and waited, his whole focus on his armored planet, his internal analytic mechanisms alert to even the slightest change in its brightness or surface.

It didn't take long. The sled was only thirty meters off the ground when his ninth planet pulsed once and shivered slightly. Then the armored casing around the top and bottom poles of the planet disengaged and retracted, revealing nothing but a wonderful clear brightness.

Blackwell gasped. His heart clamoring, he zoomed in towards the bright space it had left. And there, in letters that only glowed for a few seconds, then faded, was the image of a machine. He barely heard his own voice speaking out the word.

But Rebecca did. "A machine?"

Blackwell shuddered back into the world, though his private solar system was far more alluring than the cool of the night.

"A machine? That's the curse breaking secret? What kind of machine? Or were you thinking of the extraction device?"

Blackwell shivered as focus returned. "No, not that one. Maybe Benedict will know."

"How can a machine be the curse breaker?" Benedict said when he landed the sled and ran to them. "Nothing of this earth can break the curse."

"The Poor Men aren't of this earth," said Blackwell. "And neither is the timeslip, which would mean—"

"Sled reactors, but—"

"But there are hundreds of those! It would take us ages to check every one."

"Wait wait," said Benedict. "Tower, have you seen a reactor?"

"Yes, on my—"

"And you felt nothing? No blinding lights?"

"No."

"So it's not that, luckily for us. Which only leaves one machine. Follow me." And he led them at a run into the House and down several flights of stairs into the same deep basement that contained the modern timeslip reactor. Benedict pushed open the further wooden door, and led them into a tiny room where an ancient platform stood.

Upon it, brassy and shiny with the patina of ages, with a bewilderment of pipes, valves and glass-screened counters like an ancient steam engine, stood a machine marked with a card. 'Device for the Retarding of Time.'

Blackwell didn't even need to turn his senses inward to where his armored planet glimmered faintly in his now darkened solar system. A thrill of color flared behind his eyes. He staggered back, his armored planet shivering slightly, shedding further lines of latitude until only the middle half of the planet was still armored, and revealing, amidst a flare of brightness, a single brief image. He knew then there were only two clues left.

Strong hands on his shoulders. Potato breath.

"It's a book," he gasped.

"A book?" said Rebecca.

Benedict spun him around. "Details, please. Description, name, cover."

"I only saw it briefly. It was open, so I couldn't see the cover."

"Title? Did you see any words?"

"Nothing."

"Look again."

But even when Blackwell turned inward, Benedict's outline shimmered and faded, and the beautiful geometry of his inner solar system surrounded him, the image of the book on the planet's surface became no clearer.

Blackwell concentrated everything on the two darkened pages he saw, but if there were any words on them, they were unreadable. Nothing brightened the surface. Just two pages, old and yellowed. "Nothing, but if I can unlock this one, there's only one more clue to go."

"But how can you unlock a book you can't identify? It could be any book and there will be thousands here! None of us are from Boston, either, so we can't help you. Unless you can identify the book, we have to get out of here."

"But if we do, we won't be able to get back in!"

"There's no choice here, Poor Man. The jumpships aren't coming for a tea party. We stay here, we die." Benedict started towards the stairs.

Perth motel room

Edward Harrison, once-human, stood in the middle of his cheap motel room, waiting. After his banishment from the presence of the Second, he found he was unable to sit or lie down. Though he had looked forward so much to a glass of water and some pasta, those items remained untouched on the bedside table. Instead, in an attempt to match the Second's vile fume he now so desperately missed, fifty cigarettes burned in ashtrays around the room with the windows closed, which provided a kind of ghastly comfort, though Ed knew he could never match the Second's acrid fog. He could feel his humanity leaching out of him like sweat, and could not tell if it disturbed him.

How the Second's hand had stung his flesh as the power of the knowledge of the curse had passed into him! As he had screamed in ferocious agony, the cloud around the Second eased a little and he saw—perhaps the only human ever to have done so and lived—the whole face of the Second consider him with a kind of hungry, yearning pleasure.

And then the curse had swept through him in an rush, infecting even those parts of him that disease could not reach, changing the color of his blood, staining his character. The dim remnants of his childhood and youth drowned under its fabulously vile wickedness. After that, he did not sleep for days, and realized he might never again. He might never eat, laugh, drink or even die at all, he realized with a feral thrill. Only the last dim and weak unpolluted portion of his spirit protested at his surrender and the almost constant agony, but the riches he would gain were compensation enough for the loss of one mere spirit. He was Third of the Cabal, only one degree below the Second. There was a lot to be said for power, especially as the curse made his flesh impenetrable to harm of any kind. So attuned to the presence of the Second, he picked up the phone even before it rang.

"Go to the home of the boychild," the Second said. "Something will happen there soon. Tell me."

Camden Post Office, Perth

George stood at the counter, staring at the—finally—empty post office. Nothing settled him any more. All his music and books slowed him down and gave him time to think, but thinking was a dangerous thing these days. And every time the phone rang, he looked around for someone else to answer it, his heart going like the clappers. The loss of Harker had just about shot his confidence. He had never thought he would be an Early, but the thought had taken hold in him. Not the spirit-blackening sickness of the Earlies, but life had seemed pretty dark lately.

He jumped when his Scout beeped and knocked over his coffee, sure he had wet himself. It was a text message. Strange. He rarely received any. He fumbled for his glasses, slipped them on, and read in growing amazement as the coffee spread over the desk, reaching muddy brown fingers over his daily summary report and dripping onto his shoes. George pushed papers out of the way, and the coffee puddle just followed. *Come to my house,* the message read. Nothing amazing about that. But it was the sender that baffled and frightened him. John Smith. Harker's four year old autistic godson.

He blinked. Suddenly the coffee became much less important.

A car horn outside made him jump. When he looked out past the Australia Post posters advertising a sale for highlighter pens, DVDs and photocopy paper, it was Frank, waving madly.

George stuffed the report into a drawer, flicked lights off and security on and locked up, then couldn't remember if he had, so he turned back and rattled the door handle twice to make sure. His pulse skittered as he climbed into the car.

"Did you get it too?" blurted Frank, waving his Scout. "John's text?"

George had difficulty in framing words, let alone getting them out. "Yeah, but how? How did—"

"Dunno, mate, but come on, he wants us there."

"Yeah, but why? The kid hasn't spoken a word, and here he is sending text messages? Is this some kind of joke?" This was a couple of steps the other side of bizarre. This was the stuff of the sort of late night movies he laughed about after, but secretly enjoyed.

"Joke? Not the kind of joke Zack and Liz would play. I thought it was some kind of Scout spam —after all, John Smith's a common kind of name—but he sent a map as well, just to make sure we got it right." He waved his Scout under George's nose.

George snatched the Scout, more bewildered than annoyed. Four-year-old autistic kids weren't meant to impact his world at all. They were just peripheral, an object of compassion and sympathy, but certainly not mystery. But as they rounded the corner into Myles Street, where Zack and Liz lived, mystery turned into near-impossibility. Half a dozen or so TV vans huddled like cancer cells around the Smith house and white cars with government plates, no less, were parked diagonally across council verges like a roadblock. TV antennas forested the air.

Frank sat forward with a jolt. "What the—? They're parked outside Zack and Liz's house," said Frank, all the tone stripped out of his voice. "That's Zack's Toyota out the front."

As well as more TV technicians than either of them had ever seen in one place before, doing things with cables and headphones and Scouts neither of them had any capacity of understanding. All the major networks were there, as well as the local and national newspapers, and...George stared. *Surely that wasn't CNN and the BBC!*

They parked fifty meters away. Frank strode ahead with a grim determination that George found faintly revolting. *First to a train wreck,* he thought. *Gruesome bugger.* No-one stopped them, though

George half suspected as he followed that Frank would whip out his postie's ID and bluff everyone.

Surprisingly, the media scrum at the door parted for them. Some bloke in a suit and tie and half a face of powder asked them who they were. The powder appliers waited with their brushes.

"Friends of the family," said Frank in a voice that would have sunk battle cruisers. "Thanks," and without waiting for permission, he elbowed his way through.

The entry hall was warehoused with body odour and female perfumes as TV techs and personalities passed through. The wall-papered walls carried wedding photos of Zack in a chocolate brown suit and white ruffled shirt, grinning with all his new groom's wide-mouthed energy at the camera. Liz's smile radiated out through her skin and the fall of hair across her forehead. George had never been able to name the serenity in her eyes, and he didn't try now.

A strong grab on his forearm stopped Frank as he tried to edge his way around a wide moveable screen that blocked off the lounge room entrance. It belonged to a tall young man with a black T-shirt that read, 'Drooling is not a character flaw.' He had dreadlocks, headphones around his neck and a fistful of devices, one of which was a microphone. His aftershave blasted a path ahead of him. "Can't let you in, sorry."

"Friends of the family," said Frank.

The tech's chuckle told George what he thought of old fellas. "Sure you are, but no go. They're recording for a worldwide audience in there—it's a closed set."

Frank grabbed the tech's arm and yanked him outside onto the porch. George had half a mind to cheer, but decided wisely against it. His old mate had all the ferocity of a wronged husband."We're not trying to get on TV, you understand me?" he hissed. "You comprehend my meaning? We've. Been. Invited." The tech's face had the color of faded bedsheets on a clothesline all of a sudden. He blinked, possibly more amazed at the grunt in the old coot's bicep and fingers than anything. "I can show you the text message with the invitation," Frank said more pleasantly. "I'm sure you wouldn't want to be the one who refused us entry."

The tech found his voice. "Sure, but you still can't go in." He disengaged his arm and flexed his shoulder, though George saw no signs of the grimacing he was hoping for. "Not unless you've got a letter of intro from the station boss."

Frank paused, glanced over the tech's shoulder. "And what's suddenly so flamin' important about a four year old autistic kid? Or his parents?" The tech was silent. "Eh?" Frank jabbed his finger at the word 'Drooling.' "Never mind two old codgers just trying to do the right thing—what are *you* doing here?"

The tech stared. "Haven't you heard? The autistic kid's a painter, and everyone's wanting to see his paintings. The whole world, in fact."

"Paintings?" echoed Frank dubiously.

"Abstracts, mate, though some have got roads in 'em. He started when the comet was announced."

"He's autistic!" hissed George. "He's got two chances of the world watch him do anything—none and Buckley's! He doesn't do anything except rock back and forward! He doesn't even know what a crayon is, let alone paint! So cut the bulldust—what are you really doing here?"

The tech jerked his head towards the front door. His face was deadly serious. "Filming the kid paint a picture of the comet."

The silence was suddenly very loud to George. Frank sagged a little. "He's...the...he can't...the comet?"

The tech scratched his unshaven chin. He softened a little. It could have been a smile turning up the corners of his mouth. George thought perhaps he might not be such a bad bloke after all. "You know when they first announced the comet was coming?" the tech said.

"Yeah."

"Remember what you were doing?"

"At work, mate. What's your point?"

The tech jerked a thumb. "The kid changed dramatically, his mum said. Got busy all of a sudden, couldn't sleep, wouldn't eat. Started painting."

"Painting?"

"He painted this amazing picture showing the path of the comet and other technical data. So accurate it shocked his folks and they contacted the local news. Scientists checked it out, couldn't believe it, especially when they heard it was a four year old autistic kid. Now he's going to paint another one, news got around and everyone's here with cameras."

George was furious and frightened. "He's...that's impossible, you stupid mongrel! He can't do anything, let alone paint!"

"His folks have been told to keep quiet on all this up to now, so you wouldn't have heard. But there's something going on in the kid's head, and we're all here to find out what." He looked over his shoulder, paused as though deciding, scratched his nose and looked back. "Look," he said quietly. "I'll get you in so long as you don't speak. Stand in the corner and not a word, you hear? After we're done, you can see the parents." When George and Frank nodded, "If the kid's disturbed—"

"His name's John," said Frank. "I'm surprised you didn't know that."

The tech's eyes narrowed for a moment, and George thought he was going to refuse. "John," he said. "Yeah, I forgot. Come on." He led them back into the house and past the screen. Inside, the lounge had been transformed. A wide tarpaulin had been spread over the cream carpet and a canvas laid on it. Next to it, a plastic egg carton held paints. Not a single drop marked the tarpaulin.

Around the walls, in complete silence, men and women stood, some in shirts and ties. Most were holding cameras or Scouts, others scribbling furiously on handhelds or tablets. A film crew had set up station next to the kitchen doorway and the computer desk, with two studio lights on tall poles. Furry microphones hung from booms, though George wondered what they hoped to capture. The swish of John's paintbrush? The child had never spoken. Not once. Never made a mortal comprehensible sound. Never even smiled, which had distressed his parents more than anything. Apart from sneezing and coughing and crying, he could have lacked vocal cords altogether.

George scanned the faces until he saw Zack and Liz standing next to a woman he recognized from the news desk of one of the local TV stations. Liz was gripping Zack's arm. Her mouth was tight, her hair carefully done. She was wearing a sober blue dress, and none of her serenity was visible anywhere. She hadn't seen George. Her attention was on her son, dressed in a sunflower yellow shirt with buttons, and a pair of neat jeans and running shoes. George wondered which wardrobe director had chosen the outfit.

John. Four years old and autistic. Born late, an only child, and George knew that Liz blamed herself for John's autism. For the first month of his life, he was a perfect child, sleeping through the night, taking the breast without complaint, crying only in pain, burping on Zack's shoulder but never sicking up his baby food, for all intents and purposes the most beautiful infant imaginable.

But it became obvious within months that his internal gravity was for a different reality altogether. His poles, north and south, were aligned oddly, and his days were comprised of a peculiar silence, a waiting silence, watching for a tomorrow that never came. Yet he rarely cried and sat for hours at a time, staring at walls with a steady unerring patience, like a navigator steering through dense fog. Playgroups made no difference to him. Not therapists or bright colors, nor dancing, music, tactile explorations, swimming with Liz—none of it dented his armor.

So George stared with nothing short of amazement at the four year old boy on his hands and knees on the tarpaulin, supporting himself with one pudgy hand while his clenched teeth held one brush and his other hand held a fat brush dipped in white paint.

And on the floor before him, George saw a comet.

He sucked in air, looked away, breathed in and out twice, spread his stance a little to keep his balance, then looked back. The impact of the thing nearly floored him. As though he were out in space tracking alongside the comet. It was the closest thing to perfection he had ever seen in art. Photos could not have been clearer, not even the precise computer-generated images the TV graphics people were producing. No air out there in space to carry sound, but George swore he could almost hear the destructive roar of the thing as it blasted through vacuum.

John finished the detail he was adding to the front of the comet and considered it carefully. Then he sat back on his heels, took the second brush from his mouth, leaned forward a little, got his balance, and started painting with both hands at the same time. Someone choked down a gasp. George bit his tongue to stop from crying out. Both John's hands were painting separate parts of the comet, and his little head was steady as a conductor's in the middle. Someone swore *sotto voce* behind him, and George wondered how the sound bloke would edit it out. John didn't move. The comet burned on the canvas. No material made on Earth was strong enough to hold that heavenly blaster, thought George. It was going to lift off the surface and incinerate everything. The only thing holding it in place, its only flamin' gravity, was a four year old boy who held it there with two pudgy hands and a couple of knees.

Then things got remarkable. George forgot pretty well everything because on the canvas, overlaid on the image of the comet,

John started painting numbers and formulae in meticulous Times New Roman. Without considering or hesitating, like the sun amid planets, unmeasurable, unapproachable, unknowable, he painted numbers and equations and symbols well beyond George's high school science, pausing only to dip his brushes into black paint. Both hands deft and independent, his sandy hair going a little astray, and a faint sheen on his forehead from the studio lamps, John delivered the data with the relentless precision of a missile.

George knew then why the astronomy boffins were there with their recording devices. As John painted, covering almost the entire canvas, the watchers leaned forward with looks of intent greed. Little as George knew of science, it seemed they were all waiting for some vital bit piece of information John was yet to provide. Communal scientific breath sucked in as John paused and considered the last small blank space.

John dipped both brushes in paint, held them above the canvas, and paused, as though hearing a director's instructions. And then did something that rippled the air with shock.

With a single precise motion, he lifted his little head and fixed his stare on something in the crowd. Among gasps and surprised murmurs, all heads followed his gaze, including George's, to focus on the face of a tall, startled-looking man with a handsome face, brown eyes and dressed in a white shirt, jacket and business trousers, conservative tie and a badge that described him as Edward Harrison, Cable News.

In one hand was a camera aimed at John's painting, but Mr Harrison lifted the other almost immediately to shield his face, then turned and shouldered his way out of the press.

After the half-second of stunned silence, two men in suits followed him out and everyone turned around. George, though, remembered that instant before Mr Harrison raised his hand, where George had seen his eyes widen first in surprise, and then narrow into both fear and cunning hostility, like a trapped predator.

John was finished. Both brushes were back in the egg-carton container, and John had folded his arms across his chest. The blank spot on the canvas remained blank. George caught a glimpse of something on John's face he didn't quite believe, then the little boy lay down on the carpet, curled up like a kitten, leaned his head on his hands and closed his eyes.

Someone stepped forward, his shoes feathering on the carpet, and was pulled back. *Wait your turn,* thought George, protective as a wolf-pack leader. *There's others with more claim than you. He's a kid, for the love of Mike. Take your science and let his parents have him back.*

Zack stepped forward like a supplicant at the feet of a king and lifted his son into his arms, though George saw clearly his hesitation. John, no longer the painful boy who didn't speak, but a world-wide star, a celebrity who gave no interviews, who delivered his gift in the most awkward, beautiful silence imaginable. George wiped his eye, and saw others doing likewise. *You've lost your son, Zack,* he thought. *He belongs to the whole world now.*

Liz's eyes were wet with the kind of desolate, held-in separation and loneliness that George had always known was there behind her calm self-control. She reached out to John as he passed in Zack's arms, but the boy just didn't see her.

The producer watched her follow Zack. The instant the door closed everyone spoke at the same time. George looked over at Frank, but his friend was shaking his head slowly, side to careful side in bewilderment. Three or four men were on hands and knees on the floor, filming the painting meticulously, and one in a Swinburne University sweater was rocking back on his knees, his arms folded across his chest, whispering, "Amazing…amazing…"

The producer held out his arms. "Quiet, everyone," he said in a British accent. And when everyone was, he said, "You all know the conditions under which we're here. No-one touches the painting, and in ten minutes, everyone goes through the security barrier and collects personal effects." He looked around. "Everyone clear on that? Good. OK, if I could have some quiet, and we'll do an intro, then Doctor Harley, are you and your team ready for questions?"

A man dressed in a brown jumper, green shirt and tie, and black trousers looked up from his Scout and nodded absently.

"OK, then. Bruce, set to go?"

The anchor in his suit and tie raised a hand, though he was staring at the painting with still-wide eyes.

The producer raised his voice. "Bruce, you with us?"

"Ah, yes. Sorry." Bruce straightened his tie, stretched his lips, practised a smile, nodded to the cameras. "This is Bruce Nagle in the home of Zack and Liz Smith in Perth, Western Australia. An ordinary suburban house from the street, not one you would associate with remarkable scientific discovery, or astronomical observation.

Yet, since the first sighting of the Melcassar Comet and the wave of fear that swept the world, it has been the place of some quite extraordinary events. For this is also the home of John Smith, the son of Zack and Liz, and it is his quite remarkable achievements that have brought us here today.

"Imagine, if you will, a four year old boy who has until now been locked inside his own internal world since birth. Despite being cared for by his loving parents, he has never spoken a recognisable word, drawn a picture, or looked at a book or television."

The anchor paused a moment for effect.

"Then imagine this—that when the comet was announced, John astonished his parents by taking up paints and brushes and starting to paint, for hours at a time, day or night, first on the walls and then on canvases provided by his parents."

Nagle held up a small painting, and George leaned forward. He was expecting a few random scrawls and painted squiggles on an otherwise blank canvas, but he was surprised to see it covered in patches of yellows, blacks, whites, oranges, reds, and in one corner, the unmistakable image of a road leading into…nowhere. Nagle put it down and held up two or three similar paintings. "Although Zack and Liz were delighted and amazed, it was nothing compared to what was to come. Recently, even though he had not seen the news that the danger of the comet was past, John painted something so extraordinary that his parents notified the authorities." He pointed to a painting held up by an assistant.

"And now, young John has not only produced a stunning likeness of the comet"—the anchor shook his head in disbelief that George could see was clearly genuine—"but he has also included scientific data that representatives from the major observatories are analyzing and hope to present to the world in the very near future."

"Ladies and gentlemen, I would not have believed this if I had not seen it happen before me. Our cameras have recorded the event under strict supervision and we will be showing the entire sequence without breaks shortly. For now, I have with me Doctor Lindsay Harley from Mount Stromlo Observatory, where much of the Australian comet observation effort has been based, and he will be taking questions."

Surprisingly, the first question was about John. George was glad Zack and Liz were out of the room.

"How does a boy like this know this stuff?" It came from a local reporter with his station logo embroidered on his shirt.

Doctor Harley had a nervous laugh, George thought. "I'm not sure," he said, fiddling with a pen. "Astronomy is my field, though, and I'd be happy to take your questions on that side of things." He glanced down at the painting. "Some of his data is pretty interesting, I must say."

But the reporter would not be deterred. "But that's just it, don't you think? For an adult, providing this sort of information would be commendable. For a four year old autistic boy who can't read or speak, doesn't watch TV, and has never heard of the comet, it's frightening. Have you had psychological profiling done? Have you—?"

The producer stepped forward. "People, let's focus on the issue at hand, shall we?" He looked around at the gathering and pointed to one. "Ben?"

"How does this . . . data help us prepare, if at all?"

"After a scientific team properly analyzes it, it will be released to world governments as soon as possible."

A clamor of voices, to which Doctor Harley stepped back anxiously, then pointed again. "Wendy?"

"Do you have any idea at this stage what sort of information John has painted?"

Bruce Nagle looked across. "Doctor Harley?"

The good doctor looked pre-occupied. "Difficult to say," he said slowly. "From what I can see, there seems to be indications of the comet's…ah, metallic composition, exact weight and dimensions, origins…" His head scanned back and forward several times. "There…are other indications of…geological factors…" His voice trailed away as he forgot all his TV rules and focused on the painting. "Interesting…"

The next question dragged him back. "And what about the gap? What information is missing?" The sudden silence that followed told George it was the most important question of all. Harley stepped away from the microphone and knelt next to the painting, his lips moving soundlessly as he scanned it. "Difficult to say at this stage," he said. "I'm just amazed that all of this came from a four-year-old boy. But it could be…uhmm…given the unstable geological nature of the comet and its erratic…trajectory, possibly the…" He paused, looked up with his eyes wide, muttering, "mothers of the unborn!" and looked down again.

The anchor made an urgent hand gesture, and cameras swivelled. "Doctor, what is it?"

Cameras swivelled again, and George could see Harley's urgent finger hovering over the lines of still-wet formulae. He was silent for a moment or two, shaking his head, his fingers moving fast over the painting.

"Doctor?"

At first he didn't respond, but then, eventually, sat back and breathed out loudly. "Uhmm, well…if we could run this material through the extant comet data, it is…uhm, possible that we could extrapolate the…impact point."

The roar from the crowd was almost physical, pushing Harley back. He stared once more at the painting, then climbed to his feet, looking baffled, alarmed, but the pair of suits in the corner made a signal to the producer, who held up his arms. "People, we're out of time, I'm sorry." When George looked at his watch in surprise, sure they had another two or three minutes at least. He glanced around quickly at the Nagle bloke and the government suits in the corner, one of whom was pressing an earbud into his ear and listening intently.

"Impact point?" the press were shouting. "But it's going to miss!"

"—how can a four year old boy—"

"—no, no, no, you can't extrapolate anything from absent data—"

"—make the information available—"

The producer was waving his arms. "There will be no further questions. Please abide by the conditions of our agreement and vacate the premises immediately."

Frank pulled him outside quicker than George thought necessary. On the front lawn, amid the bottlebrush and grevilleas and morning heat, Frank was ballasted with urgency, ready to unload his thoughts on someone. George stepped aside, but Frank pulled him back. "How amazing was that?" Frank demanded. "How did he do that? How is it possible that a kid could know that? It's just not possible—he's never held a flamin' crayon before, let alone turn out a masterpiece like that, or add in all the scientific stuff! And how could he possibly know where the comet's going to hit? Who is this kid?"

George watched techs roll up long and limp cables like post-coital pythons. "Don't know, mate. Don't think Zack and Liz do, either. I'm gobsmacked…never seen anything like it before, never will again." He looked at the house, stuck his hands on his hips with an air of complete bafflement, then turned a full circle back to Frank.

"I'd really like to find out who sent that text," he muttered. "I almost forgot. Do you think we've got a chance if we sneak around the back?"

But Frank wasn't paying attention. "Sorry, mate. Hey, did you see what that reporter's badge said? The one who ran away? What network was he from?"

"Cable News," said George. "As I was saying, I wouldn't mind saying hello to Zack and Liz. What do you think?"

"Bad timing, mate," said Frank gently. "Don't really think they'll be listening to anyone at the moment. Their boy's just stunned the world and I think maybe they'll want to put him down for a sleep, and have a quiet cup of tea. Let's give them that at least."

"Oh." George searched in his pockets for his keys.

As they walked back to the car, Frank slowed down a fraction, his back suddenly very straight. "Something's not right," he hissed.

"What?"

"My neck just prickled."

George chuckled nervously. Sometimes Frank could be so irrelevant. "Seen your doctor lately?"

"Remember Army days? Out on patrol and you just know you're being watched?"

"Uhmm, yes, but who'd be watching you? Not Pat, is it? You been—"

But Frank was deadly serious. "Let's find out. Fish around in your pocket for your keys, take them out and pull out your wallet as well. Let it fall out like an accident. We'll walk on about five meters or so, then you realize, stop, turn around and look back. I'll look left and you look right. Someone's behind us, I just know it."

Feeling ridiculous, George did as he was told, although he was sure anyone watching would see through their obvious ploy. But five meters later, when he patted his pockets, put on a surprised look and turned around, he saw that Frank's prickling neck was correct. A motionless figure was standing on the other side of the road in the shadow of a large tree, although not watching Frank, but deeply intent on the Smith house. George only looked for a second, and then made a pretence of searching for his wallet. But it was enough to recognize the Cable News reporter. The trapped predator. Mr Edward Harrison. "Here it is!" said George happily as he stooped to pick it up, feeling spooked and highly exposed, almost expecting gunfire.

As he got into the car, keen to be gone from that place at all speed, the level of weirdness rose again. Ahead of them, on the grassy verge of the road, steady as though a cyclone would not move him, a ragged old man stood with a beagle at his feet. Without even checking, George knew from the angles—just knew—that the old man was watching the Cable News reporter. He stared, for a long eerie moment dislocated from reality, a witness to something far darker and bigger than his small ordinary life.

George started the engine. Frank just stared.

In the public payphone a few blocks from the autistic boy's house, Ed lifted the handset, hoping he would soon be permitted to return to the Second's room to see the curse-breaker found in Boston, and the victory of the Second. Without payment or dialling, the line to the Second came on immediately, bringing a warm rush of peculiar pleasure to Ed's mouth and the nauseous stink of pollution seeping out of the handset. The power of the Second transcended technology.

"The boy is amazing," Ed said, realizing immediately that not a single word of description of the image of the comet would interest the Second. "There is significant data from the painting to process, and I have jacked a listener into the BBC lines so you can receive the vision directly. Perhaps it will contain the information you seek." He waited for the Second to access the data.

The earpiece crackled. "It shows nothing," the Second said. "The boy is unimportant."

And the line went dead.

Brotherhood sled,
just outside Boston House timeslip boundary

Benedict landed the sled. "Rig for minimal 'slip," he ordered. "Lock everything down tight and quiet. Get comfortable, Poor Men. Nobody leaves."

"We're just going to wait?" asked Timothy.

"No, we're going to work. Tower has the curse-breaking secret locked in his head, but if we can unlock the last two clues and find the curse-breaker, the curse lifts, suicide ends, hope returns. Alright. There are four clues, the Boston House courtyard, which led to the Device, which led to the book. Two open pages of it, to be precise, without any words. Which is where our trail turns cold, but we're Poor Men! We're used to doing the impossible. So we need to work out which book. The jumpships will arrive in—how long, Tower?"

"Six hours fourteen minutes."

"If any of you have any idea, no matter how ridiculous—tell us. We're close to the House, so we can still get in, but our window of opportunity is shrinking all the time. Think fast."

For the next hour or so, the Poor Men asked Blackwell an unending stream of questions, covering everything from operational manuals to his efforts at writing a history of the Poor Men to any diaries he might have kept. Without a reliable memory, he answered as best as he could, but soon the questions stopped and the Poor Men fell silent and left for other duties.

With the sled rigged for minimal 'slip and thus minimal power, Blackwell was unable to access the Core for further research, so he wrapped his boots in cloth for quietness, and carried out a full exploration of the sled, checking every cabin, every device. He left Benedict sitting on one side of the bridge, staring out a porthole. A small group of Poor Men were huddled in the cargo hold, whispering, and Paul, wearing white gloves, was cleaning the reactor in solemn silence.

Blackwell found nothing, just as he had expected, and returned to the bridge.

When the jumpship arrival deadline arrived, Benedict went through the sled, gathered up the Poor Men and took them back to the bridge. "We're officially homeless," he said. "Outcast but fighting. Stay still and quiet until dark, get something to eat—the galley's well stocked—and then we'll be sending out patrol groups. I want to see what the jumpships are doing."

When full darkness fell, Benedict called the Poor Men together. "The first patrol group will be Philip, Antonius, Frederick, the second Nathanael, Thomas, Arthur. Poor Men, I want you to dress as black as possible, stay low to the ground, move independently. Find and plot the jumpships, identify any visible weaponry, note any movements. Tower won't be joining any patrol groups, obviously. If you are captured or spotted, escape away from the sled.

If you're not back in an hour, I'll assume you've been captured, and our position here has been compromised, in which case we will leave the sled. Our fallback meeting place will be Plymouth Rock at midnight. Questions?"

There were none. The Poor Men slipped out.

Within the hour, they returned. The ten jumpships were positioned evenly around the Boston House boundary, they said, except for a wider gap between two jumpships where a thick knot of trees prevented it. Antonius thought it was a perfect re-entry point back into the House, with the trees providing cover almost to the timeslip boundary. All the jumpships were locked down, without visible weaponry or external motion sensors, and without any Cabal soldiers moving around. It was impossible to tell if they had crossed the timeslip boundary into the House grounds.

"What class jumpship?" asked Paul.

"They looked like their latest long-range cruisers, lightweight, low on firepower and troop carrying abilities. Difficult to say without closer inspection."

"I need to know. Nathanael, Thomas, Arthur, get close to those jumpships, stay motionless, watch until midnight. Benedict and I will take the next shift, and then we'll make our plans for tomorrow night when we've got some firm observational data. In the meantime, everyone get some sleep."

Arcada

The Breakers delivered to Brisbane, Townsville, Mount Isa, Cooktown, and assisted Team Fifty-Three on a run to Tasmania, which Ivan thought was a different country until Harker showed him the Australian flag flying over Bellerive Cricket Ground. They even did a run to Macquarie Island, where the horizon of ice looked like Norse legends about the beginning of the world. The Breakers worked hard, joked like troopers, lost weight quickly and learned to sleep through almost everything. Harker slept very well and his drowsing thoughts of Ruth never lasted long before sleep unanchored him. Any post office fat melted. He transferred his hope for a golden retirement with Ruth to a hope for millions of faceless others to live free of the curse. Every night he thought of George.

In rarer moments, he saw a ragged old man standing in corners, smiling. No-one paid any attention to him, and Arcada was so strange that Harker never asked anyone how the old man was able to slip out of visibility as Harker was watching.

Ivan spoke infrequently, though in rare moments, Harker saw him practising with the cricket ball he always kept in his bag. Harker stood his cricket bat in a corner of his room and wondered as he glanced at it how much armor he would need to play ice cricket.

In rare free time, usually in the hour between returning to base and collapsing into bed, Harker and Ivan played cricket under the desert moon. Ivan's offbreak gripped and turned ferociously off any surface, but once Harker had his eye in, he clouted and lost so many cricket balls that they gave up looking, and played instead with balls that the Spanner produced in her secret workshop.

"The air's thinner here," he explained to Ivan with a straight face. "Special Australian desert air. The balls go further."

Ivan grunted. Cossacks would have taken fright at his beard. "You out many times. Australians not gentlemen in cricket."

Father Nick's Day minus nine days
Brotherhood sled
just outside Boston House timeslip boundary

With three shifts of observations, the Poor Men gathered over breakfast to realize they knew almost nothing. The jumpships had not moved, their occupants not appeared, and none of the hulls showed weaponry or tracking equipment. All the Poor Man had gained from a night of watching was wet, cold and muddy clothes.

Benedict dismissed them for the day after he had announced the patrol shifts for the next night. The Poor Men occupied themselves with a detailed walk-down of the sled, cleaning every inch of every cabin, and checking the reactor with immaculate care.

Benedict returned to his spot by the porthole, where Blackwell found him late evening. He didn't acknowledge Blackwell.

"At least they haven't come for a shooting war," Blackwell said. "The House would have burned to the ground by now. We can still get in if we need to."

Benedict was silent for many minutes before he said, "Nine days, Tower. Can you find your book and unlock the curse-breaker in that time? I really don't want to lose this war."

"Poor Men have never lost a war yet," said Blackwell and realized how trite the words sounded.

Benedict considered him with an even face. "But we've never been in this situation before. We've had a very sheltered history, very protected. It's frightening to think how the world would have ended up without the timeslip. The curse would have killed humanity centuries ago."

"I don't want to walk to Plymouth Rock."

Benedict's head jerked slightly. "Plymouth Rock," he said quietly, and then with building excitement and volume, "The Mayflower, the first Poor Men to America—Tower, I know what your book is! Listen, it makes sense! The clues all follow each other—the cobbled courtyard was a central point where all Poor Men walked, so it would make sense that you would get the first clue just crossing over it every day. The second—"

"Slow down! Start from the beginning."

"OK OK." Benedict breathed, grinning. "Plymouth Rock. Which was where the first Mayflower pilgrims arrived, and where the Brotherhood landed soon after, under the 'slip of course, in a ship not recorded in any history books or public holidays, and set about establishing a base. They knew it had to be near Boston, but in an area where settlers where unlikely to build. They considered some of the islands and outer areas, but the best place was right under their noses. The Muddy River was a polluted, filthy cesspool, perfect for them! They set up an artificial timeslip using a splinter from the original Door and years later strengthened the 'slip with the first ever reactor—the second clue—and built the Boston House around it. Alright so far?"

"Keep going."

Paul appeared on the bridge with a group of Poor Men behind him.

"Later," said Benedict, "a man called Olmsted tried to turn the Fens into parkland, but the city fathers—with some persuasion from the Poor Men—talked him out of it. It was such a good place for suicides that the city fathers didn't want them anywhere else."

"Where was the Cabal in all this?"

"Still in Europe," said Rebecca, who had just arrived, "wondering where the Poor Men had gone."

"It was one of our best covert operations ever," said Benedict. "The Poor Men laid careful and massive deceptions for months to mislead the Cabal of their intentions. For years afterwards, the Cabal had no idea that a significant portion of the Brotherhood had left Europe. A blessing in some ways, but it was almost our undoing later."

"How?"

"They got lazy. With no Cabal threat, they got careless with their deliveries. Opposition makes you strong, they say. Adversity breeds character. Well, the Poor Men thought they had no opposition, and some of them started to make deliveries under normal sight, without the timeslip. It became a wag's game, betting on who could deliver most without being seen. When the Patrons found out, the Poor Men were severely punished, but the damage was done. Questions began in the town: who are these men? What is this secret society? Are they dangerous? Are they British spies? Is this where the gifts come from? The Patrons knew they had little time before the Cabal heard the rumors and swept across into the New World. But they were crafty as foxes, those early Patrons. And the plan they devised was even better than the one they used to escape the Cabal in Europe."

"Get to the point. Where's the book in all this?"

"Stay with me. The Boston and New York Patrons devised a deception that still lasts today, though they couldn't have foreseen that then. They decided to call in some favors, and make use of their connections with the outside world. Some of the Patrons had lives both inside and outside the House then, and kept both separate. They could afford to in those days, as deliveries took so little time in the new colony. They maintained one household, one wife and family here in the House, but lived as chaste bachelors outside it, building support, establishing links with the fathers of early American society. Two such men were John Pintard, the founder of the New York Historical Society, and Washington Irving, a writer of note. They knew they had to distance Father Nicholas from the day named in his honor, so they decided to create a character and story that would move attention away from the Poor Men and explain the yearly appearances of gifts in people's homes. They also commissioned the artist Alexander Anderson, a Brotherhood supporter, to draw this character, and then to publicize him as widely as possible."

Blackwell's planet glimmered.

Benedict grinned. "Ah, it was one of the most splendid deceptions ever devised! Irving wrote his now-famous A History of New York, featuring Father Nicholas, also known as Santa Claus, the jolly pipe-smoking burgher with a full sack of gifts! It caught on. The public loved it. Even more so when Clement Clark Moore—who wasn't even a Brotherhood supporter!—wrote his famous poem, and the deception was complete. The Santa tradition spread, both in America and across the world, enabling us to continue our work in secret and out of sight of the Cabal's predatory searches. Nowadays, generations after Pintard and Irving, Santa figures in department stores all over the world dandle children on their knees while we deliver gifts in secret to those same children. Ironic, isn't it?" He chuckled. "I've always thought so."

Light flared in Blackwell's vision. "This is it! So where is this book?"

"The original is in a university collection, or maybe in the Library of Congress, I think, but Boston House has an exact copy in the Patrons' library, made at the same time as the original. Worth a fortune if it ever got out."

Blackwell scrambled up, heat generating strong and resolute purpose in every muscle. "You have to get me in! We can get in through Antonius' gap."

"Too risky," said Paul. "They'll be waiting for you."

"But they won't open fire," said Benedict. "They'll sit back and wait for Tower to get the key. That's their risk as well as ours. Like Tower said, they want it as much as we do, which is why the jumpships are here. So our best chance is to slip in, get the book, unlock the last secret and the curse-breaker, and use it."

"That's a lot of ifs," said Paul. "What if—"

"We've got nothing else!" shouted Antonius, shocking Blackwell. "Listen to you! We're hanging by a thread here—we've lost everything anyway—so what does it matter if we lose this as well? We've got nine days to finish this thing, and you're talking risk?" He pulled on his black woollen cap. "I'll take Tower in if you're too afraid."

Paul snatched the black jacket from Frederick nearby. "Not alone you won't," he growled. "Benedict?"

"Coming."

Rebecca said, "Me too."

It felt very strange indeed to Blackwell to creep, unprotected by the timeslip, through a night-darkened park, the smell of the river close at hand, the cool freshness of the park all around him. To his left, cars passed infrequently down a road, and further off, a crowd roared at something, a sports ground perhaps at one of the last defiant sporting fixtures before possible comet impact. Blackwell wondered what they would think if they knew that four people creeping through a local park were in fact planning to save them all from suicide they didn't even see coming.

Antonius motioned them all flat. Blackwell felt wet grass and mud on his chest. When he looked up, he saw two jumpships about a hundred meters apart, and a dark thicket of trees between them.

"Move separately and randomly to confuse any motion sensors," Antonius whispered. "Go slow. The 'slip boundary is just the other side of the trees. I'm first. If I'm not out in five minutes, it's clear."

Blackwell counted off five minutes on his internal clock after Antonius had disappeared, and then passed into the 'slip himself. His first sight as his heart tripped was Antonius, who had found an axe and was gripping it in a most un-Poor Man like manner, his face sweaty and fierce. *There's both steel and anger in this man,* Blackwell thought.

"If they've penetrated the 'slip," Antonius said, "I can't see them. There are no muddy footprints anywhere, apart from ours, and I don't think they're usually that precise. And I've run a circuit of the boundary, and I can't see any jumpships anywhere, either. So it seems we're here alone."

Benedict pulled Rebecca in a few minutes later. "Clear?" he said.

"Let's go," said Blackwell, already running. "The Patrons' library is upstairs, right?"

Antonius ran ahead, brandishing his axe like a gladiator, clearing every doorway they passed through. They ran through the main hall, snatched up lanterns, and bolted up the stairs towards the Patrons' chambers.

At a small landing, four doors stood closed.

"Don't know which one," Benedict said, puffing slightly. "Albuquerque House is laid out differently. I'll take this one. Take those two."

Rebecca grabbed a doorknob. "What am I looking for?"

"An archive, museum, library."

They opened their doors. Benedict and Blackwell entered, but they had only taken two steps when Rebecca gave a cry. "It's here!"

The Poor Men raced in as Antonius stood guard at the door. In front of them, lit by the moon's sullen light entering through leadlighted windows, neatly-arranged tables and bookcases held hundreds of books, boxes, paintings, and items Blackwell didn't recognize. Paul raced off to find sheets to cover the windows.

"The Brotherhood's treasure room," said Benedict, his lamplit sweat glinting. "Hundreds of years of wealth. Irreplaceable." He stepped forward. "We're looking for the name Washington Irving, but I've no idea what it looks like. It could be bound, or just a pile of papers in a box. If you find it, Tower, you'll know."

The initial noisy excitement as they compared their discoveries dimmed to a determined quietness, and then a frustrated weary silence. Weariness groaned against Blackwell's eyes—there was only so much a man could do without sleep, surrounded by jumpships or not. But then Rebecca, who had been oddly humming something that sounded like an Irish jig, gave a croaking cry. "History of New York," she said, "by Washington Irving!"

Blackwell, Benedict and Paul were at her side within seconds, the powerful warmth within Blackwell intensifying. As Blackwell took the book, his ninth planet blazed fiercely, a sustained glow that so delighted him he laughed. "It's in here!" He gripped the book far tighter than an archivist would allow.

"Start reading," said Antonius from the door.

Blackwell sat on the cold wooden floor, leaned against a wall, and did.

"From the "Evening Post" of October 26, 1809. DISTRESSING. Left his lodgings some time since, and has not since been heard of, a small elderly gentleman, dressed in an old black coat and cocked hat, by the name of Knickerbocker."

The first lines meant nothing to him.

Neither did much that followed. He read at speed, keying his eyes for words he thought important, remembering that the whole story was nothing more than a satire and would not mention the Brotherhood at all. For page after page after endless page, he read, his internal clock unwinding the minutes until the Cabal would realize where he was and what he had found.

But his ninth planet remained dim. Sleep crowded his eyes. At ten thousand words, Benedict poured water over his head.

At seventeen thousand, Benedict slapped Blackwell's face when he slumped. At twenty-two thousand, he pulled him bodily to a standing position and made him jog on the spot. At about thirty-one thousand, as Blackwell read in despair of the adroit bargain by which the Island of Manhattan was bought for sixty guilders,

Benedict made him remove his shirt and poured two jugs of cold water over him until he shivered violently.

"Keep going," growled Antonius from the door.

At Book Two, Chapter Nine, a most auspicious chapter, Blackwell thought, given the number of his planet, things changed.

"At this early period was instituted that pious ceremony, still religiously observed in all our ancient families of the right breed, of hanging up a stocking in the chimney on St. Nicholas Eve; which stocking is always found in the morning miraculously filled; for the good Fr. Nicholas has ever been a great giver of gifts, particularly to children."

Somewhere in the passage, though he was not sure of the exact point, light flared so brightly Blackwell thought it would pour from his eyes into the room. He shuddered, staggering inwards, his focus swerving towards his armored planet, which rotated slightly, shedding further latitudes until only a narrow equatorial band remained.

One clue left.

Blackwell stared at the image that glimmered there for a moment, then faded.

Blackwell leaned back, fully awake, though confused. "I know the fourth clue!"

"What?"

"Gifts."

"But everything links to gifts," said Paul. "Everything we do, everything we are."

"We need the Poor Men," Antonius announced in a voice that permitted no argument. "We should be together, helping Tower. I'll get them."

"Alone?"

"Search for your clue." He set down his axe and left.

"There's a future for that man," said Benedict when Antonius had left.

"Go back," said Paul. "Back to the point where you realized that gifts was a clue. Recreate that place for us; give us a little more information."

Blackwell opened the book, found the place and read. "At this early period was instituted that pious ceremony, still religiously observed in all our ancient families of the right breed, of hanging up a stocking in the chimney on St. Nicholas Eve; which stocking is always found in the morning miraculously filled; for the good Fr. Nicholas has ever been a great giver of gifts, particularly to children."

"That's it?"

"Courtyard, machine, book, gifts," said Blackwell. "But once I unlock the gifts clue, I'll only need to work out the last one and be able to break the curse. So something in the passage represents a place in the House linked to gifts."

"Get your shirt on, Tower." Paul handed it to him. "The common room would be a better place to discuss this when the Poor Men arrive."

They moved down to the common room and made sure every window was covered. Paul stood guard outside with Antonius' axe. Blackwell, Benedict and Rebecca sat around a table that had until recently been a safe place, laid open the book, and talked.

At about midnight, Antonius appeared with the Poor Men. Wet and muddy, they still strode into the common room with strong purpose and looked ready to search for the curse-breaker, without sleep, for the remaining four days.

Blackwell grinned. Unstinting service and loyalty was engraved deep into Poor Man DNA. Centuries of it. No desire to do anything but keep the world from a monumental landslide into despair and continental suicide. Unspoken. Unrewarded. Benedict was right. Someone should write a book about them.

The Poor Men found clean and dry clothes and sat around the table. Blackwell noticed how they considered him with steady regard, none looking aside, none frowning. They still believed in him, he realized. "This is the passage that unlocked the fourth clue," he said. "When we unlock this one, it will lead us to the last one, and that will break the curse. The jumpships are outside, but they appear to be waiting for something, or perhaps to prevent us leaving, so let's make the most of our time." He read the passage again, though none of it affected his ninth planet an atom. The armored band around it still glimmered with plated metallic defiance.

"Didn't you have to *be* in a certain place for the clue to trigger?" asked Calvin. "You did with the courtyard and the first reactor, and you had to read the book to get to the gifts clue. So one of the objects in the list should unlock the last clue."

William leaned forward. "In particular, those objects that refer to gifts! Stockings, mornings, Father Nikolas, children. There are chimneys in this House, but they're only for fires, not gifts."

"But we don't use stockings, and there aren't any children left either. Mornings and Father Nikolas are pretty irrelevant here.

So what's left?"

"Early period," said Paul, "pious ceremony, ancient families, right breed...uhmm, that's all."

"None of those," said Antonius with flat conviction.

"Maybe it's a group of words, then, or a word which sounds like a place."

But no amount of discussion resolved anything. Blackwell listened more than he spoke, waiting for even a flicker of resonance, but knew full well they would not succeed.

"Get some sleep, everyone," he said, standing. "We'll continue in the morning. I'll stand first watch. Antonius is off duty tonight."

While they were settling, he went out the Door, and looked across the yard through the faintest of rains across the line of painted yellow stones that marked the edge of the timeslip. One step across, and he would be in the outside world, trapped in human history and despair, facing the jumpships of the Cabal that wanted the thing locked in his head.

When Nathanael came to relive him, he found the Poor Men had made a bed for him in the common room. Sleep drowned him rapidly. He dreamed of children staring innocently at chimneys, enormous stockings, armoring planets, and a ceremony in which a whole host of ancient families bred with raucous, but pious, abandon.

Father Nick's Day minus eight days
Boston House

When Blackwell woke, he was surprised that a dream of any description had come from his disfigured and stunted brain. He rubbed his eyes and saw Benedict next to his bed.

"We're going to walk down the entire House," said Benedict. "Every room, just to make sure we've missed nothing. I've got your breakfast. You can eat as you walk. Everyone else is already awake and ready."

It was laborious, slow, painstaking. Blackwell knew from the start it would be difficult, but listened to every suggestion, stood in every place the Poor Men thought might trigger the last clue.

Nothing.

At this early period was instituted that pious ceremony, still religiously observed in all our ancient families of the right breed, of hanging up a stocking in the chimney on St. Nicholas Eve; which stocking is always found in the morning miraculously filled; for the good Fr. Nicholas has ever been a great giver of gifts, particularly to children.

The Poor Men repeated the passage over and over.

When evening came, they became involved in detailed discussions ranging from the architectural variations of chimneys to the pious aspects of the novice transition ceremony, grew heated over unimportances.

For the next three days, little changed. The Poor Men walked every step of the yards, climbed and examined chimneys, no matter how much Paul opposed the idea, and walked respectfully through the sleepers' rooms, every one, particularly those occupied by families, hoping that some were ancient.

Each night, Blackwell sat outside on the House doorstep, his coat snugged tightly around him.

Father Nick's Day minus five days
Boston House

Harker received a summons to Jacob's rooms. Jacob looked like he was expecting him. He was leaning against the Sentry, surrounded by the quiet glow that Harker had never figured out. The smell of smoke was stronger, and Jacob was looking weary.

Harker waited a moment. "Jacob?" "You called me?" Then Jacob's hand slipped, and he fell heavily against the rim. Something cracked, perhaps his ribs. Harker raced over and helped him up. "You alright, mate?" Bosses weren't meant to collapse in front of the workers.

Jacob nodded wearily, then stood up, still leaning against the Sentry. Harker let go of him reluctantly.

"You can't keep this up," Harker told him. "It's killing you, and how are you going to manage after we leave?"

"We have to change things," Jacob said.

"Too right, mate! Gifts are great and stop people from going Early, but what happens when you run out of gift ideas? What then? And the comet's on its way as well. How's that going to change things? You just can't keep going like this!"

"Indeed." He seemed a little sharper, and stood straighter, considering him as though he had been expecting this conversation.

"You have a solution?"

Harker snorted. "Me? Not likely. Organize some strike bombers to blow up the blokes who blew up your Scandinavian base, maybe? Though that wouldn't break the curse, and I don't think kissing a frog's going to fix things either." He sucked his teeth. "It's a big ask, mate. Harder'n pushing a boulder up a muddy hill in the rain with a pair of chopsticks."

Jacob smiled that quiet, knowing smile as though he already knew the answer. "Then what, Harker Brown?"

"Don't know, mate. You'll need a new leader for one if—"

"We need a revolution, Harker Brown."

"You said that already," Harker snorted. "But you're not going to get far with armed workers roaming the streets, burning sleds and rioting."

Jacob stood straight. "Tell your workers to be strong. Your second task is coming, bitter and dark. Be ready."

Perth

The second message to George was worse.

Come with the man to my house.

When George looked out, a man in a black suit and impenetrable sunglasses was getting out of the plain white car parked directly in front of the post office door.

"Mr Wilkins? You'll come with me, please."

"Who sent you?" babbled George, although he knew.

"I'm not at liberty to tell you," said the man, and held open the door.

The driver didn't say a word during the trip. The engine had a restrained growl. V8, thought George, desperate for something to make sense.

They pulled up at Zack's house and walked to the front door. The driver let him in.

And John Smith was standing there with his blank four-year-old face, dressed in blue shorts and a white buttoned shirt, autistic to his bones. George frowned, smiled, thought about shaking hands and decided against it.

However absurd Zack's old Toyota with its rust spots and bent aerial looked next to the immaculate white limo in the driveway, the sight of the Australian Prime Minister in a armchair in Zack and Liz's lounge room was even more so.

"Hey!" George blurted, stuck to the spot. Blinking did no good at all. There he was, parliamentary and suited, slightly balding and smiling faintly, looking taller than he did on TV, but the Prime Minister nevertheless.

John went off somewhere. Zack was standing. Liz brought in a tray with her best china and a silver teapot and placed it on the coffee table. Three tags hung out the side of the teapot. George smelled Earl Grey. Liz arranged the teacup handles so they all faced outward. She sat down, nodded weakly at George and looked at her folded hands on her lap.

"Have a seat, George," Zack said. The poor bloke looked baffled. "This is the Prime Minister."

George just stared. He put away his Scout, not knowing whether to bow or kneel, ask for a beer, invite the bloke to a barbie and discuss tax reform or just say 'G'day.' The PM smiled at him and waved off the driver. George looked around for a chair. He had never voted for the man, though seeing him there in Zack's decrepit old burgundy lounge chairs was enough to swing his vote. He hoped Zack had given him the only lounge chair that didn't have broken springs.

What the blue blazes are you doing here? George wanted to ask, but instead noticed insignificances. The PM wasn't wearing a tie, though he had an Aussie flag badge on his lapel. George wondered what sort of effect he was going for with the blue shadow on his chin and the lack of camera makeup. He wasn't wearing his glasses. His hands rested loosefingered on his knees.

The ordinary bloke effect, decided George, though it made him nervous to be sitting in the same room as Australia's most powerful man. Well, after the Test cricket captain, of course.

Zack took the teapot and poured a cup only half-full. Liz was wearing a white dress and a look of quiet sustained fright. Zack sat back in his chair, but his knees were together and his knuckles on his teacup were white.

The front door closed. The doorpanel beeped twice. Locked in, realized George. Protecting the PM.

The Prime Minister smiled. "Thank you for coming at such short notice. You may be surprised to know that John painted a remarkable likeness of you when this meeting was decided, which we interpreted as an invitation. As you know, John produced a quite...well, extraordinary painting five days ago that has drawn the media and scientific spotlight to this house. I've made a personal request that they keep their distance for this meeting, though. They'll all hear soon enough." He took a sip from his tea.

George thought the man was a fine statesman, the way he made everyone wait. George looked down at his sleeves, saw the coffee stains with guilty horror, and then realized almost immediately with huge relief that Louise would never see them. Well, not unless the PM dobbed on him.

"The data from John's painting has been tremendously important for the worldwide scientific community in learning more about the comet."

George saw that the man was thinking, working out his next words "I have been asked, on behalf of Australia's scientific community and parliament, to present an award to young John. Although it might mean little to a boy of his...gifts, and in the TIME magazine tradition, we have awarded him the honour of 'Man of All Time.'" He smiled broadly. "Had it not been for him, we would never have known about the . . . situation of the comet."

The PM reached down to where a plaque rested against his chair and stood.

That's not all, thought George. *There's got to be more. You don't come all this way to present a plaque without the media to record every smile. You don't waste that kind of good PR*. The PM's aftershave wafted against him.

But things changed right there. The look that crossed the PM's face right then was priceless, and George wished he had a camera. For little John entered the room with a painting clutched in his chubby hands and climbed onto his mother's lap.

"Ah!" the PM said in an attempt at good cheer. "Here's the Man himself!" He looked across at Zack and Liz. "Would he accept the award, now he's here? I'm happy either way."

Liz thought for a moment, then placed John on the floor, and the PM carefully approached, the plaque in one hand. George thought John looked like a kangaroo caught in spotlights on a nightbound country road.

The PM knelt, and George had to blink out the strangeness. The Prime Minister of Australia, kneeling opposite a four year old autistic boy who had just been declared Man of All Flamin' Time for painting a picture of a comet that was possibly going to end all life on Earth. *A fairly ordinary sort of day*, thought George, all things considered.

The PM wisely decided not to speak, and instead just presented the plaque to John face forward. He half-reached out a hand to shake, and then withdrew it, but John, with the concentration of a deep-sea diver, gave the plaque back.

George, holding back a surprised gasp, thought that the expression on the PM's face would easily have earned Photo of All Time.

John calmly climbed back on his mother's knee, and the PM gave the plaque to a bemused Zack with a handshake and a smile. He sat down and took a sip from his cup of tea. George saw him thinking of a jocular comment to lighten the mood, but the moment had passed, and there was no explaining such things. John's rules were John's rules, and not even the PM was permitted to break them.

"I didn't come today just to present the plaque," he said. "There's something else, far more important. We have just received the report on the data contained in John's comet painting." He paused, and looked at each of them slowly. "It has changed the situation somewhat."

"Changed?" George knew the signs of bad news—the leadership voice, the careful posture, the careful choice of words. Something sparked warning along the length of his spinal column. "What's changed?"

"The publicity factor around John's paintings has been enormously high, especially since he unaccountably left his last one incomplete." He gestured to John with a humble smile, but John didn't even move.

"So the scientific effort put into analyzing the data has been around the clock and immense. Since the nuclear device broke off part of the comet, it has become geologically unstable, fractured. Fairly soon, it is going to break in two, and while the larger of the two pieces will pass harmlessly, the smaller fragment is going to collide with Earth."

George wanted to yell at that point, but kept quiet. Zack's straight back could have been either agony, army training or terror.

The PM was speaking, even though only half of George was listening. "The Australian people owe an enormous debt of gratitude to John, and to you, his parents. Without this data, we would in all likelihood never have known, and while we cannot prevent the devastation, we can certainly save lives. We will need to put squabbles and disputes aside and co-ordinate our efforts in the days to come.

This will require a concerted effort if we are to avoid significant catastrophe."

And when George finally twigged, the PM's something else shoved a knife down his throat, nearly choked him with a terror that did away with panic and went into full body shutdown instead.

"Hang on a minute, Mister Prime Minister…ah, sir."

He saw Zack and Liz turn to him with spotlight eyes, but he pressed on, caught in a live broadcast dive ahead of which was only deep water.

"You said 'the Australian people' and 'we' and 'save lives.' Do you mean that…ah…" The words were too huge to be spoken. "…the comet is going to hit Australia?"

The Prime Minister of Australia spread his hands wide on the armrests of the couch. "Yes," he said simply. "Yes, that is what I am saying."

George swore. "Scuse the French, sir."

"Excused." The PM paused, and his expression was three thousand miles away from the green leather chairs of Parliament. For a moment, George thought he might even be a half-decent bloke. "Yes, it is going to hit. I have been informed that the impact point is going to be somewhere in the central desert region, which is extraordinarily fortunate. While we have been spared the full cometary impact, the danger from the fragment is still extreme. There is not only the danger of being in the immediate vicinity of the comet, but also the fireballs that will rain down over the Australian continent, the dust storm, the ground tremors and quakes, poisonous cloud…" He held up his politician's hands in a calming gesture. "I have spoken with the leaders of South Africa, New Zealand, the South-east Asian archipelago, and the US. Others may follow if there is need."

"Need for what, sir?" Having spoken, George wasn't about to be kept quiet.

"For evacuation. We have to evacuate Western Australia."

The last three words sounded so stupid spoken together that George laughed, and then immediately regretted it. "Sorry," he said. "But…but how?"

The PM didn't even blink, as though he had done his own disbelieving laughter in recent days. "I have asked, and received agreement, for the navies and airforces of those countries to set sail for our shores. When they arrive, they will begin shuttling citizens to aid stations set up in overseas ports. There will be significant dislocation and difficulty, but those are far better than the alternatives. Furthermore, emergency legislation has been enacted that will place many major airlines, both Australian and international, under the direct control of their governments to assist in the evacuation. Fortunately, as the most isolated capital city on the planet, Perth and Western Australia is possibly the most providential of impact points, with other population centers well distant. My Cabinet and I will work at airports and ports to assist regular staff. All suicide cults will be strictly policed to make sure they leave. We have enough time, barely, to get everyone out."

"How much time, sir?" Liz's voice had steel rods on it, George thought. Steel serenity.

"Five days. On Father Nick's Day, of all days."

George was barely listening.

The PM took another sip of his tea. "Mr and Mrs Smith and John will be on the first plane out tomorrow morning with the compliments of the Australian government. Since you have apparently touched a chord in young John's life, Mr Wilkins, you and your wife are welcome to join them."

The PM left first in his limo, with a promise to see George and his wife at the airport in the morning.

George's departure was a stunned affair. He could just think of no words apt for either the promise of devastation or a boy who did things not possible in most universes. Zack and Liz stood at the door.

But as George reached the car he had been brought in, the sound of hurried footsteps and Liz's alarmed call made him turn. It was John, running towards him, holding out something, with Liz five steps behind him, her reaching arms grabbing only air, though she halted once she realized her son had not run onto the road.

"He's fine," croaked George, raising a forced smile and realizing, as John held up a roll of paper, that John had not quite finished.

George accepted the roll with a fluttery smile and shaking hands, and little John, enclosed for four years behind an expressionless face, smiled back. His eyes focused, his mouth opened a little, his teeth gleamed. Only for an instant, but for that instant, he looked like a kid at a party, happy and engaged in the moment.

"Thank you," George said softly, but he was completely unprepared for the astonishment of the next four seconds.

John leaned forward with a look of intent eagerness bright on his face and said, "He will give up hope. You must show him this."

George just gaped. "What?" he croaked. "Show who?" but then all the cords supporting John's smile sagged, and his face reverted. Lost far off eyes, straight mouth, hanging arms. John turned and walked back to his mother as George stared, flabbergasted. He didn't even think to unroll the paper. Getting home seemed a far safer option as he got into the government car. But the strangeness of John's voice disturbed him deeply. 'You must show him this.' *Show who?* George thought, thinking it was not a kid's voice at all.

'He will give up hope. You must show him this.' The Man of All Time was warning him. Someone was going to give up hope. He had to warn someone about...about the comet, but who? He unrolled the paper, hoping it was nothing more than a blank sheet, and that he had imagined John's words. But instead, at the top of the paper, with Times New Roman characters beautifully painted, as though to verify it was really John's work and not a cheap fake, were numbers that George recognized as latitude and longitude. He frowned. Little as he understood what was going on in John's head, he knew enough to see intent. The boy knew he had to get his message out before he left the country the following day. The coordinates meant something. And so did the beautifully painted, almost photographic, picture of a brown desert hill underneath.

George turned on the Post Office computer after the driver dropped him off, found an Internet site that did such things, and typed in the coordinates.

It was a good minute or so before he could hit Enter, because at last he understood. Of all the billions of people on Earth, John wanted George, and George alone, to see the missing data from John's painting. The comet impact point.

And that hill looked scarily familiar. He hit Enter, his pulse a fluttery scramble. But when he stared at the results on the screen, and then back at the picture of the hill, his poor mature-age heart uncalibrated itself, went screaming down in a death-dive. For somehow, four year old John, with his brilliant brain imprisoned within an autistic skull, had been permitted to communicate with the world just twice. Once to save an entire nation, and once to save a single person. George's only son Murray, working on a sheep station miles north of Kalgoorlie, out on the edges of the Great Victoria Desert. With a hill overlooking the homestead building that George remembered from his last visit.

And both the coordinates and picture matched.

George leaned back, his neck throbbing. Surely it couldn't be right! This boy was squeezing all the normality out of his life, making things crazier than he could remember. Not since madmen had sent the world to war in George's youth had things been so relentlessly insane. But everything matched. And according to an autistic boy who shouldn't know anything at all, but did, something—the comet—was going to make his son give up. How did he know? Didn't matter. He had to warn Murray. From what he remembered, there were no TVs out there and an unreliable phone line. It was possible that Murray might not know about the comet until too late, and the eight hour drive back to Perth could get him back after the last planes and ships had left.

The trip home for George had no reality whatsoever. With John's paper on the passenger's seat and a formal letter of authority in his pocket personally signed by the PM, he drove home well over the speed limit, cops be damned. No way was he getting on a plane unless his family was safe. Louise he could take with him, the PM had promised as much, but he decided as he lurched the car around the corner and into his street that he would work at the airport with the government while he waited for Murray to arrive.

He flicked on the radio, wondering how quickly the PM had got the news out. None of the channels were onto it. But as he shuddered the car up the drive, the announcer said, "Stand by for important breaking news from Parliament House, Canberra. We will be crossing shortly to the Prime Minister for an announcement for all Australians."

George grabbed the paper, jumped out and ran inside. He was shaking so much when he picked up the phone and dialled the number that he had to sit down and wedge the phone against his shoulder. Louise was out the back putting scraps in the compost tumbler—he could hear her grunting as she pulled the half-full tumbler over. George felt a black wrongness steal up his throat and take up lodgings in his mouth. The place where the ordinary and the sheer downright bloody well wrong met just kept moving, and he couldn't keep track of it.

The other end of the line started ringing, an old Bakelite ring that reminded him of listless and endless afternoons on his grandfather's farm, with the sun locked in the same overhead position for months at a time.

Well, George thought. *At least the line's working.*

And kept ringing.

George was about to hang up, though he didn't quite know what he would have done next, when someone picked up in a breathless rush.

"'lo?"

George wasn't sure where his voice was for a moment. "Yes, hello, it's George Wilkins here. Is—?"

"Who? Oh, yeah…" A hand muffled the receiver. "Hey Murray, it's ya old man." Unmuffled. "Yeah, he's coming."

"Dad," Murray said in a voice that had the tail end of a laugh in it. George could hear his mates chuckling in the background.

"Murray," George said, so glad to hear his voice he almost forgot why he had called, then decided to slow down. Urgent fathers were never pleasant. "How's it going?"

"Yeah good, Dad."

George heard the tone in his son's voice, and could picture him turning to his mates sitting around on the verandah with their boots off, beers at elbows, smokes lit: *just Dad calling for a chat. Be with you soon.*

"Pretty hot. Working hard. What about you? Anything interesting happenin? How's Mum?"

"She's fine. Work's good."

And after all his urgency to get home, he didn't seem to have the right words. He cleared his throat, made some croaky beginnings, then said, "Something's happened."

Murray still had half a laugh in him. "You pregnant? Hey, good news, Dad."

"You know that comet?"

Murray went silent. "Yeah?"

"It's going to hit Australia. Scientists just discovered. It's going to break up, big piece is going to miss, but the small one is going to hit the central Australian desert. Five days. They're clearing the state. The whole place. Everyone's getting out. Five days. Turn your radio on."

Murray swore, apologised, then swore again. "Not working."

"Doesn't matter. Just pack up and get out. I've got guaranteed seats out, but I've told the…boss that I'm going to be working at Perth airport keeping track of all the evacuees until you arrive. Get yourself here as quickly as you can. You'll need ID—your driver's license will do, anything. I'm not leaving without you."

"Five days?"

"Yeah, but don't hang around! I know what you're like, you're just as likely to stop and get some photos of the comet just to see what it looks like up close."

"Yeah, no worries, Dad. I'll be there."

"How many of you are there now? You going to bring everyone?"

"Well, Neil the boss's got his car and...well, Rick's car's stuffed, Wazza rolled his last week, so...well, we've got mine, so we'll be right."

George felt all his fatherly uselessness surface as violently as a submarine. "Just. Don't. Be. Late! Better a week early than a second late, you hear me? Don't give up on me now! When you reach the airport, call me on my Scout."

"Sure, Dad. Sounds interesting though."

George's hands stopped shaking a little. He grabbed the phone with one hand, and realized the paper was still in the other. He stared at it for a moment. "Murray?"

"See ya later, D—yeah?"

"What's the name of that hill near the station?"

"That one we climbed when you were up here last? Dunno. Hey Rick, what's the name of that hill you take your girlfriend up when you're feeling frisky?"

George heard chortles and ribaldry. "Hasn't got a name, Dad. Not one we know, anyway. Why? Izzat where the comet's going to hit?"

George wondered what exactly was going on inside John's mind, what strange otherworldly architecture was there in his brain cells, how something millions of miles out in space was communicating with him. "Maybe," he said, and the word had a hollowness he could not explain. "Just get here quickly."

George hung up just as Louise came in, her hair awry and face bright with gardening sunshine and the smell of compost and potting mix. "Hello dear. You're home early. Everything alright?"

Father Nick's Day minus four days
Arcada

Jacqui toggled the sled drive control forward and the Breakers' sled rotated out of hover into a northern blast. Ahead was a quick one day run to Singapore in conjunction with eight other teams. The Breakers were exhausted. Ivan was already asleep in a corner of the cockpit.

Martin stood. "Youse blokes," he said quietly. "Something's wrong."

"I checked the course," said Jacqui. "We're fine."

"No, I mean with the schedule. Something wasn't sitting quite right with me—the numbers didn't add up—so I did some calculating." He spread out his hands. "We're going to run out of time. There's not enough workers, not enough sleds. Even if everyone worked around the clock for the next four days with all sleds in constant use, we'd still fall short."

"I thought so," said Anna.

"It's a loser's game!" shouted Graeme. "There's no point in it!"

"You've got to trust Jacob," Harker said. "I've seen what he's doing and it's not pretty. There's more at stake here than what we can see."

"Harks, you gotta talk to him." Martin's eyes were dark with resentment. "He's gotta get more workers from somewhere. I don't have anything against work, but these blokes with their history of gifts should have planned things better. It doesn't make any sense. We've got to have a reason for all this."

"There's only four more days," said Harker.

Anna's eyes were greyer than concrete. "Yeah, we can hold out for four days—everyone can—but that's not the point! We're not going to finish. We're going to get to the end and know that some people are going to miss out. The world is going to sink into suicidal darkness, and because of one man's incompetence, blithe ignorance or something else he's not saying, millions of people aren't going to get the gift due them."

"That's all he ever says," grumbled Graeme. "Get the bloody gift due them. And he doesn't seem bothered by things being so late. That bloke's cornered the market on optimism."

"Or stupidity," said Wayne. "I could do with ten hours of sleep—that's the gift due me. Ten hours straight with no wake up calls, on a bed that doesn't move, preferably after a steak and chips dinner. I'm heading straight for the pub after this."

"I don't want another Father Nick's Day gift ever again," said Frances with feeling.

Harker spread out his arms in what he hoped was a conciliatory gesture. "Stay with it," he said gently. "It's one thing my army days taught me: stick by your mates. We all promised to do this, fire or flood. Makes no difference. Jacob will work something out. Four days to go."

When the hatch opened, they slung on their packs and ran away from him, almost as one.

All except Martin.

"I didn't tell the others this," he said quietly, "but they'll work it out soon enough. None of our delivery runs have been to the places we live. I'm sure that's deliberate. So how do we know gifts have been delivered to our houses, our friends and families? If we're running short of workers, who's to say we'll miss out and get the Black Despair? I'm happy with life, Harks. I don't want to go yet. That's all."

It stopped Harker for a moment. He thought of George with a sick anger. For all his love for his mate, he had done nothing to keep George from suicide, and there was no guarantee, if time and workers were short, that George would receive anything.

He stepped out of the sled into the Singapore night and slung on his pack. *Stick by your mates*, he had told them. And here he was, running around the cavernous cold emptiness of Singapore's endless apartment blocks while the Black Despair loomed over George, and Jacob just didn't—or couldn't—provide enough workers.

When they returned to Arcada, it was not Maria waiting for them at the entrance to the chamber, but an Arcadan man Harker didn't recognize. The old man stood nearby, but he looked glimmery and insubstantial, and Harker really didn't care. But it was the way that the Arcadan nodded at the Spanner—Harker could see something passing between them—and Spanner walking away that fired Harker's anger.

"What's going on?" he demanded, anger muscling up in him despite his weariness. "Where's Maria?"

The Arcadan met Harker's glare steadily. "The Spanner is leaving your team, Harker Brown. Jacob regrets this, but promises it will be for the best. She has a vital—"

"Leaving?" snapped Harker. "What the blue blazes are you doing? We need every man! You take anyone off the teams and the deliveries won't be finished in time. George is going to kill himse… Spanner, get back here!"

Spanner kept walking with not even a hint of hesitation.

"Spanner!" But something in the Arcadan's stance and tone kept him from running after her.

The man spread out his hands. "Jacob asks you to trust him."

That was enough. Harker pushed past and strode towards the doors. The old man looked thoughtful as he went past, but Harker didn't care. Jacob had some explaining to do.

By the time he reached Jacob's sparse personal chambers, he was angry, anger comprised of eighty percent tiredness, anger he knew he shouldn't trust, though it was there anyway.

Two hooded and cloaked people were just leaving Jacob's chamber as Harker entered. He wasn't really paying attention, but after they had passed, he realized that one was rather big in the belly.

And Jacob looked exhausted, sitting on the wooden chair next to the Sentry, his head in his hands, his long fingers in his hair.

"Was that Joe and Maria? Why are they dressed strangely? Where are they going?"

Jacob's smile was wan. "They have a gift to deliver for me. Now come here."

As Harker drew near the Sentry, the stink of pollution grew stronger, as strong as an industrial sludgepond, not just contained within the well, but leaking out over it, oozing into the room, ramming gaseous fists against Harker's senses. He gasped, clapped his hand over his mouth.

"It is getting stronger," Jacob said weakly. "It will not be long now." He coughed. "The work is difficult, I know, and everyone struggles...to...to believe that it will be finished in time." He held out a hand, and Harker noticed how pale it was, how translucent. "Do not lose heart. In time, every person will have the gift due them."

"What about this?" Harker demanded, waving a fist at the Sentry, too angry to be polite. "We're pulling our weight, more than enough, working our guts out with impossible schedules, four days to go and not enough workers, the Spanner gone without explanation or warning, and now this? Seems like this is all a joke at our expense. You had me going there for a while with all the curse breaking business, but I'm seeing things more clearly now. We're all ready to walk—"

"Harker Brown, be quiet." Weak though Jacob seemed, his voice had surprising penetration.

Harker felt all his resistance subside. Jacob had the light of sunshine through rain, a glimmering like hope seen far off, his skin glowing with the incandescent softness of babies and milk and pearls. "On your first day here, I named you leader. It is now that time, time that you put aside petty things and see the manner of things beyond your team."

"Absolutely," said Harker. "I think it's about time."

"Do you?" Jacob considered him for a moment. "Very well. Give me your hands."

"What?"

"Your hands." And when Harker held them out, reluctantly, instantly suspicious, Jacob took them and laid them on the rim of the Sentry.

"This will hurt," he said, "but not injure," and plunged both Harker's hands into the well against the image of the United Kingdom.

It wasn't so much the pain that Harker afterwards remembered, but the way that the stink became force, a vast torrential wave rising up towards him, threatening to break against him, a putrid and glistening green, like a viscous discharge scumming a planetary surface.

Harker tried to pull away, but could not. A ripsaw sting scoured his hands, seemed to tear flesh from his palms. If he was screaming, he couldn't hear it. A ferocious charge of radiation swarmed through him, scorching his bones, searing his organs. His lungs were sodden paper, collapsing under the weight of the stench.

Hands pulled him back, and his relief was complete and sudden. He collapsed in Jacob's arms, panting, choking, his face dripping, his hands hanging loose, feeling no pain at all.

"What was that?" he gasped.

Jacob helped him stand, moved him away from the Sentry. "Your adversary. When the comet was announced, all his attention turned fully to Boston, waiting for a victory there, or perhaps news that would help him understand the significance of the comet. But whatever that was has failed. Six days ago, his focus turned suddenly to Perth for a moment, although that has now faded as well." He sat Harker down in the wooden chair and wiped Harker's face gently with his sleeve. Despite all the smoke and foul stench from the Sentry, the fabric smelled like clean desert wind. "And soon he will see us."

"But you've been holding him back?"

Jacob nodded. "As much as I can. But in this war, he advances and I retreat. In time, he will almost certainly break our timeslip as he has broken it in Europe and America, and then we will rely only on hope, Harker Brown."

Even in the presence of the Arcadan leader, Harker was unable to hold down a snort. "You can't just hope he won't bring his army down here! Hope's not a weapon!"

"What is it then?"

"What's hope?" Harker floundered. "Never really thought about it. But that's not the point—you can't fight with it!"

"But we have. For seventeen hundred years, in the midst of

suicide, we have hoped and striven and believed for the time when there will be no more suicides. Hope is a weapon much mightier than you may believe. For what else has fought the despair of the curse for centuries?"

"Good point. But is it mighty enough to get the job done before he declares war?"

"It has always been enough." Jacob's skin was a papery lantern, all glimmery light, his smile a faint curve of hope.

And Harker, for reasons he was never able to name, believed him. As he lay in bed later, unable to sleep, his flesh scourged but unharmed, still twitching at the memory of the rank wave about to break over him, he knew he would do anything for Jacob.

Boston House

On the fifth day of their search for the final clue, Blackwell sent the Poor Men off in pairs, hoping they would find something, even though they had walked the same corridors and rooms many times before.

It was Rebecca who came bolting back along a corridor, shouting, "Come quick, the sleepers have gone!"

Benedict was the first to run. "How gone?"

"All of them, missing from their beds. Just gone!"

"The Cabal took them?"

"But why?" demanded Benedict. "It's Tower they're after!"

The dormitories were empty, every one of them, every single sleeper gone. No signs of struggle, each of the beds left slightly body-printed, cups of water beside each bed drained and empty.

"How did they get past the jumpships?" Blackwell demanded, standing at the Door where they had all gathered. "Surely the Cabal would have seen them go!"

But a careful check by Antonius and Arthur showed the jumpships still in their places, with no signs of sleds shot down. Rattled, the Poor Men retreated deep inside the House and kept quiet. Paul doubled the guard and equipped them all with axes.

But Blackwell paced through dormitories, muttering to himself, "How did they get past the jumpships?"

NINE PLANETS

Perth International Airport

The queue of evacuees never ended, day or night, like a hungry snake, always approaching and never arriving. Children clutching gamehubs and playScouts and all manner of soft toys, harried along by parents trying unsuccessfully to be calm. Arguments flared, pets were mentioned a lot, insurance companies blamed, invoked, cursed, renovation plans discussed gloomily. Bags were checked for things left behind. One bag per person, said the signs above every exit booth. 7 kg max, no exceptions.

Amazingly, the PM and his Cabinet had kept their promises and were even now helping the regular airline staff for the night shift, the toughest, George thought, when the comet was visible through windows, and fights broke out at the sight of its tiny hurtling threat, a vertical pillar of fire off to the east.

"Fine bloody Father Nick's Day gift," said many.

At least one wedding ceremony was performed off to one side of the queue, with the only concessions to style and fashion a modest veil for the bride and a bow tie for the groom. Otherwise it was jeans and T-shirts for both, and the whole moving queue launched into the Wedding March *a capella,* cheered at the appropriate spots, and talked happily until the new couple were checked through the exit booth.

"Overseas honeymoon," yelled a young man in a fluoro road worker's vest. "Government shout. Betcha didn't expect that!"

"It was meant to be Fiji." The bride forced a smile. "Bloody comet."

"Hey, maybe next year!" called his mate as the bride turned and waved to her temporary wedding party, smiling widely and flung her veil into a group of children at the front of the queue. A boy looked at it suspiciously until his sister snatched it out of his hands.

George checked them through. "Congratulations," he said. "I'm sorry it didn't work out the way you planned," and laughed as politely as he could manage when it was someone else checking through to safety and not Murray.

An old man with a beagle was next. The beagle looked healthy, but the old bloke was dressed in rags, barefooted, filthy. "Sorry, sir, but no pets allowed," said George, pointing to the sign on the desk. "You'll have to leave your dog behind." He thought maybe the customs people could use the beagle, though no-one would be smuggling contraband into Australia for a while.

The old man said nothing for a moment. George stared at him. He would have made a good circus midget, though his eyes were calm as sunrise and his smile took up all the space on his face. George's heart flipped. "Oh, we're not going," the old man said softly. "But you are, and not on a plane."

George found that all his words had escaped him. None of them would be any good for this peculiar little man. And George didn't really notice for a moment, but all the noise in the room had dropped, quite suddenly and completely. No-one in the queue was moving. No-one was talking. The place was like a photograph. Alone in the room, only he and the man and the dog seemed to be alive.

The man smiled. "Have you shown him, as you were commanded?"

"Commanded? Yeah, I told my son. Is that what you meant? But the kid…John…that was a command? How did he know Murray… how—"

"Go," the old man said.

Then George's heart flipped again, and then there was noise and movement and an elderly woman with a walking frame.

"Excuse me," she said. "Excuse me, young man, are you alright?"

George smiled, but something peculiar in his head sparked. A recent memory, he was sure, though he couldn't pin it down. He frowned, stared around. One of those déjà vu moments, maybe, but it had been so *real!* One day, he thought, he really should get a beagle.

He processed the old lady with absent-minded courtesy, and the next person, and the next after that, but after almost every evacuee, he looked up and gazed over the heads of the queue for Murray. A shaggy mop of sunbleached hair, face and skin sundark, tufts of chest hair through the top of his battered khaki workshirt, shorts stained with oil, grease and other residues of station life, and boots probably on their last legs.

His Scout sat on the desk in front of him. A Hercules took off, and the queue cheered that they didn't have to be subjected to its horrendous internal noise for the duration of the flight. Other airliners taxied towards the terminal: QANTAS, Singapore Airlines, Thai, Cathay, Air New Zealand, British, JAL, South African. George never bothered to look around.

His Scout remained silent. Murray did not appear. The queues came and went with infuriating constancy. All noise was planes and crowd. He checked the master list on the airport's Customs database frequently, but the name of Murray Lennard Wilkins never appeared. Heart palpitations once at Murray Peter Wilkins, and also at Murray Wilkins, no middle name, pensioner. But Murray Lennard was still somewhere between George and the comet, and the worry was building that the comet would reach him first.

He called Murray's Scout several times, and hoped that the silence was just Murray passing through non-coverage zones. He left four messages before he gave up. Eight hundred and thirty odd kilometers. At normal speed, allowing for slowing down through towns…nine hours? Maybe ten if they stopped for coffee or petrol? What was keeping him?

Petrol. Mothers of the unborn. Maybe they had left with nothing but half a tank of petrol, expecting to fill up along the way, and found all the roadhouses closed. Maybe they got as far as Kalgoorlie and ran out of juice, chugged to a stop out on a desert highway, with the heat rising in waves off the road, the sun gloating, the vast horizons of silence ripping you down to primitive reactions.

Maybe they were *walking*.

George closed his file with a snap, frightening the young kids next in his queue. "I'm off," he told Harry Grant, his supervisor.

"Yer shift's not done," said Harry. "Yer need a potty break?"

"I need to get my son. He's not down from Leonora yet. He should have been here already. Give me a couple of days, and I'll be back with him and Louise."

"Hey, what about us?" shouted the father of the kids as George walked off, finding the closest exit, ignoring Harry and the yells of the crowd.

He called Louise and drove home through empty streets. Already weeds were plotting, solar roof panels expecting a long dusty-skied darkness, and cats urinating on carpets, fretting. Dogs barked, first at nothing, then each other, a lonely suburban echo. The sun warmed no-one. Vegetables wilted. Louise was on the kerb, arms crossed. Her shoulder bag sat rigid on the browning grass, packed tight with family photos, a file of important documents, and as little clothing as she could bear. *We'll be back soon*, she had promised George.

George got out of the car. "We're going," he said.

The laugh lines around her eyes crinkled, and her lipstick glimmered. George thought she still looked good, though you couldn't help gravity. Still pretty for sixty-three.

"He's back? When?"

"Not yet. He's not answering his Scout, and he hasn't called. Maybe his Scout's broke, maybe he's out of range, any number of maybes, but I'm not waiting any longer." He loaded her bag. "Get in. We're going to get him."

"George!" But she got in.

He leaned over and kissed her, tasted salt and smelled the cosmetic warmth of her old familiar wonderful cheek. "There's only one road there. It's not like he's going to wander off on side tracks. East to Kalgoorlie, then turn left. It's not rocket science. But if he's run out of petrol, he'll be walking, and odds on he hasn't got enough water. We've got enough time to get there and back."

She pulled away with wifely defiance. "What about you? Are you racing off without thinking it through? Have you got enough petrol? Water, oil, checked your tyres?"

He snorted. "You sound like the RAC. We're going to the Post Office first. The posties keep a stock of jerrycans out the back, so we should be right and we'll borrow one of the new people movers to fit in Murray and his mates." He patted her leg. "We'll be fine."

She laughed, a wicked little chuckle, and the sun glanced off her face like applause. "The PM let you go alright? He's not fretting or anything?"

George pulled out and planted it. "National security, I told him."

The boot heavy with three full jerrycans, one of water, and four liters of oil, they blazed eastward along Morley Drive past gawking stares from bumper to bumper drivers, their radiators steaming.

George said, "They're probably thinking 'Bloody idiot. He's forgotten to turn the iron off.'"

Louise laughed nervously and then was silent.

George turned on his radio, but apart from the constant reminders for people to head to airports and ports immediately, the only other news was the bizarre disappearances of the strange unknown people that had appeared so mysteriously weeks earlier. Out of hospitals and police stations, vanished without a trace.

But then his Scout buzzed, and he snatched for it so fast he whacked Louise on his follow-through.

"Murray!"

"Sorry mate, no. It's Frank. Where're you?"

"Oh. Morley Drive, coming up to Lord St. Why? I thought you were working at the airport."

"I just called the hospital to make sure they were getting Harks out OK. They were all in a flap, trying to organize all the criticals and intensive cares first…mate, it's a nightmare there."

"Get to the point."

"Harks is gone."

"That's good then. Where're they taking him? It'd be good if he could go to Joburg with us."

"No that's the point. He's gone, vanished, disappeared. The staff don't know where. They went to wheel him out, and the bed was empty. Quick search around, but no sign of him."

George wasn't sure he could handle two disasters. "He was in a coma, mate! Ya don't just wake up from those."

"Well, he's gone. One of the staff on her way to the airport said they saw him running down Riverside Drive yesterday morning."

"Running? Can't have been. Must have been someone else."

"Tall, wearing a flapping hospital gown, pulling tubes out of his nose as he ran. She recognized his face. Shocked the life out of her, almost drove into the river. It's Harker, mate, no doubt about it. Comatose one day, marathoner the next. But no-one's seen him since. There's no chance of finding him now. Only hope someone's picked him up, sorted him out, put him on a plane. Just thought I'd let you know."

"Flamin' Harks. Never happy to keep still."

"So, you're off to the airport?"

George wilted a fraction. "Murray's not down from Leonora yet. We're going to look for him. I'm getting worried."

"You told him to get down?"

"Yeah, when this was first announced."

"You'd reckon he'd be here by now."

"Could be anything: petrol, engine failure, crash." He hated each thought, especially the sight of Murray and his mates walking westward in single file along the empty Great Eastern Highway, with the sun standing guard and the comet stalking them.

Frank was silent for a moment. "You've got four days."

"I don't want to be here that long. Rather be out in two. They reckon there's gunna be fireballs hitting first." That thought was just too wild, too terrible to speak. He paused, kept his eyes on the road, knew he had to keep his throat plugged, his voice steady. Fireballs. It was too much to even put in the same sentence with Murray. He accelerated.

"Where are you now?" Frank sounded decisive.

"Great Eastern Highway, coming up to Guildford. Why?"

"Pat and I are on Roe Highway, heading to the airport. We're scheduled to go tonight. Hang on a mo." He covered the Scout and George heard muffled voices raised, most of them Pat's.

Frank came back on with a flat, decisive voice. "Pick us up on the corner of Roe and Great Eastern. We're coming with you."

"Frank! No, you—"

"Can't do it on your own, ya crazy bugger. Gotta have someone to keep ya laughing. Pat can sing a bit. We're coming."

Arcada

Jacob was waiting on the descent pad when Harker's sled landed.

Harker saw him from the cockpit. His face had the residues of battle all over it, shadowed and afraid and determined in a way that Harker recognized instantly, though he knew the Breakers wouldn't. Grenades had gone off in Jacob's eyes. The spark was missing, or bunkered deep perhaps, away from the crump of exploding shells and scream of artillery. Harker had seen concentration camp survivors with more light in their faces.

Harker climbed out of the hatch and went up and stood in front of him, feeling a strong desire to salute. It was like old army days, he thought, though this war was real, and this was an enemy whose hatred had physical impact, whose poisonous fumes reached across hemispheres.

The Breakers gathered behind Harker, though he had not asked them. Jacob's light pulsed slowly out of him, like a wounded soldier losing blood. The chamber was dim otherwise. The old man was standing near the entrance, with that odd light glimmering from his face. Harker thought he saw figures standing along the walls of the chamber, but it was too dark to tell.

Jacob found a smile somewhere. "Welcome home, Poor Men," he said quietly, as though bad news was following. "I applaud you and all you have done."

Harker heard indrawn breath behind him. The Breakers were preparing for confrontation.

"I am sorry that I took the Spanner from your team. I know the value she added. However, she has been working on a critical task, and now she has completed it successfully. So successful that I am able to return her, as well as the fruit of her efforts." He raised a hand, and five figures stepped forward from the rear of the chamber, wearing white shirts, leather aprons, brown trousers and boots. "Five new members for each team. They need no training. and they will join you tomorrow."

The noise behind him turned to a quiet murmur of approval. "Only five?" asked Anna. "That's hardly enough to—"

Jacob smiled, a little stronger, though the pain was evident. "Five, but there are thousands arriving every day, bringing with them hundreds of sleds. The Poor Men are coming home. The Brotherhood is together at last. All of them, from every continent, with all their sleds. After seventeen hundred years, we will be together at last."

Graeme coughed. "You took your time, mate."

Martin, ever the diplomat, said, "Does this mean we'll get the job done? Crikey, that's good news if so."

"Yes, the work will be finished."

"Good news, yes," said Anna, and Harker noted the careful modulation in her voice, "but we'd still like to know what's going on. We're happy to help, but we all thought this was a place of honesty, and it seems that...that you haven't been telling us the whole truth."

Harker watched Jacob carefully, keen to see how he would respond to Australian candour.

"No, I haven't," he said. "Soon I will, but not yet. For now, stay true. Your duty will be completed soon, and everyone will have the gift due him."

Great Eastern Highway, from Perth to Leonora

George and Louise and Frank and Pat pass through jarrah forests together, four last people going backwards, against the vast surging tide of humanity abandoning them. Australia is getting lighter, floating higher in the Southern Ocean as the the ships depart, and inside the planes taking off are kids snubnosed against triple layer windows, watching the country of cricket and Saturday afternoon barbecues and beaches fade under heat and low cloud. Their country. No amount of airline toys soothe that kind of loss.

George watches everything go against him as he steers. One of the last interstate road trains sways across both lanes, forcing him onto the gravel road shoulder. The women swear darkfaced, their fingers jammed down on the dashboard, their lipstick forced into tight lines. For the next minute or so, the talkspace in the car is a breathy place of relief as they debate the courtesies for and against cursing the truck driver all the way to Fremantle.

Oh, the gravity is against them out here, and the easterly as well as it leans at the car, rattling hubcaps and the bonnet latch and the plastic grille that is only a few inches away from the radiator blowing up for good. It's come curling up anticlockwise from the Great Australian Bight, leaving the whales and sharks and the vast bluewater tuna schools, and once it gets its traction on the flat face of the Nullarbor, it scratches and rips like a manic cat.

George drives. Talk is a loose thing for the first fifty kilometers or so, a random punctuation of low bursts, nothing of substance. He keeps an eye on the engine temperature, and Frank and the ladies watch the sides of the roads for any sign—any sign of Murray and the boys or his blue Holden. Anything would be good.

They pass into Northam, and when they see an identical blue Holden on the side of the road, Louise shrieks her delight, and it takes a good ten minutes to calm her down when it's not Murray's. But the damage is done now. He could have got this far, says George, and run out of juice. He could be anywhere, looking for food or water, resting up on a verandah, having a leak.

He could be safe and singing all the way to Freo with that truckie, says Frank quietly.

It's the indecision that nearly kills them. The talk fairly gets to arguing, but eyes meet, and heat settles, and when George announces that they're going to check every town just in case, no-one says a word. So it's a good half hour cruising carefully up and down streets, looking for Murray's blue Holden and seeing nothing but overturned council bins and windblown papers and crow-pecked Earlies, all abandoned before the comet.

Then it's Meckering and Cunderdin, and the sight of so many streets where only the wind walks has Louise wiping at her nose with her face turned away, and winding the window down for the road noise that will drown out her quiet sobs. There are blue Holdens around, but none have Murray's license plates. One has no wheels and a body slumped in the driver's seat.

Pat decides a song will raise the spirits. She's sung her way through many a nursing home singalong for the oldies, keeping their lungs free of fluid and tumours and other nasties, she reckons, and so she launches into some of her favorites, 'Click Go the Shears,' 'Waltzing Matilda' and 'Road to Gundagai.' As soon as she starts, though, she realizes that all the songs refer to men of the land, the very kind of man they are out looking for.

The first night on the road is one of the ugliest and loneliest nights any of them have ever spent. It beats a death in the family. It beats stillbirths, or the raving angry vacuum of divorce. The four of them go silently into a deserted motel in Tammin, hearing their own footsteps on the stain-resistant carpet where tracks have been worn by businessmen who don't really care, and husbands too drunk to get home in one piece. They take keys from the rack and let themselves into the first rooms they find. They eat and drink the food and alcohol they find in the kitchen, purely functional actions of chewing and ingestion. It's all silent. There are no words for this kind of emptiness.

George hates stopping. He'd drive all day and all night loaded up with No-Doz, with the headlights on hi-beam and the CD player blaring. He drinks one red wine too many, doesn't taste it, but as it sends him off, he's thinking that somewhere out in the desert, if they don't find Murray, he'll share the last of the bottle with Louise, watching fireballs.

Pat weeps at the tiny tourist brochures in a plastic rack on the reception desk for places that might very well be just atomised dust in a few days time. She wonders if she would have come with George and Louise if she and Frank had been able to have kids. She wonders many things as she lies on top of the orange quilted bedspread with Frank in the next bed, both fully dressed, their shoes lined up neatly on the floor beside them, and she tells Frank none of them. This isn't the sort of place for conversation. She wants to leave no trace of herself here, not body imprint, not words, not even her smell. She doesn't belong here; she belongs on a plane travelling at great speed away from this country, and even the great sturdy ramshackle structure of their lifelong friendship with George and Louise is not enough to dissuade her. Sleep comes eventually, but it sure takes its time.

In the morning, when she wakes with the orange quilted bedspread scattered on the floor, she makes the bed carefully before they leave.

The next day, they search Kellerberrin, and then the two houses and petrol station at Hines Hill and then Merredin after that, and there are scatterings of conversation for as long as they can maintain humour or good cheer, and then it dies in the space between breaths. The day turns the color of chlorine.

With three days to go before the comet hits, as they drive into Kalgoorlie, George decides to be open and honest about his calculations. He lays them out on the dashboard for everyone to see and the sun to fade.

The last plane goes thirty-six hours before impact, he says. We have to give ourselves ten hours to get back from Leonora, so we have a day to find Murray.

And we're heading the wrong bloody way, says Frank, and although there is a hiccup of embarrassment for a second, they chortle like schoolkids, and the resonances of their laughter are better than food and wine for the next hour or so.

But George, as they head out northwards from Kalgoorlie, past the last great abandoned city before the endless desert, is starting to wonder.

If he doesn't find Murray, he will connect a pipe from the exhaust into the cabin, then wind up the windows, kiss Louise whom he loves, and wait for that last sleep.

Father Nick's Day minus three days
Boston House

Rattled as they were by the disappearance of the sleepers, the Poor Men searched the Boston House for their missing brethren. Everywhere. Every room, workshop, rooftop, attic, basement, cupboard, crevice. Every hangar, outbuilding, storeroom. Twice. Then again. For men who had continued a millennial tradition of invisible charity all their lives, the idea that their own brethren could be silently stolen from within their midst was deeply disturbing. Even Antonius seemed shaken, and seemed glad when it was his guard duty that another Poor Man was standing with him. Paul even suggested the sleepers might have collectively given up hope and crossed the line of yellow stones into the outside world, but that was loudly shouted down. Poor Men always hope. Poor Men never surrender.

Nevertheless, the talk in quiet huddles turned to arcane witcheries and supernaturals, and when Blackwell went by, they looked up at him, most unlike Poor Men, with hollow eyes of fright.

None of them moved apart from meals.

Blackwell continued the search for his last clue himself. He walked the corridors alone, repeating the passage to himself as though mere sound would deliver meaning.

And still the question overrode everything.

How did they get past the jumpships?

NINE PLANETS

Satson Station, Leonora

Murray Lennard Wilkins sat on the verandah and stared out at the no-name hill drinking down the sun, treeshadows laid flat on the brown earth like snakes dying. There was beer in the fridge, and it would stay cold as long as the electricity kept going. Neil the fat mongrel boss, before he drained Murray's ute and both motorbikes of their fuel and took off with the only other working vehicle in the early hours, had just stocked up with food on his last trip to town, so they had enough to last them.

Oh, they had considered their options. None of the phone lines out of the station were working since his father had called and sent that strange picture that had taken ages to download. Satson Station was way outside Scout range, and the brief radio message they had managed only reached some random fella who hardly spoke any English, so that didn't seem to have done any good. Even when that quiet bloke Joe who said he was from a construction camp somewhere had arrived with his pregnant wife Maria, their beat-up old Holden was on empty as well.

So that was that. Three days before impact and they didn't have many other choices. They could hope they'd survive the two hundred kilometer walk into town and hope there was someone left there to give them a lift to Perth, when they knew full well there wasn't. Mark out the words 'SOS' in the dirt, and hope someone flying past saw it. And hope that the scientist blokes were wrong, that they had got their calculations out by a degree or whatever it was they measured these things by.

Lots of hoping. Not much hope.

Murray held out the grainy picture of the painting of the hill his Dad had emailed.

"Waddya reckon?" he asked Rick.

Rick put down his beer. "Who'd he say did this? Some kid?"

"Four year old. Autistic."

"Yeah?" said Wazza. "Doesn't look that artistic to me."

"Autistic. His lights are out; he doesn't connect with the world."

Rick looked hard at the picture, held it up against the hill. "Connected pretty well to paint that. It's exactly the same hill. Spittin' image! Has he been up here for a paintin' class or something?"

"Maybe. Seems strange though he'd paint this hill, then give the painting to the old man. Like he meant something by it."

"Artistic kids got their lights switched off, you said," grunted John. "So he couldn't've meant nothin'."

Murray drank the last of his beer. "I'm going up there, take a look. I reckon that kid's got something goin on in his little brain."

"Alien landing site, ya reckon?"

"Touchdown and take over the world."

"Secret government plot. Clear everyone out, then let every other country dump their nuclear waste there."

Murray laughed.

"Be dark soon," said Rick.

"Moon's out. Ya wanna come? Better'n sitting here waiting for the end of the world."

Wazza put down his beer. "I'll get me boots on. Don't want to be stubbin' me toe. Could take weeks to heal."

Murray laughed, and almost felt good about it, but heard something beautiful, beautiful enough to distract him from continental disasters.

A soft voice from the verandah, singing. Murray turned slowly, shushing his mates with a finger to his lips. It was Maria, her dark hair luminous under lamplight, singing to her unborn child.

Murray listened for a while, and thought to himself, *Bloody beautiful. A new family, but a doomed one.*

Father Nick's Day minus twenty-eight hours
Arcada

Exhausted, Harker Brown climbed out of the sled, the last to leave, and left the hatch open for the loaders to prepare the sled for the next run. He desperately wanted more than six hours sleep, but knew someone would rouse him after only three. Father Nick's Day was only a day or so away, and even with the extra Poor Men, it was going to be tight.

But the hangar was very quiet. Harker stared. Strangely quiet.

"Harker Brown."

Harker turned quickly to see Jacob near the nose of the sled. "Yes, sir," he said, with all the conviction of a guilty child. He could not meet those eyes, bruised as they were. *It was London,* he thought. Jacob had been packing sandbags against his courage, building defences Harker knew would never stand. Jacob breathed out, and Harker smelled something sickly, like week-old meat. The old army training stood him up straight because slouching brought the sarge's rod down on his shoulders, and he had learned discipline despite himself.

Jacob raised a hand that he no doubt meant to be calming, but which twitched like a heart patient on the table, and Harker knew immediately why the hangar was empty, why Jacob was waiting.

The second task. He had dreaded it, remembering how his hands had throbbed at the touch of the Sentry. He thought of the vast leering poison of London, and wondered where he would find the strength. Nothing would compare, not the loss of Ruth on that day the world had turned its back on him. At least there he had held Ruth's hand as it had grown cool. Here, his hands on the image of London would ache with a whole continent of agonies.

Jacob said, "Come," and led Harker through a deserted Arcada. About fifty meters from the Sentry chamber, he stopped at a heavily-armored and open door Harker had never seen before. It looked like a bank vault, and when Harker looked inside, he saw nothing but a straight tunnel stretching into blackness.

"Remember this door," said Jacob. "You will need it later."

Then he led Harker to the Sentry chamber. "This is your second task," he said quietly at the door. "I regret it will be alone."

Harker stepped in. The stench of the Sentry assaulted him as he knew it would, but he also saw on a nearby table, as though to distract him, a brass chronometer, as well as a plate of fresh fruit and vegetables, some cheese and sausage, a loaf of new bread, a glass jug of milk and a dark green bottle, unlabelled. Harker's Father Nick's Day book lay next to them and his cricket bat stood in a corner. The bed was newly made. Harker smelled clean milk and soap. He thought he saw a ghostly blur of the strange old man in the corner, but he didn't really care anymore.

"This will be your home until it is all over," Jacob said. "When I go, I will shut you in. You will have everything you need here. There is water in the next room for washing. Do you understand?"

"So far, yes."

Jacob's face reminded Harker of the Kokoda Trail heroes. "I chose you for this task for your resilience, your refusal to give up. Even when your beloved wife died, you did not surrender and take your own life, as so many would have done."

Harker nodded.

"So I ask you now—you must obey my command. For the sake of hope in the world, you must. Promise me this."

"Without telling me what you want me to do?"

"Promise me."

Harker hesitated, more afraid than he had ever been. "I promise I will obey your command."

Jacob closed his eyes slowly, like a patient dying, and roused himself slowly. "You will remain in this room until your task is complete. You will not have human contact or sleep. The Sentry will not permit slumber, believe me. You will stand with your hands on the Sentry, focusing solely on our adversary in London, and resisting him with all your strength of character. He knows me now, and knows my weaknesses, but he does not know you. So you can withstand him for a while. But when the chronometer reads 'zero,' you must do the first of two things. I regret that you will find the first against your nature." He held Harker's gaze with what Harker knew was the last of his strength. "I must ask you to surrender."

The moment collapsed. Harker opened his mouth, all his protests lined up and armed. "What?" he shouted. "And let him in? What the blue blazes for? He'll destroy you! You're going to wipe out everything we've worked for, all the busting our guts, all our… we haven't slept, we've done what you asked, we've done *more* than what you've asked, and now you want me to throw it all away?" He was expanding, his anger swelling out, loading up his ammo, lining up his tanks and artillery. He wanted to shake the stupidity out of Jacob. The work had got to him, the lack of workers, the pressure of the Sentry. He'd crossed over from leadership into insanity. "Are you *mad?*"

"Whether you see it or not, there is still hope."

"There's no hope in surrender!"

Jacob reached out and took Harker's hands, although Harker pulled away twice and Jacob gently pulled them back. "Hear me well. Resist the adversary. Do not sleep. Eat quickly and only when you need to. And when the chronometer reads 'zero,' surrender. Open the timeslip. Permit the adversary entry. End your resistance. Step away from the Sentry."

Harker yanked his hands away, stepped back. "And everything will end! You're bloody mad!"

"For the sake of hope in the world, you must honor your promise."

"It's a crazy promise! I didn't—"

"This is not a game for children, Harker Brown," said Jacob, pulling his hands back.

Harker exhaled, and with it went a greater portion of what he believed was his integrity. "How can I trust you?"

"You trusted us when you willingly entered into our labours. Has this changed?"

Oddly, Harker thought then of Ruth. *Come on, Harks,* she would have said. *It'll do you good. You'll turn into a grumpy old bugger otherwise.* "What's the other task?" he said.

"When you have completed the first task, you must flee through the door I showed you. Do not waste time by attempting to close it. Do not stop until you are out of the tunnel. You will be safe then. Now I must leave you. Do you understand and agree?"

"I understand." He sighed. "Yes, I agree."

"Do you trust me?"

"I must be mad." Harker shook his head. "Yes, I trust you."

"Begin now." And he thrust Harker's hands into poison.

Six

The Final Day

Father Nick's Day minus twenty-two hours
Boston House

When Blackwell woke soon after he had gone to sleep, he knew—just *knew*—how the sleepers had disappeared. Somewhere deep in sleep, neural connections must have attached, he realized with a grin. He sat up, keen to tell the Poor Men.

The common room was empty.

His heart and throat emptied together in a choking cry.

He leaped out of bed. "Hey!" he called, and almost instantly thought better of it. The Cabal could have invaded at last, killed or taken the Poor Men and be even now hunting for him. He looked to the doorway where Antonius usually left his axe, and saw it was gone.

He had to find the Poor Men, re-establish certainty. Possibly it was nothing, and they had all resumed their searches of chimneys for the curse-breaker. Blackwell didn't think so.

He crept to the door, peered around.

Silence. Not a sound, neither of Poor Men or Cabal boots. He took up a broom he found leaning against a wall and slipped quietly along the hall towards the front of the House. If nothing else, he would at least check the 'slip boundary for any Cabal incursions.

A moonlight-framed figure stood in the doorway.

Blackwell dropped to an attacking posture and brandished his broom.

And Timothy laughed. "The key words were 'miraculously filled,'" he said, with a smile that could have been granted him by angels.

"Timothy?" croaked Blackwell, laying down his broom. "What are you doing there?"

"Coming back for you. We're all waiting for you to unlock the last clue and break the curse."

"Break? You know where it is?"

"I'll take you there now."

"The jumpships?"

"No movement yet, but there will be when you unlock the curse-breaker. We'll need to be ready for it."

Timothy led him at a striding walk across the courtyard towards the hangar. They passed into its cool expanses, past the rows of pallets and boxes still waiting there among the trolleys, both small and large, and manifests and pencils lying neatly on work tables.

"I asked myself how gifts were linked with each of the groups of words," said Timothy. "None of the first half of the passage made any sense, but when you link gifts with miraculously filled, what do you get? Which place in the House is filled with gifts as if with a miracle?"

They rounded a corner, and Blackwell saw the Poor Men, all dressed identically in white shirts, black trousers and leather aprons, even Rebecca, their hair neat, their faces alight as Blackwell appeared.

"It's the Rooms of Delivery," said Timothy, beaming, "where the Arcadan gifts appear once a month through their miraculous timeslip."

"Tower," welcomed Paul as Blackwell reached them, Timothy behind him. "We think you'll find the curse-breaker inside."

And memory burst open in Blackwell's mind in a wonderful rush—the pleasure of standing guard with Caroline, the jasmine woman outside the locked doors of the Rooms of Delivery where the Arcadan gifts appeared.

No-one was permitted inside the rooms except for that one day of the month when, in careful and precise ceremony, the Patrons unlocked the doors and went in to see thousands of boxes stacked in wonderful architectures and a fabulous glow of color. Fairy tale and legend and magic all wrapped up in these marvelous rooms: Rumpelstiltskin, Ali Baba, echoes of Fahrettin's joyful amazement when he saw Father Nikolas' first gifts.

Only after the Patrons had conferred in quiet voices were he and other novices permitted in with their trolleys to begin ferrying the gifts to the hangar to be listed on the manifests and prepared for loading onto sleds.

"But we need a Patron to get in," he said, remembering.

"Axes beat Patrons," said Antonius, with one in his hand.

The Chamber, when they hacked down the door, contained nothing. Bare walls, bare floor.

Benedict wiped his mouth. "This is it?"

But Blackwell needed no more words. Wondrous color flared behind his eyes.

"It's here!" He leaned back against the euphoric gust as he slipped below reality into that secret place within him, where the geometric and lovely order of his inner solar system sang, and the armored planet grew more radiant than ever before. There, with its gears disengaging and humming in marvelous concord, triggering open and detaching its equatorial belt, a great splendor of novatic light pouring out, his ninth planet revealed her final secret.

Blackwell gazed in, eager beyond words—the curse breaker at last! An end to suicide! Hope for humanity!

Yet what he saw was none of those.

Amid the brightness, the face of the old man stared out, grim and defiant, speaking words Blackwell only heard in his mind.

"No. You will come no further."

Father Nick's Day minus twenty-one hours thirty minutes
Arcada

With no idea where Jacob and the Arcadans were, Harker hoped the Breakers at least were all safe. He ate an apple he did not taste, drank milk that meant nothing to his tongue or belly.

He was so afraid. It wasn't the silence that unsettled him; he was used to the bush, and there was enough quiet in his soul.

Even the vicious force of the adversary's poison had not weakened him. Early in his duty, as his hands screamed and the vast wave of foul fume almost swamped him, he remembered that morning on Ocean Beach, that transcendent moment, when all the world's noises shrank down small enough to fit into a back pocket, and the balance of things re-established itself. The horizon dividing sky and sea, the waves bringing the horizon towards him bit by bit. Sky above, sea below. That moment when something pinged on his radar, when all the lamps in his heart lit up at the same time.

It was that same transcendence that defeated the viciousness of the adversary.

But he was terrified of surrender. Giving up Ruth had almost broken him, letting her go, when all of his height and strength and experience had counted for nothing. Giving up a hill, a command post during war games in army training, even that had been hard.

But giving up Father Nick's Day, the source of hope for millions? Surrendering Arcada to the Cabal army waiting—just waiting—for a moment of weakness? Surrendering George, in whom he had focused all his hope and strength? Surrendering *himself?*

At zero on the chronometer, he stood, deciding things. He laid his hands on the Sentry, felt the instant surge of foul venom drive into his skin. He held it there for a moment, resisting, then let the thoughts of Ocean Beach drop, all the transcendence evaporate.

And, hating himself, hating Jacob, hating everything, he said the words aloud.

"I surrender."

Father Nick's Day minus twenty-one hours thirty minutes
Perth

Ed stood.

He had barely moved for days, not even to relieve himself in the toilet of the abandoned motel or to sleep, bodily functions which had been replaced by the constant and ferocious pleasure of the curse's agony. Water, food, warmth, rest. All were now long-ago memories of the human he had been, of that distant era of his life bound by frailty, no matter what he had called it then. Now the curse consumed him so fully, so completely! Only one degree below the Second, he was Third of the Cabal, and would be so forever.

He sensed the signal from the phone before it rang, picked it up, and gorged himself on the message from the Second with ravenous hunger. Then he left the motel and took the first car he found.

Leonora, he thought. There he would witness massive continental despair as the curse flooded out of his body into the whole world.

The Second's gift to humanity.

Suicide.

Father Nick's Day minus twenty-one hours
Boston House

Benedict, Rebecca and Blackwell headed back towards the House.

"I'm so close!" Blackwell snarled. "One last clue and it's done! Why stop me with time so short? This is the secret to break the curse, stop suicide, restore hope to humanity, so why?"

"He must have a reason," said Rebecca.

Blackwell whirled. "What? And why not tell me? If it was all a hoax, then why not stop me earlier? He was the one who told me I had the secret on which so much balanced, so why let me get to the end and then intervene?"

Rebecca held up a hand, her eyes narrowing. "Wait wait wait! He told you what?"

"That I had the secret that would break the curse. He was the one who started me going! The old man who knew everything. And I believed him!"

Rebecca laid a hand on his shoulder, an assassin's hand, he thought.

"What else did he say? Come on, I'm curious. Tell us the whole story. I don't think we've heard this before."

"It's not important now—it's over!"

"Not yet, Poor Man," said Benedict quietly. "If the secret is here in Boston, maybe we can bypass this old man of yours. We've still got time. And the jumpships are still there, waiting."

"So tell us," said Rebecca. "Everything. From the beginning. We've never really had time to hear the story of your nine planets."

Blackwell was surprised to realize, for the first time since his coma, that he could read something in her tone. Courteous affection.

After all, thrust into a desperate circumstance, a man with a history of head injury and coma could easily deceive himself by constructing a fictional curse-breaking secret. Not only could the clues Blackwell had announced be easily fabricated, but the whole story of his armored planet could never be proved, one way or the other.

He paused, cautious, suddenly aware of their inner presences. "You've been very kind."

She frowned. "No, I believe you. Both of us do. But I'm not interested in your self-pity. Just the story of the nine planets. So speak, Tower."

Tower. Much as he wanted it to stiffen his spine, it didn't. Surprised his responses had been so easily identified and rejected, he looked at Benedict, who nodded.

"Alright," he said. "The day after I woke from my coma, the old man met me at home—he knew where I lived—and told me that in my head was the secret that would break the curse. It was also what the Cabal was hunting for, and with that secret, they would bring down a suicidal darkness on Earth from which it would never recover."

"No, stop. Go back. The nine planets, please. They came first, yes?"

Blackwell stepped back a little. "Yes. Moscow, stars—"

"No, I know all of them. But who put them there? Are there any more?"

"No-one put them there—they're just memories of my life before the comet, triggered by events, sounds, words, sights. I suppose they stuck in my head and escaped the brain damage. Are there any more? I don't know. Maybe. But if the armored planet is the last one, then I guess not."

"And you've sucked all the meaning out of these planets?"

"Yes."

"And only the ninth planet remains."

"You know all this already."

"Just getting my bearings. So the old man meets you, announces you have the curse-breaker—"

"—as if he wanted you to find it and end the curse—" said Rebecca.

"But then stops you from reaching it. Sounds contradictory."

"Illogical, bizarre, strange, stupid—"

"But with a reason. Strange as it may seem, there must be a reason. And if the old man only saw you once, then somewhere in that meeting might be some clue as to the reason. So what do you remember from that meeting?"

"You want me to tell you what happened?"

"I know it's probably a blur, but even a small clue might help."

No blur for Blackwell. He went back to where the memory. "First he said, 'You are so different to the man you once were.'

"Then I said, 'Who are you?'

"And he said, 'I know who I am. But it is you upon whom the light rests. Do you know who you are?'

"I answered, 'Tower? Is that who you mean? What Doctor Cox called me?'

"'Some call you that. The good Doctor was one. The good Doctor that others have ridiculed and mocked, whose warnings you have been unable to ignore. Did you not believe him?'"

Benedict's eyes were wide.

"Stop stop!" Rebecca said. "You remember all this? Everything?"

"Every word. Accents, intonation, everything. My brain's wired up differently. The effects of the head injury."

"You weren't like that before," said Rebecca.

"Before?" demanded Benedict, and even Blackwell with his stunted ability to read faces and voices, knew he was shocked. "How did you know him before? You were in the Cabal!"

And before Rebecca could speak, Blackwell took his courage in his mouth and spoke. "Before this, I was a Cabal assassin and top-level spy planted here to get this curse-breaking secret. I was meant to deliver it to the Second and end the Brotherhood of Poor Men and hope in the world forever, but I fell in love with a Brotherhood woman and decided to defect."

Benedict's eyes were like white vaults of astonishment, but Blackwell pressed on.

"I'm not going back. Neither is Rebecca. We're safe. The head injury changed me. Rebecca tastes of limes."

Benedict was silent for a spiky second but then, to Blackwell's surprise, he leaned back and laughed, a great roar of amusement that shook his hands. "Ah my," he said, wiping his cheeks, still chuckling. "Just think how absurd we have been! Thousands of men and women, hidden completely from the world, never acknowledged, never thanked, giving gifts for almost two millennia to keep Mr and Mrs Public from suicide! Ah, someone ought to write a book about us!"

Bewildered didn't even begin to explain it for Blackwell. It was his turn to stare.

Benedict wiped his face. "No, no, don't worry." He chuckled.

"Laughing just keeps me sane, keeps the nightmares away. The job's impossible, but we have been doing the impossible for centuries. If almost two millennia of surreal, and completely secret dedication, charity and war is true, then your little double game, perfect recall and assassins with limey skin is fine. I just want to know where Rebecca's going with this."

"Keep going with the perfect recall, Tower," she said. "I need to hear everything."

He repeated the conversation exactly as he remembered it, with Rebecca and Benedict listening intently. When he came to the old man's command to keep silent for fourteen days, she stopped him.

"Only for fourteen days?"

"Yes."

"After that?"

"He said, 'And it will be soon, within fourteen days. In that time, you must keep your silence. Now I must go. Trust no-one and be cautious who you befriend, for there are more than two players in this game, Tower.'"

"More than two?" she breathed. "How could there be? There's Cabal and Brotherhood, who else? Benedict? Who else is involved in this?"

"The Arcadans, maybe. But we've had no contact with them for centuries."

"But they're still in the Brotherhood. They're working to the same end. Unless they've defected recently, and we've certainly had some of that."

"None of this is going to help, though," said Blackwell. The anger had gone, replaced by a flat hopelessness. "It's only making it more complicated. We still have to find the key, and the only one who might help is the old man, who's made his position clear. We've run out of time, the jumpships will probably kill us all soon, and there's the comet as well. Thank you for your kindness, but I'll take responsibility for this myself."

"You go on," Rebecca said. "There's something I want to check in my jumpship. I'll be back in a moment."

Blackwell barely heard her. With only one day before Father Nick's Day, most likely the last one in history, the last one before a suicidal darkness from which the world would never again emerge, his hope was dead.

The old man had prevented him from going further and was not there to explain why. The curse breaker was inaccessible. Blackwell and his Twelve—he had never been quite able to include Rebecca in that number—were alone in the world. Even the sleepers, whom he had hoped would revive and help with the restoration of the Brotherhood, were gone. He snugged his coat tighter, though no amount of wool would ever warm the cold stone of his heart. There were only so many times he could batter his grim, blunt anger against the blank wall of hopelessness.

Benedict turned, and nodded at the door. "Nathanael's cooking tonight."

Blackwell jammed his hands in his pockets, feeling the defiance build.

Benedict's slow easy breath misted in the cold. "We're still alive, Poor Man." His smile came after a pause. "The jumpships didn't attack. And Rebecca didn't kill you. She's turned out alright."

She had. Blackwell had to give her that. Yet he was still surprised that her perfume had not raised even the faintest breath of desire in him. He must have been a different man to have loved her then, for he certainly didn't now.

And neither would he be pacified. "I've failed."

Someone at the House door called out, "Are you boys coming?"

Benedict called out with his eyes on Blackwell, "We'll be there soon."

The door closed, and with it, Blackwell realized, went the only real companionship he had known in his broken, disjointed life. He wanted to follow them in, but something had hardened in him, desperation gone to grim resolve, and he knew the weight of his failure could not be shared. He stayed where he was, in the cold, thinking of yellow stones.

Benedict placed an arm around his shoulders and guided him to the doorstep. "Sit," he said, and pulled Blackwell down. "Tell me you haven't lost hope."

The defiance became anger. "It's over!" he gritted, and found he could say no more. That was it, his entire stock of words. All of his life, ground down to a few miserable syllables.

Benedict was quiet for much longer than Blackwell expected. Then he took his arm from around Blackwell's shoulder, rubbed his hands together and pointed to the sunset. "Pretty, isn't it?"

Blackwell looked up, surprised, then over at Benedict for clarification. The sky was a variety of colors, but all he saw was a chrono counting down the minutes before Father Nick's Day fell like a building collapsing.

"Some people say night is only a period of darkness, like a waiting time before the light comes around again," Benedict said softly. "I've always thought that makes it sound second rate, like an absence of something, or an ending. But here's what I think. Evening's a woman in her pretty dress, gorgeous and colorful, and keen to be admired. She draws the crowds. She's a party girl." He clapped his hands once. "But night! Ah, night is a woman with her own mind. She doesn't mind what men think. She dresses with stars, she moves with silence, she dances across the universe. She's equal to the day; she's not just the space between days."

For Blackwell, counting hours and minutes, it meant nothing. He hunched into his coat, looking over at the border of yellow stones and the waiting jumpships.

Benedict glanced at him, then chuckled. "A bit too poetic? Never mind. I've never told anyone that before, but the point is that it's not over. We've run out of time, and the suicide agents will make millions this year but we're still here. Your curse breaker is still out there…somewhere. Don't lose hope, Poor Man." He stood, opened the door and leaned inside. "Smells good," he said. "Potato soup, garlic bread, stew, good Poor Man fare."

Blackwell realized Benedict was waiting for him, but he felt something give way in his heart, a landslip. "I'll be there soon," he said. "I want to see your lady of the night first." It shocked him, for a man incapable of untruth, that the lie had slipped out so naturally.

Benedict paused a moment, then said, "Alright. I'll tell them to keep yours hot."

Blackwell waited until Benedict had closed the door, then stood, turned towards the yellow stones of the House border, and started running. If he was going to abandon friends, purpose and hope, he was going to do it quickly.

When he reached the border, he didn't break stride. He heard a cry of alarm behind him—Rebecca?—and the sound of running, but his heart was already slamming madly in his chest as he stepped across the yellow stones into the outside world.

Rebecca's mind was all excitement and possibility and darkness.

Maybe Peter still didn't trust her, even after her stripping. She didn't trust herself either, and moulded against her ankle in a skin-colored sheath was a secret knife that scraped at her conscience, abraded the parts that had been healing. There was hurt in that, though hurt she knew she deserved.

But her jumpship screens showed something that Peter had to see.

She leaped down from the jumpship and went looking for him.

Behind Blackwell was only wetlands and the quiet sound of water-birds. The Boston House might well have never existed. All of his life, a failure, a waste of hope and time. And with the comet due to hit in a day, his future held little more.

And then something slammed into him from behind, knocking him down onto the wet muddy grass.

Aside from the shock, he knew immediately it was Rebecca by her smell. She rolled off him and onto her feet. He thought morosely that she was perhaps joining him in his abandonment.

Instead, as she jerked him up, she snarled, "What are you doing out here? Giving up? Where's your hope now?"

"There's no hope!" Blackwell yelled. "It's over! We've got no time-slip, no time, no hope! It's a hoax; the old man blocked the last clue!"

He was surprised to see her grinning.

"There's *every* hope." She grabbed his hand and turned. "The jumpships have gone."

Father Nick's Day
minus twenty hours twenty-nine minutes
Arcada

Harker was stupid to have listened to Jacob, stupid to have surrendered. What good was decency, trust and integrity when the Cabal would arrive within hours?

He shoved his Father Nick's Day book into his pocket and hoisted his cricket bat. There could be no hope now, no matter what Jacob had said, and everything was surrender, hopelessness and the fiery atomic annihilation of the comet.

He staggered a little as he made for the door. He was so tired.

After over a day without sleep, and exposed to the vile ferocity of London, his eyes shuddered into heavy blackness with the ghoulish inevitable horror of a car crash.

He shook himself, took another step, reached out dimly for support. Poison clouded his vision, truncated his senses.

Clear air, he thought frantically even as he sank, the surface just one more breath away than he had in his lungs.

He stumbled, fell to his knees, dragged himself along on legs that had already abandoned him, the door getting no closer, a toxic green fume rising up in his eyes.

His head hit the floor. Fine dirt inhaled up his nose irritated him dimly.

Ruth, he thought with vague concern. *She wouldn't have let the floor get so dirty…*

Boston House

"That's *hopeful*?" Blackwell shouted. He spoke the five words, wrenched Rebecca back across the House boundary, and bolted to her jumpship.

"Why withdraw the troops?" he demanded as they ran. "What does the Second know that we don't?"

In the cockpit, the navigator screen showed blank spaces where the jumpships had been. Grim and alarmed, Blackwell barely noticed his own Cabal-trained fingers bringing up screens that showed the jumpships on flightpaths to London, or accessing the Cabal communication channels that revealed command traffic buzzing around London.

Assault Group Two prepare for immediate embarkation. Alert Level One…

"Assault Group?" cried Rebecca. "That's a mothership and ten troop carriers, a fast attack force, a thousand heavily armed men on highest alert!"

…Weaponry Code White…

Rebecca blanched. One hand grabbed Blackwell's wrist, locked tight, nearly dragged him down.

And Blackwell realized in shock, perhaps through the proximity of Cabal technology, that he was thinking like a Cabal agent again. And how strange it was, when he had grabbed her hand that her touch had no taste! No lime of truth.

"He's using Mothers!" she gritted.

"What?"

"Mothers! Mass destruction chemical weapon, eats flesh, burns on organic material, they're going to burn us!"

"You know these weapons?"

"I trained in them—we used one to destroy Kavonatur! We've got to get out of here now!"

"He's not coming here," said Blackwell, his mind assassin-clear, "or the jumpships would have destroyed us already. It doesn't take chemical weapons to kill thirteen Poor Men. So where's he going?"

It shocked Blackwell how quickly he made the connections. Considering all the factors, events and possibilities with a cold analytic precision, he brought everything together—comet, old man, nine planets, assassin, angles, distances and times—and when he…

…understood…

…it all made sense. Blinding, destructive sense for the insane evil of the Second. He had no idea what his face was showing as he thought, but he read Rebecca's face perfectly in a way Corporal Peter Blackwell of NASAD never had. She was confused, and she desperately wanted him to trust her.

"The Second's not after us anymore. He knows the curse-breaker's not here, but now—I don't know how—he's found out where it really is, and he knows if he can destroy it before the comet hits, he'll have won forever. Humanity will never be free of the curse, and with Father Nick's Day annihilated, hope will die first, and the human race second." His mind and heart a peculiar union of Cabal analyst and Brotherhood servant, he made some rapid decisions. "What's the top speed and range of this jumpship?" he demanded, and when she told him, pulled her out and ran towards the hangar.

"Where are we going?"

"The sleds are faster, better range."

"The Poor Men?" she asked.

"No time! We have to leave now. And you're coming with me.

You're going to tell me about the surgery you had just before this mission."

"Wha—surgery? And where are we going?"

"We're going to stop the Second."

He chose one of the Patron sleds, sprinted up onto the bridge and fired it up. Within a minute, he had set deceptors to a local shuttle, taxied the sled onto the hangar apron, and toggled it into a rapid ascent.

At a thousand meters, he rotated out of hover, set their speed to maximum and blasted south-west.

Rebecca said, "What was that about surgery?"

"You went under the knife, didn't you?"

"No."

"Nothing? No procedures of any kind?"

"Only the dentist for the regular six-monthlies."

"And they used a general anesthetic, yes? And you were puzzled about it?"

"Yes, but you just don't ask these things."

He held up a hand. "How good are you with pain?"

Her mouth tightened. "I'm an assassin."

"Good. I need to do this now, give you time to recover. Wait here." He ran down to the equipment locker and took out a number of tools and a wad of clean cloth, then ran back to the bridge and laid them on the floor, his task-oriented Cabal identity speaking. "Open up." Without waiting for her, he opened her mouth, angled her towards the lights. "They were good," he said after a quick check, "but there's evidence on this molar of recent intervention."

"A filling?" She nearly bit his finger off.

"False tooth. Slightly different color, or I never would have spotted it. Microphone and transmitter combined. Must have driven the Cabal listeners nuts listening to you eat. Now open up. Let's have some silence in this treachery."

It only took a few tugs with pliers to pull it out and crush it. Rebecca explored the empty spot with her tongue. "How did you know I was bugged?"

"We didn't find it when we stripped you, so it had to have been implanted."

"Yes, but how did you know?"

"Tell you soon. We need to make some plans first. Scan London airspace, get a fix on him. He'll set deceptors to a major cargo carrier, probably TransBaltic." He was surprised at how quickly the knowledge appeared in his head, and realized it was because the deceptor initiative in Cabal planning sessions had first been his. It had been easy to be the Brotherhood Poor Man when he could not remember his Cabal life, but now he was both. Soon, he realized, he would have to choose.

She checked. "There's traffic, but he's not moving yet. So how do you know where he's heading?"

"Comet impact time?"

"From now? A little over twenty-four hours. Now finish the story," she said. "I don't like the idea of being bugged."

"I would have bugged you too," he said, quite without thinking, and realized he was reasoning more as Cabal Third than Poor Man. "Sorry," he said with effort, seeing hurt on her face. "OK, these are the five questions that got me thinking. Why did the Second act so strangely when all this started? Since he had already penetrated the timeslip, destroyed Kavonatur and wiped out the Brotherhood, why didn't he just send his jumpships in to kill the last thirteen Poor Men? Why didn't he act when you killed your partner? Why wait when he was so close to complete destruction of the Brotherhood and the end of all hope on Earth?"

"Because he was waiting for something."

"Because he still wanted the curse-breaker, and you were bait. He was dangling you, counting on you to lure me in with our past relationship so when I found the curse-breaker, I would voluntarily share it with you. He knew you wanted to leave the Cabal, join the Brotherhood and have me back. He knew he couldn't force something out of me I didn't know myself. So he took the soft approach. He had you miked, then waited patiently, as he has been waiting for centuries, listening to everything, and hoping you would be close to me when I found the curse breaker."

"Bait," said Rebecca with quiet disgust.

"Second question was this: Who is this old man?"

"The Defier, the Serpent, Deathless. The single most hated figure among the Cabal, and most certainly not human. No-one loves the Second, but he gives good rewards. The old man just defies the Cabal, been standing in their way for centuries, since the very first night in Patara when he protected Father Nikolas from the curse and certain death, gave him the timeslip, and thus got the Brotherhood of Poor Men started. A figure of incorruptible goodness, unkillable, unstoppable."

"Exactly! So if anyone on the planet knew the existence or location of the curse-breaker, it would be him. The single bit of information that would destroy the Second and Cabal forever, stop suicides. And the Second knew it was real, which drove him to kill as many stupid humans as possible to make up for those protected by Poor Man gifts. Our lion and your lamb, he said. So there is a curse-breaker. It's real, alright."

With a shiver, Rebecca nodded.

"Third question: If it is real, why did he tell me, a top Cabal agent, where it was? You yourself told me it was strange. More than strange, it was the single most stupid, counterproductive destructive action in human history."

"Because it's a hoax."

"Yes, but not for us! When the comet appeared, and the Second started moving, the old man knew he had to keep him distracted until the comet hit. He must have realized that he had a unique opportunity to deceive the Second, so he set up an amazingly elaborate hoax, and told me the curse-breaker was in Boston. And why there? Because it focused the Cabal's attention there for as long as possible and as far away as possible from the real location of the curse-breaker. And here's the fourth question: Why didn't the old man reveal it much earlier? Why wait seventeen hundred years?"

Her eyes narrowed a little. "Because the comet is the turning point."

"And both the Second and the old man knew it. The old man knew if he could protect the curse-breaker until that point, humanity would be safe, and the Second knew he had to destroy the curse-breaker before the comet hit. So this is the last question: who's been hiding the curse-breaker for seventeen hundred years?"

"The old man, of course."

"But if he has, and given he's unkillable, then why send a heavily-armed Assault Group?"

"And not the Poor Men, or someone would have done something about it by now. The Patrons wouldn't have sat on it if they'd known it would end the curse."

"So how has it stayed off the Second's radar for so long? He would have found it if humans were hiding it."

She cocked her head, thinking, and then realisation lit up her eyes. "The Arcadans! They're hiding it under their timeslip!"

"As well as the sleepers they took. But that's another story. And where are they hiding?"

"You said as far away from Boston as possible. Which would be…where? Singapore…ish? India?"

"Not quite." Blackwell quickly keyed in the coordinates, and the screen blanked briefly before focusing in on what appeared to be ocean.

"You've lost me," said Rebecca.

"That's the exact geographic opposite of Boston," said Blackwell, "but we're not heading there." He swept the screen eastwards until it crossed into land again, and further into a desert region, within which a small black diamond appeared, which expanded to show a tiny township of gridded streets, a single-runway airport off to the west and an arid landscape like the soles of an old man's feet. Leonora, Australia, the attached dataframe read.

"Leonora!" Rebecca caught her breath. "That's too much of a coincidence."

"For the Second's lion and lamb? Yes, I thought so too. But here's the scary part."

He marked Leonora with a bright yellow tag, then zoomed out until the Australian continent was visible, and overlaid the first screen with a second, where a bold arc marked Melcassar and calibrated with date/time markings terminated at the same black diamond.

"The best hiding place on the planet," said Blackwell. "They've hidden the curse-breaker exactly where the comet's going to hit."

"You're insane! The Arcadans won't still be there! They'll have removed the curse-breaker and everyone to safety!"

"Then why's the Second arming up an Assault Group with chemical weapons? He does everything for a reason. Look, he's located the Arcadan base, which means he's penetrated their timeslip, which means he believes he has a chance to destroy it all. And if the Arcadans don't know they've been compromised, then their only chance is us. We have to beat the Cabal there. And even if we don't know what the curse-breaker is, at least we can warn the Arcadans to get it out before the Second arrives." He manipulated controls. "He's still in London."

"He's closer to the impact point than us, though." She calculated. "About three thousand five hundred kilometers."

"But we're moving and he's not. And if this is the first he's heard of the curse-breaker's location, and he has to assemble his army and load weaponry onto one of the motherships. We'll have a headstart, three hours max, I would think."

She calculated quickly. "Which will put us on the ground at the same time."

"Run the sims then. The Brotherhood have the mothership data in here; I've seen it. Configure for their three hour load time, and our running this sled reactor at safety plus ten, eleven, twelve and thirteen. Zero cargo."

"Thirteen is redlining."

"We won't get a second chance at this."

The sims took barely two minutes to configure. "Their load time of three hours with running this sled on safety plus ten, and we'll arrive together. Safety plus eleven will give us a one minute advantage, twelve gives us nineteen minutes, and thirteen gives us thirty seven minutes."

"Should be enough," he said, more strong hope in his heart than cold Cabal analysis.

She looked over at him. "Enough?" she whispered. "Even with the comet?"

"It's all we've got. Life's nothing without it."

She watched him closely for a moment. "I'm still getting used to that idea."

"Get used to it." He stood. "I'm going to override the reactor safeties. Back soon."

He went down to the reactor, toggled off the overrides and set it to safety plus twelve, so that even the slightest shudder in the reactor would tear it apart. He then checked every failsafe on the reactor itself, and set all the early warnings to give them enough time to eject. On his way back, he closed every intermediate hatch to keep the noise bearable.

When he re-entered the hatch, she had found some food in a locker, a few handfuls of nuts, barely enough to ease Blackwell's growing hunger.

"We don't know what the curse-breaker is," she said. "Person, place, thing, book, a series of words, it could be anything! And how are we going to get in if we can't penetrate their timeslip?"

"The old man knows. And I'm thinking we'll meet him there, when it comes down to it."

"In our tiny window, if the reactor holds. But will he tell you or will he just keep his secret until the comet hits? He didn't trust you before, so how can he trust you now?"

That caught Blackwell, stopped him. *Who was he, Cabal super-agent or Poor Man?*

She was silent for a moment before she said, "The least we can do is keep the Cabal away until it hits. We're visible to them now with the 'slip gone, so we'll play the lure if we need to."

"Sacrifice ourselves?"

"If we must. We've done enough damage already, you and I. This would redeem us a little."

"Maybe, but we won't be dying doing it. The Second knows we're coming, be sure of that, but I don't think he'll be distracted by a single sled when he's got his target so close."

An hour after take-off, Rebecca checked her screens. "Still no movement in London."

"Another two hours," breathed Blackwell. "Just give me that."

The Second gave him one hour twenty.

Rebecca swore, softly and murderously as the airspace around London pulsed on her screens. "He's taken off. Deceptors set to a merchant aircraft, but it's the Assault Group, sure of it."

"Heading?"

"Same as us. Comet impact site."

Blackwell raced down to the reactor and slid the safety toggle to thirteen.

Father Nick's Day minus eleven hours

George empties the jerrycan into the petrol tank and whacks the latch closed with a wild desperate anger. Murray's nowhere, his blue Holden's nowhere, there's no Scout reception up here, and the whole of Australia has left him. He's the biggest fool anywhere, and all his mates will talk for years about stupid George who raced off to Leonora, looking for his son, when his son was safe and well in Perth, having got a lift back with a truckie. The tears on his cheeks do standup battle with the thought that—No! He's still out here somewhere, and I've just Got. To. Get. Him. Back!

When he gets back into the car, they are all talking happily, a conversation that has sprung up while he was standing out on the scorching bitumen. They're happy as puppies, giggling away about being teenagers and the times they larrikinized around in the strong young years, when all the horizons were pushed back, and rules were scanty things, about as brief as the hours of sleep they got. Long hot days at the beach, hormones strong enough to taste on salt-rimed lips, and the quiet cool valleys up in the dunes where things got even scantier.

Oh, they're laughing, sharing things they've never shared before. All the escapades! Cruising along Rokeby Road with sunglasses dark and cool for people on the sidewalks to admire, or their summerbrown arms resting on the wound-down windows as they drive down West Coast Highway, the sun all over them like a lover. Or parked with lovers in quiet places in Kings Park, with the smells of eucalyptus and perfume and desire throbbing, exploring by night, making contact in ways soft and wild and mysterious.

They're talking like there's no tomorrow, George thinks, and then his chortle becomes a geyserous laugh, and he's in there with them, shouting out the wonderful years of his wild oats, making it known, releasing the goodness of it, and all the while holding back the awful sick knowing that he will kill himself soon. All hope is gone, he knows.

And without hope there is only death.

Father Nick's Day minus eight hours

Murray stood outside, hands in pockets, a belly full of steak and baked beans, staring up at the comet. "Bloody beautiful," he whispered, and finished his beer. "That kid's amazing. Whatever's going on in that little head of his, I'd like to know how he does it."

Rick burped. "We oughta get a camera, get some pictures. If it misses, we could make a fortune. Hey Wazza, you still got that camera? Waddya reckon we get the end of the world on film?"

John came out from the house. "Power's just gone off. Get your beer while it's cold." He handed out some cans.

Murray shook his can. "Any Little Creatures left?"

"Last one, mate." He threw over a can.

"Last one in Australia!" chortled Warren. "Make the most of it, mate!" He waved his hands around. "Savour every exquisite nuance of flavour, with a rich creamy head, an oaky palate and a dry pleasing aftertaste. Voted Number One by the Comet Watchers' Beer Appreciation Society." He drank deeply then belched, a long deliberate beersnort that Murray knew was the beginning of a fine competition. They'd be at it all night, burping out the alphabet, their lower jaws executing fine tucks and rolls, and their throats and bellies absolutely sticking the dismount. "Yeah." A flurry of supplementary belches followed for good measure.

John said, "That bloke Joe and his missus have gone. Can't find 'em anywhere."

"No-one told me. Where'd they go?"

"Away from here, ya twit. Out into the desert, maybe. Nobloodywhere else to go, is there?"

"Yeah, but why?"

"Dunno. 'Spose they wanted to be alone."

"Yeah, 'spose so."

Father Nick's Day minus three hours

Ed the traitor stood alone in the Australian desert night with the stolen helicopter's rotor blades slowing, the engine ticking, and the billion unnameable stars turning away their faces.

He had never seen a night sky so vast. Nothing in London was even remotely comparable, not even since all the city had died and all its lights gone out. He had only looked up once at the comet's line of approach, then turned to the distant sight of the mothership and troopships approaching from the north-west, a black mass extinguishing stars.

Make a gift of the seven Mothers, the Second had said. *Let her smother them with her soft kisses. Let us make a conflagration that is truly legendary. Make an end to it, curse-breaker and all.*

Ed could feel the pulse of the curse-breaker close by. Close by, but obscured. Unborn, he realized. His flesh ached for it.

An end to human hope.

That was all Edward Harrison, once-human, wanted.

Father Nick's Day minus thirty-seven minutes

Blackwell brought the sled down to a hundred meters altitude and skimmed along the rolling desert floor to a point a few hundred meters from the impact zone. A low hill stood before them.

With the reactor on idle and the cargo hatch open for a quick escape, they left the sled, sprinted to the top of the hill, dropped and looked out over the desert below. The ten Cabal carriers, mothership, a curiously civilian-looking helicopter and a wide ring of troopers stood around a large square hole in the ground, shadowed with what might have been a staircase.

"How…how did they find the base?" Rebecca hissed. "And how is it visible? Even if the Second penetrated the 'slip, we didn't! We shouldn't be able to see it!"

"The Cabal must have disabled the reactor," said Blackwell. "It doesn't matter. We have to get in. We'll need night vision helmets, weapons and jackets for camouflage."

Rebecca pointed to where Cabal crews were unloading a large crate from the mothership and setting it with great care on the desert sand. "One of the Mothers. They'll set a short delay to give themselves time to escape—"

"So we'll follow them in." He rose to a crouch. "Let's go."

At the foot of the hill, with a merciless precision that disgusted him, Blackwell disabled two soldiers on the outer ring of sentries, removed their jackets and helmets, drilled neat Cabal laser holes between Cabal eyes and dragged them behind rocks.

"Quiet," whispered Rebecca. "Their helmet comms channels are locked open. How much time?"

"Thirty minutes three seconds."

"Should be enough. Helmets on. Let's go."

They fell into step at the rear of the squad guarding the last of the Mothers, and entered the base.

At the foot of the stairs, they found themselves in a stone-walled chamber with a single wide passage leading forward. Blackwell could see no light sources, but the light was there regardless, a soft, even honey-colored glow.

But even as he followed, he sensed—smelled?—something unusual deep inside the base and away to the left, something more complex than ordinary sense. He shook his head. Was it possible that part of his old NASAD nature could smell the curse-breaker? He halted.

Rebecca grabbed his arm, lifted her helmet and mouthed, *What?*

He pulled her into a doorway, removed his helmet and motioned for her to do the same.

"I can sense something," he whispered, "maybe the curse-breaker.

It's down below us, maybe about two hundred meters or so."

She hesitated, nodded at the Cabal squad. "Shouldn't we follow?"

"Not enough time. And the Second's not above killing a troop or two if it suits his needs, so the last Mother could go off while we're following. Come on, I have to know what this thing is! Helmets on."

But as he pulled her out into the corridor, the scent of the thing strong in secret chambers behind his eyes, the last Cabal trooper turned and saw them.

"Hey!" he called. "Get back into formation!"

Blackwell briefly considered shooting, but realized he couldn't risk detonating the Mother if the troopers dropped it. They would have to rejoin the squad before resuming their search for the curse-breaker.

He sprinted forward with Rebecca. "Thought we saw Poor Men targets down there," he grunted.

"I've got your numbers," a voice snarled. "Report on mission completion for re-discipline."

"Acknowledged," said Rebecca.

"Acknowledged," said Blackwell without thinking, so focused on the smell of the curse-breaker rise up in him that the next voice he heard on the command channel, cutting across chatter, familiar though it was, almost passed him by.

"Blackwell?" said the voice. "Rebecca?" and then, a moment later, "Squad leader, abandon mission. Repeat, abandon mission immediately. Immobilize troopers 3462 and 5894 for my interrogation."

Ed? Blackwell realized, but Rebecca was already firing, taking down the rearmost pair, then the next two before Blackwell pulled her into a doorway. The smell rose powerfully in him as he yanked off his helmet and flung it behind him, hoping for harm or distraction, then rose to a sprint. The smell loomed up like mountains in his vision, like a dark cliff of sense, in a way he had only felt pursuing his nine planets.

Behind him, Cabal voices shouted, and the air hissed with laserfire but he and Rebecca had rounded a corner, and the shots crackled against walls behind them.

"Find this thing, Poor Man!" Rebecca hissed.

"Clear my back! We're close."

"Your laser!" demanded Rebecca and Blackwell passed it back.

At the next corner, Rebecca halted, took a firing position, loosed streams of laserfire, then leaped up and sprinted after Blackwell.

"Four still following," she said.

"It's below us," panted Blackwell. "Must be stairs somewhere."

Fifty meters further along, Blackwell felt drawn left into a narrow passage, which dropped almost immediately down stairs, lit by the soft golden glow. Rebecca waited at the entrance, a laser at each hip. Seconds later, as Blackwell plunged downwards, exchanges of fire, cries and the noises of falling bodies sounded behind him.

At the foot of the stairs, they entered a narrow corridor that extended both left and right. Without hesitation, Blackwell turned left as Rebecca leaped down beside him, already turning to fire up the stairs.

Blackwell smelled scorched plastic and pain. One laser dangled loosely from her left hand.

"Two more down," she panted.

"You OK?"

"Fine," she said, although the stink of burned flesh was clear.

He grabbed her left-hand laser and bolted along the corridor to a door, feeling the smell of the curse-breaker nearly consume him.

Someone was shaking Harker awake.

He opened his eyes to the grit of dust dry in his nose and throat and scratching his eyeballs. His arms ached, his neck, his lower back, and almost every other body part still functional. He closed his eyes and drifted back into sleep.

Someone shook him again, insistently this time, until he stirred. He coughed, spat out dirt, licked the inside of his arid mouth.

"Get out, Poor Man!" someone was saying. "Get out now!"

For a moment, he wondered what he was doing spreadeagled on a dirt floor. He scrambled to his knees, thinking perhaps his benefactor would help him stand, although when he looked around, the room was empty.

But when he heard footsteps in the corridor outside, reality hit hard. He felt sick, defiled, stupid.

The Cabal had arrived.

If Harker was to die, he would take out some of them first. He and his cricket bat, and all the signatures of his mates on it.

For the first and last time, the Australian Post Office would go to war.

Death and destruction?

He would cause some before they got him.

Hearing footsteps outside, his last thoughts were of Ruth before he leaped out swinging.

As Blackwell reached the door, it burst open and a tall figure sprang out, swinging a club of some kind. Blackwell swung his laser then yelled to Rebecca, "Hold fire!"

It only took a single glance at the tall man's face to recognize him.

"You're the man at the Door in Patara!" he breathed. "You were taking your vows at the Door! You're an Arcadan!"

The tall man peered at him, eyes narrowed. "The man in black running for the door," he whispered in a strange accent. "Cabal?"

"Poor Man."

The tall man stared, his face contorting. "Doesn't matter!" he snapped. "Jacob's a lunatic…it was a sacrifice! He's bloody let the Cabal in!"

Blackwell lowered his laser as a distant impact shuddered the ground and walls. Dirt fell. "It's in there!" he whispered. "I can feel it."

"What? Come on, let's get out of here—there's a tunnel close by!"

But then laser blasts scorched the walls near Rebecca. She ran to Blackwell and the stranger, pushed them inside the door and pulled it to.

Blackwell scanned the room and saw what looked like a stone well from which a faint light pulsed. He knew instantly it was what he had sensed.

Only a few seconds later, though, the door was wrenched open and three Cabal soldiers burst in. Laser blasts hissed. Blackwell heard a heavy body thud, and as he was trying to swing his weapon around, he was astonished to see the Poor Man leap out from behind him, making solid contact with a Cabal neck with a vicious clout. The soldier dropped and Blackwell put an extra orifice in his face. Rebecca shot the other one.

"Well aimed!" Blackwell told the stranger. "What is that thing?"

"Cricket bat," said the man. "You're American, you wouldn't understand. Any more Cabal coming?"

Rebecca slipped carefully out the door into a crouch and sighted both ways along the passage. "Clear," she said after a few seconds.

"What's that?" demanded Blackwell, pointing to the well.

"The Sentry," said the stranger. "Jacob used it to keep London out, but then he told me to surrender!"

"Surrender?" said Rebecca. "So that's how the Second found you! But why surrender if you have the curse-breaker?"

"It's a trap," said Blackwell, realizing instantly. "Your Jacob set a trap, which means he's already removed the curse-breaker to safety so he could lure the Cabal in. Did he say anything? Any clues? And where is he now?"

"No idea, but I'd rather survive if you don't mind. There's a tunnel close by, unless—"

A massive impact collapsed walls only meters away, shuddered the air with dust and debris, stopped all voices.

"Fireballs!" yelled Rebecca. "Let's go! Where's this tunnel?"

The stranger led them towards a heavily-armored and open door about forty meters away.

Moments later, another impact rocked the floor, and a blast of heat washed over them.

They entered the tunnel, steel-lined, Blackwell noted.

"Where does this tunnel lead?" Blackwell asked. "How deep are we? Are there bunkers somewhere?" Though he knew the chances of surviving depended not only on the depth and strength of any bunker, but their ability to dig their way through tonnes of rubble after the comet impact.

"Safety, wherever that is!" shouted the stranger above the roar of nearby blasts.

The tunnel ran slightly upwards, without doorways on either side. The blasts behind them became more frequent and louder; the floor trembled, and heat scorched their backs.

They ran, the stranger surprisingly fast. Blackwell and Rebecca dropped their weapons and leaned into the sprint.

"How much further?" gritted Rebecca.

A blast rocked the tunnel, knocked them off their feet. Blackwell was surprised to see the stranger leap up and help up Rebecca. "Come on!" he yelled. "I'm not going to get killed by a cave-in!"

But then the whole world broke apart with a ferocious roar, bulging and screaming and groaning all around them, knocking Blackwell down. As his face slammed into the ground, he was dimly aware of a hand grabbing him and pulling him upright, and then his eyes opened to see a great white blast of fire vomiting along the tunnel behind them, a mighty coruscation of heat and noise and ferocity that shocked the air from his lungs.

Without any warning, his heart rises to a wild sprint, gallops at a rate he thinks must surely kill him, then slows. He stumbles, shocked, his chest swelling with space that it cannot possibly hold. His vision blurs.

The noise of the blast is cut off cleanly. Knife-clean. Without echo.

The wind drops.

And Peter Blackwell turns to behold, only a handspan from his face, what appears to be the inside of a star.

Alive and astonished, Blackwell breathed out.

On the further side of the timeslip's impenetrable skin, for he was sure that the Arcadans had raised it again and saved him in the process, the comet had come down to Earth, marrying heaven and earth with all the violence and malice that the laws of physics could produce.

And when he realized what had happened, he climbed to his feet, roused Rebecca and the stranger and helped them stand.

They saw first the roiling white blast behind them. Rebecca screamed and hid her face from it and the stranger recoiled. "What the blue blazes?" he muttered. "How?"

"Come on," said Blackwell, "I'll explain everything soon, but there's something you need to see, and you're not going to believe it."

"You've found the curse-breaker?"

"Not yet," he said, "but I'll know as soon as I see her."

"Her?" echoed Rebecca. "It's a woman?"

"Actually, no."

"I'm not following you, sorry."

"Lion and the lamb, Rebecca. Lamb means newborn, innocent. You'll see soon."

"Sheep station pretty close by, mate," said the stranger. "Bigger than some European countries. If you're after a lamb, that is."

Blackwell led them along the last fifty meters of the tunnel into the immense silence of the Australian desert night. "We were almost there," he said.

"Get back in!" hissed Rebecca. "They'll see us!"

"Come on," said Blackwell, grinning. He removed his Cabal jacket, dropped it on the saltbush and led his companions up the hill.

The air smelled so beautifully pure, he thought, and the night had taken on garments of silent wonder and magnificence, the whole of it watching and waiting in calm expectation. Just like Benedict's lady of the night, he remembered.

At the top of the hill, about ten meters from where their jump-ship still idled, Blackwell waited until Rebecca and the stranger joined him. "What can you see?" he asked, pointing to the desert floor about a hundred meters below them.

It gave Blackwell enormous pleasure when Rebecca saw it. Her face widened in a kind of luminous shock. "Where's the comet crater?" she whispered. "The base entrance? The Cabal ships? Didn't the comet just hit?" She jerked her gaze upwards, but the galaxy still blazed, only one less astronomical body in number. "Or was that the Mothers?"

"That was both. And the Cabal haven't gone anywhere. The Arcadans raised the timeslip again just as the comet hit—"

"But I surrendered!" said the stranger. "All the defences were down!"

"Yes, but not because the Second broke in! You opened the door, but once the Cabal were in—a brilliant trap that the Second never spotted—it was a simple matter for the Arcadans to close the door again. Which they kindly did just as the comet hit, keeping us out and trapping the Cabal in." He pointed to the valley floor. "Somewhere down there are a thousand Assault Group troops, a mothership, ten carriers and seven Mothers, all blown into a million pieces, and unless the Arcadans lift their 'slip again, the pieces will stay hidden for the next seventeen hundred years. No-one will ever know."

"Bloo—dy," said the stranger, with enormous feeling.

"So we're safe," said Rebecca quietly. "It's over."

"Not yet. The curse-breaker's still out there. We've still got to find it."

"No need," said a voice behind them. "I have her already."

Blackwell whirled to see and recognize, even in the moonlight and at fifty meters distance, the fine wispy hair of his once-friend.

Ed.

Beside him was a woman whose dark hair and fair skin shone with far more radiance than the moon could possibly have offered. And her belly, shadowed with wondrous beauty under the moon, was full with child.

Whoever she was, she would need protection from Ed. Even as he calculated attack vectors and angles, realizing they had left their weapons below ground in the Arcadan base, a portion of him was remembering Benedict.

...a woman with her own mind. She doesn't mind what men think. She dresses with stars, she moves with silence, she dances across the universe.

"Move right and distract him," whispered Rebecca. "I'll attack from the left."

"Maria!" cried the stranger, taking a single step forwards. "You're the curse-breaker?"

Maria shook her head, one hand on her belly.

"Indeed not," said Ed loudly, his voice timbred as though filtered through poison. "It's the child within her."

"But nothing of this earth can break the curse!" shouted Blackwell, taking a step sideways up the hill towards the sled, then another and another. As Ed tracked him, Rebecca moved slowly down the hill towards a knot of low scrubby trees.

"But the comet is not of this earth, Tower," Ed snarled. "So our sweet Maria here needed only stand beneath it and permit its unearthly light and power to pass into her unborn child, son of the many sons of Nikolas of Patara, who began your foolish Brotherhood. Now the child has a fatherhood not of this earth, and so has the power to break the curse forever." He laughed, a sound like drowning in a glass tank with an audience of thousands turning their faces away. "Unless I kill him first."

Blackwell realized how little of the human Ed remained, and how much the Second had possessed him. He thought quickly. "You've lost already, traitor! You had to destroy the curse-breaker before the comet—you're too late!"

As he spoke, he took another two steps, and saw in the corner of his eye that Rebecca and the stranger would soon be hidden by the tree.

"Consider her well," said Ed. "Is she not smiling, as though simple happiness alone could stand against the curse that now occupies me fully and completely? I am Third, just as you should have been, Peter. But I have her now, and you do not. And when I touch her and the curse passes into her, most certainly killing her, the work of the Second will be complete. Humanity will perish."

Ed was only an arms-reach from Maria, and Blackwell realized that if Ed was correct, and a simple touch would kill the child, then nothing he could do would prevent it. At twenty meters, Rebecca was too far away to launch a running attack. Maria seemed far too calm for a woman about to lose both her own life and uncounted billions of humankind, and Blackwell wondered if Ed had worked some dark Cabal control over her.

Delay, he told himself, until Rebecca had found a weapon. He dared not take his eyes off Ed. "How did you find her?" he asked Ed.

"It was not difficult to find a woman standing in the comet impact zone, her arms raised, as though expecting to be blasted."

"You've still failed!" shouted Blackwell. "You didn't get her before the comet impact!"

But now Maria makes her first sound, a most pregnant groan. She leans forward, grabbing her belly with both hands, her knees bending. Ed turns towards her, one hand reaching out, and Blackwell sees in the moment the wonderful opportunity granted him by the throwing knife he does not have.

But Rebecca does. From out of the cover of the tree, in a moment caught only by the beholding moon, she unbends her arms, and a knife leaps into the night. The moon catches its glimmer but does not hinder it. Blackwell has only the moment for a single held breath before the knife completes its track, embedding itself in the chest of Ed the traitor.

Ed staggers, and in the moment before a Cabal malediction streams from his mouth, he turns to consider Blackwell with an expression of quite human hurt and shock.

But he is the Third of the Cabal, only one degree below the Second, and it will take much more than a mere human knife to kill him.

Rebecca was in full motion an instant after the knife, Harker Brown with her, and Blackwell a second later. Blackwell landed on Ed and drove him down onto the loose red dirt, where they both skidded downhill through saltbush, Blackwell smelling the sharp copper bitterness of Ed's blood, and refusing to let go.

With surprising strength for an older man, Harker swept Maria up into his arms and carried her into the sled.

"Rebecca, rope!" Blackwell yelled, wondering how long Ed would resist. "Then get Maria into the sled and down to that sheep ranch!"

To Ed, when he had rolled him over, shoved his face into the dirt and pinned both his hands behind his back, he said, "Kill me if you must, traitor, but you're not getting the child."

It made surprising little noise for an aircraft, Murray thought, though he'd just seen a comet disappear into the nearby hill in complete silence, so a stealth aircraft appearing out of nowhere with its back hatch open and a man and woman sitting there was nothing out of the ordinary. Neither was the quiet bloke Joe, who had walked up out of the scrub only half an hour before, saying his wife Maria was dead, having walked into the path of the comet that seemed not to have hit at all.

But that wasn't a dead Maria getting helped out of the aircraft by the old codger, Murray saw, yelling for the other blokes to come see, and could they get a fire going and some hot water underway? And maybe some blankets as well? Looked like the kid was going to get born any second.

Rick and John got a bed arranged swiftish, and Warren had a fire going within a minute or two with old newspapers, some kero and his lighter. Joe rustled up some tea in a second billy, to which the men gave all their attention as the woman helped Maria onto the bed and into a birthing position. There were some things a bloke just shouldn't see.

But it was the movement in the back of the aircraft that Murray knew he had to see. Two blokes were wrestling in there, and one had a knife, even though his chest seemed to be covered in something dark. Blood?

"You OK in there?" Murray yelled, even as he started running, John alongside him. Bloody bizarre night and just getting bizarrer with blokes having a stoush when they should have been respecting the mother and keeping the noise down. One of the two fellas looked like he'd been wounded, and that knife didn't look promising. The wounded bloke brought the knife down, the other bloke fended it away, and then the wounded man leaped out of the aircraft, the knife in one fist, and came bolting across the ground towards Maria, his wispy hair covered in dirt and blood, his face locked in a horror movie snarl.

"You're doing fine," said the other woman to Maria—Murray was going to have to get some names pretty soon—"the head and shoulders are out."

The bloke in the hatch yelled out, 'Stop him!" but Murray didn't need telling twice. Anyone aiming a knife at a woman giving birth wasn't in it for the Nobel Peace Prize, so Murray made the most of his Australian football training and landed a great tackle, knocked the knife out of his hand and brought him down, expecting he would stay down.

But the bloke was clearly possessed. Even after John landed on him, and Warren and Rick had added their bulk as well, the man struggled with incredible strength, reaching for the knife, blood pouring from his chest, his eyes glazing and foul green fluid oozing from his mouth, his nose, his ears. He made no sound at all.

The other woman, on the other hand, could have been a midwife for the amazing calm in her voice. "Almost done," she said to Maria, and then, a moment later, with a last groan from Maria and a soft cry from the newborn child, "It's a boy."

The change in the wounded man was instant. His eyes hardened green as dirty copper, the blood streaming from his chest congealed like dried mud, and every muscle in his face locked as hard and ugly as concrete.

His last breath stank.

Murray and John dragged his corpse away downwind, poured petrol over it, and hoped the wind would carry the stench away.

And then, after seventeen hundred years of secrecy and murder, hatred and vengeance, hopelessness and defiance, the night just stopped.

The whole universe focused down on a newborn child, still purple and greasy at his mother's breast and wrapped in the cleanest sheets and blankets they could find.

Rick broke into the national anthem, the only song he could think of for such an amazing moment. Warren jabbed him in the ribs, then looked around, saw no-one was at all offended, so cleared his throat and joined in.

Harker took out his Father Nick's Day book and thought the story he had lived through just had to be told. A mystery? he thought. Not any more.

Rebecca the once-assassin, all her life to this moment denied affection, gave it all to the child as she wiped it clean with the most adoring gentleness Blackwell had ever seen.

Murray just stood there, unable to work out how the birth of a kid just made him so amazingly, unbelievably, outrageously happy.

But Blackwell did.

Kid not of this earth breaks the curse, he thought.

Hope at last.

Seven

After Father Nick's Day

I.

All the news from the major media channels is strange and wonderful. A waiting world sees footage of the the comet disappearing, and the Australian PM declares a national holiday.

In a palatial mansion on the French Riviera and in other hotels and private clubs, carousing hordes of Cabal assassins feel, almost as one, and so unexpectedly as to cause an abrupt and bewildered silence, that all this partying is rather pointless. One by one, or in groups, bottles and glasses and all manner of substance delivery devices fall from hands or are set down. Into those same hands weapons find their way, and then there is blood on the floor and walls, their own, and in great quantities. Seventeen hundred years of it, measured not in liters but with the needlessly truncated lives of those gone Early.

Outside, an old man waits patiently, and when all is done, he nods once and leads his beagle away.

Describing himself as a representative of the Father Nick's Day gift-givers in a pre-recorded segment, a sober-looking Ed gives a CNN press conference to announce that Father Nick's Day, with its magically appearing gifts, has been indefinitely postponed. However, the major retailing chains have offered huge discounts in a kind act of charity to cover all future losses, and stores will have extended trading hours for the foreseeable future. Father Nick's Day will continue in spirit, if not in tradition.

In his dingy flat, the Second is troubled. Not only does the strange silence from the Third not please him at all, but now the First is in the world. Plans will need to be made.

But the world doesn't care. Free of the curse, a wave of euphoria and adventurous abandon sweeps continents. Their lives once again their own, people take up polar trekking and bungee jumping, cave diving and surfing, learning languages and crossing oceans on windsurfers. Random huggers laugh their way along streets and subways, parks and piazzas. Shoppers break into rapturous song in supermarket aisles.

On the last kilometer to Leonora, soon after he sees the comet vanish into the ground, there is an odd disconnect in George's head, a clearing, a soft wind easing out sludged chambers and pathways. Suicide? he thinks. What a stupid idea that was.

And to restore that great sturdy ramshackle structure of their friendship, Harker takes George and Louise and Frank and Pat back to Perth in a Brotherhood sled, the first non Poor Men ever to do so. Louise takes the controls for the (mostly automated) descent and lands it in her back yard, roaring with laughter the whole way.

Suicide agents go out of business within a month. Governments assign larger portions of annual budgets than ever before to aged care. There is work to be done, much work, but now there is a stable workforce to do it.

The Australian Government citizenship office is overwhelmed by men and women in sand colored tunics as well as white shirts, leather aprons and brown trousers, all requesting citizenship. Oddly enough, not only does the PM endorse every claim, but sets aside some of the Nullarbor's vast natural caves for a new base.

The Boston House becomes a museum. No-one is charged entry.

The worldwide scientific community, amazed at the timeslip, discovers the secrets of the Bermuda Triangle.

At the top of every bestseller list is a debut work by an ordinary Australian postie. It sells tens of millions, and is translated into hundreds of languages almost overnight. Chat show hosts are amazed at the original manuscript, with its beautifully serifed characters, that appears to have been written without correction. The postie gives every cent of the advances and commissions to the Poor Men, and chuckles every time he sees Benedict.

Peter, the man with two memories, finds an army to lead in a mighty revolution of hope that sweeps the world. As leader of the united Poor Men, with Book and Valentina and Carl with him, he is the subject of news stories, biographies, TV shows, documentaries, websites and discussions for years. Not only have the Poor Men seemingly sprung from nothing, but under Peter's white-hot enthusiasm, good humour and warmth, they help orphans and the destitute, the needy and the sick, the victims of war, crime, broken families and any number of sins. In their white shirts and brown trousers and leather aprons, they give their wonderful gifts without stint, and overcome difficulties and obstacles with strong arms and laughter and the kind of free hope the world has not seen for centuries.

On a remote part of the Californian coast, a bungalow smiles at the shouts and laughter of orphaned children playing cricket on the beach with a postie, a Russian man and his kids. Standing on the sand, her sunbrown feet bare, her laughter and endless embraces as good as any medicine, is a woman whose right hand bears the marks of a skin graft. Emerging from the ocean, his blond hair dripping, is a man whose soft salty gentleness is more than enough for the years she has left. There are vegetables in pots and bikes leaning against walls. An easel stands with an unfinished painting, and Toby and Matilda are curled up asleep on windowsills, adored by sunshine.

In Russia, the local village council name a street and ice cricket ground after Ivan the Magnificent, and erect a statue that shows off his great Cossack beard and pale face. Harker is present at the unveiling and cheers the loudest.

Under skies completely free of comets, Joe and Maria move to Perth with their newborn son.

II.

And in the most isolated capital city on the face of the planet, a four year old once-autistic boy opens the front door of his house one quiet Sunday morning with only the sun watching him. With the Man of All Time plaque under one arm and a honey sandwich in his other hand, he walks four blocks with unerring navigation to an ordinary suburban house he has never before seen. There at the front door, he carefully places the plaque and the honey sandwich on the doorstep as his gifts. Standing up, he smiles broadly. He will be doing a lot more smiling, he thinks.

Voices and the smell of newly-cut wood from the tiny workshop in the garage stop him as he crosses the front lawn. He looks back and sees the father sawing timber with the infant son asleep in a sling on his back.

"He's here," John whispers, and runs a short way on his chubby legs. "Get ready!"

Painting won't be sufficient for this news. He laughs all the way home.

Unseen by anyone but the sun, a ragged old man watches, a beagle by his side. The man's smile takes up all the space on his face.

Ah, he thinks. The world is right at last.

Now it begins.

Acknowledgements

Nine Planets owes its existence to a Korean student. In an ESL class I was teaching about Christmas in late December 2006, he said, "Santa can't possibly deliver all the presents the night before Christmas, so he hires a network of retired postmen to help him." Within ten minutes of glorious inspiration / epiphany / revelation, the novel was in my head, a gift almost fully formed, one I felt I had been commanded to write down and then give again.

I have been enormously blessed in the writing journey by my family, my greatest treasure. I must also thank, with a great smile of delight, all my long-standing writing buddies (several published) from the Online Writing Workshop for Science Fiction, Fantasy and Horror, the marvellous writing community that nourished my writing skills and thinking for so many years: Jesse Bangs, Elizabeth Bear, Susan Elizabeth Curnow, Marlene Dotterer, Charlie Finlay, David Fortier, Kyri Freeman, Rhonda Garcia, John Hoddy, Michael Keyton, Lindsay Kitson, Leo Korogodski, Ranke Lidyek, Christine Lucas, Elizabeth Shack, Gene Spears, Jeff Stanley, Stelios Touchtidis, Walter Williams, the esteemed members of The Round Table and the PA, as well as Brad Beaulieu, Gareth Davies and Ays Marin. Without your keen shaping, advice, encouragement and necessary kicks, Nine Planets would have never reached publication. I must also thank Charles Salzberg for his collegiate support and Dawei Dong at Dragonwell for realising the hopes of an author who had dreamed of little else for many *many* years.

For the one who deserves most thanks, read the book.

About the Author

Greg Byrne loved stories, words and languages as soon as he knew what crayons were for, and was writing with them soon after. He recalls, quite distinctly, the place and time as a young boy when his heart opened in unexpected ways to the *otherness* of The Hobbit, and he spent his early years both reading Tolkien, Le Guin, Clarke, Lewis, Asimov, Moorcock, Herbert, McCaffrey and others and then trying to copy them. He also remembers the exact moment and place where the story of Nine Planets dropped, almost in its entirety, into his head in a ten minute period in late 2006 as he was teaching a class of ESL students in Perth. In between his other duties as a university tutor and lecturer, ESL teacher, and grammar consultant, and in the little free time he has, he enjoys watching his beloved Wallabies, exploring places, ideas, history, languages and science, reading, traveling, dinner with friends, watching his family grow, and living life's great adventure.

His next projects are a YA thriller with a twist and developing a grammar teaching system for ESL students. He lives in Perth, Western Australia, with his beloved wife and family and an overweight British Blue, and wouldn't live anywhere else.

More from Dragonwell Publishing:

The Garden at the Roof of the World
by W. B. J. Williams

a medieval quest of healing, magic, and love

Lex Talionis
by R. S. A. Garcia

"A stunning debut"
—*Publishers Weekly*

www.dragonwellpublishing.com

More from Dragonwell Publishing:

Mistress of the Solstice
by Anna Kashina

a dark romantic tale
based on Russian
folklore

The Chocolatier's Wife
by Cindy Lynn Speer

a rich tale of romance,
magic, mystery
... and chocolate

CPSIA information can be obtained at www.ICGtesting.com
Printed in the USA
LVOW07s1743141214
418773LV00009B/1045/P
9 781940 076171